HENRY FIELDING

JONATHAN WILD

EDITED BY
DAVID NOKES

PENGUIN BOOKS

PENGUIN BOOKS

Published by the Penguin Group
Penguin Books Ltd, 27 Wrights Lane, London W8 5TZ, England
Penguin Books USA Inc., 375 Hudson Street, New York, New York 10014, USA
Penguin Books Australia Ltd, Ringwood, Victoria, Australia
Penguin Books Canada Ltd, 10 Alcorn Avenue, Toronto, Ontario, Canada M4V 3B2
Penguin Books (NZ) Ltd, 182–190 Wairau Road, Auckland 10, New Zealand

Penguin Books Ltd, Registered Offices: Harmondsworth, Middlesex, England

First published 1743
Published in the Penguin English Library 1982
Reprinted in Penguin Classics 1986
9 10 8

Printed in England by Clays Ltd, St Ives plc
Filmset in Monophoto Plantin

CONTENTS

INTRODUCTION

The crowd which gathered to line the route from Newgate prison to the gallows at Tyburn on the morning of 24 May 1725 was of quite unprecedented proportions. 'Never was there seen so prodigious a concourse of people before, not even upon the most popular occasions of that nature.' They had gathered to witness the final appearance of London's public enemy number one, the gang-leader, receiver and racketeer, Jonathan Wild. What was remarkable, according to the eye-witness Defoe, was the crowd's universal detestation of the man who was to be executed.

> In all that innumerable crowd, there was not one pitying eye to be seen, nor one compassionate word to be heard; but, on the contrary, wherever he came, there was nothing but hollowing and huzzas, as if it had been upon a triumph.

So ended the career of the man who, seven years earlier, had proclaimed himself 'Thief-Taker General of Great Britain and Ireland', the most notorious criminal of his generation, the man who had elevated criminality, if not quite to the status of an art, at least to that of a branch of politics. The death of Wild the man was only the beginning of Wild the legend. For several weeks the press was full of elegies, epitaphs, 'last farewells', narratives, histories and lives of Wild. Defoe, having provided an account of the execution for *Applebee's Journal*, published his own *True and Genuine Account of the Life and Actions of the Late Jonathan Wild* a fortnight later. To counter any suspicions of staleness he was careful to slap on the journalist's 'exclusive' tag to his version of the now familiar tale. 'Not made up of *Fiction* and *Fable*, but taken from his own mouth, and collected from PAPERS of his own writing.' The accuracy of this claim is open to question; nor was Defoe alone in making it. The author of a highly derivative *Life of Jonathan Wilde* published in Northampton attempted to pep up his work with supposed excerpts from 'Jonathan's Diary'. However, Defoe's account does appear to be the most detailed and accurate of the many versions of the life of Wild.

Criminal biographies enjoyed a considerable vogue at this time. Well spiced with sex and violence, including exploits of outrageous bravado or of ingenious cunning, and concluding with either a penitent confession and conversion or a swaggering defiance of the hangman's noose, they comprised a highly popular and easily identifiable *genre*. It was for such a market that Defoe wrote *Moll Flanders* in 1722, and both a *History* and a *Narrative* of Jack Sheppard in 1724; that Captain Alexander Smith wrote his *Complete History of the Lives of the Most Notorious Highwaymen* in 1714; and that John Applebee published pamphlet accounts of the Hawkins gang, and of Martin Bellamy, John Dyer, John Everett, and so on. Criminal biographies have enjoyed a perennial popularity, from Robin Hood to the Great Train Robbers, but rarely if ever have they figured as pre-eminently in publishers' lists as in the first three decades of the eighteenth century.

This surge of interest was partly caused by an increase in the incidence of crime itself. The rapid expansion of London since the Great Fire had taken place in a haphazard, undisciplined way, and the increased population of the 'great Wen' was protected merely by a system of purely local constables and watches which had been inadequate to the needs of a far smaller community and was now hopelessly overwhelmed. While the Jacobite rebellion of 1715 and the South Sea Bubble of 1720 seemed to threaten the established order of the nation's superstructure, a kind of gang warfare erupted in London as an underworld counterpart to this disorder. Nor were the disturbances confined to London and the urban areas; rick-burning and cattle-stealing also increased, resulting in the notorious Black Act of 1723. Part of the increase in 'crime' was, however, statistical, reflecting the increase in the number of activities deemed to be criminal. Between 1688 and 1820 the number of capital offences rose from about 50 to over 200. Pat Rogers writes:

Hanging crimes ranged from murder, rape, sodomy, arson and forgery through burglary, house-breaking, maiming cattle and shooting at a revenue officer to cutting down trees in an avenue, concealing the death of a bastard child, destroying turnpikes and sending threatening letters.*

---

*Pat Rogers, *The Augustan Vision*, Weidenfeld & Nicolson, 1974.

Equally important was the fact that crimes were now far better reported than ever before. The daily press in London always included a section of sensational accounts of highway robberies, cold-blooded murders, ingenious burglaries, and so on. Such reports added to the drama and romance of a life of crime, and a certain minority of criminals began to pride themselves on carrying out their activities with a finesse or bravado that would look well in print. In 1712 the violent activities of a gang of upper-class hooligans, the Mohocks, were almost entirely a 'media-event', the result of a sudden panic in the Tory press.

Similarly, just as many other activities were becoming institutionalized at this time, with the emergence of banks, joint-stock companies, societies and clubs, so criminals too began forming fraternities for mutual assistance. Apart from Wild's own organization, there were Jack Hall's gang, Obadiah Lemon's gang, William Field's gang and the largely Irish Carrick gang, all operating in London. In the second decade of the century the *Daily Journal* published reports that mail robberies were costing the government more than £10,000 per annum (approaching £500,000 in 1980 currency). In 1712 Under City-Marshal Charles Hitchen declared that he personally knew 2,000 people in London who lived by theft alone. By the 1720s the number of criminals in the capital was almost certainly not less than 10,000.

Among that 10,000 a few men acquired the glamour and notoriety of Chicago bootleggers or Mafia godfathers. Three men in particular caught the public imagination in 1724: Wild, Jack Sheppard and Joe 'Blueskin' Blake. Wild had gained fame and fortune as head of an organization that was a model of business efficiency. Stripped of the various disguises and ruses that Defoe describes so well in his *True and Genuine Account*, Wild's business was simplicity itself. He instructed his thieves what to steal, received the stolen goods from them, and then returned the goods to the persons robbed for a fee. Thieves who refused to co-operate with the scheme were easily caught and 'framed' by Wild, who sent more than sixty of them to the gallows. It was this 'public service' aspect of his career that he emphasized in arrogating to himself the title of 'Thief-Taker General'. In the absence of any really effective police force, Wild's cynical system of 'private vices/public benefits' was tolerated, even condoned. Part of his success was due to a remarkable flair for publicity, coupled with an audacious clarity in identifying the symbiotic relationship between criminal and police activities. Reports like the following in the *Weekly Journal* for 13 June 1719 presented him as a fearless law-enforcement agent, travelling the country in pursuit of wrong-doers:

> Jonathan Wild, the British Thief-Taker, going down last week into Oxfordshire with a Warrant from the Lord Chief Justice to apprehend two notorious Highwaymen, who infested that country, met them within a few miles of Oxford on the road. But they hearing of his design met him, and one of them fired a pistol at him: but Jonathan having on the old Proverb for Armour, received no Hurt, and then he discharged a Pistol at them, which wounded one of them so terribly that his life is in great danger: the other was pursued and taken and committed to Oxford Gaol, and Jonathan has given Security to appear the next Assizes to justify his Conduct.

In 1720 the Privy Council consulted him about ways and means of checking the increase in highway robberies. He immediately advised an increase in the rewards paid for apprehending highwaymen. Accordingly in May a Royal Proclamation raised the reward from £40 to £100, and again subsequently to £140, giving Wild a very handsome salary increase. However, his actual position was less secure than this makes it appear. In 1718 the laws relating to the receiving of stolen goods were tightened, with his own activities in mind. Advertisements such as the following, in the *Daily Post* for 2 November 1724, continued to appear, but Wild was treading on dangerous ground.

> Lost, the 1st of October, a black shagreen Pocket-Book, edged with Silver, with some Notes of Hand. The said Book was lost in the Strand, near the Fountain Tavern, about 7 or 8 o'clock at Night. If any Person will bring the aforesaid Book to Mr Jonathan Wild, in the Old Bailey, he shall have a Guinea reward.

Decoded, this means that Wild already had the pocket-book and was offering to return it for an appropriate fee. The mention of 'notes of hand' implies that he already knew the owner's name, and, since the Fountain Tavern was a notorious brothel, probably amounts to a threat of blackmail. This is a fine example of Wild's method at its most sophisticated – and at the point when the precarious balance he maintained between law-breaking and law-enforcing was about to topple over into disaster.

Between 23 July and 4 August Wild was responsible for the arrest of twenty-one members of the Carrick gang. It was a coup which earned him considerable public respect and over £800 in reward money. But one member of the gang, Joseph Blake, was released. Wild, ruthless with those who opposed him, continued to pursue Blake and had him arrested once more in October. Blake was quickly charged, tried, convicted and sentenced on evidence supplied by Wild. However, when Wild added insult to injury by gloating over his victim in the condemned cell, Blake rebelled and, as the *British Journal* reported (17 October), 'seized Wild by the Neck, and with a little Clasp-Knife cut his Throat in a very dangerous Manner'. The incident became instant folklore, the subject of ballads, prints and moralizing broadsheets.

An even more famous struggle took place between Wild and the cockney housebreaker Jack Sheppard. In February 1724 Sheppard was imprisoned for the first time in St Giles' Roundhouse. He promptly escaped. In May Wild had him arrested and imprisoned in the New Prison. Within a week he had escaped from that too. Wild recaptured him in July. This time he was tried, convicted and placed in the secure incarceration of Newgate's condemned hold. However, on the night that the Dead Warrant arrived for him, 30 August, Sheppard managed to escape again. By this time he had become a celebrity. His quips – such as 'a file is worth all the bibles in the world' – were circulated as catchphrases. He was free for ten days, until some of Wild's men discovered him on Finchley Common. He was placed in the 'Castle', the strongest room in Newgate, and chained to the floor with manacles and fetters. Five nights later, when he escaped again, there was general celebration in all the underworld alehouses of London. Ballads were composed; Defoe interviewed the incredulous turnkeys, who showed how he had broken loose of chains and padlocks and had got through six iron-barred doors, several of which had been padlocked on the *far* side. However, Wild was just as determined to capture Sheppard as Sheppard was to escape. He pursued him all over again, and found him at the end of October in a Drury Lane gin-shop. This time Sheppard was placed in the middle stone room of Newgate and loaded with 300 pounds of iron. Here he was visited by hundreds of society tourists, missionary vicars, and even the fashionable portrait painter Sir James Thornhill, who did him in oils. His turnkeys charged each visitor 1s. 6d. for the privilege of meeting the famous escapologist. Sheppard was hanged on 16 November, and Wild had his reward.

If these escapes had turned Sheppard into a hero, they had no less certainly cast Wild in the role of villain. This, together with increasing evidence of his ruthlessness, and his barely concealed contempt for legal authority, began to undermine his position. In February 1725 he used force to rescue a gang member, Roger Johnson, from custody. It was a rash move, for which he was himself arrested a few days later. Even in Newgate he continued to advertise for business, apparently unconcerned by threats of prosecution. However, his former associates, emboldened by his imprisonment, began to bring forward evidence to damn him. Even then it was possible that the authorities might have shown leniency, in view of his long record of 'public service', had not Wild's gang been particularly greedy in stealing jewellery during the installment ceremony for Knights of the Garter at Windsor the previous August. It was noted by many that Wild's trial in May 1725 coincided with the impeachment proceedings against the Lord Chancellor, the Earl of Macclesfield, for accepting bribes of £100,000 and embezzling public funds. Wild was hanged on 24 May. The Earl of Macclesfield was fined £30,000.

The political analogy between Wild's organization and Walpole's administration was there from the beginning. Just after Wild's trial, the Tory paper *Mist's Weekly Journal* published two long mock-serious articles on the life and opinions of 'that celebrated Statesman and Politician Jonathan Wild'. The thief–statesman parallel soon became a stock element in opposition attacks on Walpole, receiving its most memorable and effective expression in Gay's *Beggar's Opera* (1728). There Peachum and

Macheath are clearly modelled on Wild and Sheppard, and the words of the Beggar make explicit the political accusation:

> Through the whole piece you may observe such a similitude of manners in high or low life, that it is difficult to determine whether (in the fashionable vices) the fine gentlemen imitate the gentlemen of the road, or the gentlemen of the road the fine gentlemen.

When Fielding came to use the thief–statesman parallel in *Jonathan Wild* it was not merely unoriginal, it was positively old hat.

Born in 1707 and educated at Eton and, briefly, at the University of Leyden, Henry Fielding had begun writing stage comedies – mainly in the burlesque style – in 1730. Dubbing himself 'Scriblerus Secundus', he declared his allegiance to the school of Tory satirists headed by Pope, Swift and Gay, and his plays mocked in turn the bombastic histrionics of neoclassical tragedy and the corrupt machinations of Walpolean politics. When the Licensing Act of 1737 cut short his career as a playwright, he turned to the law and to journalism, starting to edit the *Champion*, under the pseudonym 'Captain Hercules Vinegar'. In November 1740 the first section of Richardson's enormously popular novel *Pamela* appeared, giving a new motivation to Fielding's career. In April he published *An Apology for the Life of Mrs Shamela Andrews*, combining attacks on both Richardson and Colley Cibber, and in February 1742 *Joseph Andrews*. Throughout 1741 Walpole's political fortunes had been in evident decline, and he finally lost power in 1742. So, when the first edition of *The History of the Life of the Late Mr Jonathan Wild the Great* appeared in the third volume of the *Miscellanies* the following year, it may already have seemed out of date. It contained an attack on a politician who had now been removed, in the *persona* of a man hanged eighteen years earlier. Hardly the most effective of political satires, one might think.

A feeling of redundancy is not the only objection some readers have raised to *Jonathan Wild*. Many who delight in the elaborate jests of that 'comic-epic-poem in prose', *Joseph Andrews*, find the ironies of *Jonathan Wild* crude and over-insistent. In place of the warm humanity of Parson Adams, there is a crude contrast between the 'good' man Heartfree and the 'great' man Wild. The crudity, however, is deliberate, and represents a technique with which we have become more familiar in the satires of our own century.

In Brecht's play *The Resistible Rise of Arturo Ui*, the central character, Ui, is a small-time Chicago gangster with ambitions to run a protection racket for the entire city's greengrocery trade. He enlists the aid of a Shakespearean ham-actor to teach him to strut and declaim in what he calls 'the grand style'. 'Julius Caesar, Hamlet, Romeo – that's Shakespeare, Mr Ui. You've come to the right man', the actor assures him as Ui practises in the mirror. When Ui's associate, Givola, objects to Ui's goose-stepping, arguing, 'you can't walk like that in front of Cauliflower men. It ain't natural,' Ui retorts, 'What do you mean, it ain't natural? Nobody's natural in this day and age. When I walk, I want people to know I'm walking.'* He goes on to explain that the image he wishes to project is the little man's image of his master, and he uses Shakespearean bombast to achieve this. In the play's prologue, the announcer, introducing the characters, asks us directly about Ui, 'doesn't he make you think of Richard III?', and throughout the play Brecht echoes scenes from *Macbeth*, *Richard III* and *Julius Caesar* to insist that his gangster's career of murder, intimidation and extortion is in the 'grand style' of these great men of the past.

Brecht, who had great success with his own version of Gay's *Beggar's Opera*, found something particularly congenial about the political mock-heroics of the early eighteenth century. The satires of Gay and Fielding taught him techniques that he was keen to adapt and develop, and the close similarities between *Jonathan Wild* and *Arturo Ui* suggest a direct influence. Ui stands for Hitler as Wild stands for Walpole; Brecht makes the same comparison between the methods of Hitler and Al Capone as Fielding makes between politicians and 'prigs'. More specifically, both Ui and Wild are small men who jack themselves up with a 'grand style'; they become performers who deliberately elevate their own self-interest by garbing it in the rhetoric and imagery of a heroic

---

*Translated by Ralph Manheim, Eyre Methuen, 1976.

tradition. Wild constantly refers to those two models of greatness, Alexander and Julius Caesar. At school, we are told, 'He was a passionate admirer of heroes, particularly of Alexander the Great, between whom, and the late King of Sweden he would frequently draw parallels.' He does not scruple to echo the sentiments of an even more illustrious forbear. His boast that he 'had rather stand on the summit of a dunghill, than at the bottom of a hill in paradise' is a direct allusion to Satan's declaration of independence in *Paradise Lost*, 'Better to reign in Hell, than serve in Heaven.'

As he first gathers his gang together, Wild makes the point that had become a commonplace of Tory propaganda:

> Conquerors, absolute princes, statesmen and prigs . . . differ from each other in greatness only as they employ more or fewer hands. And Alexander the Great was only greater than a captain of one of the Tartarian or Arabian hordes, as he was at the head of a larger number.

The comparison with Brecht may help us to understand Fielding's own technique, for he parades GREATNESS in *Jonathan Wild* like one of Brecht's placards. The words 'Great' or 'Greatness' appear in 20 of the 56 chapter headings, for instance, 'Containing many surprising adventures which our hero, with GREAT GREATNESS, achieved' (II.v). The narrator of the novel draws attention to its manipulative crudity. Having begun a conventional enough simile on the 'world's a stage' theme, he checks himself abruptly:

> To say the truth, a puppet show will illustrate our meaning better, where it is the master of the show (the great man) who dances and moves everything: whether it be the king of muscovy, or whatever other potentate, alias puppet, which we hold on the stage; but he himself wisely keeps out of sight; for should he once appear, the whole motion would be at an end. Not that any one is ignorant of his being there, or supposes that the puppets are not mere sticks of wood, and he himself the sole mover; but as this (tho' everyone knows it) doth not appear visibly, i.e. to their eyes, no one is ashamed of consenting to be imposed upon; of helping on the drama, by calling the several sticks or puppets by the names which the master hath allotted to them, and by assigning to each the characters which the great man is pleased they shall move in, or rather in which he himself is pleased to move them.

A puppet-show is the perfect analogy for *Jonathan Wild*, just as the fuller conventions of the stage provide a rich metaphorical source for the devices of *Tom Jones*. The narrator pulls the strings behind Wild just as obviously as Wild and Walpole seek to pull the strings that make their dependants dance. For example, when Wild, showing a truly great determination to stick to his purposes, attempts to rape Mrs Heartfree aboard a sinking ship, he is prevented by the ship's captain and cast adrift in an open boat. There he demonstrates his noble defiance of death by leaping into the sea. However he was 'miraculously within two minutes after replaced in his boat'. The narrator draws attention to the 'miracle', which was achieved 'without the assistance of dolphin, or a sea-horse, or any other fish or animal, who are always as ready at hand when a poet or historian pleases to call for them to carry a hero through a sea, as any chairman at a coffee-house door near St James's'. In fact, Nature, having originally intended Wild for 'final exaltation' (that is, hanging) 'would by no means be diverted from her purpose and softly whispered in his ear' to scramble back into the boat. For 'Nature' we are to understand the natural impulse of fear; but, naturally, the narrator cannot admit such a weakness in his Great Man's character. He concludes, ironically: 'We hope our hero is justified from that imputation of want of resolution, which must have been fatal to the greatness of his character.'

In fact, what we see is Wild being bandied back and forth like a shuttlecock according to authorial whims which are grandly identified as 'Greatness' and 'Nature'. He is a puppet, a comic automaton. Now, no one doubts that the characters of *Tom Jones* and *Joseph Andrews* are equally at the disposal of the benevolent despots that control the narrative structures of those novels. But they are never flung about in quite this un-ceremonious manner, to demonstrate that disposability. There's a more gentlemanly pressure, a less overt manipulation of authorities, befitting the more genial tones of those works. In *Jonathan Wild* we are shown the puppet-master's strings. As Rawson writes, 'the verbal mock-heroics concerning Greatness are not sustained by a live core of mock-heroic fiction'.* Showing

---

* C. J. Rawson, *Henry Fielding and the Augustan Ideal under Stress*, Routledge & Kegan Paul, 1972.

us the strings is a fundamental part of the challenge of Fielding's satire.

Like *Arturo Ui*, Max Frisch's play *The Fire Raisers* attacks Nazi methods of intimidation in the 1930s. Eisenring, like Wild, is a cunning, plausible rogue; Biedermann is his timid, gullible middle-class victim. While a chorus of firemen chant continually about the dangers of arson, houses are burned down all around, and Biedermann lives in terror that his house will be the next. Nevertheless two complete strangers, Eisenring and Schmitz, talk their way into Biedermann's attic, which, with his knowledge, they proceed to fill with drums of petrol and long fuses. Finally they ask for matches:

> *Eisenring*: Give us matches.
> *Biedermann*: Do what?
> *Eisenring*: We've none left.
> *Biedermann*: You want me to –
> *Eisenring*: Yes. If you don't think we're fire-raisers.
> *Biedermann*: Matches?
> *Schmitz*: As a sign of trust . . .*

Biedermann gives them the matches. When his wife protests he offers this marvellously comic rationalization: 'if they were really fire-raisers, do you think they wouldn't have matches?' With this excellent encapsulation of anguished liberalism the house bursts into flames. Earlier, the ice-cool Eisenring has explained his methods of conning people to an incredulous Biedermann:

> Joking is the third best method of hoodwinking people. The second best is sentimentality. But the best and safest method – in my opinion – is to tell the plain unvarnished truth. Oddly enough. No one believes it.

It's precisely this point, the willingness, the positive desire of people to be deceived, that Fielding aims at in the strident ironies of *Jonathan Wild*. Hitler himself admitted the importance of this factor in his rise to power: '*In der Grosse der Luge liegt immer ein Faktor des Geglaubtwerdens*' – 'If the lie is big enough, it is sure to be believed.'

---

* Translated by Michael Bullock, Methuen, 1962.

Fielding develops his simile of the puppet-show by drawing a closer analogy with the farce of politics:

> It would be to suppose thee, gentle reader, one of very little knowledge in the world, to imagine thou hast never seen some of these puppet-shows, which are so frequently acted on the great stage. But tho' thou shouldst have resided all thy days in those remote parts of the island, which great men seldom visit; yet, if thou hast any penetration, thou must have had some occasion to admire both the solemnity of count-enance in the actor, and the gravity in the spectator, while some of those farces are carried on, which are acted almost daily in every village in the kingdom. He must have a very despicable opinion of mankind indeed who can conceive them to be imposed on as often as they appear to be so.

There's a telling irony in that last sentence, for the alternative, that 'mankind' are not imposed on by the devices of the puppet-eers, alias great men, but willingly *deceive :hemselves*, makes a political point different from and more important than the con-ventional one. There was indeed nothing new or provocative about the Wild/Walpole parallel in 1743; on the contrary, it had become something of a political cliché. That is Fielding's starting point: the recognition that we *know* that politicians are merely rogues on a grand scale, but are prepared to acquiesce in a pre-tence of their altruism and probity, granting them the epithet 'right honourable', merely for a quiet life. Fielding's target is therefore not so much Walpole himself as the combination of popular apathy and political opportunism that allowed such a man as Walpole to succeed so easily and for so long.

Fielding was particularly exercised by the abuses and corrup-tions of language, both through simple ignorance and, more in-sidiously, by the institutionalized euphemisms which assisted corrupt politicians to maintain themselves in power. His reading of Locke told him that abstract terms used without clarity and distinction ceased to have any meaning at all. This was par-ticularly worrying in the case of those words of moral value – honour, virtue, truth, love, goodness, greatness, duty – upon which a civilized society depended, but which had no concrete referents in the material world. His works are full of examples of characters making euphemistic use of such terms to convert them from moral absolutes to social conveniences. In his *Covent Garden Journal* he provided a 'Modern Glossary' of the new meanings that such words had acquired in fashionable society: 'honour' = duelling; 'learning' = pedantry; 'a patriot' = 'a candidate for a place at court', and 'politics' = 'the art of getting such a place'; 'worth' amounts to no more than 'power, rank, wealth', and 'wisdom', correspondingly, 'the art of acquiring all three'. The irony here follows the Scriblerian axioms of *The Art of Sinking in Poetry*, where it is stated that 'every man is honourable, who is so by law, custom or title'. In other words, members of the House of Commons, high court judges and maids of honour are honourable, privy councillors and Lord Mayors are right honourable, and holders of the Order of the Bath are most honourable.

There was a well-established humanist tradition of attacks upon 'greatness' that Fielding's *Jonathan Wild* draws upon. Boileau, Samuel Clark, Voltaire and Pope had all denounced the vain ambitions of such tyrants as Alexander, Julius Caesar, Louis XIV and Charles XII of Sweden. In his *Essay on Man*, Pope wrote:

> Look next on Greatness: say where Greatness lies.
> 'Where but among the heroes and the wise?'
> Heroes are much the same, the point's agreed
> From Macedonia's madman to the Swede;
> The whole strange purpose of their lives to find,
> Or make, an enemy of all mankind.
> (EPISTLE IV, 217–22)

Yet there is also another, less illustrious but equally significant literary genre behind *Jonathan Wild*: that of the defenders not simply of greatness but of the *realpolitik* that legitimizes the suppression of truth in the national interest – the tradition of Machiavelli and Mandeville.

Before the consummation of his greatness – at Tyburn – Wild commits to paper fifteen maxims 'as the certain methods of attaining greatness'. They include the following:

To know no distinction of men from affection; but to sacrifice all with equal readiness to his interest.

Never to communicate more of an affair than was necessary to the person who was to execute it.

To forgive no enemy; but to be cautious and often dilatory in revenge.

As examples of statecraft, these maxims bear comparison with the set of Machiavellian precepts that secret agent Daniel Defoe prepared for Secretary of State Robert Harley in 1704, which included such advice as this:

A popular statesman should have the obtaining of all the favours, and let others have the management of offences, and the distribution of justice.

When a Prince is to act anything doubtful, or anything likely to be disputed either at law or in parliament, the Council is a necessary screen to the Secretaries of State.

Defoe was a staunch advocate of the political lie. 'This hypocrisy', he claimed, 'is a virtue ... which is not unlike what the Apostle says of himself; becoming all things to all men, that he might gain some.' Wild himself could not have offered a more plausible justification of criminal means for corporate ends.

In the Appendix to *1984*, Orwell, who shared with Fielding a lifelong determination to rescue moral vocabulary from the pressures of propaganda, explained the principles of 'Newspeak', the language of *1984*. In 'Newspeak', a forced-labour camp is a 'Joycamp', the Ministry of War is 'Minipax', the Ministry of Propaganda is 'Minitrue'. The similarities with Fielding's 'Modern Glossary' are clear; behind both there exists a common anxiety at the wilful self-deception of people which allows such obvious untruths to gain wide currency and acceptance.

From all of which it's evident that Fielding's Jonathan Wild bears very little relation to the thief-taker born at Wolverhampton in 1683 and hanged at Tyburn in May 1725. Instead Fielding provides his hero with an appropriately mock-heroic ancestry of pickpockets and highwaymen stretching back to Saxon times. Even when a historical figure, such as Roger Johnson, is mentioned, his role is entirely fictionalized. Fielding's Johnson is the head of all the prigs of Newgate until Wild arrives and forms his own party to oppose him, arguing, in a delightful paradox, that

Johnson's rule is 'undermining the liberties of Newgate'. Wild cites Johnson's finery as a symbol of corruption: 'Witness that silk night-gown, that robe of shame, which to his eternal dishonour, he publicly wears; that gown which I will not scruple to call the winding sheet of the liberties of Newgate.' It comes as no surprise that, having displaced Johnson as leader of the prigs, Wild promptly assumes these despised garments for himself, despite the fact that they 'fitted him very ill, being infinitely too big for him; and the cap was so heavy that it made his head ache'. Like Macbeth he finds his borrowed robes 'hang loose upon him, like a giant's robes / upon a dwarfish thief'. The image of Wild in his ill-fitting clothes and uncomfortable cap is one of those many touches of ridicule which deflate his heroic pretensions and reveal him as more like a posturing actor waving a wooden sword.

Unlike Defoe, Fielding shows little interest in the actual details of Wild's career. Perhaps surprisingly for one who was soon (1748) to become a Bow Street magistrate and who wrote in 1751 a detailed and constructive *Enquiry into the Causes of the Late Increase in Robberies*, he pays no attention to the specific tricks and devices used by Wild. Where Defoe takes a journalist's interest in reproducing the authentic cant terms of underworld slang, Fielding uses them as part of his general attack on abuses of language.

As in his other criminal biographies, Defoe's interests and sympathies are split. For the greater part of his *True and Genuine Account* he describes, with fascination, the ingenuity of Wild's various schemes. His life, according to Defoe, was 'a perfectly new scene' and he demonstrated 'a kind of brutal courage' in his audacity and enterprise. Towards the end of the pamphlet, however, the tone changes to one of moral outrage. This is particularly the case when he deals with Wild's Fagin-like scheme for enticing destitute young boys into a life of crime, only to betray them subsequently for the £40 reward.

> First to tempt and then accuse, which is the very nature of the devil; first to make poor desolate vagabond boys thieves, and then betray them to the gallows! Who can think of such a thing without a just abhorrence? Who can think it to be less than the worst sort of murder?

Overt moralizing of this kind is quite foreign to Fielding's purpose. In formal terms the moral pattern of his *Jonathan Wild* is presented as the allegorical antithesis of the good man Heart-free to the great man Wild. In the Preface to the *Miscellanies* Fielding argues that no two qualities can be more distinct than goodness and greatness:

> For as it cannot be doubted but that benevolence, honour, honesty, & charity make a good man; and that parts and courage are the efficient qualities of a great man, so must it be confessed, that the ingredients which compose the former of these characters, bear no analogy to, nor dependence on those which constitute the latter.

'Good nature' is an essential and invariable element in the morality of Fielding's novels. A combination of geniality and in-nocence, it preserves his heroes as saintly fools in a world of knaves. Behind the Heartfrees lurks a theory of human benevol-ence associated with the name of the Earl of Shaftesbury; behind Wild, the Hobbesian view of the primacy of self-love. However, if the novel had no more to offer than these highly exaggerated contrasts, it would indeed be a failure. What sustains our interest is the far more subtle ironic examination of the ambiguous nature of greatness itself.

For all his ingenuity, Wild frequently suffers bathetic humilia-tions. While, with the narrator's complicity, he constantly com-pares himself to Caesar and Alexander, the narrator often trips him with a far more lowly simile: 'Not the highest-fed footman of the highest-bred woman of quality knocks with more impetuosity than Wild did at the count's door ...' The comparison becomes even more humiliating when Wild is turned away by a *real* footman, 'a well-dressed livery man, who answered that his master was not at home'. The great manipulator is frequently out-manipulated, most notably by women – Laetitia Snap, Molly Straddle, even Mrs Heartfree. Wild's constant comic failures with women make him appear not only as less than a hero, but also as less than a full adult; his schemes seem less like criminal master-strokes than the pranks of a malicious schoolboy.

The point is that Wild is as much a victim of his own great-ness as the agent of it. Greatness doesn't serve him, in the sense of satisfying his desires; it's he who serves the cause of Greatness.

He is dedicated to it even at the cost of his own comfort and self-interest, as this soliloquy, after another defeat, indicates:

> How vain is human Greatness! What avail superior abilities and a noble defiance of those narrow rules and bounds which confine the vulgar, when our best-concerted schemes are liable to be defeated! How unhappy is the state of Priggism! ... But can I acquit myself of all neglect? Did I not misbehave in putting it into the power of others to outwit me? But that is impossible to be avoided. In this a prig is more unhappy than any other: a cautious man may, in a crowd, preserve his own pockets by keeping his hands in them: but while the prig employs his hands in another's pockets, how shall he be able to defend his own? Indeed, in this light, what can be imagined more miserable than a prig? How dangerous are his acquisitions! how unsafe, how unquiet his possessions! Why then should any man wish to be a prig, or where is his greatness? I answer, in his mind: 'tis the inward glory, the secret consciousness of doing great and wonderful actions which can alone support the truly GREAT man, whether he be a conqueror, a tyrant, a statesman, or a prig. These must bear him up against the private curse and public imprecation, and, while he is hated and despised by all mankind, must make him inwardly satisfied with himself.

Bernard Harrison remarks of this passage that Wild is sustained by a kind of black, or inverse, puritanism. 'Wild's "inward glory" which buoys him up against vilification and misfortune is the mirror image of the inner satisfaction in his own justification which buoys up the puritan in his not dissimilar isolation.'* Such a meditative soliloquy seems at first to enhance Wild's view of himself as a tragic hero; yet, when contrasted with the more opportunistic self-interest of his associates, it also makes him comic. The great man's dedication to his ideal makes him rigid, comically inflexible in the Bergsonian sense. He is the victim of all those mechanical operations which Fielding, like Swift, identified as the real basis of the inner light of puritanism. The automatism of his pocket-picking, leaving his own pockets vulnerable, is emphasized at the beginning and ending of the book. In his early conversations with Count La Ruse over cards, Wild's hands 'made frequent visits to the count's pocket', as if by fatalistic

---

* B. Harrison, *Henry Fielding's Tom Jones*, Sussex University Press, 1975.

attraction. Finally, even on the scaffold, he is subject to his ruling passion: '. . . Wild, in the midst of the shower of stones etc., which played upon him, applied his hands to the parson's pocket, and emptied it of its bottle-screw, which he carried out of the world in his hand.'

Fielding examines the paradoxical qualities of this charismatic concept, greatness, which has such a paralysing effect on the self-interest both of its followers and of its victims. Swift wrote that 'when a man's fancy gets astride on his reason . . . the first proselyte he makes is himself.' Wild is the first victim of his own greatness; being great means, for him, being little, limited, an automaton.

Fielding's novel, then, is not just an attack on the corruption of politicians, though it is that; it is not simply a traditional humanist attack on the vanity of human wishes, though it is partly that too. More subtly it is an exposure of the deeply paradoxical nature of our responses to power. Like Eisenring, Fielding knows that the best way to deceive people is to tell them the truth, and the best way to be believed is to tell really monstrous lies.

At the end of *1984*, it is with tears of relief trickling down his cheeks into his Victory gin that Winston Smith finally learns to love Big Brother. He has given up the lonely misanthropic moral struggle and learned to accept the benevolent face of greatness, that freedom is slavery, and that $2 + 2 = 5$. Wild, on his scaffold, no less than Winston Smith, loves the Greatness which carries him out of the world with the parson's bottle-screw in his hand. But at least, in Fielding's view of the world, the puppet-show is still continuing, and the audience can rise and leave if it wishes.

NOTE ON THE TEXTS

The text of this edition follows that of the first separate edition of the novel in 1754. *Jonathan Wild* had earlier appeared in the third volume of the *Miscellanies* in 1743. The 1754 edition was considerably revised from that of 1743, and details of the major alterations will be found among the notes at the end of the present volume. Where necessary, punctuation, typography and spelling have been silently amended to conform with modern conventions. The text is otherwise unaltered and unabridged. Also included is an extract from the Preface to the *Miscellanies* (1743), and the 'Advertisement from the Publisher to the Reader' prefixed to the 1754 edition and almost certainly by Fielding.

The text of the *True and Genuine Account of the Life and Actions of the late Jonathan Wild* follows the first edition of 1725, with amendments to punctuation, spelling and typography as above. The work has been attributed to Defoe by the common consent of modern scholars.

FURTHER READING

BIOGRAPHY

W. L. Cross, *The History of Henry Fielding*, 3 vols., Yale University Press, New Haven, 1918

Pat Rogers, *Henry Fielding*, Elek, 1979

GENERAL CRITICISM

Robert Alter, *Fielding and the Nature of the Novel*, Harvard University Press, Cambridge, Mass., 1968

B. Harrison, *Henry Fielding's Tom Jones*, Sussex University Press, 1975

G. W. Hatfield, *Henry Fielding and the Language of Irony*, University of Chicago Press, 1968

Ronald Paulson and Thomas Lockwood (eds.), *Henry Fielding: The Critical Heritage*, Routledge & Kegan Paul, 1969

C. J. Rawson, *Henry Fielding and the Augustan Ideal under Stress*, Routledge & Kegan Paul, 1972

ON JONATHAN WILD

Gerald Howson, *Thief-Taker General*, Hutchinson, 1970

W. R. Irwin, *The Making of Jonathan Wild*, New York, 1941

J. Preston, 'The Ironic Mode, A Comparison of *Jonathan Wild* and *The Beggar's Opera*', *Essays in Criticism*, vol. xvi, 1966

J. E. Wells, 'Fielding's Political Purpose in *Jonathan Wild*', *PMLA*, vol. xxviii, 1913

Allan Wendt, 'The Moral Allegory of *Jonathan Wild*', *ELH*, vol. xxiv, 1970

BACKGROUND

M. D. George, *London Life in the Eighteenth Century*, Kegan Paul, Trench, Trubner & Co., 1925; Penguin, 1966

D. Hay, et al., *Albion's Fatal Tree*, Allen Lane, 1975; Penguin, 1977

Pat Rogers, *The Augustan Vision*, Weidenfeld & Nicolson, 1974

Ian Watt, *The Rise of the Novel*, Chatto & Windus, 1957; Penguin, 1963

MISCELLANIES.

THE
LIFE
OF
Mᵣ JONATHAN WILD
THE GREAT.

VOL. III.

By HENRY FIELDING, Esq;

LONDON,

Printed for the AUTHOR; and sold by A. MILLAR, opposite to *Catharine-street* in the *Strand.*

M DCC XLIII.

EXTRACT FROM FIELDING'S
PREFACE TO THE *MISCELLANIES*

(1743)

I come now to the third and last volume, which contains the history of Jonathan Wild. And here it will not, I apprehend, be necessary to acquaint my reader, that my design is not to enter the lists with that excellent historian, who from authentic papers and records, etc., hath already given so satisfactory an account of the life and actions of this great man. I have not indeed the least intention to depreciate the veracity and impartiality of that history; nor do I pretend to any of those lights, not having, to my knowledge, ever seen a single paper relating to my hero, save some short memoirs, which about the time of his death were published in certain chronicles called newspapers, the authority of which hath been sometimes questioned, and in the Ordinary of Newgate his account, which generally contains a more particular relation of what the heroes are to suffer in the next world, than of what they did in this.

To confess the truth, my narrative is rather of such actions which he might have performed, or would, or should have performed, than what he really did; and may, in reality, as well suit any other such great man, as the person himself whose name it bears.

A second caution I would give my reader is, that as it is not a very faithful portrait of Jonathan Wild himself, so neither is it intended to represent the features of any other person. Roguery, and not a rogue, is my subject; and as I have been so far from endeavouring to particularize any individual, that I have with my utmost art avoided it; so will any such application be unfair in my reader, especially if he knows much of the great world, since he must then be acquainted, I believe, with more than one on whom he can fix the resemblance.

In the third place, I solemnly protest, I do by no means intend in the character of my hero to represent nature in general. Such insinuations must be attended with very dreadful conclu-

29

sions; nor do I see any other tendency they can naturally have, but to encourage and soothe men in their villainies, and to make every well-disposed man disclaim his own species, and curse the hour of his birth into such a society. For my part, I understand those writers who describe human nature in this depraved character, as speaking only of such persons as Wild and his gang; and I think it may be justly inferred, that they do not find in their own bosoms any deviation from the general rule. Indeed it would be an insufferable vanity in them to conceive themselves as the only exception to it.

But without considering Newgate as no other than human nature with its mask off, which some very shameless writers have done, a thought which no price should purchase me to entertain, I think we may be excused for suspecting, that the splendid palaces of the great are often no other than Newgate with the mask on. Nor do I know any thing which can raise an honest man's indignation higher than that the same morals should be in one place attended with all imaginable misery and infamy, and in the other, with the highest luxury and honour. Let any impartial man in his senses be asked, for which of these two places a composition of cruelty, lust, avarice, rapine, insolence, hypocrisy, fraud and treachery, was best fitted, surely his answer must be certain and immediate; and yet I am afraid all these ingredients glossed over with wealth and a title, have been treated with the highest respect and veneration in the one, while one or two of them have been condemned to the gallows in the other.

If there are then any men of such morals who dare to call themselves great, and are so reputed, or called at least, by the deceived multitude, surely a little private censure by the few is a very moderate tax for them to pay, provided no more was to be demanded. But I fear this is not the case. However the glare of riches, and awe of title, may dazzle and terrify the vulgar; nay, however hypocrisy may deceive the more discerning, there is still a judge in every man's breast, which none can cheat nor corrupt, though perhaps it is the only uncorrupt thing about him. And yet, inflexible and honest as this judge is (however polluted the bench be on which he sits), no man can, in my opinion, enjoy any applause which is not thus adjudged to be his due.

Nothing seems to me more preposterous than that, while the way to true honour lies so open and plain, men should seek false by such perverse and rugged paths: that while it is so easy and safe, and truly honourable, to be good, men should wade through difficulty and danger, and real infamy, to be *great*, or, to use a synonymous word, *villains*.

Nor hath goodness less advantage in the article of pleasure, than of honour over this kind of greatness. The same righteous judge always annexes a bitter anxiety to the purchases of guilt, whilst it adds a double sweetness to the enjoyments of innocence and virtue: for fear, which all the wise agree is the most wretched of human evils, is, in some degree, always attending on the former, and never can in any manner molest the happiness of the latter.

This is the doctrine which I have endeavoured to inculcate in this history, confining myself at the same time within the rules of probability. (For except in one chapter, which is visibly meant as a burlesque on the extravagant accounts of travellers, I believe I have not exceeded it.) And though perhaps it sometimes happens, contrary to the instances I have given, that the villain succeeds in his pursuit, and acquires some transitory imperfect honour or pleasure to himself for his iniquity; yet I believe he oftener shares the fate of my hero, and suffers the punishment, without obtaining the reward.

As I believe it is not easy to teach a more useful lesson than this, if I have been able to add the pleasant to it, I might flatter myself with having carried every point.

But perhaps some apology may be required of me, for having used the word *Greatness*, to which the world have affixed such honourable ideas, in so disgraceful and contemptuous a light. Now if the fact be, that the greatness which is commonly worshipped is really of that kind which I have here represented, the fault seems rather to lie in those who have ascribed it to those honours, to which it hath not in reality the least claim.

The truth, I apprehend, is, we often confound the ideas of goodness and greatness together, or rather include the former in our idea of the latter. If this be so, it is surely a great error, and no less than a mistake of the capacity for the will. In reality, no qualities can be more distinct: for as it cannot be doubted but that benevolence, honour, honesty, and charity, make a good man; and that parts and courage, are the efficient qualities of a great man, so must it be confessed, that the ingredients which compose the former of these characters, bear no analogy to, nor dependence on, those which constitute the latter. A man may therefore be great without being good, or good without being great.

However, though the one bear no necessary dependence on the other, neither is there any absolute repugnancy among them which may totally prevent their union so that they may, though not of necessity, assemble in the same mind, as they actually did, and all in the highest degree, in those of Socrates and Brutus, and perhaps in some among us. I at least know one to whom nature could have added no one great or good quality more than she hath bestowed on him.

Here then appear three distinct characters; the great, the good, and the great and good.

The last of these is the *true sublime* in human nature. That elevation by which the soul of man, raising and extending itself above the order of this creation, and brightened with a certain ray of divinity, looks down on the condition of mortals. This is indeed a glorious object, on which we can never gaze with too much praise and admiration. A perfect work! the *Iliad* of Nature! ravishing and astonishing, and which at once fills us with love, wonder, and delight.

The second falls greatly short of this perfection, and yet hath its merit. Our wonder ceases; our delight is lessened; but our love remains; of which passion, goodness hath always appeared to me the only true and proper object. On this head I think proper to observe, that I do not conceive my good man to be absolutely a fool or a coward; but that he often partakes too little of parts or courage, to have any pretensions to greatness.

Now as to that greatness which is totally devoid of goodness, it seems to me in Nature to resemble the *false sublime* in poetry; whose bombast is, by the ignorant and ill-judging vulgar, often mistaken for solid wit and eloquence, whilst it is in effect the very reverse. Thus pride, ostentation, insolence, cruelty, and every kind of villainy, are often construed into true greatness of mind, in which we always include an idea of goodness.

This bombast greatness then is the character I intend to expose; and the more this prevails in and deceives the world, taking to itself not only riches and power, but often honour, or at least the shadow of it, the more necessary is it to strip the monster of these false colours, and show it in its native deformity: for by suffering vice to possess the reward of virtue, we do a double injury to society, by encouraging the former, and taking away the chief incentive to the latter. Nay, though it is, I believe, impossible to give vice a true relish of honour and glory, or though we give it riches and power, to give it the enjoyment of them, yet it contaminates the food it can't taste, and sullies the robe which neither fits nor becomes it, 'till virtue disdains them both.

ADVERTISEMENT FROM THE PUBLISHER
TO THE READER
(1754)

The following pages are the corrected edition of a book which was first published in the year 1743.

That any personal application could have ever been possibly drawn from them, will surprise all who are not deeply versed in the black art (for so it seems most properly to be called), of deciphering men's meaning when couched in obscure, ambiguous, or allegorical expressions: this art hath been exercised more than once on the author of our little book, who hath contracted a considerable degree of odium from having had the scurrility of others imputed to him. The truth is, as a very corrupt state of morals is here represented, the scene seems very properly to have been laid in Newgate; nor do I see any reason for introducing any allegory at all: unless we all agree that there are without those walls, some other bodies of men of worse morals than those within; and who have, consequently, a right to change places with its present inhabitants.

To such persons, if any such there be, I would particularly recommend the perusal of the third chapter of the fourth book of the following history, and more particularly still the speech of the grave man in pages 195, 196 of that book (pages 174–5 of the present edition).

CONTENTS

BOOK I

35

BOOK II

BOOK III

BOOK IV

CONTENTS

BOOK I

CHAPTER I

Shewing the wholesome uses drawn from recording the achievements of those wonderful productions of nature called
GREAT MEN

As it is necessary that all great and surprising events, the designs of which are laid, conducted, and brought to perfection by the utmost force of human invention and art, should be produced by great and eminent men, so the lives of such may be justly and properly styled the quintessence of history. In these, when delivered to us by sensible writers, we are not only most agreeably entertained, but most usefully instructed; for, besides the attaining hence a consummate knowledge of human nature in general; of its secret springs, various windings, and perplexed mazes; we have here before our eyes lively examples of whatever is amiable or detestable, worthy of admiration or abhorrence, and are consequently taught, in a manner infinitely more effectual than by precept, what we are eagerly to imitate or carefully to avoid.

But besides the two obvious advantages of surveying, as it were in a picture, the true beauty of virtue and deformity of vice, we may moreover learn from Plutarch, Nepos, Suetonius,[1] and other biographers, this useful lesson, not too hastily, nor in the gross, to bestow either our praise or censure; since we shall often find such a mixture of good and evil in the same character that it may require a very accurate judgement and a very elaborate enquiry to determine on which side the balance turns, for though we sometimes meet with an Aristides or a Brutus, a Lysander or a Nero,[2] yet far the greater number are of the mixt kind, neither totally good nor bad; their greatest virtues being obscured and allayed by their vices, and those again softened and coloured over by their virtues.

Of this kind was the illustrious person whose history we now undertake; to whom, though nature had given the greatest and most shining endowments, she had not given them absolutely pure and without alloy. Though he had much of the admirable in his character, as much perhaps as is usually to be found in a hero, I will not yet venture to affirm that he was entirely free from all defects, or that the sharp eyes of censure could not spy out some little blemishes lurking amongst his many great perfections.

We would not therefore be understood to affect giving the reader a perfect or consummate pattern of human excellence; but rather, by faithfully recording some little imperfections which shadowed over the lustre of those great qualities which we shall here record, to teach the lesson we have above mentioned, to induce our reader with us to lament the frailty of human nature, and to convince him that no mortal, after a thorough scrutiny, can be a proper object of our adoration.

But before we enter on this great work we must endeavour to remove some errors of opinion which mankind have, by the disingenuity of writers, contracted: for these, from their fear of contradicting the obsolete and absurd doctrines of a set of simple fellows, called, in derision, sages or philosophers, have endeavoured, as much as possible, to confound the ideas of greatness and goodness; whereas no two things can possibly be more distinct from each other, for greatness consists in bringing all manner of mischief on mankind, and goodness in removing it from them. It seems therefore very unlikely that the same person should possess them both; and yet nothing is more usual with writers, who find many instances of greatness in their favourite hero, than to make him a compliment of goodness into the bargain; and this, without considering that by such means they destroy the great perfection called uniformity of character. In the histories of Alexander and Cæsar[3] we are frequently, and indeed impertinently, reminded of their benevolence and generosity, of their clemency and kindness. When the former had with fire and sword overrun a vast empire, had destroyed the lives of an immense number of innocent wretches, had scattered ruin and desolation like a whirlwind, we are told, as an example of his clemency, that he did not cut the throat of an old woman, and ravish her daughters, but was content with only undoing them. And when the mighty Cæsar, with wonderful greatness of mind, had destroyed the liberties of his country, and with all the means of fraud and force had placed himself at the head of his equals, had corrupted and enslaved the greatest people whom the sun ever saw, we are reminded, as an evidence of his generosity, of his largesses to his followers and tools, by whose means he had accomplished his purpose, and by whose assistance he was to establish it.

Now, who doth not see that such sneaking qualities as these are rather to be bewailed as imperfections than admired as ornaments in these great men; rather obscuring their glory, and holding them back in their race to greatness, indeed unworthy the end for which they seem to have come into the world, viz. of perpetrating vast and mighty mischief?

We hope our reader will have reason justly to acquit us of any such confounding ideas in the following pages; in which, as we are to record the actions of a great man, so we have nowhere mentioned any spark of goodness which had discovered itself either faintly in him, or more glaringly in any other person, but as a meanness and imperfection, disqualifying them for undertakings which lead to honour and esteem among men.

As our hero had as little as perhaps is to be found of that meanness, indeed only enough to make him partaker of the imperfection of humanity, instead of the perfection of diabolism, we have ventured to call him *The Great*;[4] nor do we doubt but our reader, when he hath perused his story, will concur with us in allowing him that title.

CHAPTER II

Giving an account of as many of our hero's ancestors as can be gathered out of the rubbish of antiquity, which hath been carefully sifted for that purpose

It is the custom of all biographers, at their entrance into their work, to step a little backwards (as far, indeed, generally as they are able) and to trace up their hero, as the ancients did the River

Nile, till an incapacity of proceeding higher puts an end to their search.

What first gave rise to this method is somewhat difficult to determine. Sometimes I have thought that the hero's ancestors have been introduced as foils to himself. Again, I have imagined it might be to obviate a suspicion that such extraordinary personages were not produced in the ordinary course of nature, and may have proceeded from the author's fear that, if we are not told who their fathers were, they might be in danger, like Prince Pretty-man,[5] of being supposed to have had none. Lastly, and perhaps more truly, I have conjectured that the design of the biographer hath been no more than to shew his great learning and knowledge of antiquity. A design to which the world hath probably owed many notable discoveries, and indeed most of the labours of our antiquarians.

But whatever original this custom had, it is now too well established to be disputed. I shall therefore conform to it in the strictest manner.

Mr Jonathan Wild, or Wyld, then (for he himself did not always agree in one method of spelling his name), was descended from the great Wolfstan Wild, who came over with Hengist, and distinguished himself very eminently at that famous festival, where the Britons were so treacherously murdered by the Saxons; for when the word was given, i.e. *Nemet eour Saxes, take out your swords*, this gentleman, being a little hard of hearing, mistook the sound for *Nemet her sacs, take out their purses*;[6] instead therefore of applying to the throat, he immediately applied to the pocket of his guest, and contented himself with taking all that he had, without attempting his life.

The next ancestor of our hero who was remarkably eminent was Wild, surnamed Langfanger, or Longfinger. He flourished in the reign of Henry III, and was strictly attached to Hubert de Burgh, whose friendship he was recommended to by his great excellence in an art of which Hubert was himself the inventor; he could, without the knowledge of the proprietor, with great ease and dexterity, draw forth a man's purse from any part of his garment where it was deposited, and hence he derived his surname. This gentleman was the first of his family who had the honour to suffer for the good of his country: on whom a wit of that time made the following epitaph:

> O shame o' justice! Wild is hang'd,
> For thatten he a pocket fang'd,
> While safe old Hubert, and his gang,
> Doth pocket o' the nation fang.

Langfanger left a son named Edward, whom he had carefully instructed in the art for which he himself was so famous. This Edward had a grandson, who served as a volunteer under the famous Sir John Falstaff, and by his gallant demeanour so recommended himself to his captain, that he would have certainly been promoted by him, had Harry the Fifth kept his word with his old companion.

After the death of Edward the family remained in some obscurity down to the reign of Charles the First, when James Wild distinguished himself on both sides the question in the civil wars, passing from one to t' other, as Heaven seemed to declare itself in favour of either party. At the end of the war, James not being rewarded according to his merits, as is usually the case of such impartial persons, he associated himself with a brave man of those times, whose name was Hind, and declared open war with both parties. He was successful in several actions, and spoiled many of the enemy: till at length, being overpowered and taken, he was, contrary to the law of arms, put basely and cowardly to death by a combination between twelve men of the enemy's party, who, after some consultation, unanimously agreed on the said murder.

This Edward took to wife Rebecca, the daughter of the above-mentioned John Hind, Esq., by whom he had issue John, Edward, Thomas, and Jonathan, and three daughters, namely, Grace, Charity, and Honour. John followed the fortunes of his father, and, suffering with him, left no issue. Edward was so remarkable for his compassionate temper that he spent his life in soliciting the causes of the distressed captives in Newgate, and is reported to have held a strict friendship with an eminent divine who solicited the spiritual causes of the said captives. He married Editha, daughter and co-heiress of Geoffry Snap,[7] gent., who long enjoyed an office under the High Sheriff of London and Middlesex, by which, with great reputation, he acquired a handsome fortune: by her he had no issue. Thomas went very young abroad to one of our American colonies,[8] and hath not been since heard of. As for the daughters, Grace was married to a merchant of Yorkshire who dealt in horses. Charity took to husband an eminent gentleman, whose name I cannot learn, but who was famous for so friendly a disposition that he was bail for above a hundred persons in one year. He had likewise the remarkable humour of walking in Westminster Hall[9] with a straw in his shoe. Honour, the youngest, died unmarried. She lived many years in this town, was a great frequenter of plays, and used to be remarkable for distributing oranges[10] to all who would accept of them.

Jonathan married Elizabeth, daughter of Scragg Hollow, of Hockley-in-the-Hole,[11] Esq.; and by her had Jonathan, who is the illustrious subject of these memoirs.

CHAPTER III

The birth, parentage, and education of Mr Jonathan Wild the Great

It is observable that Nature seldom produces any one who is afterwards to act a notable part on the stage of life, but she gives some warning of her intention; and, as the dramatic poet generally prepares the entry of every considerable character with a solemn narrative, or at least a great flourish of drums and trumpets, so doth this our Alma Mater by some shrewd hints pre-admonish us of her intention, giving us warning, as it were, and crying:

– Venienti occurrite morbo.[12]

Thus Astyages, who was the grandfather of Cyrus, dreamt that his daughter was brought to bed of a vine, whose branches overspread all Asia, and Hecuba, while big with Paris, dreamt that she was delivered of a firebrand that set all Troy in flames;[13] so did the mother of our great man, while she was with child of him, dream that she was enjoyed in the night by the gods Mercury

44

and Priapus. This dream puzzled all the learned astrologers of her time, seeming to imply in it a contradiction; Mercury being the god of ingenuity, and Priapus[14] the terror of those who practised it. What made this dream the more wonderful, and perhaps the true cause of its being remembered, was a very extraordinary circumstance, sufficiently denoting something preternatural in it; for though she had never heard even the name of either of these gods, she repeated these very words in the morning, with only a small mistake of the quantity of the latter, which she chose to call *Priăpus* instead of *Priāpus*; and her husband swore that, though he might possibly have named Mercury to her (for he had heard of such an heathen god), he never in his life could anywise have put her in mind of that other deity, with whom he had no acquaintance.

Another remarkable incident was, that during her whole pregnancy she constantly longed for everything she saw; nor could be satisfied with her wish unless she enjoyed it clandestinely; and as nature, by true and accurate observers, is remarked to give us no appetites without furnishing us with the means of gratifying them; so had she at this time a most marvellous glutinous quality attending her fingers, to which, as to birdlime, everything closely adhered that she handled.

To omit other stories, some of which may be perhaps the growth of superstition, we proceed to the birth of our hero, who made his first appearance on this great theatre the very day when the plague first broke out in 1665. Some say his mother was delivered of him in an house of an orbicular or round form[15] in Covent Garden; but of this we are not certain. He was some years afterwards baptized by the famous Mr Titus Oates.[16]

Nothing very remarkable passed in his years of infancy, save that, as the letters *th* are the most difficult of pronunciation, and the last which a child attains to the utterance of, so they were the first that came with any readiness from young Master Wild. Nor must we omit the early indications which he gave of the sweetness of his temper; for though he was by no means to be terrified into compliance, yet might he, by a sugar-plum, be brought to your purpose; indeed, to say the truth, he was to be bribed to anything, which made many say he was certainly born to be a great man.

He was scarce settled at school before he gave marks of his lofty and aspiring temper; and was regarded by all his schoolfellows with that deference which men generally pay to those superior geniuses who will exact it of them. If an orchard was to be robbed Wild was consulted, and, though he was himself seldom concerned in the execution of the design, yet was he always concerter of it, and treasurer of the booty, some little part of which he would now and then, with wonderful generosity, bestow on those who took it. He was generally very secret on these occasions; but if any offered to plunder of his own head, without acquainting Master Wild, and making a deposit of the booty, he was sure to have an information against him lodged with the schoolmaster, and to be severely punished for his pains.

He discovered so little attention to school-learning that his master, who was a very wise and worthy man, soon gave over all care and trouble on that account, and, acquainting his parents that their son proceeded extremely well in his studies, he permitted his pupil to follow his own inclinations, perceiving they led him to nobler pursuits than the sciences, which are generally acknowledged to be a very unprofitable study, and indeed greatly to hinder the advancement of men in the world. But though Master Wild was not esteemed the readiest at making his exercise, he was universally allowed to be the most dexterous at stealing it of all his schoolfellows, being never detected in such furtive compositions, nor indeed in any other exercitations of his great talents, which all inclined the same way, but once, when he had laid violent hands on a book called *Gradus ad Parnassum*,[17] i.e. *A Step towards Parnassus*; on which account his master, who was a man of most wonderful wit and sagacity, is said to have told him he wished it might not prove in the event *Gradus ad Patibulum*, i.e. *A step towards the gallows*.

But, though he would not give himself the pains requisite to acquire a competent sufficiency in the learned languages, yet did he readily listen with attention to others, especially when they translated the classical authors to him; nor was he in the least backward, at all such times, to express his approbation. He was wonderfully pleased with that passage in the eleventh Iliad where Achilles is said to have bound two sons of Priam upon a mountain, and afterwards to have released them for a sum of money.[18] This was, he said, alone sufficient to refute those who affected a contempt for the wisdom of the ancients, and an undeniable testimony of the great antiquity of priggism.* He was ravished with the account which Nestor gives in the same book of the rich booty which he bore off (i.e. stole) from the Eleans.[19] He was desirous of having this often repeated to him, and at the end of every repetition he constantly fetched a deep sigh, and said *it was a glorious booty*.

When the story of Cacus was read to him out of the eighth Æneid he generously pitied the unhappy fate of that great man, to whom he thought Hercules much too severe: one of his schoolfellows commending the dexterity of drawing the oxen backward by their tails into his den, he smiled, and with some disdain said, *He could have taught him a better way*.[20]

He was a passionate admirer of heroes, particularly of Alexander the Great, between whom and the late King of Sweden[21] he would frequently draw parallels. He was much delighted with the accounts of the Czar's retreat from the latter, who carried off the inhabitants of great cities to people his own country. *This*, he said, *was not once thought of by* Alexander; *but*, added, *perhaps he did not want them*.

Happy had it been for him if he had confined himself to this sphere; but his chief, if not only blemish, was, that he would sometimes, from an humility in his nature too pernicious to true greatness, condescend to an intimacy with inferior things and persons. Thus the *Spanish Rogue* was his favourite book, and the *Cheats of Scapin* his favourite play.[22]

The young gentleman being now at the age of seventeen, his father, from a foolish prejudice to our universities, and out of a false as well as excessive regard to his morals, brought his son to town, where he resided with him till he was of age to travel. Whilst he was here, all imaginable care was taken of his instruction, his father endeavouring his utmost to inculcate principles of honour and gentility into his son.

---

* This word, in the cant language, signifies thievery.

CHAPTER IV

*Mr Wild's first entrance into the world. His acquaintance with
Count la Ruse*

An accident soon happened after his arrival in town which almost
saved the father his whole labour on this head, and provided
Master Wild a better tutor than any care or expense could have
furnished him with. The old gentleman, it seems, was a
FOLLOWER of the fortunes of Mr Snap,[23] son of Mr Geoffry
Snap, whom we have before mentioned to have enjoyed a reputable office under the Sheriff of London and Middlesex, the
daughter of which Geoffry had intermarried with the Wilds. Mr
Snap the younger, being thereto well warranted, had laid violent
hands on, or, as the vulgar express it, arrested one Count la Ruse,
a man of considerable figure in those days, and had confined him
to his own house till he could find two seconds who would in a
formal manner give their words that the count should, at a certain
day and place appointed, answer all that one Thomas Thimble, a
taylor, had to say to him; which Thomas Thimble, it seems,
alleged that the count had, according to the law of the realm, made
over his body to him as a security for some suits of clothes to him
delivered by the said Thomas Thimble. Now as the count, though
perfectly a man of honour, could not immediately find these
seconds, he was obliged for some time to reside at Mr Snap's
house: for it seems the law of the land is, that whoever owes
another £10, or indeed £2, may be, on the oath of that person,
immediately taken up and carried away from his own house and
family, and kept abroad till he is made to owe £50, whether he
will or no; for which he is perhaps afterwards obliged to lie in gaol;
and all these without any trial had, or any other evidence of the
debt than the abovesaid oath, which if untrue, as it often happens,
you have no remedy against the perjurer; he was, forsooth, mistaken.

But though Mr Snap would not (as perhaps by the nice rules
of honour he was obliged) discharge the count on his parole, yet

did he not (as by the strict rules of law he was enabled) confine him to his chamber. The count had his liberty of the whole house, and Mr Snap, using only the precaution of keeping his doors well locked and barred, took his prisoner's word that he would not go forth.

Mr Snap had by his second lady two daughters, who were now in the bloom of their youth and beauty. These young ladies, like damsels in romance, compassionated the captive count, and endeavoured by all means to make his confinement less irksome to him; which, though they were both very beautiful, they could not attain by any other way so effectually as by engaging with him at cards, in which contentions, as will appear hereafter, the count was greatly skilful.

As whisk and swabbers[24] was the game then in the chief vogue, they were obliged to look for a fourth person in order to make up their parties. Mr Snap himself would sometimes relax his mind from the violent fatigues of his employment by these recreations; and sometimes a neighbouring young gentleman or lady came in to their assistance: but the most frequent guest was young Master Wild, who had been educated from his infancy with the Miss Snaps, and was, by all the neighbours, allotted for the husband of Miss Tishy, or Lætitia, the younger of the two; for though, being his cousin-german, she was perhaps, in the eye of a strict conscience, somewhat too nearly related to him, yet the old people on both sides, though sufficiently scrupulous in nice matters, agreed to overlook this objection.

Men of great genius as easily discover one another as freemasons can. It was, therefore, no wonder that the count soon conceived an inclination to an intimacy with our young hero, whose vast abilities could not be concealed from one of the count's discernment; for though this latter was so expert at his cards that he was proverbially said to *play the whole game*,[25] he was no match for Master Wild, who, inexperienced as he was, notwithstanding all the art, the dexterity, and often the fortune of his adversary, never failed to send him away from the table with less in his pocket than he brought to it; for indeed Langfanger himself could not have extracted a purse with more ingenuity than our young hero.

His hands made frequent visits to the count's pocket before the latter had entertained any suspicion of him, imputing the several losses he sustained rather to the innocent and sprightly frolic of Miss Doshy, or Theodosia, with which, as she indulged him with little innocent freedoms about her person in return, he thought himself obliged to be contented; but one night, when Wild imagined the count asleep, he made so unguarded an attack upon him, that the other caught him in the fact: however, he did not think proper to acquaint him with the discovery he had made, but, preventing him from any booty at that time, he only took care for the future to button his pockets, and to pack the cards with double industry.

So far was this detection from causing any quarrel between these two prigs,* that in reality it recommended them to each other; for a wise man, that is to say a rogue, considers a trick in life as a gamester doth a trick at play. It sets him on his guard, but he admires the dexterity of him who plays it. These, therefore, and many other such instances of ingenuity, operated so violently on the count, that, notwithstanding the disparity which age, title, and above all, dress, had set between them, he resolved to enter into an acquaintance with Wild. This soon produced a perfect intimacy, and that a friendship, which had a longer duration than is common to that passion between persons who only propose to themselves the common advantages of eating, drinking, whoring, or borrowing money; which ends, as they soon fail, so doth the friendship founded upon them. Mutual interest, the greatest of all purposes, was the cement of this alliance, which nothing, of consequence, but superior interest, was capable of dissolving.

CHAPTER V

A dialogue between young Master Wild and Count la Ruse, which having extended to the rejoinder, had a very quiet, easy, and natural conclusion

One evening, after the Miss Snaps were retired to rest, the count thus addressed himself to young Wild: 'You cannot, I

---

* Thieves.

apprehend, Mr Wild, be such a stranger to your own great capacity, as to be surprised when I tell you I have often viewed, with a mixture of astonishment and concern, your shining qualities confined to a sphere where they can never reach the eyes of those who would introduce them properly into the world, and raise you to an eminence where you may blaze out to the admiration of all men. I assure you I am pleased with my captivity, when I reflect I am likely to owe to it an acquaintance, and I hope friendship, with the greatest genius of my age; and, what is still more, when I indulge my vanity with a prospect of drawing from obscurity (pardon the expression) such talents as were, I believe, never before like to have been buried in it: for I make no question but, at my discharge from confinement, which will now soon happen, I shall be able to introduce you into company, where you may reap the advantage of your superior parts.

'I will bring you acquainted, sir, with those who, as they are capable of setting a true value on such qualifications, so they will have it both in their power and inclination to prefer you for them. Such an introduction is the only advantage you want, without which your merit might be your misfortune; for those abilities which would entitle you to honour and profit in a superior station may render you only obnoxious to danger and disgrace in a lower.'

Mr Wild answered: 'Sir, I am not insensible of my obligations to you, as well for the over-value you have set on my small abilities, as for the kindness you express in offering to introduce me among my superiors. I must own my father hath often persuaded me to push myself into the company of my betters; but, to say the truth, I have an awkward pride in my nature, which is better pleased with being at the head of the lowest class than at the bottom of the highest. Permit me to say, though the idea may be somewhat coarse, I had rather stand on the summit of a dunghill than at the bottom of a hill in Paradise.[26] I have always thought it signifies little into what rank of life I am thrown, provided I make a great figure therein, and should be as well satisfied with exerting my talents well at the head of a small party or gang, as in the command of a mighty army; for I am far from agreeing with you, that great parts are often lost in a low situation; on the contrary, I am convinced it is impossible they should be lost. I have often persuaded myself that there were not fewer than a thousand in Alexander's troops capable of performing what Alexander himself did.

'But, because such spirits were not elected or destined to an imperial command, are we therefore to imagine they came off without a booty? or that they contented themselves with the share in common with their comrades? Surely, no. In civil life, doubtless, the same genius, the same endowments, have often composed the statesman and the prig, for so we call what the vulgar name a thief. The same parts, the same actions, often promote men to the head of superior societies, which raise them to the head of lower; and where is the essential difference if the one ends on Tower Hill and the other at Tyburn?[27] Hath the block any preference to the gallows, or the axe to the halter, but was given them by the ill-guided judgement of men? You will pardon me, therefore, if I am not so hastily inflamed with the common outside of things, nor join the general opinion in preferring one state to another. A guinea is as valuable in a leathern as in an embroidered purse; and a cod's head is a cod's head still, whether in a pewter or a silver dish.'

The count replied as follows: 'What you have now said doth not lessen my idea of your capacity, but confirms my opinion of the ill effects of bad and low company. Can any man doubt whether it is better to be a great statesman or a common thief? I have often heard that the devil used to say, where or to whom I know not, that it was better to reign in Hell than to be a valet de chambre in Heaven, and perhaps he was in the right; but sure, if he had had the choice of reigning in either, he would have chosen better. The truth therefore is, that by low conversation we contract a greater awe for high things than they deserve. We decline great pursuits not from contempt but despair. The man who prefers the high road to a more reputable way of making his fortune doth it because he imagines the one easier than the other; but you yourself have asserted, and with undoubted truth, that the same abilities qualify you for undertaking, and the same means will bring you to your end in both journeys – as in music it is the same tune, whether you play it in a higher or a lower key. To instance in some particulars: is it not the same qualification

which enables this man to hire himself as a servant, and to get into
the confidence and secrets of his master in order to rob him, and
that to undertake trusts of the highest nature with a design to
break and betray them? Is it less difficult by false tokens to
deceive a shopkeeper into the delivery of his goods, which you
afterwards run away with, than to impose upon him by outward
splendour and the appearance of fortune into a credit by which
you gain and he loses twenty times as much? Doth it not require
more dexterity in the fingers to draw out a man's purse from his
pocket, or to take a lady's watch from her side, without being perceived of any (an excellence in which, without flattery, I am persuaded you have no superior), than to cog a die[28] or to shuffle a
pack of cards? Is not as much art, as many excellent qualities,
required to make a pimping porter at a common bawdy-house as
would enable a man to prostitute his own or his friend's wife or
child? Doth it not ask as good a memory, as nimble an invention,
as steady a countenance, to forswear yourself in Westminster Hall
as would furnish out a complete tool of state, or perhaps a statesman himself? It is needless to particularize every instance; in all
we shall find that there is a nearer connexion between high and
low life than is generally imagined, and that a highwayman is
entitled to more favour with the great than he usually meets with.
If, therefore, as I think I have proved, the same parts which
qualify a man for eminence in a low sphere, qualify him likewise
for eminence in a higher, sure it can be no doubt in which he
would choose to exert them. Ambition, without which no one can
be a great man, will immediately instruct him, in your own
phrase, to prefer a hill in Paradise to a dunghill; nay, even fear, a
passion the most repugnant to greatness, will shew him how much
more safely he may indulge himself in the free and full exertion
of his mighty abilities in the higher than in the lower rank; since
experience teaches him that there is a crowd oftener in one year
at Tyburn than on Tower Hill in a century.' Mr Wild with much
solemnity rejoined, 'That the same capacity which qualifies a
mill-ken, a bridle-cull, or a buttock-and-file,* to arrive at any

----

*A housebreaker; a highwayman; a shoplifter. Terms used in the Cant Diction-
ary.[29]

degree of eminence in his profession, would likewise raise a man in what the world esteem a more honourable calling, I do not deny; nay, in many of your instances it is evident that more ingenuity, more art, are necessary to the lower than the higher proficients. If, therefore, you had only contended that every prig might be a statesman if he pleased, I had readily agreed to it; but when you conclude that it is his interest to be so, that ambition would bid him take that alternative, in a word, that a statesman is greater or happier than a prig, I must deny my assent. But, in comparing these two together, we must carefully avoid being misled by the vulgar erroneous estimation of things; for mankind err in disquisitions of this nature as physicians do who in considering the operations of a disease have not a due regard to the age and complexion of the patient. The same degree of heat which is common in this constitution may be a fever in that; in the same manner that which may be riches or honour to me may be poverty or disgrace to another: for all these things are to be estimated by relation to the person who possesses them. A booty of £10 looks as great in the eye of a bridle-cull, and gives as much real happiness to his fancy, as that of as many thousands to the statesman; and doth not the former lay out his acquisitions in whores and fiddles with much greater joy and mirth than the latter in palaces and pictures? What are the flattery, the false compliments of his gang to the statesman, when he himself must condemn his own blunders, and is obliged against his will to give fortune the whole honour of success? What is the pride resulting from such sham applause, compared to the secret satisfaction which a prig enjoys in his mind in reflecting on a well-contrived and well-executed scheme? Perhaps, indeed, the greater danger is on the prig's side; but then you must remember that the greater honour is so too. When I mention honour, I mean that which is paid them by their gang; for that weak part of the world which is vulgarly called THE WISE see both in a disadvantageous and disgraceful light; and as the prig enjoys (and merits too) the greater degree of honour from his gang, so doth he suffer the less disgrace from the world, who think his misdeeds, as they call them, sufficiently at last punished with a halter, which at once puts an end to his pain and infamy; whereas the other is not only hated in power, but detested and contemned at the scaffold; and future ages vent their malice on his fame, while the other sleeps quiet and forgotten. Besides, let us a little consider the secret quiet of their consciences: how easy is the reflection of having taken a few shillings or pounds from a stranger, without any breach of confidence, or perhaps any great harm to the person who loses it, compared to that of having betrayed a public trust, and ruined the fortunes of thousands, perhaps of a great nation! How much braver is an attack on the highway than at a gaming-table; and how much more innocent the character of a b—dy-house than a c—t pimp!' He was eagerly proceeding, when, casting his eyes on the count, he perceived him to be fast asleep; wherefore, having first picked his pocket of three shillings, then gently jogged him in order to take his leave, and promised to return to him the next morning to breakfast, they separated: the count retired to rest, and Master Wild to a night-cellar.[30]

CHAPTER VI

Further conferences between the count and Master Wild,
with other matters of the GREAT *kind*

The count missed his money the next morning, and very well knew who had it; but, as he knew likewise how fruitless would be any complaint, he chose to pass it by without mentioning it. Indeed it may appear strange to some readers that these gentlemen, who knew each other to be thieves, should never once give the least hint of this knowledge in all their discourse together, but, on the contrary, should have the words honesty, honour, and friendship as often in their mouths as any other men. This, I say, may appear strange to some; but those who have lived long in cities, courts, gaols, or such places, will perhaps be able to solve the seeming absurdity.

When our two friends met the next morning the count (who, though he did not agree with the whole of his friend's doctrine, was, however, highly pleased with his argument) began to bewail the misfortune of his captivity, and the backwardness of friends to assist each other in their necessities; but what vexed him, he said, most, was the cruelty of the fair: for he entrusted Wild with the secret of his having had an intrigue with Miss Theodosia, the elder of the Miss Snaps, ever since his confinement, though he could not prevail with her to set him at liberty. Wild answered, with a smile: 'It was no wonder a woman should wish to confine her lover where she might be sure of having him entirely to herself'; but added, he believed he could tell him a method of certainly procuring his escape. The count eagerly besought him to acquaint him with it. Wild told him bribery was the surest means, and advised him to apply to the maid. The count thanked him, but returned: 'That he had not a farthing left besides one guinea, which he had then given her to change.' To which Wild said: 'He must make it up with promises, which he supposed he was courtier enough to know how to put off.' The count greatly applauded the advice, and said he hoped he should be able in time to persuade him to condescend to be a great man, for which he was so perfectly well qualified.

This method being concluded on, the two friends sat down to cards, a circumstance which I should not have mentioned but for the sake of observing the prodigious force of habit; for though the count knew if he won ever so much of Mr Wild he should not receive a shilling, yet could he not refrain from packing the cards; nor could Wild keep his hands out of his friend's pockets, though he knew there was nothing in them.

When the maid came home the count began to put it to her; offered her all he had, and promised mountains *in futuro*; but all in vain – the maid's honesty was impregnable. She said: 'She would not break her trust for the whole world; no, not if she could gain a hundred pounds by it.' Upon which Wild stepping up and telling her, 'She need not fear losing her place, for it would never be found out; that they could throw a pair of sheets into the street, by which it might appear he got out at a window; that he himself would swear he saw him descending; that the money would be so much gains in her pocket; that, besides his promises, which she might depend on being performed, she would receive from him twenty shillings and ninepence in ready money (for she had only laid out threepence in plain Spanish);[31]

and lastly, that, besides his honour, the count should leave a pair of gold buttons (which afterwards turned out to be brass) of great value, in her hands, as a further pawn.'

The maid still remained inflexible, till Wild offered to lend his friend a guinea more, and to deposit it immediately in her hands. This reinforcement bore down the poor girl's resolution, and she faithfully promised to open the door to the count that evening.

Thus did our young hero not only lend his rhetoric, which few people care to do without a fee, but his money too (a sum which many a good man would have made fifty excuses before he would have parted with), to his friend, and procured him his liberty.

But it would be highly derogatory from the GREAT character of Wild, should the reader imagine he lent such a sum to a friend without the least view of serving himself. As, therefore, the reader may easily account for it in a manner more advantageous to our hero's reputation, by concluding that he had some interested view in the count's enlargement, we hope he will judge with charity, especially as the sequel makes it not only reasonable but necessary to suppose he had some such view.

A long intimacy and friendship subsisted between the count and Mr Wild, who, being by the advice of the count dressed in good clothes, was by him introduced into the best company. They constantly frequented the assemblies, auctions, gaming-tables, and playhouses; at which last they saw two acts every night, and then retired without paying – this being, it seems, an immemorial privilege which the beaus of the town prescribe for themselves. This, however, did not suit Wild's temper, who called it a cheat, and objected against it as requiring no dexterity, but what every blockhead might put in execution. He said it was a custom very much savouring of the sneaking-budge,*32 but neither so honourable nor so ingenious.

Wild now made a considerable figure, and passed for a gentleman of great fortune in the funds. Women of quality treated him with great familiarity, young ladies began to spread their charms for him, when an accident happened that put a stop to his con-

---

* Shoplifting

tinuance in a way of life too insipid and inactive to afford employment for those great talents which were designed to make a much more considerable figure in the world than attends the character of a beau or a pretty gentleman.

CHAPTER VII

Master Wild sets out on his travels, and returns home again. A very short chapter, containing infinitely more time and less matter than any other in the whole story

We are sorry we cannot indulge our reader's curiosity with a full and perfect account of this accident; but as there are such various accounts, one of which only can be true, and possibly and indeed probably none; instead of following the general method of historians, who in such cases set down the various reports, and leave to your own conjecture which you will choose, we shall pass them all over.

Certain it is that, whatever this accident was, it determined our hero's father to send his son immediately abroad for seven years; and, which may seem somewhat remarkable, to His Majesty's plantations in America[33] – that part of the world being, as he said, freer from vices than the courts and cities of Europe, and consequently less dangerous to corrupt a young man's morals. And as for the advantages, the old gentleman thought they were equal there with those attained in the politer climates; for travelling, he said, was travelling in one part of the world as well as another; it consisted in being such a time from home, and in traversing so many leagues; and [he] appealed to experience whether most of our travellers in France and Italy did not prove at their return that they might have been sent as profitably to Norway and Greenland.

According to these resolutions of his father, the young gentleman went aboard a ship, and with a great deal of good company set out for the American hemisphere. The exact time of his stay is somewhat uncertain; most probably longer than was intended. But howsoever long his abode there was, it must be a blank in this history, as the whole story contains not one adventure worthy the reader's notice; being indeed a continued scene of whoring, drinking, and removing from one place to another.

To confess a truth, we are so ashamed of the shortness of this chapter, that we would have done a violence to our history, and have inserted an adventure or two of some other traveller; to which purpose we borrowed the journals of several young gentlemen who have lately made the tour of Europe; but to our great sorrow, could not extract a single incident strong enough to justify the theft to our conscience.

When we consider the ridiculous figure this chapter must make, being the history of no less than eight years, our only comfort is, that the histories of some men's lives, and perhaps of some men who have made a noise in the world, are in reality as absolute blanks as the travels of our hero. As, therefore, we shall make sufficient amends in the sequel for this inanity, we shall hasten on to matters of true importance and immense greatness. At present we content ourselves with setting down our hero where we took him up, after acquainting our reader that he went abroad, stayed seven years, and then came home again.

CHAPTER VIII

An adventure where Wild, in the division of the booty, exhibits an astonishing instance of GREATNESS

The count was one night very successful at the hazard-table,[34] where Wild, who was just returned from his travels, was then present; as was likewise a young gentleman whose name was Bob Bagshot,[35] an acquaintance of Mr Wild's, and of whom he entertained a great opinion; taking, therefore, Mr Bagshot aside, he advised him to provide himself (if he had them not about him) with a case of pistols, and to attack the count in his way home, promising to plant himself near with the same arms, as a *corps de reserve*, and to come up on occasion. This was accordingly executed, and the count obliged to surrender to savage force what he had in so genteel and civil a manner taken at play.

And as it is a wise and philosophical observation, that one mis-fortune never comes alone, the count had hardly passed the examination of Mr Bagshot when he fell into the hands of Mr Snap, who, in company with Mr Wild the elder and one or two more gentlemen, being, it seems, thereto well warranted, laid hold of the unfortunate count and conveyed him back to the same house from which, by the assistance of his good friend, he had formerly escaped.

Mr Wild and Mr Bagshot went together to the tavern, where Mr Bagshot (generously, as he thought) offered to share the booty, and, having divided the money into two unequal heaps, and added a golden snuff-box to the lesser heap, he desired Mr Wild to take his choice.

Mr Wild immediately conveyed the larger share of the ready into his pocket, according to an excellent maxim of his: 'First secure what share you can before you wrangle for the rest'; and then, turning to his companion he asked him with a stern coun-tenance whether he intended to keep all that sum to himself? Mr Bagshot answered, with some surprise, that he thought Mr Wild had no reason to complain; for it was surely fair, at least on his part, to content himself with an equal share of the booty, who had taken the whole. 'I grant you took it,' replied Wild; 'but, pray, who proposed or counselled the taking it? Can you say that you have done more than executed my scheme? and might not I, if I had pleased, have employed another, since you well know there was not a gentleman in the room but would have taken the money if he had known how, conveniently and safely, to do it?' 'That is very true,' returned Bagshot, 'but did not I execute the scheme, did not I run the whole risk? Should not I have suffered the whole punishment if I had been taken, and is not the labourer worthy of his hire?'[36] 'Doubtless,' says Jonathan, 'he is so, and your hire I shall not refuse you, which is all that the labourer is entitled to or ever enjoys. I remember when I was at school to have heard some verses which for the excellence of their doctrine made an impression on me, purporting that the birds of the air and the beasts of the field work not for themselves. It is true, the farmer allows fodder to his oxen and pasture to his sheep; but it is for his own service, not theirs. In the same manner the ploughman, the shepherd, the weaver, the builder, and the soldier, work not for themselves but others; they are contented with a poor pittance (the labourer's hire), and permit us, the GREAT, to enjoy the fruits of their labours. Aristotle, as my master told us, hath plainly proved, in the first book of his politics, that the low, mean, useful part of mankind are born slaves to the wills of their superiors, and are indeed as much their property as the cattle.[37] It is well said of us, the higher order of mortals, that we are born only to devour the fruits of the earth; and it may be as well said of the lower class, that they are born only to produce them for us. Is not the battle gained by the sweat and danger of the common soldier? Are not the honour and fruits of the victory the general's who laid the scheme? Is not the house built by the labour of the carpenter and the bricklayer? Is it not built for the profit of the architect and for the use of the inhabitant, who could not easily have placed one brick upon another? Is not the cloth or the silk wrought into its form and variegated with all the beauty of colours by those who are forced to content themselves with the coarsest and vilest part of their work, while the profit and enjoyment of their labours fall to the share of others? Cast your eye abroad, and see who is it lives in the most magnificent buildings, feasts his palate with the most luxurious dainties, his eyes with the most beautiful sculptures and delicate paintings, and clothes himself in the finest and richest apparel; and tell me if all these do not fall to his lot who had not any the least share in producing all these conveniences, nor the least ability so to do? Why then should the state of a prig differ from all others? Or why should you, who are the labourer only, the executor of my scheme, expect a share in the profit? Be advised, therefore; deliver the whole booty to me, and trust to my bounty for your reward.' Mr Bagshot was some time silent, and looked like a man thunderstruck, but at last, recovering himself from his surprise, he thus began: 'If you think, Mr Wild, by the force of your arguments, to get the money out of my pocket, you are greatly mistaken. What is all this stuff to me? D—n me, I am a man of honour, and, though I can't talk as well as you, by G— you shall not make a fool of me; and if you take me for one, I must tell you, you are a rascal.' At which words he laid his hand to his pistol. Wild, perceiving the little success the great strength of his arguments had met with, and the hasty temper of his friend, gave over his design for the present, and told Bagshot he was only in jest. But this coolness with which he treated the other's flame had rather the effect of oil than of water. Bagshot replied in a rage: 'D—n me, I don't like such jests; I see you are a pitiful rascal and a scoundrel.' Wild, with a philosophy worthy of great admiration, returned: 'As for your abuse, I have no regard to it; but, to convince you I am not afraid of you, let us lay the whole booty on the table, and let the conqueror take it all.' And having so said, he drew out his shining hanger,[38] whose glittering so dazzled the eyes of Bagshot, that, in a tone entirely altered, he said: 'No! he was contented with what he had already; that it was mighty ridiculous in them to quarrel among themselves; that they had common enemies enough abroad, against whom they should unite their common force; that if he had mistaken Wild he was sorry for it; and that as for a jest, he could take a jest as well as another.' Wild, who had a wonderful knack of discovering and applying the passions of men, beginning now to have a little insight into his friend, and to conceive what arguments would make the quickest impression on him, cried out in a loud voice: 'That he had bullied him into drawing his hanger, and, since it was out, he would not put it up without satisfaction.' 'What satisfaction would you have?' answered the other. 'Your money or your blood,' said Wild. 'Why, look ye, Mr Wild,' said Bagshot, 'if you want to borrow a little of my part, since I know you to be a man of honour, I don't care if I lend you; for, though I am not afraid of any man living, yet rather than break with a friend, and as it may be necessary for your occasions – ' Wild, who often declared that he looked upon borrowing to be as good a way of taking as any, and, as he called it, the genteelest kind of sneaking-budge, putting up his hanger, and shaking his friend by the hand, told him he had hit the nail on the head; it was really his present necessity only that prevailed with him against his will, for that his honour was concerned to pay a considerable sum the next morning. Upon which, contenting himself with one half of Bagshot's share, so that he had three parts in four of the whole, he took leave of his companion and retired to rest.

CHAPTER IX

Wild pays a visit to Miss Lætitia Snap. A description of that lovely young creature, and the successless issue of Mr Wild's addresses

The next morning when our hero waked he began to think of paying a visit to Miss Tishy Snap, a woman of great merit and of as great generosity; yet Mr Wild found a present was ever most welcome to her, as being a token of respect in her lover. He therefore went directly to a toy-shop, and there purchased a genteel snuff-box, with which he waited upon his mistress, whom he found in the most beautiful undress. Her lovely hair hung wantonly over her forehead, being neither white with, nor yet free from, powder; a neat double clout, which seemed to have been worn a few weeks only, was pinned under her chin; some remains of that art with which ladies improve nature shone on her cheeks; her body was loosely attired, without stays or jumps, so that her breasts had uncontrolled liberty to display their beauteous orbs, which they did as low as her girdle; a thin covering of a rumpled muslin handkerchief almost hid them from the eyes, save in a few parts, where a good-natured hole gave opportunity to the naked breast to appear. Her gown was a satin of a whitish colour, with about a dozen little silver spots upon it, so artificially interwoven at great distance, that they looked as if they had fallen there by chance. This, flying open, discovered a fine yellow petticoat, beautifully edged round the bottom with a narrow piece of half gold lace, which was now almost become fringe: beneath this appeared another petticoat stiffened with whalebone, vulgarly called a hoop, which hung six inches at least below the other; and under this again appeared an undergarment of that colour which Ovid intends when he says:

– *Qui color albus erat nunc est contrarius albo.*[39]

She likewise displayed two pretty feet covered with silk and adorned with lace, and tied, the right with a handsome piece of blue ribbon; the left, as more unworthy, with a piece of yellow stuff, which seemed to have been a strip of her upper petticoat. Such was the lovely creature whom Mr Wild attended. She received him at first with some of that coldness which women of strict virtue, by a commendable though sometimes painful restraint, enjoin themselves to their lovers. The snuff-box, being produced, was at first civilly, and indeed gently, refused; but on a second application accepted. The tea-table was soon called for, at which a discourse passed between these young lovers, which, could we set it down with any accuracy, would be very edifying as well as entertaining to our reader; let it suffice then that the wit, together with the beauty, of this young creature, so inflamed the passion of Wild, which, though an honourable sort of a passion, was at the same time so extremely violent, that it transported him to freedoms too offensive to the nice chastity of Lætitia, who was, to confess the truth, more indebted to her own strength for the preservation of her virtue than to the awful respect or backwardness of her lover; he was indeed so very urgent in his addresses, that, had he not with many oaths promised her marriage, we could scarce have been strictly justified in calling his passion honourable; but he was so remarkably attached to decency, that he never offered any violence to a young lady without the most earnest promises of that kind, these being, he said, a ceremonial due to female modesty, which cost so little, and were so easily pronounced, that the omission could arise from nothing but the mere wantonness of brutality. The lovely Lætitia, either out of prudence, or perhaps religion, of which she was a liberal professor, was deaf to all his promises, and luckily invincible by his force; for, though she had not yet learnt the art of well clenching her fist, nature had not, however, left her defenceless, for at the ends of her fingers she wore arms, which she used with such admirable dexterity, that the hot blood of Mr Wild soon began to appear in several little spots on his face, and his fullblown cheeks to resemble that part which modesty forbids a boy to turn up anywhere but in a public school, after some pedagogue, strong of arm, hath exercised his talents thereon. Wild now retreated from the conflict, and the victorious Lætitia with becoming triumph and noble spirit, cried out: 'D—n your eyes, if this be your way of shewing your love, I'll warrant I gives you enough on 't.' She then proceeded to talk of her virtue, which Wild bid her carry to the devil with her, and thus our lovers parted.

CHAPTER X

A discovery of some matters concerning the chaste Lætitia which must wonderfully surprise, and perhaps affect, our reader

Mr Wild was no sooner departed than the fair conqueress, opening the door of a closet, called forth a young gentleman whom she had there enclosed at the approach of the other. The name of this gallant was Tom Smirk. He was clerk to an attorney, and was indeed the greatest beau and the greatest favourite of the ladies at the end of the town where he lived. As we take dress to be the characteristic or efficient quality of a beau, we shall, instead of giving any character of this young gentleman, content ourselves with describing his dress only to our readers. He wore, then, a pair of white stockings on his legs, and pumps on his feet: his buckles were a large piece of pinchbeck plate,[40] which almost covered his whole foot. His breeches were of red plush, which hardly reached his knees; his waistcoat was a white dimity,[41] richly embroidered with yellow silk, over which he wore a blue plush coat with metal buttons, a smart sleeve, and a cape reaching half-way down his back. His wig was of a brown colour, covering almost half his pate, on which was hung on one side a little laced hat, but cocked with great smartness. Such was the accomplished Smirk, who, at his issuing forth from the closet, was received with open arms by the amiable Lætitia. She addressed him by the tender name of dear Tommy, and told him she had dismissed the odious creature whom her father intended for her husband, and had now nothing to interrupt her happiness with him.

Here, reader, thou must pardon us if we stop a while to lament the capriciousness of nature in forming this charming part of the creation designed to complete the happiness of man; with their soft innocence to allay his ferocity, with their sprightliness to soothe his cares, and with their constant friendship to relieve all the troubles and disappointments which can happen to him. Seeing then that these are the blessings chiefly sought after and generally found in every wife, how must we lament that disposition in these lovely creatures which leads them to prefer in their favour those individuals of the other sex who do not seem intended by nature as so great a masterpiece! For surely, however useful they may be in the creation, as we are taught that nothing, not even a louse, is made in vain,[42] yet these beaus, even that most splendid and honoured part which in this our island nature loves to distinguish in red, are not, as some think, the noblest work of the Creator. For my own part, let any man choose to himself two beaus, let them be captains or colonels, as well-dressed men as ever lived, I would venture to oppose a single Sir Isaac Newton, a Shakespear, a Milton, or perhaps some few others, to both these beaus; nay, and I very much doubt whether it had not been better for the world in general that neither of these beaus had ever been born than that it should have wanted the benefit arising to it from the labour of any one of those persons.

If this be true, how melancholy must the consideration that any single beau, especially if he have but half a yard of ribbon in his hat, shall weigh heavier in the scale of female affection than twenty Sir Isaac Newtons! How must our reader, who perhaps had wisely accounted for the resistance which the chaste Lætitia had made to the violent addresses of the ravished (or rather ravishing) Wild from that lady's impregnable virtue – how he must blush, I say, to perceive her quit the strictness of her carriage, and abandon herself to those loose freedoms which she indulged to Smirk! But alas! when we discover all, as to preserve the fidelity of our history we must, when we relate that every familiarity had passed between them, and that the FAIR Lætitia (for we must, in this single instance, imitate Virgil when he drops the *pius* and the *pater*, and drop our favourite epithet of *chaste*), the FAIR Lætitia had, I say, made Smirk as happy as Wild desired to be, what must then be our reader's confusion! We will, therefore, draw a curtain over this scene, from that philogyny which is in us, and proceed to matters which, instead of dishonouring the human species, will greatly raise and ennoble it.

CHAPTER XI

Containing as notable instances of human greatness as are to be met with in ancient or modern history. Concluding with some wholesome hints to the gay part of mankind

Wild no sooner parted from the chaste Lætitia than, recollecting that his friend the count was returned to his lodgings in the same house, he resolved to visit him; for he was none of those half-bred fellows who are ashamed to see their friends when they have plundered and betrayed them; from which base and pitiful temper many monstrous cruelties have been transacted by men, who have sometimes carried their modesty so far as to the murder or utter ruin of those against whom their consciences have suggested to them that they have committed some small trespass, either by the debauching a friend's wife or daughter, belying or betraying the friend himself, or some other such trifling instance. In our hero there was nothing not truly great: he could, without the least abashment, drink a bottle with the man who knew he had the moment before picked his pocket; and, when he had stripped him of everything he had, never desired to do him any further mischief; for he carried good-nature to that wonderful and uncommon height that he never did a single injury to man or woman by which he himself did not expect to reap some advantage. He would often indeed say that by the contrary party men often made a bad bargain with the devil, and did his work for nothing.

Our hero found the captive count, not basely lamenting his fate nor abandoning himself to despair, but, with due resignation, employing himself in preparing several packs of cards for future exploits. The count, little suspecting that Wild had been the sole contriver of the misfortune which had befallen him, rose up and eagerly embraced him, and Wild returned his embrace with equal warmth. They were no sooner seated than Wild took an occasion, from seeing the cards lying on the table, to inveigh against gaming, and, with an usual and highly commendable freedom, after first exaggerating the distressed circumstances in which the count was then involved, imputed all his misfortunes to that cursed itch of play which, he said, he concluded had brought his present confinement upon him, and must unavoidably end in his destruction. The other, with great alacrity, defended his favourite amusement (or rather employment), and, having told his friend the great success he had after his unluckily quitting the room, acquainted him with the accident which followed, and which the reader, as well as Mr Wild, hath had some intimation of before; adding, however, one circumstance not hitherto mentioned, viz. that he had defended his money with the utmost bravery, and had dangerously wounded at least two of the three men that had attacked him. This behaviour Wild, who not only knew the extreme readiness with which the booty had been delivered, but also the constant frigidity of the count's courage, highly applauded, and wished he had been present to assist him. The count then proceeded to animadvert on the carelessness of the watch, and the scandal it was to the laws that honest people could not walk the streets in safety; and, after expatiating some time on the subject, he asked Mr Wild if he ever saw so prodigious a run of luck (for so he chose to call his winning, though he knew Wild was well acquainted with his having loaded dice in his pocket). The other answered it was indeed prodigious, and almost sufficient to justify any person who did not know him better in suspecting his fair play. 'No man, I believe, dares call that in question,' replied he. 'No, surely,' says Wild; 'you are well known to be a man of more honour; but pray, sir,' continued he, 'did the rascals rob you of all?' 'Every shilling,' cries the other, with an oath; 'they did not leave me a single stake.'

While they were thus discoursing, Mr Snap, with a gentleman who followed him, introduced Mr Bagshot into the company. It seems Mr Bagshot, immediately after his separation from Mr Wild, returned to the gaming-table, where having trusted to fortune that treasure which he had procured by his industry, the faithless goddess committed a breach of trust, and sent Mr Bagshot away with as empty pockets as are to be found in any laced coat in the kingdom. Now, as that gentleman was walking to a certain reputable house or shed in Covent Garden Market he

fortuned to meet with Mr Snap, who had just returned from conveying the count to his lodgings, and was then walking to and fro
before the gaming-house door; for you are to know, my good
reader, if you have never been a man of wit and pleasure about
town, that, as the voracious pike lieth snug under some weed
before the mouth of any of those little streams which discharge
themselves into a large river, waiting for the small fry which issue
thereout, so hourly, before the door or mouth of these gaming-
houses, doth Mr Snap, or some other gentleman of his occupation, attend the issuing forth of the small fry of young gentlemen,
to whom they deliver little slips of parchment, containing invita-
tions of the said gentlemen to their houses, together with one Mr
John Doe,* a person whose company is in great request. Mr Snap,
among many others of these billets, happened to have one directed
to Mr Bagshot, being at the suit or solicitation of one Mrs Anne
Sample, spinster, at whose house the said Bagshot had lodged
several months, and whence he had inadvertently departed without taking a formal leave, on which account Mrs Anne had taken
this method of *speaking with* him.[43]

Mr Snap's house being now very full of good company, he
was obliged to introduce Mr Bagshot into the count's apartment,
it being, as he said, the only chamber he had to *lock up* in. Mr
Wild no sooner saw his friend than he ran eagerly to embrace
him, and immediately presented him to the count, who received
him with great civility.

CHAPTER XII

*Further particulars relating to Miss Tishy, which perhaps may
not greatly surprise after the former. The description of a very
fine gentleman. And a dialogue between Wild and the count, in
which public virtue is just hinted at, with, etc.*

Mr Snap had turned the key a very few minutes before a servant of the family called Mr Bagshot out of the room, telling him

---

*This is a fictitious name which is put into every writ; for what purpose the
lawyers best know.

there was a person below who desired to speak with him; and this was no other than Miss Lætitia Snap, whose admirer Mr Bagshot had long been, and in whose tender breast his passion had raised a more ardent flame than that of any of his rivals had been able to raise. Indeed, she was so extremely fond of this youth, that she often confessed to her female confidents, if she could ever have listened to the thought of living with any one man, Mr Bagshot was he. Nor was she singular in this inclination, many other young ladies being her rivals in this lover, who had all the great and noble qualifications necessary to form a true gallant, and which nature is seldom so extremely bountiful as to indulge to any one person. We will endeavour, however, to describe them all with as much exactness as possible. He was then six feet high, had large calves, broad shoulders, a ruddy complexion, with brown curled hair, a modest assurance, and clean linen. He had indeed, it must be confessed, some small deficiencies to counter-balance these heroic qualities; for he was the silliest fellow in the world, could neither write nor read, nor had he a single grain or spark of honour, honesty, or good-nature, in his whole composition.

As soon as Mr Bagshot had quitted the room the count, taking Wild by the hand, told him he had something to communicate to him of very great importance. 'I am very well convinced,' said he, 'that Bagshot is the person who robbed me.' Wild started with great amazement at this discovery, and answered, with a most serious countenance: 'I advise you to take care how you cast any such reflections on a man of Mr Bagshot's nice honour for I am certain he will not bear it.' 'D—n his honour!' quoth the enraged count; 'nor can I bear being robbed; I will apply to a justice of the peace.' Wild replied, with great indignation: 'Since you dare entertain such a suspicion against my friend, I will henceforth disclaim all acquaintance with you. Mr Bagshot is a man of honour, and my friend, and consequently it is impossible he should be guilty of a bad action.' He added much more to the same purpose, which had not the expected weight with the count; for the latter seemed still certain as to the person, and resolute in applying for justice, which, he said, he thought he owed to the public as well as to himself. Wild then changed his countenance into a kind of derision, and spoke as follows: 'Suppose it should be possible that

Mr Bagshot had, in a frolic (for I will call it no other), taken this method of borrowing your money, what will you get by prosecuting him? Not your money again, for you hear he was stripped at the gaming-table (of which Bagshot had during their short confabulation informed them); you will get then an opportunity of being still more out of pocket by the prosecution. Another advantage you may promise yourself is the being blown up[44] at every gaming-house in town, for that I will assure you of; and then much good may it do you to sit down with the satisfaction of having discharged what it seems you owe the public. I am ashamed of my own discernment when I mistook you for a great man. Would it not be better for you to receive part (perhaps all) of your money again by a wise concealment: for, however *seedy** Mr Bagshot may be now, if he hath really played this frolic with you, you may believe he will play it with others, and when he is in cash you may depend on a restoration; the law will be always in your power, and that is the last remedy which a brave or a wise man would resort to. Leave the affair therefore to me; I will examine Bagshot, and, if I find he hath played you this trick, I will engage my own honour you shall in the end be no loser.' The count answered: 'If I was sure to be no loser, Mr Wild, I apprehend you have a better opinion of my understanding than to imagine I would prosecute a gentleman for the sake of the public. These are foolish words of course, which we learn a ridiculous habit of speaking, and will often break from us without any design or meaning. I assure you, all I desire is a reimbursement; and if I can by your means obtain that, the public may –' concluding with a phrase too coarse to be inserted in a history of this kind.

They were now informed that dinner was ready, and the company assembled below stairs, whither the reader may, if he please, attend these gentlemen.

There sat down at the table Mr Snap, and the two Miss Snaps his daughters, Mr Wild the elder, Mr Wild the younger, the count, Mr Bagshot, and a grave gentleman who had formerly had the honour of carrying arms in a regiment of foot, and who was now engaged in the office (perhaps a more profitable one) of

---

* Poor.

assisting or following Mr Snap in the execution of the laws of his country.

Nothing very remarkable passed at dinner. The conversation (as is usual in polite company) rolled chiefly on what they were then eating and what they had lately eaten. In this the military gentleman, who had served in Ireland, gave them a very particular account of a new manner of roasting potatoes, and others gave an account of other dishes. In short, an indifferent bystander would have concluded from their discourse that they had all come into this world for no other purpose than to fill their bellies; and indeed, if this was not the chief, it is probable it was the most innocent design nature had in their formation.

As soon as *the dish* was removed, and the ladies retired, the count proposed a game at hazard, which was immediately assented to by the whole company, and, the dice being immediately brought in, the count took up the box and demanded who would set him: to which no one made any answer, imagining perhaps the count's pockets to be more empty than they were; for, in reality, that gentleman (notwithstanding what he had heartily swore to Mr Wild) had, since his arrival at Mr Snap's, conveyed a piece of plate to pawn, by which means he had furnished himself with ten guineas. The count, therefore perceiving this backwardness in his friends, and probably somewhat guessing at the cause of it, took the said guineas out of his pocket, and threw them on the table; when lo (such is the force of example), all the rest began to produce their funds, and immediately, a considerable sum glittering in their eyes, the game began.

CHAPTER XIII

*A chapter of which we are extremely vain, and which indeed
we look on as our chef-d'œuvre; containing a wonderful story
concerning the devil, and as nice a scene of honour as ever happened*

My reader, I believe, even if he be a gamester, would not thank me for an exact relation of every man's success; let it suffice then that they played till the whole money vanished from the table.

Whether the devil himself carried it away, as some suspected, I will not determine; but very surprising it was that every person protested he had lost, nor could any one guess who, unless *the devil*, had won.

But though very probable it is that this arch-fiend had some share in the booty, it is likely he had not all; Mr Bagshot being imagined to be a considerable winner, notwithstanding his assertions to the contrary; for he was seen by several to convey money often into his pocket; and what is still a little stronger presumption is, that the grave gentleman whom we have mentioned to have served his country in two honourable capacities, not being willing to trust alone to the evidence of his eyes, had frequently dived into the said Bagshot's pocket, whence (as he tells us in the apology for his life afterwards published*), though he might extract a few pieces, he was very sensible he had left many behind. The gentleman had long indulged his curiosity in this way before Mr Bagshot, in the heat of gaming, had perceived him; but, as Bagshot was now leaving off play, he discovered this ingenious feat of dexterity; upon which, leaping up from his chair in violent passion he cried out: 'I thought I had been among gentlemen and men of honour, but d—n me, I find we have a pickpocket in company.' The scandalous sound of this word extremely alarmed the whole board, nor did they all shew less surprise than the *Conv—n*[45] (whose not sitting of late is much lamented) would express at hearing there was an atheist in the room; but it more particularly affected the gentleman at whom it was levelled, though it was not addressed to him. He likewise started from his chair, and, with a fierce countenance and accent, said: 'Do you mean me? D—n your eyes, you are a rascal and a scoundrel!' Those words would have been immediately succeeded by blows had not the company interposed, and with strong arm withheld the two antagonists from each other. It was, however, a long time before they could be prevailed on to sit down; which being at last happily brought about, Mr Wild the elder, who was a well-disposed

---

*Not in a book by itself, in imitation of some other such persons,[46] but in the ordinary's account, etc., where all the apologies for the lives of rogues and whores which have been published within these twenty years should have been inserted.

old man, advised them to shake hands and be friends; but the gentleman who had received the first affront absolutely refused it, and swore *he would have the villain's blood*. Mr Snap highly applauded the resolution, and affirmed that the affront was by no means to be put up by any who bore the name of a gentleman, and that unless his friend resented it properly he would never execute another warrant in his company; that he had always looked upon him as a man of honour, and doubted not but he would prove himself so; and that, if it was his own case, nothing should persuade him to put up such an affront without proper satisfaction. The count likewise spoke on the same side, and the parties themselves muttered several short sentences purporting their intentions.[47] At last Mr Wild, our hero, rising slowly from his seat, and having fixed the attention of all present, began as follows: 'I have heard with infinite pleasure everything which the two gentlemen who spoke last have said with relation to honour, nor can any man possibly entertain a higher and nobler sense of that word, nor a greater esteem of its inestimable value, than myself. If we have no name to express it by in our Cant Dictionary, it were well to be wished we had. It is, indeed, the essential quality of a gentleman, and which no man who ever was great in the field or on the road (as others express it) can possibly be without. But alas! gentlemen, what pity is it that a word of such sovereign use and virtue should have so uncertain and various an application that scarce two people mean the same thing by it? Do not some by honour mean good-nature and humanity, which weak minds call virtues? How then! Must we deny it to the great, the brave, the noble; to the sackers of towns, the plunderers of provinces, and the conquerors of kingdoms! Were not these men of honour? and yet they scorned those pitiful qualities I have mentioned. Again, some few (or I am mistaken) include the idea of honesty in their honour. And shall we then say that no man who withholds from another what law, or justice perhaps, calls his own, or who greatly and boldly deprives him of such property, is a man of honour? Heaven forbid I should say so in this, or, indeed, in any other good company! Is honour truth? No; it is not in the lie's going from us,[48] but in its coming to us, our honour is injured. Doth it then consist in what the vulgar call cardinal virtues?

It would be an affront to your understandings to suppose it, since we see every day so many men of honour without any. In what then doth the word honour consist? Why, in itself alone. A man of honour is he that is called a man of honour; and while he is so called he so remains, and no longer. Think not anything a man commits can forfeit his honour. Look abroad into the world; the PRIG, while he flourishes, is a man of honour; when in gaol, at the bar, or the tree, he is so no longer. And why is this distinction? Not from his actions; for those are often as well known in his flourishing estate as they are afterwards; but because men, I mean those of his own party or gang, call him a man of honour in the former, and cease to call him so in the latter condition. Let us see then; how hath Mr Bagshot injured the gentleman's honour? Why, he hath called him a pickpocket; and that, probably, by a severe construction and a long roundabout way of reasoning, may seem a little to derogate from his honour, if considered in a very nice sense. Admitting it, therefore, for argument's sake, to be some small imputation on his honour, let Mr Bagshot give him satisfaction; let him doubly and triply repair this oblique injury by directly asserting that he believes he is a man of honour.' The gentleman answered he was content to refer it to Mr Wild, and whatever satisfaction he thought sufficient he would accept. 'Let him give me my money again first,' said Bagshot, 'and then I will call him a man of honour with all my heart.' The gentleman then protested he had not any, which Snap seconded, declaring he had his eyes on him all the while; but Bagshot remained still unsatisfied, till Wild, rapping out a hearty oath, swore he had not taken a single farthing, adding that whoever asserted the contrary gave him the lie, and he would resent it. And now, such was the ascendancy of this great man, that Bagshot immediately acquiesced, and performed the ceremonies required: and thus, by the exquisite address of our hero, this quarrel, which had so fatal an aspect, and which between two persons so extremely jealous of their honour would most certainly have produced very dreadful consequences, was happily concluded.

Mr Wild was, indeed, a little interested in this affair, as he himself had set the gentleman to work, and had received the greatest part of the booty: and as to Mr Snap's deposition in his favour, it was the usual height to which the ardour of that worthy person's friendship too frequently hurried him. It was his constant maxim that he was a pitiful fellow who would stick at a little rapping* for his friend.

CHAPTER XIV

In which the history of GREATNESS *is continued*

Matter being thus reconciled, and the gaming over, from reasons before hinted, the company proceeded to drink about with the utmost cheerfulness and friendship; drinking healths, shaking hands, and professing the most perfect affection for each other. All which were not in the least interrupted by some designs which they then agitated in their minds, and which they intended to execute as soon as the liquor had prevailed over some of their understandings. Bagshot and the gentleman intending to rob each other; Mr Snap and Mr Wild the elder meditating what other creditors they could find out to charge the gentleman then in custody with; the count hoping to renew the play, and Wild, our hero, laying a design to put Bagshot out of the way, or, as the vulgar express it, to hang him with the first opportunity. But none of these great designs could at present be put in execution, for, Mr Snap being soon after summoned abroad on business of great moment, which required likewise the assistance of Mr Wild the elder and his other friend, and as he did not care to trust to the nimbleness of the count's heels, of which he had already had some experience, he declared he must *lock up* for that evening. Here, reader, if thou pleasest, as we are in no great haste, we will stop and make a simile. As when their lap is finished, the cautious huntsman to their kennel gathers the nimble-footed hounds, they with lank ears and tails slouch sullenly on, whilst he, with his whippers-in, follows close at their heels, regardless of their dogged humour, till, having seen them safe within the door, he turns the key, and then retires to whatever business or pleasure calls him

---

* Rapping is a cant word for perjury.

thence; so with louring countenance and reluctant steps mounted the count and Bagshot to their chamber, or rather kennel, whither they were attended by Snap and those who followed him, and where Snap, having seen them deposited, very contentedly locked the door and departed. And now, reader, we will, in imitation of the truly laudable custom of the world, leave these our good friends to deliver themselves as they can, and pursue the thriving fortunes of Wild, our hero, who, with that great aversion to satisfaction and content which is inseparably incident to great minds, began to enlarge his views with his prosperity. For this restless, amiable disposition, this noble avidity which increases with feeding, is the first principle or constituent quality of these our great men; to whom, in their passage on to greatness, it happens as to a traveller over the Alps, or, if this be a too far-fetched simile, to one who travels westward over the hills near Bath,[49] where the simile was indeed made. He sees not the end of his journey at once; but, passing on from scheme to scheme, and from hill to hill, with noble constancy, resolving still to attain the summit on which he hath fixed his eye, however dirty the roads may be through which he struggles, he at length arrives – at some vile inn, where he finds no kind of entertainment nor conveniency for repose. I fancy, reader, if thou hast ever travelled in these roads, one part of my simile is sufficiently apparent (and, indeed, in all these illustrations, one side is generally much more apparent than the other); but, believe me, if the other doth not so evidently appear to thy satisfaction, it is from no other reason than because thou art unacquainted with these great men, and hast not had sufficient instruction, leisure, or opportunity, to consider what happens to those who pursue what is generally understood by GREATNESS: for surely, if thou hadst animadverted, not only on the many perils to which great men are daily liable while they are in their progress, but hadst discerned, as it were through a microscope (for it is invisible to the naked eye), that diminutive speck of happiness which they attain even in the consummation of their wishes, thou wouldst lament with me the unhappy fate of these great men, on whom nature hath set so superior a mark, that the rest of mankind are born for their use and emolument only, and be apt to cry out: 'It is pity that THOSE for whose pleasure and profit mankind are to labour and sweat, to be hacked and hewed, to be pillaged, plundered, and every way destroyed, should reap so LITTLE advantage from all the miseries they occasion to others.' For my part, I own myself of that humble kind of mortals who consider themselves born for the behoof of some great man or other, and could I behold his happiness carved out of the labour and ruin of a thousand such reptiles as myself, I might with satisfaction exclaim, *Sic, sic juvat*:[50] but when I behold one GREAT MAN starving with hunger and freezing with cold, in the midst of fifty thousand who are suffering the same evils for his diversion; when I see another, whose own mind is a more abject slave to his own greatness, and is more tortured and racked by it, than those of all his vassals; lastly, when I consider whole nations rooted out only to bring tears into the eyes of a GREAT MAN,[51] not indeed because he hath extirpated so many, but because he had no more nations to extirpate, then truly I am almost inclined to wish that Nature had spared us this her MASTERPIECE, and that no GREAT MAN had ever been born into the world.

But to proceed with our history, which will, we hope, produce much better lessons, and more instructive, than any we can preach: Wild was no sooner retired to a night-cellar than he began to reflect on the sweets he had that day enjoyed from the labours of others, viz. first, from Mr Bagshot, who had for his use robbed the count; and, secondly, from the gentleman, who, for the same good purpose, had picked the pocket of Bagshot. He then proceeded to reason thus with himself: 'The art of policy is the art of multiplication, the degrees of greatness being constituted by those two little words *more* and *less*. Mankind are first properly to be considered under two grand divisions, those that use their own hands, and those who employ the hands of others. The former are the base and rabble; the latter, the genteel part of the creation. The mercantile part of the world, therefore, wisely use the term *employing hands*, and justly prefer each other as they employ more or fewer; for thus one merchant says he is greater than another because he employs more hands. And now, indeed, the merchant should seem to challenge some character of greatness, did we not necessarily come to a second division, viz. of

those who employ hands for the use of the community in which
they live, and of those who employ hands merely for their own
use, without any regard to the benefit of society. Of the former
sort are the yeoman, the manufacturer, the merchant, and
perhaps the gentleman. The first of these being to manure and
cultivate his native soil, and to employ hands to produce the fruits
of the earth. The second being to improve them by employing
hands likewise, and to produce from them those useful commodities which serve as well for the conveniences as necessaries
of life. The third is to employ hands for the exportation of the redundance of our own commodities, and to exchange them with
the redundance of foreign nations, that thus every soil and every
climate may enjoy the fruits of the whole earth. The gentleman is,
by employing hands, likewise to embellish his country with the
improvement of arts and sciences, with the making and executing
good and wholesome laws for the preservation of property and the
distribution of justice, and in several other manners to be useful
to society. Now we come to the second part of this division,
viz. of those who employ hands for their own use only; and this
is that noble and great part who are generally distinguished into
conquerors, *absolute princes*, *statesmen*, and *prigs*.* Now all these
differ from each other in greatness only – they employ *more* or
fewer hands. And Alexander the Great was only *greater* than a
captain of one of the Tartarian or Arabian hordes, as he was at
the head of a larger number. In what then is a single *prig* inferior
to any other great men, but because he employs his own hands
only; for he is not on that account to be levelled with the base and
vulgar, because he employs his hands for his own use only. Now,
suppose a *prig* had as many tools as any prime minister ever had,
would he not be as great as any prime minister whatsoever?
Undoubtedly he would. What then have I to do in the pursuit
of greatness but to procure a gang, and to make the use of this gang
centre in myself? This gang shall rob for me only, receiving very
moderate rewards for their actions; out of this gang I will prefer
to my favour the boldest and most iniquitous (as the vulgar
express it); the rest I will, from time to time, as I see occasion,

---

* Thieves.

transport and hang at my pleasure; and thus (which I take to be the highest excellence of a *prig*) convert those laws which are made for the benefit and protection of society to my single use.'

Having thus preconceived his scheme, he saw nothing wanting to put it in immediate execution but that which is indeed the beginning as well as the end of all human devices: I mean money. Of which commodity he was possessed of no more than sixty-five guineas, being all that remained from the double benefits he had made of Bagshot, and which did not seem sufficient to furnish his house, and every other convenience necessary for so grand an undertaking. He resolved, therefore, to go immediately to the gaming-house, which was then sitting, not so much with an intention of trusting to fortune as to play the surer card of attacking the winner in his way home. On his arrival, however, he thought he might as well try his success at the dice, and reserve the other resource as his last expedient. He accordingly sat down to play; and as Fortune, no more than others of her sex, is observed to distribute her favours with strict regard to great mental endowments, so our hero lost every farthing in his pocket. This loss, however, he bore with great constancy of mind, and with as great composure of aspect. To say truth, he considered the money as only lent for a short time, or rather indeed as deposited with a banker. He then resolved to have immediate recourse to his surer stratagem; and, casting his eyes round the room, he soon perceived a gentleman sitting in a disconsolate posture, who seemed a proper instrument or tool for his purpose. In short (to be as concise as possible in these least shining parts of our history), Wild accosted this man, sounded him, found him fit to execute, proposed the matter, received a ready assent, and, having fixed on the person who seemed that evening the greatest favourite of Fortune, they posted themselves in the most proper place to surprise the enemy as he was retiring to his quarters, where he was soon attacked, subdued, and plundered; but indeed of no considerable booty; for it seems this gentleman played on a common stock, and had deposited his winnings at the scene of action, nor had he any more than two shillings in his pocket when he was attacked.

This was so cruel a disappointment to Wild, and so sensibly

affects us, as no doubt it will the reader, that, as it must disqualify us both from proceeding any farther at present, we will now take a little breath, and therefore we shall here close this book.

BOOK II

CHAPTER I

*Characters of silly people, with the proper uses for which
such are designed*

One reason why we chose to end our first book, as we did, with
the last chapter, was, that we are now obliged to produce two
characters of a stamp entirely different from what we have
hitherto dealt in. These persons are of that pitiful order of mortals
who are in contempt called good-natured; being indeed sent
into the world by nature with the same design with which men
put little fish into a pike-pond, in order to be devoured by that
voracious water-hero.

But to proceed with our history: Wild, having shared the
booty in much the same manner as before, i.e. taken three-fourths
of it, amounting to eighteenpence, was now retiring to rest, in no
very happy mood, when by accident he met with a young fellow
who had formerly been his companion, and indeed intimate
friend, at school. It hath been thought that friendship is usually
nursed by similitude of manners, but the contrary had been the
case between these lads; for whereas Wild was rapacious and in-
trepid, the other had always more regard for his skin than his
money; Wild, therefore, had very generously compassionated this
defect in his schoolfellow, and had brought him off from many
scrapes, into most of which he had first drawn him, by taking
the fault and whipping to himself. He had always indeed been well
paid on such occasions; but there are a sort of people who,
together with the best of the bargain, will be sure to have the
obligation too on their side; so it had happened here: for this
poor lad had considered himself in the highest degree obliged to
Mr Wild, and had contracted a very great esteem and friendship
for him; the traces of which an absence of many years had not

in the least effaced in his mind. He no sooner knew Wild, there-fore, than he accosted him in the most friendly manner, and in-vited him home with him to breakfast (it being now near nine in the morning), which invitation our hero with no great difficulty consented to. This young man, who was about Wild's age, had some time before set up in the trade of a jeweller, in the materials or stock for which he had laid out the greatest part of a little fortune, and had married a very agreeable woman for love, by whom he then had two children. As our reader is to be more acquainted with this person, it may not be improper to open somewhat of his character, especially as it will serve as a kind of foil to the noble and great disposition of our hero, and as the one seems sent into this world as a proper object on which the talents of the other were to be displayed with a proper and just success.

Mr Thomas Heartfree[52] then (for that was his name) was of an honest and open disposition. He was of that sort of men whom experience only, and not their own natures, must inform that there are such things as deceit and hypocrisy in the world, and who, consequently, are not at five-and-twenty so difficult to be imposed upon as the oldest and most subtle. He was possessed of several great weaknesses of mind, being good-natured, friendly, and generous to a great excess. He had, indeed, too little regard to common justice, for he had forgiven some debts to his acquaintance only because they could not pay him, and had entrusted a bankrupt, on his setting up a second time, from having been convinced that he had dealt in his bankruptcy with a fair and honest heart, and that he had broke through misfortune only, and not from neglect or imposture. He was withal so silly a fellow that he never took the least advantage of the ignorance of his cus-tomers, and contented himself with very moderate gains on his goods; which he was the better enabled to do, notwithstanding his generosity, because his life was extremely temperate, his expenses being solely confined to the cheerful entertainment of his friends at home, and now and then a moderate glass of wine, in which he indulged himself in the company of his wife, who, with an agreeable person, was a mean-spirited, poor, domestic, low-bred animal, who confined herself mostly to the care of her family, placed her happiness in her husband and her children, followed no expensive fashions or diversions, and indeed rarely went abroad, unless to return the visits of a few plain neighbours, and twice a year afforded herself, in company with her husband, the diversion of a play, where she never sat in a higher place than the pit.

To this silly woman did this silly fellow introduce the GREAT WILD, informing her at the same time of their school acquaintance, and the many obligations he had recieved from him. This simple woman no sooner heard her husband had been obliged to her guest than her eyes sparkled on him with a benevolence which is an emanation from the heart, and of which great and noble minds, whose hearts never swell but with an injury, can have no very adequate idea; it is, therefore, no wonder that our hero should misconstrue, as he did, the poor, innocent, and simple affection of Mrs Heartfree towards her husband's friend, for that great and generous passion, which fires the eyes of a modern heroine, when the colonel is so kind as to indulge his city creditor with partaking of his table to-day, and of his bed to-morrow. Wild, therefore, instantly returned the compliment as he understood it, with his eyes, and presently after bestowed many encomiums on her beauty, with which perhaps she, who was a woman, though a good one, and misapprehended the design, was not displeased any more than the husband.

When breakfast was ended, and the wife retired to her household affairs, Wild, who had a quick discernment into the weaknesses of men, and who, besides the knowledge of his good (or foolish) disposition when a boy, had now discovered several sparks of goodness, friendship, and generosity in his friend, began to discourse over the accidents which had happened in their childhood, and took frequent occasions of reminding him of those favours which we have before mentioned his having conferred on him; he then proceeded to the most vehement professions of friendship, and to the most ardent expressions of joy in this renewal of their acquaintance. He at last told him, with great seeming pleasure, that he believed he had an opportunity of serving him by the recommendation of a gentleman to his custom, who was then on the brink of marriage. 'And, if he be not already engaged, I will,' says he, 'endeavour to prevail on him to furnish his lady with jewels at your shop.'

Heartfree was not backward in thanks to our hero, and, after many earnest solicitations to dinner, which were refused, they parted for the first time.

But here, as it occurs to our memory that our readers may be surprised (an accident which sometimes happens in histories of this kind) how Mr Wild the elder, in his present capacity, should have been able to maintain his son at a reputable school, as this appears to have been, it may be necessary to inform him that Mr Wild himself was then a tradesman in good business, but, by misfortunes in the world, to wit, extravagance and gaming, he had reduced himself to that honourable occupation which we have formerly mentioned.

Having cleared up this doubt, we will now pursue our hero, who forthwith repaired to the count, and, having first settled preliminary articles concerning distributions, he acquainted him with the scheme which he had formed against Heartfree; and after consulting proper methods to put it in execution, they began to concert measures for the enlargement of the count; on which the first, and indeed only point to be considered, was to raise money, not to pay his debts, for that would have required an immense sum, and was contrary to his inclination or intention, but to procure him bail; for as to his escape, Mr Snap had taken such precautions that it appeared absolutely impossible.

CHAPTER II

Great examples of GREATNESS *in Wild, shewn as well by his behaviour to Bagshot as in a scheme laid, first, to impose on Heartfree by means of the count, and then to cheat the count of the booty*

Wild undertook, therefore, to extract some money from Bagshot, who, notwithstanding the depredations made on him, had carried off a pretty considerable booty from their engagement at dice the preceding day. He found Mr Bagshot in expectation of his bail, and, with a countenance full of concern, which he could at any time, with wonderful art, put on, told him that all was discovered; that the count knew him, and intended to prosecute him for the robbery, 'had not I exerted (said he) my utmost interest, and with great difficulty prevailed on him in case you refund the money – ' 'Refund the money!' cried Bagshot, 'that is in your power: for you know what an inconsiderable part of it fell to my share.' 'How!' replied Wild, 'is this your gratitude to me for saving your life? For your own conscience must convince you of your guilt, and with how much certainty the gentleman can give evidence against you.' 'Marry come up!' quoth Bagshot; 'I believe my life alone will not be in danger. I know those who are as guilty as myself. Do you tell me of conscience?' 'Yes, sirrah!' answered our hero, taking him by the collar; 'and since you dare threaten me I will shew you the difference between committing a robbery and conniving at it, which is all I can charge myself with. I own indeed I suspected, when you shewed me a sum of money, that you had not come honestly by it.' 'How!' says Bagshot, frightened out of one half of his wits, and amazed out of the other, 'can you deny?' 'Yes, you rascal,' answered Wild, 'I do deny everything; and do you find a witness to prove it: and, to shew you how little apprehension I have of your power to hurt me, I will have you apprehended this moment.' – At which words he offered to break from him; but Bagshot laid hold of his skirts, and, with an altered tone and manner, begged him not to be so impatient. 'Refund then, sirrah,' cries Wild, 'and perhaps I may take pity on you.' 'What must I refund?' answered Bagshot. 'Every farthing in your pocket,' replied Wild; 'then I may have some compassion on you, and not only save your life, but, out of an excess of generosity, may return you something.' At which words Bagshot seeming to hesitate, Wild pretended to make to the door, and rapt out an oath of vengeance with so violent an emphasis, that his friend no longer presumed to balance, but suffered Wild to search his pockets and draw forth all he found, to the amount of twenty-one guineas and a half, which last piece our generous hero returned him again, telling him he might now sleep secure, but advised him for the future never to threaten his friends.

Thus did our hero execute the greatest exploits with the utmost ease imaginable, by means of those transcendent qualities which nature had indulged him with, viz. a bold heart, a thundering voice, and a steady countenance.

Wild now returned to the count, and informed him that he had got ten guineas of Bagshot; for, with great and commendable prudence, he sunk the other eleven into his own pocket, and told him with that money he would procure him bail, which he after prevailed on his father, and another gentleman of the same occupation, to become, for two guineas each; so that he made lawful prize of six more, making Bagshot debtor for the whole ten; for such were his great abilities, and so vast the compass of his understanding, that he never made any bargain without over-reaching (or, in the vulgar phrase, cheating) the person with whom he dealt.

The count being, by these means, enlarged, the first thing they did, in order to procure credit from tradesmen, was the taking a handsome house ready furnished in one of the new streets; in which as soon as the count was settled, they proceeded to furnish him with servants and equipage, and all the *insignia* of a large estate proper to impose on poor Heartfree. These being all obtained, Wild made a second visit to his friend, and with much joy in his countenance acquainted him that he had succeeded in his endeavours, and that the gentleman had promised to deal with him for the jewels which he intended to present to his bride, and which were designed to be very splendid and costly; he therefore appointed him to go to the count the next morning, and carry with him a set of the richest and most beautiful jewels he had, giving him at the same time some hints of the count's ignorance of that commodity, and that he might extort what price of him he pleased; but Heartfree told him, not without some disdain, that he scorned to take any such advantage; and, after expressing much gratitude to his friend for his recommendation, he promised to carry the jewels at the hour and to the place appointed.

I am sensible that the reader, if he hath but the least notion of greatness, must have such a contempt for the extreme folly of this fellow, that he will be very little concerned at any misfortunes which may befal him in the sequel; for to have no suspicion that an old schoolfellow, with whom he had, in his tenderest years, contracted a friendship, and who, on the accidental renewing of their acquaintance, had professed the most passionate regard for him, should be very ready to impose on him; in short, to conceive that a friend should, of his own accord, without any view to his own interest, endeavour to do him a service, must argue such weakness of mind, such ignorance of the world, and such an artless, simple, undesigning heart, as must render the person possessed of it the lowest creature and the properest object of contempt imaginable, in the eyes of every man of understanding and discernment.

Wild remembered that his friend Heartfree's faults were rather in his heart than in his head; that, though he was so mean a fellow that he was never capable of laying a design to injure any human creature, yet was he by no means a fool, nor liable to any gross imposition, unless where his heart betrayed him. He, therefore, instructed the count to take only one of his jewels at the first interview, and reject the rest as not fine enough, and order him to provide some richer. He said this management would prevent Heartfree from expecting ready money for the jewel he brought with him, which the count was presently to dispose of, and by means of that money, and his great abilities at cards and dice, to get together as large a sum as possible, which he was to pay down to Heartfree at the delivery of the set of jewels, who would be thus void of all manner of suspicion, and would not fail to give him credit for the residue.

By this contrivance, it will appear in the sequel that Wild did not only propose to make the imposition on Heartfree, who was (hitherto) void of all suspicion, more certain; but to rob the count himself of this sum. This double method of cheating the very tools who are our instruments to cheat others is the superlative degree of greatness, and is probably, as far as any spirit crusted over with clay can carry it, falling little short of diabolism itself.

This method was immediately put in execution, and the count the first day took only a single brilliant, worth about three hundred pounds, and ordered a necklace, earrings, and solitaire, of the value of three thousand more, to be prepared by that day sevennight.

The interval was employed by Wild in prosecuting his scheme of raising a gang, in which he met with such success, that within a few days he had levied several bold and resolute fellows, fit for any enterprise, how dangerous or great soever.

We have before remarked that the truest mark of greatness is insatiability. Wild had covenanted with the count to receive three-fourths of the booty, and had, at the same time, covenanted with himself to secure the other fourth part likewise, for which he had formed a very great and noble design; but he now saw with concern that sum which was to be received in hand by Heartfree in danger of being absolutely lost. In order, therefore, to possess himself of that likewise, he contrived that the jewels should be brought in the afternoon, and that Heartfree should be detained before the count could see him; so that the night should overtake him in his return, when two of his gang were ordered to attack and plunder him.

CHAPTER III

Containing scenes of softness, love, and honour, all in the great style

The count had disposed of his jewel for its full value, and this he had by dexterity raised to a thousand pounds; this sum, therefore, he paid down to Heartfree, promising him the rest within a month. His house, his equipage, his appearance, but, above all, a certain plausibility in his voice and behaviour would have deceived any, but one whose great and wise heart had dictated to him something within, which would have secured him from any danger of imposition from without. Heartfree, therefore, did not in the least scruple giving him credit; but, as he had in reality procured those jewels of another, his own little stock not being able to furnish anything so valuable, he begged the count would be so kind to give his note for the money, payable at the time he mentioned; which that gentleman did not in the least scruple; so he paid him the thousand pound in specie, and gave his note for two thousand eight hundred pounds more to Heartfree, who burnt with gratitude to Wild for the noble customer he had recommended to him.

As soon as Heartfree was departed, Wild, who waited in another room, came in and received the casket from the count, it having been agreed between them that this should be deposited in his hands, as he was the original contriver of the scheme, and was to have the largest share. Wild, having received the casket, offered to meet the count late that evening to come to a division, but such was the latter's confidence in the honour of our hero, that he said, if it was any inconvenience to him, the next morning would do altogether as well. This was more agreeable to Wild, and accordingly, an appointment being made for that purpose, he set out in haste to pursue Heartfree to the place where the two gentlemen were ordered to meet and attack him. Those gentlemen with noble resolution executed their purpose; they attacked and spoiled the enemy of the whole sum he had received from the count.

As soon as the engagement was over, and Heartfree left sprawling on the ground, our hero, who wisely declined trusting the booty in his friends' hands, though he had good experience of their honour, made off after the conquerors: at length, they being all at a place of safety, Wild, according to a previous agreement, received nine-tenths of the booty: the subordinate heroes did indeed profess some little unwillingness (perhaps more than was strictly consistent with honour) to perform their contract; but Wild, partly by argument, but more by oaths and threatenings, prevailed with them to fulfil their promise.

Our hero having thus, with wonderful address, brought this great and glorious action to a happy conclusion, resolved to relax his mind after his fatigue, in the conversation of the fair. He therefore set forwards to his lovely Lætitia; but in his way accidentally met with a young lady of his acquaintance, Miss Molly Straddle,[53] who was taking the air in Bridges Street. Miss Molly, seeing Mr Wild, stopped him, and with a familiarity peculiar to a genteel town education, tapped, or rather slapped him on the back, and asked him to treat her with a pint of wine at a neighbouring tavern. The hero, though he loved the chaste Lætitia with excessive tenderness, was not of that low snivelling breed of mortals who, as it is generally expressed, *tie themselves to a woman's apron-strings*; in a word, who are tainted with that mean, base, low vice, or virtue as it is called, of constancy; therefore he immediately consented, and attended her to a tavern famous for excellent wine, known by the name of the Rummer and Horseshoe,[54] where they retired to a room by themselves. Wild was very vehement in his addresses, but to no purpose; the young lady declared she would grant no favour till he had made her a present; this was immediately complied with, and the lover made as happy as he could desire.

The immoderate fondness which Wild entertained for his dear Lætitia would not suffer him to waste any considerable time with Miss Straddle. Notwithstanding, therefore, all the endearments and caresses of that young lady, he soon made an excuse to go downstairs, and thence immediately set forward to Lætitia without taking any formal leave of Miss Straddle, or indeed of the drawer, with whom the lady was afterwards obliged to come to an account for the reckoning.

Mr Wild, on his arrival at Mr Snap's, found only Miss Doshy at home, that young lady being employed alone, in imitation of Penelope, with her thread or worsted, only with this difference, that whereas Penelope unravelled by night what she had knit or wove or spun by day, so what our young heroine unravelled by day she knit again by night. In short, she was mending a pair of blue stockings with red clocks;[55] a circumstance which perhaps we might have omitted, had it not served to shew that there are still some ladies of this age who imitate the simplicity of the ancients.

Wild immediately asked for his beloved, and was informed that she was not at home. He then inquired where she was to be found, and declared he would not depart till he had seen her, nay, not till he had married her; for, indeed, his passion for her was truly honourable; in other words, he had so ungovernable a desire for her person, that he would go any length to satisfy it. He then pulled out the casket, which he swore was full of the finest jewels, and that he would give them all to her, with other promises, which so prevailed on Miss Doshy, who had not the common failure of sisters in envying, and often endeavouring to disappoint, each other's happiness, that she desired Mr Wild to sit down for a few

minutes, whilst she endeavoured to find her sister and to bring
her to him. The lover thanked her, and promised to stay till her
return; and Miss Doshy, leaving Mr Wild to his meditations,
fastened him in the kitchen by barring the door (for most of the
doors in this mansion were made to be bolted on the outside),
and then, slapping to the door of the house with great violence,
without going out at it, she stole softly upstairs where Miss
Lætitia was engaged in close conference with Mr Bagshot. Miss
Letty, being informed by her sister in a whisper of what Mr
Wild had said, and what he had produced, told Mr Bagshot that
a young lady was below to visit her whom she would dispatch with
all imaginable haste and return to him. She desired him, therefore, to stay with patience for her in the meantime, and that she
would leave the door unlocked, though her papa would never
forgive her if he should discover it. Bagshot promised on his
honour not to step without his chamber; and the two young ladies
went softly downstairs, when, pretending first to make their entry
into the house, they repaired to the kitchen, where not even the
presence of the chaste Lætitia could restore that harmony to the
countenance of her lover which Miss Theodosia had left him
possessed of; for, during her absence, he had discovered the
absence of a purse containing bank-notes for £900, which had
been taken from Mr Heartfree, and which, indeed, Miss Straddle
had, in the warmth of his amorous caresses, unperceived drawn
from him. However, as he had that perfect mastery of his temper,
or rather of his muscles, which is as necessary to the forming a
great character as to the personating it on the stage, he soon conveyed a smile into his countenance, and, concealing as well his
misfortune as his chagrin at it, began to pay honourable addresses
to Miss Letty. This young lady, among many other good ingredients, had three very predominant passions; to wit, vanity,
wantonness, and avarice. To satisfy the first of these she employed
Mr Smirk and company; to the second, Mr Bagshot and company; and our hero had the honour and happiness of solely en-
grossing the third. Now, these three sorts of lovers she had very
different ways of entertaining. With the first she was all gay and
coquette; with the second all fond and rampant; and with the
last all cold and reserved. She, therefore, told Mr Wild, with a

most composed aspect, that she was glad he had repented of his manner of treating her at their last interview, where his behaviour was so monstrous that she had resolved never to see him any more; that she was afraid her own sex would hardly pardon her the weakness she was guilty of in receding from that resolution, which she was persuaded he never should have brought herself to, had not her sister, who was there to confirm what she said (as she did with many oaths), betrayed her into his company, by pretending it was another person to visit her: but, however, as he now thought proper to give her more convincing proofs of his affections (for he had now the casket in his hand), and since she perceived his designs were no longer against her virtue, but were such as a woman of honour might listen to, she must own – and then she feigned an hesitation, when Theodosia began: 'Nay, sister, I am resolved you shall counterfeit no longer. I assure you, Mr Wild, she hath the most violent passion for you in the world; and indeed, dear Tishy, if you offer to go back, since I plainly see Mr Wild's designs are honourable, I will betray all you have ever said.' 'How, sister!' answered Lætitia; 'I protest you will drive me out of the room: I did not expect this usage from you.' Wild then fell on his knees, and, taking hold of her hand, repeated a speech, which, as the reader may easily suggest it to himself, I shall not here set down. He then offered her the casket, but she gently rejected it; and on a second offer, with a modest countenance and voice, desired to know what it contained. Wild then opened it, and took forth (with sorrow I write it, and with sorrow will it be read) one of those beautiful necklaces with which, at the fair of Bartholomew,[56] they deck the well-bewhitened neck of Thalestris Queen of Amazons, Anna Bullen, Queen Elizabeth, or some other high princess in Drollic story. It was indeed composed of that paste which Derdæus Magnus,[57] an ingenious toyman, doth at a very moderate price dispense of to the second-rate beaus of the metropolis. For, to open a truth, which we ask our reader's pardon for having concealed from him so long, the sagacious count, wisely fearing lest some accident might prevent Mr Wild's return at the appointed time, had carefully conveyed the jewels which Mr Heartfree had brought with him into his own pocket, and in their stead had placed in the casket these artificial stones, which, though of equal value to a philosopher, and perhaps of a much greater to a true admirer of the compositions of art, had not, however, the same charms in the eyes of Miss Letty, who had indeed some knowledge of jewels; for Mr Snap, with great reason, considering how valuable a part of a lady's education it would be to be well instructed in these things, in an age when young ladies learn little more than how to dress themselves, had in her youth placed Miss Letty as the handmaid (or housemaid as the vulgar call it) of an eminent pawnbroker. The lightning, therefore, which should have flashed from the jewels, flashed from her eyes, and thunder immediately followed from her voice. She be-knaved, be-rascalled, be-rogued the unhappy hero, who stood silent, confounded with astonishment, but more with shame and indignation, at being thus outwitted and overreached. At length he recovered his spirits, and, throwing down the casket in a rage, he snatched the key from the table, and, without making any answer to the ladies, who both very plentifully opened upon him, and without taking any leave of them, he flew out at the door, and repaired with the utmost expedition to the count's habitation.

CHAPTER IV

In which Wild, after many fruitless endeavours to discover his friend, moralizes on his misfortune in a speech, which may be of use (if rightly understood) to some other considerable speech-makers

Not the highest-fed footman of the highest-bred woman of quality knocks with more impetuosity than Wild did at the count's door, which was immediately opened by a well-drest liveryman, who answered that his master was not at home. Wild, not satisfied with this, searched the house, but to no purpose; he then ransacked all the gaming-houses in town, but found no count: indeed, that gentleman had taken leave of his house the same instant Mr Wild had turned his back, and, equipping himself with boots and a post-horse, without taking with him either servant, clothes, or any necessaries for the journey of a great man, made such mighty expedition that he was now upwards of twenty miles on his way to Dover.

Wild, finding his search ineffectual, resolved to give it over for that night; he then retired to his seat of contemplation, a night-cellar, where, without a single farthing in his pocket, he called for a sneaker[58] of punch, and, placing himself on a bench by himself, he softly vented the following soliloquy:

'How vain is human GREATNESS! What avail superior abilities, and a noble defiance of those narrow rules and bounds which confine the vulgar, when our best-concerted schemes are liable to be defeated! How unhappy is the state of PRIGGISM! How impossible for human prudence to foresee and guard against every circumvention! It is even as a game of chess, where, while the rook, or knight, or bishop, is busied in forecasting some great enterprise, a worthless pawn interposes and disconcerts his scheme. Better had it been for me to have observed the simple laws of friendship and morality than thus to ruin my friend for the benefit of others. I might have commanded his purse to any degree of moderation: I have now disabled him from the power of serving me. Well! but that was not my design. If I cannot arraign my own conduct, why should I, like a woman or a child, sit down and lament the disappointment of chance? But can I acquit myself of all neglect? Did I not misbehave in putting it into the power of others to outwit me? But that is impossible to be avoided. In this a *prig* is more unhappy than any other: a cautious man may, in a crowd, preserve his own pockets by keeping his hands in them; but while the *prig* employs his hands in another's pocket, how shall he be able to defend his own? Indeed, in this light, what can be imagined more miserable than a *prig*? How dangerous are his acquisitions! how unsafe, how unquiet his possessions! Why then should any man wish to be a *prig*, or where is his greatness? I answer, in his mind: 'tis the inward glory, the secret consciousness of doing great and wonderful actions, which can alone support the truly GREAT man, whether he be a CONQUEROR, a TYRANT, a STATESMAN, or a PRIG. These must bear him up against the private curse and public imprecation, and, while he is hated and detested by all mankind, must make him inwardly satisfied with himself. For what but some such inward satisfaction as this could inspire men possessed of power, of wealth, of every human blessing which pride, avarice, or luxury could desire, to forsake their homes, abandon ease and repose, and at the expense of riches and pleasures, at the price of labour and hardship, and at the hazard of all that fortune hath liberally given them, could send them at the head of a multitude of *prigs*, called an army, to molest their neighbours; to introduce rape, rapine, bloodshed, and every kind of misery among their own species? What but some such glorious appetite of mind could inflame princes, endowed with the greatest honours, and enriched with the most plentiful revenues, to desire maliciously to rob those subjects of their liberties who are content to sweat for the luxury, and to bow down their knees to the pride, of those very princes? What but this can inspire them to destroy one half of their subjects, in order to reduce the rest to an absolute dependence on their own wills, and on those of their brutal successors? What other motive could seduce a subject, possessed of great property in his community, to betray the interest of his fellow-subjects, of his brethren, and his posterity, to the wanton disposition of such princes? Lastly, what less inducement could persuade the *prig* to forsake the methods of acquiring a safe, an honest, and a plentiful livelihood, and, at the hazard of even life itself, and what is mistakenly called dishonour, to break openly and bravely through the laws of his country, for uncertain, unsteady, and unsafe gain? Let me then hold myself contented with this reflection, that I have been wise though unsuccessful, and am a GREAT though an unhappy man.'

His soliloquy and his punch concluded together; for he had at every pause comforted himself with a sip. And now it came first into his head that it would be more difficult to pay for it than it was to swallow it; when, to his great pleasure, he beheld at another corner of the room one of the gentlemen whom he had employed in the attack on Heartfree, and who, he doubted not, would readily lend him a guinea or two; but he had the mortification, on applying to him, to hear that the gaming-table had stript him of all the booty which his own generosity had left in his possession. He was, therefore, obliged to pursue his usual method on such occasions; so, cocking his hat fiercely, he marched out of the room without making any excuse, or any one daring to make the least demand.

CHAPTER V

Containing many surprising adventures, which our hero, with GREAT GREATNESS, *achieved*

We will now leave our hero to take a short repose, and return to Mr Snap's, where, at Wild's departure, the fair Theodosia had again betaken herself to her stocking, and Miss Letty had retired upstairs to Mr Bagshot; but that gentleman had broken his parole, and, having conveyed himself below stairs behind a door, he took the opportunity of Wild's sally to make his escape. We shall only observe that Miss Letty's surprise was the greater, as she had, notwithstanding her promise to the contrary, taken the precaution to turn the key; but, in her hurry, she did it ineffectually. How wretched must have been the situation of this young creature, who had not only lost a lover on whom her tender heart perfectly doted, but was exposed to the rage of an injured father, tenderly jealous of his honour, which was deeply engaged to the Sheriff of London and Middlesex for the safe custody of the said Bagshot, and for which two very good responsible friends had given not only their words but their bonds.

But let us remove our eyes from this melancholy object, and survey our hero, who, after a successless search for Miss Straddle, with wonderful greatness of mind and steadiness of countenance went early in the morning to visit his friend Heartfree, at a time when the common herd of friends would have forsaken and avoided him. He entered the room with a cheerful air, which he presently changed into surprise on seeing his friend in a night-gown, with his wounded head bound about with linen, and looking extremely pale from a great profusion of blood. When Wild was informed by Heartfree what had happened he first expressed great sorrow, and afterwards suffered as violent agonies of rage against the robbers to burst from him. Heartfree, in compassion to the deep impression his misfortunes seemed to make on his friend, endeavoured to lessen it as much as possible, at the same time exaggerating the obligation he owed to Wild, in which his wife likewise seconded him, and they breakfasted with more comfort than was reasonably to be expected after such an accident; Heartfree expressing great satisfaction that he had put the count's note in another pocket-book; adding, that such a loss would have been fatal to him; 'for, to confess the truth to you, my dear friend,' said he, 'I have had some losses lately which have greatly perplexed my affairs; and though I have many debts due to me from people of great fashion, I assure you I know not where to be certain of getting a shilling.' Wild greatly felicitated him on the lucky accident of preserving his note, and then proceeded, with much acrimony, to inveigh against the barbarity of people of fashion, who kept tradesmen out of their money.

While they amused themselves with discourses of this kind, Wild meditating within himself whether he should borrow or steal from his friend, or indeed whether he could not effect both, the apprentice brought a bank-note of £500 in to Heartfree, which he said a gentlewoman in the shop, who had been looking at some jewels, desired him to exchange. Heartfree, looking at the number, immediately recollected it to be one of those he had been robbed of. With this discovery he acquainted Wild, who, with the notable presence of mind and unchanged complexion so essential to a great character, advised him to proceed cautiously; and offered (as Mr Heartfree himself was, he said, too much flustered to examine the woman with sufficient art) to take her into a room in his house alone. He would, he said, personate the master of the shop, would pretend to shew her some jewels, and would undertake to get sufficient information out of her to secure the rogues, and most probably all their booty. This proposal was readily and thankfully accepted by Heartfree. Wild went immediately upstairs into the room appointed, whither the apprentice, according to appointment, conducted the lady.

The apprentice was ordered downstairs the moment the lady entered the room; and Wild, having shut the door, approached her with great ferocity in his looks, and began to expatiate on the complicated baseness of the crime she had been guilty of; but though he uttered many good lessons of morality, as we doubt whether from a particular reason they may work any very good effect on our reader, we shall omit his speech, and only mention his conclusion, which was by asking her what mercy she could now expect from him? Miss Straddle, for that was the young lady, who had had a good education, and had been more than once present at the Old Bailey, very confidently denied the whole charge, and said she had received the note from a friend. Wild then, raising his voice, told her she should be immediately committed, and she might depend on being convicted; 'but,' added he, changing his tone, 'as I have a violent affection for thee, my dear Straddle, if you will follow my advice, I promise you, on my honour, to forgive you, nor shall you be ever called in question on this account.' 'Why, what would you have me to do, Mr Wild?' replied the young lady, with a pleasanter aspect. 'You must know then,' said Wild, 'the money you picked out of my pocket (nay, by G—d you did, and if you offer to flinch you shall be convicted of it) I won at play of a fellow who it seems robbed my friend of it; you must, therefore, give an information on oath against one Thomas Fierce, and say that you received the note from him, and leave the rest to me. I am certain, Molly, you must be sensible of your obligations to me, who return good for evil to you in this manner.' The lady readily consented, and advanced to embrace Mr Wild, who stepped a little back and cried, 'Hold, Molly; there are two other notes of £200 each to be accounted for – where are they?' The lady protested with the most solemn asseverations that she knew of no more; with which, when Wild was not satisfied, she cried: 'I will stand search.' 'That you shall,' answered Wild, 'and stand strip too.' He then proceeded to tumble and search her, but to no purpose, till at last she burst into tears, and declared she would tell the truth (as indeed she did); she then confessed that she had disposed of the one to Jack Swagger, a great favourite of the ladies, being an Irish gentleman, who had been bred clerk to an attorney, afterwards whipt out of a regiment of dragoons, and was then a Newgate solicitor, and a bawdyhouse bully; and, as for the other, she had laid it all out that very morning in brocaded silks and Flanders lace. With this account Wild, who indeed knew it to be a very probable one, was forced to be contented: and now, abandoning all further thoughts of what he saw was irretrievably lost, he gave the lady some further instructions, and then, desiring her to stay a few minutes behind him, he returned to his friend, and acquainted him that he had discovered the whole roguery; that the woman had confessed from whom she had received the note, and promised to give an information before a justice of peace; adding, he was concerned he could not attend him thither, being obliged to go to the other end of the town to receive thirty pounds, which he was to pay that evening. Heartfree said that should not prevent him of his company, for he could easily lend him such a trifle. This.was accordingly done and accepted, and Wild, Heartfree, and the lady went to the justice together.

The warrant being granted, and the constable being acquainted by the lady, who received her information from Wild, of Mr Fierce's haunts, he was easily apprehended, and, being confronted by Miss Straddle, who swore positively to him, though she had never seen him before, he was committed to Newgate, where he immediately conveyed an information to Wild of what had happened, and in the evening received a visit from him.

Wild affected great concern for his friend's misfortune, and as great surprise at the means by which it was brought about. However, he told Fierce that he must certainly be mistaken in that point of his having had no acquaintance with Miss Straddle: but added, that he would find her out, and endeavour to take off her evidence, which, he observed, did not come home enough to endanger him; besides, he would secure him witnesses of an alibi, and five or six to his character; so that he need be under no apprehension, for his confinement till the sessions would be his only punishment.

Fierce, who was greatly comforted by these assurances of his friend, returned him many thanks, and, both shaking each other very earnestly by the hand, with a very hearty embrace they separated.

The hero considered with himself that the single evidence of Miss Straddle would not be sufficient to convict Fierce, whom he resolved to hang, as he was the person who had principally refused to deliver him the stipulated share of the booty; he therefore went in quest of Mr James Sly, the gentleman who had assisted in the exploit, and found and acquainted him with the apprehending of Fierce. Wild then, intimating his fear least Fierce should impeach Sly, advised him to be beforehand, to surrender himself to a justice of peace and offer himself as an evidence. Sly approved Mr Wild's opinion, went directly to a magistrate, and was by him committed to the Gate House, with a promise of being admitted evidence against his companion.

Fierce was in a few days brought to his trial at the Old Bailey, where, to his great confusion, his old friend Sly appeared against him, as did Miss Straddle. His only hopes were now in the assistances which our hero had promised him. These unhappily failed him: so that, the evidence being plain against him, and he making no defence, the jury convicted him, the court condemned him, and Mr Ketch[59] executed him.

With such infinite address did this truly great man know how to play with the passions of men, to set them at variance with each other, and to work his own purposes out of those jealousies and apprehensions which he was wonderfully ready at creating by means of those great arts which the vulgar call treachery, dissembling, promising, lying, falsehood, etc., but which are by great men summed up in the collective name of policy, or politics,[60] or rather *pollitrics*; an art of which, as it is the highest excellence of human nature, perhaps our great man was the most eminent master.

CHAPTER VI

Of hats

Wild had now got together a very considerable gang, composed of undone gamesters, ruined bailiffs, broken tradesmen, idle apprentices, attorneys' clerks, and loose and disorderly youths, who, being born to no fortune, nor bred to any trade or profession, were willing to live luxuriously without labour. As these persons wore different *principles*, i.e. *hats*, frequent dissensions grew among them. There were particularly two parties, viz. those who wore hats *fiercely* cocked, and those who preferred the *nab* or trencher hat,[61] with the brim flapping over their eyes. The former were called *cavaliers* and *tory rory ranter boys*, etc.; the latter went by the several names of *wags*, roundheads, shakebags, oldnolls,[62] and several others. Between these, continual jars arose, insomuch that they grew in time to think there was something essential in their differences, and that their interests were incompatible with each other, whereas, in truth, the difference lay only in the fashion of their hats. Wild, therefore, having assembled them all at an alehouse on the night after Fierce's execution, and perceiving evident marks of their misunderstanding, from their behaviour to each other, addressed them in the following gentle, but forcible manner:* 'Gentlemen, I am ashamed to see men embarked in so great and glorious an undertaking, as that of robbing the public, so foolishly and weakly dissenting among themselves. Do you think the first inventors of hats, or at least of the distinctions between them, really conceived that one form of hats should inspire a man with divinity, another with law, another with learning, or another with bravery? No, they meant no more by these outward signs than to impose on the vulgar, and, instead of putting great men to the trouble of acquiring or maintaining the substance, to make it sufficient that they condescend to wear the type or shadow of it. You do wisely, therefore, when in a crowd, to amuse the mob by quarrels on such accounts, that while they are listening to

---

*There is something very mysterious in this speech, which probably that chapter written by Aristotle on this subject, which is mentioned by a French author, might have given some light into; but that is unhappily among the lost works of that philosopher. It is remarkable that *galerus*, which is Latin for a hat, signifies likewise a dog-fish, as the Greek word κυνέη doth the skin of that animal; of which I suppose the hats or helmets of the ancients were composed, as ours at present are of the beaver or rabbit. Sophocles, in the latter end of his *Ajax*, alludes to a method of cheating in hats, and the scholiast on the place tells us of one Crephontes, who was a master of the art. It is observable likewise that Achilles, in the first Iliad of Homer, tells Agamemnon, in anger, that he had dog's eyes. Now, as the eyes of a dog are handsomer than those of almost any other animal, this could be no term of reproach. He must, therefore, mean that he had a hat on, which, perhaps, from the creature it was made of, or from some other reason, might have been a mark of infamy. This superstitious opinion may account for that custom, which hath descended through all nations, of shewing respect by pulling off this covering, and that no man is esteemed fit to converse with his superiors with it on. I shall conclude this learned note with remarking that the term *old hat* is at present used by the vulgar in no very honourable sense.[63]

your jargon you may with the greater ease and safety pick their pockets: but surely to be in earnest, and privately to keep up such a ridiculous contention among yourselves, must argue the highest folly and absurdity. When you know you are all *prigs*, what difference can a broad or a narrow brim create? Is a *prig* less a *prig* in one hat than in another? If the public should be weak enough to interest themselves in your quarrels, and to prefer one pack to the other, while both are aiming at their purses, it is your business to laugh at, not imitate their folly. What can be more ridiculous than for gentlemen to quarrel about hats, when there is not one among you whose hat is worth a farthing? What is the use of a hat farther than to keep the head warm, or to hide a bald crown from the public? It is the mark of a gentleman to move his hat on every occasion; and in courts and noble assemblies no man ever wears one. Let me hear no more, therefore, of this childish disagreement, but all toss up your hats together with one accord, and consider that hat as the best, which will contain the largest booty.' He thus ended his speech, which was followed by a murmuring applause, and immediately all present tossed their hats together as he had commanded them.

CHAPTER VII

Shewing the consequence which attended Heartfree's adventures with Wild; all natural and common enough to little wretches who deal with GREAT MEN; together with some precedents of letters, being the different methods of answering a dun

Let us now return to Heartfree, to whom the count's note, which he had paid away, was returned, with an account that the drawer was not to be found, and that, on inquiring after him, they had heard he had run away, and consequently the money was now demanded of the endorser. The apprehension of such a loss would have affected any man of business, but much more one whose unavoidable ruin it must prove. He expressed so much concern and confusion on this occasion, that the proprietor of the note was frightened, and resolved to lose no time in securing what he could.

So that in the afternoon of the same day Mr Snap was commissioned to pay Heartfree a visit, which he did with his usual formality, and conveyed him to his own house.

Mrs Heartfree was no sooner informed of what had happened to her husband than she raved like one distracted; but after she had vented the first agonies of her passion in tears and lamentations she applied herself to all possible means to procure her husband's liberty. She hastened to beg her neighbours to secure bail for him. But, as the news had arrived at their houses before her, she found none of them at home, except an honest Quaker, whose servants durst not tell a lie. However, she succeeded no better with him, for unluckily he had made an affirmation the day before that he would never be bail for any man. After many fruitless efforts of this kind she repaired to her husband, to comfort him at least with her presence. She found him sealing the last of several letters, which he was despatching to his friends and creditors. The moment he saw her a sudden joy sparkled in his eyes, which, however, had a very short duration; for despair soon closed them again; nor could he help bursting into some passionate expressions of concern for her and his little family, which she, on her part, did her utmost to lessen, by endeavouring to mitigate the loss, and to raise in him hopes from the count, who might, she said, be possibly only gone into the country. She comforted him likewise with the expectation of favour from his acquaintance, especially from those whom he had in a particular manner obliged and served. Lastly, she conjured him, by all the value and esteem he professed for her, not to endanger his health, on which alone depended her happiness, by too great an indulgence of grief; assuring him that no state of life could appear unhappy to her with him, unless his own sorrow or discontent made it so.

In this manner did this weak poor-spirited woman attempt to relieve her husband's pains, which it would have rather become her to aggravate, by not only painting out his misery in the liveliest colours imaginable, but by upbraiding him with that folly and confidence which had occasioned it, and by lamenting her own hard fate in being obliged to share his sufferings.

Heartfree returned this goodness (as it is called) of his wife with the warmest gratitude, and they passed an hour in a scene of tenderness too low and contemptible to be recounted to our great readers. We shall, therefore, omit all such relations, as they tend only to make human nature low and ridiculous.

Those messengers who had obtained any answers to his letters now returned. We shall here copy a few of them, as they may serve for precedents to others who have an occasion, which happens commonly enough in genteel life, to answer the impertinence of a dun.

LETTER I

MR HEARTFREE, – My lord commands me to tell you he is very much surprised at your assurance in asking for money which you know hath been so little while due; however, as he intends to deal no longer at your shop, he hath ordered me to pay you as soon as I shall have cash in hand, which, considering many disbursements for bills long due, etc., can't possibly promise any time, etc., at present. And am your humble servant,

ROGER MORECRAFT.

LETTER II

DEAR SIR, – The money, as you truly say, hath been three years due, but upon my soul I am at present incapable of paying a farthing; but as I doubt not, very shortly not only to content that small bill, but likewise to lay out very considerable further sums at your house, hope you will meet with no inconvenience by this short delay in, dear sir, your most sincere humble servant,

CHA. COURTLY.

LETTER III

MR HEARTFREE, – I beg you would not acquaint my husband of the trifling debt between us; for, as I know you to be a very good-natured man, I will trust you with a secret; he gave me the money long since to discharge it, which I had the ill luck to lose at play. You may be assured I will satisfy you the first opportunity, and am, sir, your very humble servant,

CATH. RUBBERS.

Please to present my compliments to Mrs Heartfree.

LETTER IV

MR THOMAS HEARTFREE, Sir, – Yours received: but as to sum mentioned therein, doth not suit at present. Your humble servant,

PETER POUNCE.[64]

LETTER V

SIR, – I am sincerely sorry it is not at present possible for me to comply with your request, especially after so many obligations received on my side, of which I shall always entertain the most grateful memory. I am very greatly concerned at your misfortunes, and would have waited upon you in person, but am not at present very well, and besides, am obliged to go this evening to Vauxhall. I am, sir, your most obliged humble servant.

CHA. EASY.

P.S. – I hope good Mrs Heartfree and the dear little ones are well.

There were more letters to much the same purpose; but we proposed giving our readers a taste only. Of all these, the last was infinitely the most grating to poor Heartfree, as it came from one to whom, when in distress, he had himself lent a considerable sum, and of whose present flourishing circumstances he was well assured.

CHAPTER VIII

In which our hero carries GREATNESS *to an immoderate height*

Let us remove, therefore, as fast as we can, this detestable picture of ingratitude, and present the much more agreeable portrait of that assurance to which the French very properly annex the epithet of good. Heartfree had scarce done reading his letters when our hero appeared before his eyes; not with that aspect with which a pitiful parson meets his patron after having opposed him at an election, or which a doctor wears when sneaking away from a door where he is informed of his patient's death; not with that downcast countenance which betrays the man who, after a strong conflict between virtue and vice, hath surrendered his mind to the latter, and is discovered in his first treachery; but with that noble, bold, great confidence with which a prime minister assures his dependent that the place he promised him was disposed of before. And such concern and uneasiness as he expresses in his looks on those occasions did Wild testify on the first meeting of his friend. And as the said prime minister chides you for neglect of your interest in not having asked in time, so did our hero attack Heartfree for his giving credit to the count; and, without suffering him to make any answer, proceeded in a torrent of words to overwhelm him with abuse, which, however friendly its intention might be, was scarce to be outdone by an enemy. By these means Heartfree, who might perhaps otherwise have vented some little concern for that recommendation which Wild had given him to the count, was totally prevented from any such endeavour; and, like an invading prince, when attacked in his own dominions, forced to recall his whole strength to defend himself at home. This indeed he did so well, by insisting on the figure and outward appearance of the count and his equipage, that Wild at length grew a little more gentle, and with a sigh said: 'I confess I have the least reason of all mankind to censure another for an imprudence of this nature, as I am myself the most easy to be imposed upon, and indeed have been so by this count, who, if he be insolvent, hath cheated me of five hundred pounds. But, for my own part,' said he, 'I will not yet despair, nor would I have you. Many men have found it convenient to retire or abscond for a while, and afterwards have paid their debts, or at least handsomely compounded them. This I am certain of, should a composition take place, which is the worst I think that can be apprehended, I shall be the only loser; for I shall think myself obliged in honour to repair your loss, even though you must confess it was principally owing to your own folly. Z—ds! had I imagined it necessary, I would have cautioned you, but I thought the part of the town where he lived sufficient caution not to trust him. And such a sum! – The devil must have been in you certainly!'

This was a degree of impudence beyond poor Mrs Heartfree's imagination. Though she had before vented the most violent execrations on Wild, she was now thoroughly satisfied of his innocence, and begged him not to insist any longer on what he perceived so deeply affected her husband. She said trade could not be carried on without credit, and surely he was sufficiently justified in giving it to such a person as the count appeared to be. Besides, she said, reflections on what was past and irretrievable would be of little service; that their present business was to consider how to prevent the evil consequences which threatened, and first to endeavour to procure her husband his liberty. 'Why doth he not procure bail?' said Wild. 'Alas! sir,' said she, 'we have applied to many of our acquaintance in vain; we have met with excuses even where we could least expect them.' 'Not bail!' answered Wild, in a passion; 'he shall have bail, if there is any in the world. It is now very late, but trust me to procure him bail to-morrow morning.'

Mrs Heartfree received these professions with tears, and told Wild he was a friend indeed. She then proposed to stay that evening with her husband, but he would not permit her on account of his little family, whom he would not agree to trust to the care of servants in this time of confusion.

A hackney-coach was then sent for, but without success; for these, like hackney-friends, always offer themselves in the sunshine, but are never to be found when you want them. And as for a chair, Mr Snap lived in a part of the town which chairmen very little frequent. The good woman was, therefore, obliged to walk home, whither the gallant Wild offered to attend her as a protector. This favour was thankfully accepted, and, the husband and wife having taken a tender leave of each other, the former was locked in and the latter locked out by the hands of Mr Snap himself.

As this visit of Mr Wild's to Heartfree may seem one of those passages in history which writers, Drawcansir-like,[65] introduce only *because they dare*; indeed, as it may seem somewhat contradictory to the greatness of our hero, and may tend to blemish his character with an imputation of that kind of friendship which savours too much of weakness and imprudence, it may be necessary to account for this visit, especially to our more sagacious readers, whose satisfaction we shall always consult in the most especial manner. They are to know then that at the first interview with Mrs Heartfree Mr Wild had conceived that passion, or affection, or friendship, or desire, for that handsome creature, which the gentlemen of this our age agreed to call LOVE, and which is indeed no other than that kind of affection which, after the exercise of the dominical day is over, a lusty divine is apt to conceive for the well-drest sirloin or handsome buttock which the well-edified squire in gratitude sets before him, and which, so violent is his love, he devours in imagination the moment he sees it. Not less ardent was the hungry passion of our hero, who, from the moment he had cast his eyes on that charming dish, had cast about in his mind by what method he might come at it. This, as he perceived, might most easily be effected after the ruin of Heartfree, which, for other considerations, he had intended. So he postponed all endeavours for this purpose till he had first effected what, by order of time, was regularly to precede this latter design; with such regularity did this our hero conduct all his schemes, and so truly superior was he to all the efforts of passion, which so often disconcert and disappoint the noblest views of others.

CHAPTER IX

More GREATNESS *in Wild. A low scene between Mrs Heartfree and her children, and a scheme of our hero worthy the highest admiration, and even astonishment*

When first Wild conducted his flame (or rather his dish, to continue our metaphor) from the proprietor, he had projected a design of conveying her to one of those eating-houses in Covent Garden, where female flesh is deliciously drest and served up to the greedy appetites of young gentlemen; but, fearing lest she should not come readily enough into his wishes, and that, by too eager and hasty a pursuit, he should frustrate his future expectations, and luckily at the same time a noble hint suggesting itself to him, by which he might almost inevitably secure his pleasure, together with his profit, he contented himself with waiting on Mrs Heartfree home, and, after many protestations of friendship and service to her husband, took his leave, and promised to visit her early in the morning, and to conduct her back to Mr Snap's.

Wild now retired to a night-cellar, where he found several of his acquaintance, with whom he spent the remaining part of the night in revelling; nor did the least compassion for Heartfree's misfortunes disturb the pleasure of his cups. So truly great was his soul, that it was absolutely composed, save that an apprehension of Miss Tishy's making some discovery (as she was then in no good temper towards him) a little ruffled and disquieted the perfect serenity he would otherwise have enjoyed. As he had, therefore, no opportunity of seeing her that evening, he wrote her a letter full of ten thousand protestations of honourable love, and (which he more depended on) containing as many promises, in order to bring the young lady into good humour, without acquainting her in the least with his suspicion, or giving her any caution; for it was his constant maxim never to put it into any one's head to do you a mischief by acquainting him that it is in his power.

We must now return to Mrs Heartfree, who passed a sleepless night in as great agonies and horror for the absence of her husband as a fine well-bred woman would feel at the return of hers from a long voyage or journey. In the morning the children being brought to her, the eldest asked where dear papa was? At which she could not refrain from bursting into tears. The child, perceiving it, said: 'Don't cry, mamma; I am sure papa would not stay abroad if he could help it.' At these words she caught the child in her arms, and, throwing herself into the chair in an agony of passion, cried out: 'No, my child; nor shall all the malice of hell keep us long asunder.'

These are circumstances which we should not, for the amusement of six or seven readers only, have inserted, had they not served to shew that there are weaknesses in vulgar life to which great minds are so entirely strangers that they have not even an idea of them; and, secondly, by exposing the folly of this low creature, to set off and elevate that greatness of which we endeavour to draw a true portrait in this history.

Wild, entering the room, found the mother with one child in her arms, and the other at her knee. After paying her his compliments, he desired her to dismiss the children and servant, for that he had something of the greatest moment to impart to her.

She immediately complied with his request, and, the door

being shut, asked him with great eagerness if he had succeeded in his intentions of procuring the bail. He answered he had not endeavoured at it yet, for a scheme had entered into his head by which she might certainly preserve her husband, herself, and her family. In order to which he advised her instantly to remove with the most valuable jewels she had to Holland, before any statute of bankruptcy issued to prevent her; that he would himself attend her thither and place her in safety, and then return to deliver her husband, who would be thus easily able to satisfy his creditors. He added that he was that instant come from Snap's, where he had communicated the scheme to Heartfree, who had greatly approved of it, and desired her to put it in execution without delay, concluding that a moment was not to be lost.

The mention of her husband's approbation left no doubt in this poor woman's breast; she only desired a moment's time to pay him a visit in order to take her leave. But Wild peremptorily refused; he said by every moment's delay she risked the ruin of her family; that she would be absent only a few days from him, for that the moment he had lodged her safe in Holland he would return, procure her husband his liberty, and bring him to her. 'I have been the unfortunate, the innocent cause of all my dear Tom's calamity, madam,' said he, 'and I will perish with him or see him out of it.' Mrs Heartfree overflowed with acknowledgements of his goodness, but still begged for the shortest interview with her husband. Wild declared that a minute's delay might be fatal; and added, though with the voice of sorrow rather than of anger, that if she had not resolution enough to execute the commands he brought her from her husband, his ruin would lie at her door; and, for his own part, he must give up any farther meddling in his affairs.

She then proposed to take her children with her; but Wild would not permit it, saying they would only retard their flight, and and that it would be properer for her husband to bring them. He at length absolutely prevailed on this poor woman, who immediately packed up the most valuable effects she could find, and, after taking a tender leave of her infants, earnestly commended them to the care of a very faithful servant. Then they called a hackney-coach, which conveyed them to an inn, where they were furnished with a chariot and six, in which they set forward for Harwich.

Wild rode with an exulting heart, secure, as he now thought himself, of the possession of that lovely woman, together with a rich cargo. In short, he enjoyed in his mind all the happiness which unbridled lust and rapacious avarice could promise him. As to the poor creature who was to satisfy these passions, her whole soul was employed on reflecting on the condition of her husband and children. A single word scarce escaped her lips, though many a tear gushed from her brilliant eyes, which, if I may use a coarse expression, served only as delicious sauce to heighten the appetite of Wild.

CHAPTER X

Sea-adventures very new and surprising

When they arrived at Harwich they found a vessel, which had put in there, just ready to depart for Rotterdam. So they went immediately on board, and sailed with a fair wind; but they had hardly proceeded out of sight of land when a sudden and violent storm arose and drove them to the south-west; insomuch that the captain apprehended it impossible to avoid the Goodwin Sands, and he and all his crew gave themselves up for lost. Mrs Heartfree, who had no other apprehensions from death but those of leaving her dear husband and children, fell on her knees to beseech the Almighty's favour, when Wild, with a contempt of danger truly great, took a resolution as worthy to be admired perhaps as any recorded of the bravest hero, ancient or modern; a resolution which plainly proved him to have these two qualifications so necessary to a hero, to be superior to all the energies of fear or pity. He saw the tyrant death ready to rescue from him his intended prey, which he had yet devoured only in imagination. He, therefore, swore he would prevent him, and immediately attacked the poor wretch, who was in the utmost agonies of despair, first with solicitation, and afterwards with force.

Mrs Heartfree, the moment she understood his meaning, which, in her present temper of mind, and in the opinion she held of him, she did not immediately, rejected him with all the repulses which indignation and horror could animate: but when he attempted violence she filled the cabin with her shrieks, which were so vehement that they reached the ears of the captain, the storm at this time luckily abating. This man, who was a brute rather from his education and the element he inhabited than from nature, ran hastily down to her assistance, and, finding her struggling on the ground with our hero, he presently rescued her from her intended ravisher, who was soon obliged to quit the woman, in order to engage with her lusty champion, who spared neither pains nor blows in the assistance of his fair passenger.

When the short battle was over, in which our hero, had he not been overpowered with numbers, who came down on their captain's side, would have been victorious, the captain rapped out a hearty oath, and asked Wild, if he had no more Christianity in him than to ravish a woman in a storm? To which the other greatly and sullenly answered: 'It was very well; but d—m him if he had not satisfaction the moment they came on shore.' The captain with great scorn replied: 'Kiss — ' etc., and then, forcing Wild out of the cabin, he, at Mrs Heartfree's request, locked her into it, and returned to the care of his ship.

The storm was now entirely ceased, and nothing remained but the usual ruffling of the sea after it, when one of the sailors spied a sail at a distance, which the captain wisely apprehended might be a privateer (for we were then engaged in a war with France), and immediately ordered all the sail possible to be crowded; but his caution was in vain, for the little wind which then blew was directly adverse, so that the ship bore down upon them, and soon appeared to be what the captain had feared, a French privateer. He was in no condition of resistance, and immediately struck[66] on her firing the first gun. The captain of the Frenchman, with several of his hands, came on board the English vessel, which they rifled of everything valuable, and, amongst the rest, of poor Mrs Heartfree's whole cargo; and then taking the crew, together with the two passengers, aboard his own ship, he determined, as the other would be only a burthen to him, to sink her, she being very old and leaky, and not worth going back with to Dunkirk. He preserved, therefore, nothing but the boat, as his own was none of the best, and then, pouring a broadside into her, he sent her to the bottom.

The French captain, who was a very young fellow, and a man of gallantry, was presently enamoured to no small degree with his beautiful captive; and imagining Wild, from some words he dropt, to be her husband, notwithstanding the ill affection towards him which appeared in her looks, he asked her if she understood French. She answered in the affirmative, for indeed she did perfectly well. He then asked her how long she and that gentleman (pointing to Wild) had been married. She answered, with a deep sigh and many tears, that she was married indeed, but not to that villain, who was the sole cause of all her misfortunes. That appellation raised a curiosity in the captain, and he importuned her in so pressing but gentle a manner to acquaint him with the injuries she complained of, that she was at last prevailed on to recount to him the whole history of her afflictions. This so moved the captain, who had too little notions of greatness, and so incensed him against our hero, that he resolved to punish him; and, without regard to the laws of war, he immediately ordered out his shattered boat, and, making Wild a present of half a dozen biscuits to prolong his misery, he put him therein, and then, committing him to the mercy of the sea, proceeded on his cruise.

CHAPTER XI

The great and wonderful behaviour of our hero in the boat

It is probable that a desire of ingratiating himself with his charming captive, or rather conqueror, had no little share in promoting this extraordinary act of illegal justice; for the Frenchman had conceived the same sort of passion or hunger which Wild himself had felt, and was almost as much resolved, by some means or other, to satisfy it. We will leave him, however, at present in the pursuit of his wishes, and attend our hero in his boat, since it is in circumstances of distress that true greatness appears most wonderful. For that a prince in the midst of his courtiers, all ready to compliment him with his favourite character or title, and indeed with everything else, or that a conqueror, at the head of a hundred thousand men, all prepared to execute his will, how ambitious, wanton, or cruel soever, should in the giddiness of their pride, elevate themselves many degrees above those their tools, seems not difficult to be imagined, or indeed accounted for. But that a man in chains, in prison, nay, in the vilest dungeon, should, with persevering pride and obstinate dignity, discover that vast superiority in his own nature over the rest of mankind, who to a vulgar eye seem much happier than himself; nay, that he should discover heaven and providence (whose peculiar care, it seems, he is) at that very time at work for him; this is among the arcana of greatness, to be perfectly understood only by an adept in that science.

What could be imagined more miserable than the situation of our hero at this season, floating in a little boat on the open sea, without oar, without sail, and at the mercy of the first wave to overwhelm him? nay, this was indeed the fair side of his fortune, as it was a much more eligible fate than that alternative which threatened him with almost unavoidable certainty, viz. starving with hunger, the sure consequence of a continuance of the calm.

Our hero, finding himself in this condition, began to ejaculate a round of blasphemies, which the reader, without being over-pious, might be offended at seeing repeated. He then accused the whole female sex, and the passion of love (as he called it), particularly that which he bore to Mrs Heartfree, as the unhappy occasion of his present sufferings. At length, finding himself descending too much into the language of meanness and complaint, he stopped short, and soon after broke forth as follows: 'D—n it, a man can die but once! what signifies it? Every man must die, and when it is over it is over. I never was afraid of anything yet, nor I won't begin now; no, d—n me, won't I. What signifies fear? I shall die whether I am afraid or not: who's afraid then, d—n me?' At which words he looked extremely fierce, but, recollecting that no one was present to see him, he relaxed a little the terror of his countenance, and, pausing a while, repeated the word, 'D—n!' 'Suppose I should be d—ned at last,' cries he, 'when I never thought a syllable of the matter? I have often laughed and made a jest about it, and yet it may be so, for anything which I know to the contrary. If there should be another world it will go hard with me, that is certain. I shall never escape for what I have done to Heartfree. The devil must have me for that undoubtedly. The devil! Pshaw! I am not such a fool to be frightened at him neither. No, no; when a man's dead there's an end of him. I wish I was certainly satisfied of it though: for there are some men of learning, as I have heard, of a different opinion. It is but a bad chance, methinks, I stand. If there be no other world, why I shall be in no worse condition than a block or a stone: but if there should – d—n me I will think no longer about it. – Let a pack of cowardly rascals be afraid of death, I dare look him in the face. But shall I stay and be starved? – No, I will eat up the biscuits the French son of a whore bestowed on me, and then leap into the sea for drink, since the unconscionable dog hath not allowed me a single dram.' Having thus said, he proceeded immediately to put his purpose in execution, and, as his resolution never failed him, he had no sooner dispatched the small quantity of provision which his enemy had with no vast liberality presented him, than he cast himself headlong into the sea.

CHAPTER XII[67]

The strange and yet natural escape of our hero

Our hero, having with wonderful resolution thrown himself into the sea, as we mentioned at the end of the last chapter, was miraculously within two minutes after replaced in his boat; and this without the assistance of a dolphin or a seahorse, or any other fish or animal, who are always as ready at hand when a poet or historian pleases to call for them to carry a hero through a sea, as any chairman at a coffee-house door near St James's to convey a beau over a street, and preserve his white stockings. The truth is, we do not choose to have any recourse to miracles, from the strict observance we pay to that rule of Horace:

Nec Deus intersit, nisi dignus vindice nodus.[68]

The meaning of which is, do not bring in a supernatural agent when you can do without him; and indeed we are much deeper read in natural than supernatural causes. We will, therefore, endeavour to account for this extraordinary event from the former of these; and in doing this it will be necessary to disclose some profound secrets to our reader, extremely well worth his knowing, and which may serve him to account for many occurrences of the phenomenous kind which have formerly appeared in this our hemisphere.

Be it known then that the great Alma Mater, Nature, is of all other females the most obstinate, and tenacious of her purpose. So true is that observation:

Naturam expellas furca licet, usque recurret.[69]

Which I need not render in English, it being to be found in a book which most fine gentlemen are forced to read. Whatever Nature, therefore, purposes to herself, she never suffers any reason, design, or accident to frustrate. Now, though it may seem to a shallow observer that some persons were designed by Nature for no use or purpose whatever, yet certain it is that no man is born into the world without his particular allotment, viz. some to be kings, some statesmen, some ambassadors, some bishops, some generals, and so on. Of these there be two kinds; those to whom Nature is so generous to give some endowment qualifying them for the parts she intends them afterwards to act on this stage, and those whom she uses as instances of her unlimited power, and for whose preferment to such and such stations Solomon himself could have invented no other reason than that Nature designed them so. These latter some great philosophers have, to shew them to be the favourites of Nature, distinguished by the honourable appellation of NATURALS.[70] Indeed, the true reason of the general ignorance of mankind on this head seems to be this; that, as Nature chooses to execute these her purposes by certain second causes, and as many of these second causes seem so totally foreign to her design, the wit of man, which, like his eye, sees best directly forward, and very little and imperfectly what is oblique, is not able to discern the end by the means. Thus, how a handsome wife or daughter should contribute to execute her original designation of a general, or how flattery or half a dozen houses in a borough-town should denote a judge, or a bishop, he is not capable of comprehending. And, indeed, we ourselves, wise as we are, are forced to reason *ab effectu*;[71] and if we had been asked what Nature had intended such men for, before she herself had by the event demonstrated her purpose, it is possible we might sometimes have been puzzled to declare; for it must be confessed that at first sight, and to a mind uninspired, a man of vast natural capacity and much acquired knowledge may seem by Nature designed for power and honour, rather than one remarkable only for the want of these, and indeed all other qualifications; whereas daily experience convinces us of the contrary, and drives us as it were into the opinion I have here disclosed.

Now, Nature having originally intended our great man for that final exaltation which, as it is the most proper and becoming end of all great men, it were heartily to be wished they might all arrive at, would by no means be diverted from her purpose. She, therefore, no sooner spied him in the water than she softly whispered in his ear to attempt the recovery of his boat, which call he immediately obeyed, and, being a good swimmer, and it being a perfect calm, with great facility accomplished it.

Thus we think this passage in our history, at first so greatly surprising, is very naturally accounted for, and our relation rescued from the Prodigious, which, though it often occurs in biography, is not to be encouraged nor much commended on any occasion, unless when absolutely necessary to prevent the history's being at an end. Secondly, we hope our hero is justified from that imputation of want of resolution which must have been fatal to the greatness of his character.

CHAPTER XIII

The conclusion of the boat adventure, and the end of the second book

Our hero passed the remainder of the evening, the night, and the next day, in a condition not much to be envied by any passion of the human mind, unless by ambition; which, provided it can only entertain itself with the most distant music of fame's trumpet, can disdain all the pleasures of the sensualist, and those more solemn, though quieter comforts, which a good conscience suggests to a Christian philosopher.

He spent his time in contemplation, that is to say, in blaspheming, cursing, and sometimes singing and whistling. At last, when cold and hunger had almost subdued his native fierceness, it being a good deal past midnight and extremely dark, he thought he beheld a light at a distance, which the cloudiness of the sky prevented his mistaking for a star: this light, however, did not seem to approach him, at least it approached by such imperceptible degrees that it gave him very little comfort, and at length totally forsook him. He then renewed his contemplation as before, in which he continued till the day began to break, when, to his inexpressible delight, he beheld a sail at a very little distance, and which luckily seemed to be making towards him. He was likewise soon espied by those in the vessel, who wanted no signals to inform them of his distress, and, as it was almost a calm, and their course lay within five hundred yards of him, they hoisted out their boat and fetched him aboard.

The captain of this ship was a Frenchman; she was laden with deal from Norway, and had been extremely shattered in the late storm. This captain was of that kind of men who are actuated by general humanity, and whose compassion can be raised by the distress of a fellow-creature, though of a nation whose king hath quarrelled with the monarch of their own. He, therefore, commiserating the circumstances of Wild, who had dressed up a story proper to impose upon such a silly fellow, told him that, as himself well knew, he must be a prisoner on his arrival in France, but that he would endeavour to procure his redemption; for which our hero greatly thanked him. But, as they were making very slow sail (for they had lost their mainmast in the storm), Wild saw a little vessel at a distance, they being within a few leagues of the English shore, which, on enquiry, he was informed was probably an English fishing-boat. And, it being then perfectly calm, he proposed that, if they would accommodate him with a pair of scullers, he could get within reach of the boat, at least near enough to make signals to her; and he preferred any risk to the certain fate of being a prisoner. As his courage was somewhat restored by the provisions (especially brandy) with which the Frenchmen had supplied him, he was so earnest in his entreaties, that the captain, after many persuasions, at length complied, and he was furnished with scullers, and with some bread, pork, and a bottle of brandy. Then, taking leave of his preservers, he again betook himself to his boat, and rowed so heartily that he soon came within the sight of the fisherman, who immediately made towards him and took him aboard.

No sooner was Wild got safe on board the fisherman than he begged him to make the utmost speed into Deal, for that the vessel which was still in sight was a distressed Frenchman, bound for Havre de Grace, and might easily be made a prize if there was any ship ready to go in pursuit of her. So nobly and greatly did our hero neglect all obligations conferred on him by the enemies of his country, that he would have contributed all he could to the taking his benefactor, to whom he owed both his life and his liberty.

The fisherman took his advice, and soon arrived at Deal, where the reader will, I doubt not, be as much concerned as Wild was, that there was not a single ship prepared to go on the expedition.

Our hero now saw himself once more safe on terra firma, but unluckily at some distance from that city where men of ingenuity can most easily supply their wants without the assistance of money, or rather can most easily procure money for the supply of their wants. However, as his talents were superior to every difficulty, he framed so dexterous an account of his being a merchant, having been taken and plundered by the enemy, and of his great effects in London, that he was not only heartily regaled by the fisherman at his house, but made so handsome a booty by way of borrowing, a method of taking which we have before mentioned to have his approbation, that he was enabled to provide himself with a place in the stage-coach; which (as God permitted it to perform the journey) brought him at the appointed time to an inn in the metropolis.

And now, reader, as thou canst be in no suspense for the fate of our great man, since we have returned him safe to the principal scene of his glory, we will a little look back on the fortunes of Mr Heartfree, whom we left in no very pleasant situation; but of this we shall treat in the next book.

BOOK III

CHAPTER I

The low and pitiful behaviour of Heartfree; and the foolish conduct of his apprentice

His misfortunes did not entirely prevent Heartfree from closing his eyes. On the contrary, he slept several hours the first night of his confinement. However, he perhaps paid too severely dear both for his repose and for a sweet dream which accompanied it, and represented his little family in one of those tender scenes which had frequently passed in the days of his happiness and prosperity, when the provision they were making for the future fortunes of their children used to be one of the most agreeable topics of discourse with which he and his wife entertained themselves. The pleasantness of this vision, therefore, served only, on his awaking, to set forth his present misery with additional horror, and to heighten the dreadful ideas which now crowded on his mind.

He had spent a considerable time after his first rising from the bed on which he had, without undressing, thrown himself, and now began to wonder at Mrs Heartfree's long absence; but as the mind is desirous (and perhaps wisely too) to comfort itself with drawing the most flattering conclusions from all events, so he hoped the longer her stay was the more certain was his deliverance. At length his impatience prevailed, and he was just going to dispatch a messenger to his own house when his apprentice came to pay him a visit, and on his enquiry informed him that his wife had departed in company with Mr Wild many hours before, and had carried all his most valuable effects with her; adding at the same time that she had herself positively acquainted him she had her husband's express orders for so doing, and that she was gone to Holland.

It is the observation of many wise men, who have studied the anatomy of the human soul with more attention than our young physicians generally bestow on that of the body, that great and violent surprise hath a different effect from that which is wrought in a good housewife by perceiving any disorders in her kitchen; who, on such occasions, commonly spreads the disorder, not only over her whole family, but over the whole neighbourhood. – Now, these great calamities, especially when sudden, tend to stifle and deaden all the faculties, instead of rousing them; and accordingly Herodotus tells us a story of Crœsus, King of Lydia, who, on beholding his servants and courtiers led captive, wept bitterly, but, when he saw his wife and children in that condition, stood stupid and motionless;[72] so stood poor Heartfree on this relation of his apprentice, nothing moving but his colour, which entirely forsook his countenance.

The apprentice, who had not in the least doubted the veracity of his mistress, perceiving the suprise which too visibly appeared in his master, became speechless likewise, and both remained silent some minutes, gazing with astonishment and horror at each other. At last Heartfree cried out in an agony: 'My wife deserted me in my misfortunes!' 'Heaven forbid, sir!' answered the other. 'And what is become of my poor children?' replied Heartfree. 'They are at home, sir,' said the apprentice. 'Heaven be praised! She hath forsaken them too!' cries Heartfree: 'fetch them hither this instant. Go, my dear Jack, bring hither my little all which remains now: fly, child, if thou dost not intend likewise to forsake me in my afflictions.' The youth answered he would die sooner than entertain such a thought, and, begging his master to be comforted, instantly obeyed his orders.

Heartfree, the moment the young man was departed, threw himself on his bed in an agony of despair; but, recollecting himself after he had vented the first sallies of his passion, he began to question the infidelity of his wife as a matter impossible. He ran over in his thoughts the uninterrupted tenderness which she had always shewn him, and, for a minute, blamed the rashness of his belief against her; till the many circumstances of her having left him so long, and neither writ nor sent to him since her departure with all his effects and with Wild, of whom he was not before without suspicion, and, lastly and chiefly, her false pretence to his commands, entirely turned the scale, and convinced him of her disloyalty.

While he was in these agitations of mind the good apprentice, who had used the utmost expedition, brought his children to him. He embraced them with the most passionate fondness, and imprinted numberless kisses on their little lips. The little girl flew to him with almost as much eagerness as he himself exprest at her sight, and cried out: 'O papa, why did you not come home to poor mamma all this while! I thought you would not have left your little Nancy so long.' After which he asked her for her mother, and was told she had kissed them both in the morning, and cried very much for his absence. All which brought a flood of tears into the eyes of this weak, silly man, who had not greatness sufficient to conquer these low efforts of tenderness and humanity.

He then proceeded to enquire of the maidservant, who acquainted him that she knew no more than that her mistress had taken leave of her children in the morning with many tears and kisses, and had recommended them in the most earnest manner to her care; she said she had promised faithfully to take care of them, and would, while they were entrusted to her, fulfil her promise. For which profession Heartfree expressed much gratitude to her, and, after indulging himself with some little fondnesses which we shall not relate, he delivered his children into the good woman's hands, and dismissed her.

CHAPTER II

A soliloquy of Heartfree's, full of low and base ideas,
without a syllable of GREATNESS

Being now alone, he sat some short time silent, and then burst forth into the following soliloquy:

'What shall I do? Shall I abandon myself to a dispirited despair, or fly in the face of the Almighty? Surely both are unworthy of a wise man; for what can be more vain than weakly to lament my fortune if irretrievable, or, if hope remains, to offend that Being who can most strongly support it? but are my passions then voluntary? Am I so absolutely their master that I can resolve with myself, so far only will I grieve? Certainly no. Reason, however we flatter ourselves, hath not such despotic empire in our minds, that it can, with imperial voice, hush all our sorrow in a moment. Where then is its use? For either it is an empty sound, and we are deceived in thinking we have reason, or it is given us to some end, and hath a part assigned it by the all-wise Creator. Why, what can its office be other than justly to weigh the worth of all things, and to direct us to that perfection of human wisdom which proportions our esteem of every object by its real merit, and prevents us from over or undervaluing whatever we hope for, we enjoy, or we lose. It doth not foolishly say to us, Be not glad, or, Be not sorry, which would be as vain and idle as to bid the purling river cease to run, or the raging wind to blow. It prevents us only from exulting, like children, when we receive a toy, or from lamenting when we are deprived of it. Suppose then I have lost the enjoyments of this world, and my expectation of future pleasure and profit is for ever disappointed, what relief can my reason afford? What, unless it can shew me I had fixed my affections on a toy; that what I desired was not, by a wise man, eagerly to be affected, nor its loss violently deplored? for there are toys adapted to all ages, from the rattle to the throne; and perhaps the value of all is equal to their several possessors; for if the rattle pleases the ear of the infant, what can the flattery of sycophants give more to the prince? The latter is as far from examining into the reality and source of his pleasure as the former; for if both did, they must both equally despise it. And surely, if we consider them seriously, and compare them together, we shall be forced to conclude all those pomps and pleasures of which men are so fond, and which, through so much danger and difficulty, with such violence and villainy they pursue, to be as worthless trifles as any exposed to sale in a toyshop. I have often noted my little girl viewing, with eager eyes, a jointed baby; I have marked the pains and solicitations she hath used till I have been prevailed on to indulge her with it. At her first obtaining it, what joy hath sparkled in her countenance! with what raptures hath she taken possession! but how little satisfaction hath she found in it! What pains to work out her amusement from it! Its dress must be varied; the tinsel ornaments which first caught her eyes produce no longer pleasure; she endeavours to make it stand and walk in vain, and is constrained herself to supply it with conversation. In a day's time it is thrown by and neglected, and some less costly toy preferred to it. How like the situation of this child is that of every man! What difficulties in the pursuit of his desires! what inanity in the possession of most, and satiety in those which seem more real and substantial! The delights of most men are as childish and as superficial as that of my little girl; a feather or a fiddle are their pursuits and their pleasures through life, even to their ripest years, if such men may be said to attain any ripeness at all. But let us survey those whose understandings are of a more elevated and refined temper; how empty do they soon find the world of enjoyments worth their desire or attaining! How soon do they retreat to solitude and contemplation, to gardening and planting, and such rural amusements, where their trees and they enjoy the air and the sun in common, and both vegetate with very little difference between them. But suppose (which neither truth nor wisdom will allow) we could admit something more valuable and substantial in these blessings, would not the uncertainty of their possession be alone sufficient to lower their price? How mean a tenure is that at the will of fortune, which chance, fraud, and rapine are every day so likely to deprive us of, and often the more likely by how much the greater worth our possessions are of! Is it not to place our affections on a bubble in the water, or on a picture in the clouds! What madman would build a fine house or frame a beautiful garden on land in which he held so uncertain an interest? But again, was all this less undeniable, did Fortune, the lady of our manor, lease to us for our lives, of how little consideration must even this term appear! For, admitting that these pleasures were not liable to be torn from us, how certainly must we be torn from them! Perhaps to-morrow – nay, or even sooner; for as the excellent poet says:[73]

> Where is to-morrow? – In the other world.
> To thousands this is true, and the reverse
> Is sure to none.

But if I have no further hope in this world, can I have none beyond it? Surely those laborious writers, who have taken such infinite pains to destroy or weaken all the proofs of futurity, have not so far succeeded as to exclude us from hope. That active principle in man which with such boldness pushes us on through every labour and difficulty, to attain the most distant and most improbable event in this world, will not surely deny us a little flattering prospect of those beautiful mansions which, if they could be thought chimerical, must be allowed the loveliest which can entertain the eye of man; and to which the road, if we understand it rightly, appears to have so few thorns and briars in it, and to require so little labour and fatigue from those who shall pass through it, that its ways are truly said to be ways of pleasantness, and all its paths to be those of peace. If the proofs of Christianity be as strong as I imagine them, surely enough may be deduced from that ground only, to comfort and support the most miserable man in his afflictions. And this I think my reason tells me, that, if the professors and propagators of infidelity are in the right, the losses which death brings to the virtuous are not worth their lamenting; but if these are, as certainly they seem, in the wrong, the blessings it procures them are not sufficiently to be coveted and rejoiced at.

'On my own account, then, I have no cause for sorrow, but on my children's! – Why, the same Being to whose goodness and power I entrust my own happiness is likewise as able and as willing to procure theirs. Nor matters it what state of life is allotted for them, whether it be their fate to procure bread with their own labour, or to eat it at the sweat of others. Perhaps, if we consider the case with proper attention, or resolve it with due sincerity, the former is much the sweeter. The hind may be more happy than the lord, for his desires are fewer, and those such as are attended with more hope and less fear. I will do my utmost to lay the foundations of my children's happiness, I will carefully avoid educating them in a station superior to their fortune, and for the event trust to that Being in whom whoever rightly confides, must be superior to all worldly sorrows.'

In this low manner did this poor wretch proceed to argue, till he had worked himself up into an enthusiasm which by degrees soon became invulnerable to every human attack; so that when

Mr Snap acquainted him with the return of the writ, and that he must carry him to Newgate, he received the message as Socrates did the news of the ship's arrival, and that he was to prepare for death.[74]

CHAPTER III

Wherein our hero proceeds in the road to GREATNESS

But we must not detain our reader too long with these low characters. He is doubtless as impatient as the audience at the theatre till the principal figure returns on the stage; we will therefore indulge his inclination, and pursue the actions of the Great Wild.

There happened to be in the stage-coach in which Mr Wild travelled from Dover a certain young gentleman who had sold an estate in Kent, and was going to London to receive the money. There was likewise a handsome young woman who had left her parents at Canterbury, and was proceeding to the same city, in order (as she informed her fellow-travellers) to make her fortune. With this girl the young spark was so much enamoured that he publicly acquainted her with the purpose of his journey, and offered her a considerable sum in hand and a settlement if she would consent to return with him into the country, where she would be at a safe distance from her relations. Whether she accepted this proposal or no we are not able with any tolerable certainty to deliver: but Wild, the moment he heard of this money, began to cast about in his mind by what means he might become master of it. He entered into a long harangue about the methods of carrying money safely on the road, and said: 'He had at that time two bank-bills of a hundred pounds each sewed in his coat; which,' added he, 'is so safe a way, that it is almost impossible I should be in any danger of being robbed by the most cunning highwayman.'

The young gentleman, who was no descendant of Solomon, or, if he was, did not, any more than some other descendants of wise men, inherit the wisdom of his ancestor, greatly approved Wild's ingenuity, and, thanking him for his information, declared he would follow his example when he returned into the country; by which means he proposed to save the premium commonly taken for the remittance. Wild had then no more to do but to inform himself rightly of the time of the gentleman's journey, which he did with great certainty before they separated.

At his arrival in town he fixed on two whom he regarded as the most resolute of his gang for this enterprise; and, accordingly, having summoned the principal, or most desperate, as he imagined him, of these two (for he never chose to communicate in the presence of more than one), he proposed to him the robbing and murdering this gentleman.

Mr Marybone (for that was the gentleman's name to whom he applied) readily agreed to the robbery, but he hesitated at the murder. He said, as to robbery, he had, on much weighing and considering the matter, very well reconciled his conscience to it; for, though that noble kind of robbery which was executed on the highway was, from the cowardice of mankind, less frequent, yet the baser and meaner species, sometimes called cheating, but more commonly known by the name of *robbery within the law*, was in a manner universal. He did not, therefore, pretend to the reputation of being so much honester than other people; but could by no means satisfy himself in the commission of murder, which was a sin of the most heinous nature, and so immediately prosecuted by God's judgement that it never passed undiscovered or unpunished.

Wild, with the utmost disdain in his countenance, answered as follows: 'Art thou he whom I have selected out of my whole gang for this glorious undertaking, and dost thou cant of God's revenge against murder?[75] You have, it seems, reconciled your conscience (a pretty word) to robbery, from its being so common. Is it then the novelty of murder which deters you? Do you imagine that guns, and pistols, and swords, and knives, are the only instruments of death? Look into the world and see the numbers whom broken fortunes and broken hearts bring untimely to the grave. To omit those glorious heroes who, to their immortal honour, have massacred whole nations, what think you of private persecution, treachery, and slander, by which the very souls of men are in a manner torn from their bodies? Is it not more generous, nay, more good-natured, to his send a man to his rest, than, after having plundered him of all he hath, or from malice or malevolence deprived him of his character, to punish him with a languishing death, or, what is worse, a languishing life? Murder, therefore, is not so uncommon as you weakly conceive it, though, as you said of robbery, that more noble kind which lies within the paw of the law may be so. But this is the most innocent in him who doth it, and the most eligible to him who is to suffer it. Believe me, lad, the tongue of a viper is less hurtful than that of a slanderer, and the gilded scales of a rattlesnake less dreadful than the purse of the oppressor. Let me, therefore, hear no more of your scruples; but consent to my proposal without further hesitation, unless, like a woman, you are afraid of blooding your clothes, or, like a fool, are terrified with the apprehensions of being hanged in chains. Take my word for it, you had better be an honest man than half a rogue. Do not think of continuing in my gang without abandoning yourself absolutely to my pleasure; for no man shall ever receive a favour at my hands who sticks at anything, or is guided by any other law than that of my will.'

Wild then ended his speech, which had not the desired effect on Marybone: he agreed to the robbery, but would not undertake the murder, as Wild (who feared that, by Marybone's demanding to search the gentleman's coat, he might hazard suspicion himself) insisted. Marybone was immediately entered by Wild in his black-book, and was presently after impeached and executed as a fellow on whom his leader could not place sufficient dependence; thus falling, as many rogues do, a sacrifice, not to his roguery, but to his conscience.

CHAPTER IV

In which a young hero, of wonderful good promise, makes his first appearance, with many other GREAT MATTERS

Our hero next applied himself to another of his gang, who instantly received his orders, and, instead of hesitating at a single murder, asked if he should blow out the brains of all the passengers, coachman and all. But Wild, whose moderation we have before noted, would not permit him; and, therefore, having given him an exact description of the devoted person, with his other necessary instructions, he dismissed him, with the strictest orders to avoid, if possible, doing hurt to any other person.

The name of this youth, who will hereafter make some figure in this history, being the Achates of our Æneas, or rather the Hephæstion of our Alexander,[76] was Fireblood. He had every qualification to make a second-rate GREAT MAN; or, in other words, he was completely equipped for the tool of a real or first-rate GREAT MAN. We shall therefore (which is the properest way of dealing with this kind of GREATNESS) describe him negatively, and content ourselves with telling our reader what qualities he had not; in which number were humanity, modesty, and fear, not one grain of any of which was mingled in his whole composition.

We will now leave this youth, who was esteemed the most promising of the whole gang, and whom Wild often declared to be one of the prettiest lads he had ever seen, of which opinion, indeed, were most other people of his acquaintance; we will, however, leave him at his entrance on this enterprise, and keep our attention fixed on our hero, whom we shall observe taking strides towards the summit of human glory.

Wild, immediately at his return to town, went to pay a visit to Miss Lætitia Snap; for he had that weakness of suffering himself to be enslaved by women, so naturally incident to men of heroic disposition; to say the truth, it might more properly be called a slavery to his own appetite; for, could he have satisfied that, he had not cared three farthings what had become of the little tyrant for whom he professed so violent a regard. Here he was informed that Mr Heartfree had been conveyed to Newgate the day before, the writ being then returnable. He was somewhat concerned at this news; not from any compassion for the misfortunes of Heartfree, whom he hated with such inveteracy that one would have imagined he had suffered the same injuries from him which he had done towards him. His concern, therefore, had another motive; in fact he was uneasy at the place of Mr Heartfree's confinement, as it was to be the scene of his future glory, and where consequently he should be frequently obliged to see a face which hatred, and not shame, made him detest the sight of.

To prevent this, therefore, several methods suggested themselves to him. At first he thought of removing him out of the way by the ordinary method of murder, which he doubted not but Fireblood would be very ready to execute; for that youth had, at their last interview, sworn, 'D—n his eyes, he thought there was no better pastime than blowing a man's brains out.' But, besides the danger of this method, it did not look horrible nor barbarous enough for the last mischief which he should do to Heartfree. Considering, therefore, a little farther with himself, he at length came to a resolution to hang him, if possible, the very next session.

Now, though the observation – how apt men are to hate those they injure, or how unforgiving they are of the injuries they do themselves, be common enough, yet I do not remember to have ever seen the reason of this strange phenomenon as at first it appears. Know, therefore, reader, that with much and severe scrutiny we have discovered this hatred to be founded on the passion of fear, and to arise from an apprehension that the person whom we have ourselves greatly injured will use all possible endeavours to revenge and retaliate the injuries we have done him. An opinion so firmly established in bad and great minds (and those who confer injuries on others have seldom very good or mean ones) that no benevolence, nor even beneficence, on the injured side, can eradicate it. On the contrary they refer all these acts of kindness to imposture and design of lulling their suspicion, till an opportunity offers of striking a surer and severer blow; and thus, while the good man who hath received it hath truly forgotten the injury, the evil mind which did it hath it in lively and fresh remembrance.

As we scorn to keep any discoveries secret from our readers, whose instruction, as well as diversion, we have greatly considered in this history, we have here digressed somewhat to communicate the following short lesson to those who are simple and well inclined: though as a Christian thou art obliged, and we advise thee, to forgive thy enemy, NEVER TRUST THE MAN WHO HATH REASON TO SUSPECT THAT YOU KNOW HE HATH INJURED YOU.

CHAPTER V

More and more GREATNESS, *unparalleled in history or romance*

In order to accomplish this great and noble scheme, which the vast genius of Wild had contrived, the first necessary step was to regain the confidence of Heartfree. But, however necessary this was, it seemed to be attended with such insurmountable difficulties, that even our hero for some time despaired of success. He was greatly superior to all mankind in the steadiness of his countenance, but this undertaking seemed to require more of that noble quality than had ever been the portion of a mortal. However, at last he resolved to attempt it, and from his success I think we may fairly assert that what was said by the Latin poet of labour,[77] that it conquers all things, is much more true when applied to impudence.

When he had formed his plan he went to Newgate, and burst resolutely into the presence of Heartfree, whom he eagerly embraced and kissed; and then, first arraigning his own rashness, and afterwards lamenting his unfortunate want of success, he acquainted him with the particulars of what had happened; concealing only that single incident of his attack on the other's wife, and his motive to the undertaking, which, he assured Heartfree, was a desire to preserve his effects from a statute of bankruptcy.

The frank openness of this declaration, with the composure of countenance with which it was delivered; his seeming only ruffled by the concern for his friend's misfortune; the probability of truth attending it, joined to the boldness and disinterested appearance of this visit, together with his many professions of immediate service at a time when he could not have the least visible motive from self-love; and above all, his offering him money, the last and surest token of friendship, rushed with such united force on the well-disposed heart, as it is vulgarly called, of this simple man, that they instantly staggered and soon subverted all the determination he had before made in prejudice of Wild, who, perceiving the balance to be turning in his favour, presently threw in a hundred imprecations on his own folly and ill-advised forwardness to serve his friend, which had thus unhappily produced his ruin; he added as many curses on the count, whom he vowed to pursue with revenge all over Europe; lastly, he cast in some grains of comfort, assuring Heartfree that his wife was fallen into the gentlest hands, that she would be carried no farther than Dunkirk, whence she might very easily be redeemed.

Heartfree, to whom the lightest presumption of his wife's fidelity would have been more delicious than the absolute restoration of all his jewels, and who, indeed, had with the utmost difficulty been brought to entertain the slightest suspicion of her inconstancy, immediately abandoned all distrust of both her and his friend, whose sincerity (luckily for Wild's purpose) seemed to him to depend on the same evidence. He then embraced our hero, who had in his countenance all the symptoms of the deepest concern, and begged him to be comforted; saying that the intentions, rather than the actions of men, conferred obligations; that as to the event of human affairs, it was governed either by chance or some superior agent; that friendship was concerned only in the direction of our designs; and suppose these failed of success, or produced an event never so contrary to their aim, the merit of a good intention was not in the least lessened, but was rather entitled to compassion.

Heartfree, however, was soon curious enough to inquire how Wild had escaped the captivity which his wife then suffered. Here, likewise, he recounted the whole truth, omitting only the motive to the French captain's cruelty, for which he assigned a very different reason, namely, his attempt to secure Heartfree's jewels. Wild, indeed, always kept as much truth as was possible in everything; and this he said was turning the cannon of the enemy upon themselves.

Wild, having thus with admirable and truly laudable conduct achieved the first step, began to discourse on the badness of the world, and particularly to blame the severity of creditors, who seldom or never attended to any unfortunate circumstances, but without mercy inflicted confinement on the debtor, whose body the law, with very unjustifiable rigour, delivered into their power. He added, that for his part, he looked on this restraint to be as heavy a punishment as any appointed by the law for the greatest offenders. That the loss of liberty was, in his opinion, equal to, if not worse, than the loss of life; that he had always determined, if by any accident or misfortune he had been subjected to the former, he would run the greatest risk of the latter to rescue himself from it; which he said, if men did not want resolution, was always easy enough; for that it was ridiculous to conceive that two or three men could confine two or three hundred, unless the prisoners were either fools, or cowards, especially when they were neither chained nor fettered. He went on in this manner till, perceiving the utmost attention in Heartfree, he ventured to propose to him an endeavour to make his escape, which he said might easily be executed; that he would himself raise a party in the prison, and that, if a murder or two should happen in the attempt, he (Heartfree) might keep free from any share in the guilt or in the danger.

There is one misfortune which attends all great men and their schemes, viz. that, in order to carry them into execution, they are obliged, in proposing their purpose to their tools, to discover themselves to be of that disposition in which certain little writers have advised mankind to place no confidence; an advice which hath been sometimes taken. Indeed, many inconveniences arise to the said great men from these scribblers publishing without restraint their hints or alarms to society; and many great and glorious schemes have been thus frustrated; wherefore it were to be wished that in all well-regulated governments such liberties should be by some wholesome laws restrained, and all writers inhibited from venting any other instructions to the people than what should be first approved and licensed by the said great men,[78] or their proper instruments or tools; by which means nothing would ever be published but what made for the advancing their most noble projects.

Heartfree, whose suspicions were again raised by this advice, viewing Wild with inconceivable disdain, spoke as follows: 'There is one thing the loss of which I should deplore infinitely beyond that of liberty and of life also; I mean that of a good conscience; a blessing which he who possesses can never be thoroughly unhappy; for the bitterest potion of life is by this so sweetened, that it soon becomes palatable; whereas, without it, the most delicate enjoyments quickly lose all their relish, and life itself grows insipid, or rather nauseous, to us. Would you then lessen my misfortunes by robbing me of what hath been my only comfort under them, and on which I place my dependence of being relieved from them? I have read that Socrates refused to save his life by breaking the laws of his country, and departing from his prison when it was open.[79] Perhaps my virtue would not go so far; but heaven forbid liberty should have such charms to tempt me to the perpetration of so horrid a crime as murder! As to the poor evasion of committing it by other hands, it might be useful indeed to those who seek only the escape from temporal punishment, but can be of no service to excuse me to that Being whom I chiefly fear offending; nay, it would greatly aggravate my guilt by so impudent an endeavour to impose upon Him, and by so wickedly involving others in my crime. Give me, therefore, no more advice of this kind; for this is my great comfort in all my afflictions, that it is in the power of no enemy to rob me of my conscience, nor will I ever be so much my own enemy as to injure it.'

Though our hero heard all this with proper contempt, he made no direct answer, but endeavoured to evade his proposal as much as possible, which he did with admirable dexterity: this method of getting tolerably well off, when you are repulsed in your attack on a man's conscience, may be styled the art of retreating, in which the politician, as well as the general, hath sometimes a wonderful opportunity of displaying his great abilities in his profession.

Wild, having made this admirable retreat, and argued away all design of involving his friend in the guilt of murder, concluded, however, that he thought him rather too scrupulous in not attempting his escape; and then, promising to use all such means as the other would permit in his service, took his leave for the present. Heartfree, having indulged himself an hour with his children, repaired to rest, which he enjoyed quiet and undisturbed; whilst Wild, disdaining repose, sat up all night, consulting how he might bring about the final destruction of his friend, without being beholden to any assistance from himself, which he now despaired of procuring. With the result of these consultations we shall acquaint our reader in good time, but at present we have matters of much more consequence to relate to him.

CHAPTER VI

*The event of Fireblood's adventure; and a treaty of marriage,
which might have been concluded either at Smithfield[80] or
St James's*

Fireblood returned from his enterprise unsuccessful. The gentleman happened to go home another way than he had intended; so that the whole design miscarried. Fireblood had indeed robbed the coach, and had wantonly discharged a pistol into it, which slightly wounded one of the passengers in the arm. The booty he met with was not very considerable, though much greater than that with which he acquainted Wild; for of eleven pounds in money, two silver watches, and a wedding-ring, he produced no more than two guineas and the ring, which he protested with numberless oaths was his whole booty. However, when an advertisement of the robbery was published, with a reward promised for the ring and the watches, Fireblood was obliged to confess the whole, and to acquaint our hero where he had pawned the watches; which Wild, taking the full value of them for his pains, restored to the right owner.

He did not fail catechizing his young friend on this occasion. He said he was sorry to see any of his gang guilty of a breach of honour; that without honour *priggery* was at an end; that if a *prig* had but honour he would overlook every vice in the world. 'But, nevertheless,' said he, 'I will forgive you this time, as you are a hopeful lad; and I hope never afterwards to find you delinquent in this great point.'

Wild had now brought his gang to great regularity: he was obeyed and feared by them all. He had likewise established an office, where all men who were robbed, paying the value only (or a little more) of their goods, might have them again. This was of notable use to several persons who had lost pieces of plate they had received from their grandmothers; to others who had a particular value for certain rings, watches, heads of canes, snuff-boxes, etc., for which they would not have taken twenty times as much as they were worth, either because they had them a little while or a long time, or that somebody else had had them before, or from some other such excellent reason, which often stamps a greater value on a toy than the great Bubble-boy[81] himself would have the impudence to set upon it.

By these means he seemed in so promising a way of procuring a fortune, and was regarded in so thriving a light by all the gentlemen of his acquaintance, as by the keeper and turnkeys of Newgate, by Mr Snap, and others of his occupation, that Mr Snap one day, taking Mr Wild the elder aside, very seriously proposed what they had often lightly talked over, a strict union between their families, by marrying his daughter Tishy to our hero. This proposal was very readily accepted by the old gentleman, who promised to acquaint his son with it.

On the morrow on which this message was to be delivered, our hero, little dreaming of the happiness which, of its own accord, was advancing so near towards him, had called Fireblood to him; and, after informing that youth of the violence of his passion for the young lady, and assuring him what confidence he reposed in him and his honour, he dispatched him to Miss Tishy with the following letter; which we here insert, not only as we take it to be extremely curious, but to be a much better pattern for that epistolary kind of writing which is generally called love-letters than any to be found in the *academy of compliments*,[82] and which we challenge all the beaus of our time to excel either in matter or spelling.

MOST DEIVINE and ADWHORABLE CRETURE, – I doubt not but those IIs, briter than the son, which have kindled such a flam in my hart, have likewise the faculty of seeing it. It would be the hiest preassumption to imagin you eggnorant of my loav. No, madam, I sollemly purtest, that of all the butys in the unavarsal glob, there is none kapable of hater-acting my IIs like you. Corts and pallaces would be to me deserts without your kumpany, and with it a wilderness would have more charms than haven itself. For I hope you will believe me when I sware every place in the univarse is a haven with you. I am konvinced you must be sinsibel of my violent passion for you, which, if I endevored to hid it, would be as impossible as for you, or the son, to hid your buty's. I assure you I have not slept a wink since I had the hapness of seeing you last; therefore hop you will, out of Kumpassion, let me have the honour of seeing you this afternune; for I am, with the greatest adwhor-ation,

Most deivine creeture,

Iour most pessionate amirer,

Adwhorer, and slave,

JOHANATAN WYLD.

If the spelling of this letter be not so strictly orthographical, the reader will be pleased to remember that such a defect might be worthy of censure in a low and scholastic character, but can be no blemish in that sublime greatness of which we endeavour to raise a complete idea in this history. In which kind of composition spelling, or indeed any kind of human literature, hath never been thought a necessary ingredient; for if these sort of great person-ages can but complot and contrive their noble schemes, and hack and hew mankind sufficiently, there will never be wanting fit and able persons who can spell to record their praises. Again, if it should be observed that the style of this letter doth not exactly correspond with that of our hero's speeches, which we have here recorded, we answer, it is sufficient if in these the historian ad-heres faithfully to the matter, though he embellishes the diction with some flourishes of his own eloquence, without which the excellent speeches recorded in ancient historians (particularly in Sallust) would have scarce been found in their writings. Nay, even amongst the moderns, famous as they are for elocution, it may be doubted whether those inimitable harangues published in the monthly magazines came literally from the mouths of the HUR-GOS,[83] etc., as they are there inserted, or whether we may not rather suppose some historian of great eloquence hath borrowed the matter only, and adorned it with those rhetorical flowers for which many of the said HURGOS are not so extremely eminent.

CHAPTER VII

Matters preliminary to the marriage between
Mr Jonathan Wild and the chaste Lætitia

But to proceed with our history; Fireblood, having received this letter, and promised on his honour, with many voluntary asseverations, to discharge his embassy faithfully, went to visit the fair Lætitia. The lady, having opened the letter and read it, put on an air of disdain, and told Mr Fireblood she could not conceive what Mr Wild meant by troubling her with his impertinence; she begged him to carry the letter back again, saying, had she known from whom it came, she would have been d—d before she had opened it. 'But with you, young gentleman,' says she, 'I am not in the least angry. I am rather sorry that so pretty a young man should be employed in such an errand.' She accompanied these words with so tender an accent and so wanton a leer, that Fireblood, who was no backward youth, began to take her by the hand, and proceeded so warmly, that, to imitate his actions with the rapidity of our narration, he in a few minutes ravished this fair creature, or at least would have ravished her, if she had not, by a timely compliance, prevented him.

Fireblood, after he had ravished as much as he could, returned to Wild, and acquainted him, as far as any wise man would, with what had passed; concluding with many praises of the young lady's beauty, with whom, he said, if his honour would have permitted him, he should himself have fallen in love; but, d—n him if he would not sooner be torn in pieces by wild horses than even think of injuring his friend. He asserted indeed, and swore so heartily, that, had not Wild been so thoroughly convinced of the impregnable chastity of the lady, he might have suspected his success; however, he was, by these means, entirely satisfied of his friend's inclination towards his mistress.

Thus constituted were the love affairs of our hero, when his father brought him Mr Snap's proposal. The reader must know very little of love, or indeed of anything else, if he requires any information concerning the reception which this proposal met with. *Not guilty* never sounded sweeter in the ears of a prisoner at the bar, nor the sound of a reprieve to one at the gallows, than did every word of the old gentleman in the ears of our hero. He gave his father full power to treat in his name, and desired nothing more than expedition.

The old people now met, and Snap, who had information from his daughter of the violent passion of her lover, endeavoured to improve it to the best advantage, and would have not only declined giving her any fortune himself, but have attempted to cheat her of what she owed to the liberality of her relations, particularly of a pint silver caudle-cup, the gift of her grandmother. However, in this the young lady herself afterwards took care to prevent him. As to the old Mr Wild, he did not sufficiently attend to all the designs of Snap, as his faculties were busily employed in designs of his own, to overreach (or, as others express it, to cheat) the said Mr Snap, by pretending to give his son a whole number for a chair, when in reality he was entitled to a third only.

While matters were thus settling between the old folks the young lady agreed to admit Mr Wild's visits, and, by degrees, began to entertain him with all the shew of affection which the great natural reserve of her temper, and the greater artificial reserve of her education, would permit. At length, everything being agreed between their parents, settlements made, and the lady's fortune (to wit, seventeen pounds and nine shillings in money and goods) paid down, the day for their nuptials was fixed, and they were celebrated accordingly.

Most private histories, as well as comedies, end at this period; the historian and the poet both concluding they have done enough for their hero when they have married him; or intimating rather that the rest of his life must be a dull calm of happiness, very delightful indeed to pass through, but somewhat insipid to relate;

and matrimony in general must, I believe, without any dispute, be allowed to be this state of tranquil felicity, including so little variety, that, like Salisbury Plain, it affords only one prospect, a very pleasant one it must be confessed, but the same.

Now there was all the probability imaginable that this contract would have proved of such happy note, both from the great accomplishments of the young lady, who was thought to be possessed of every qualification necessary to make the marriage state happy, and from the truly ardent passion of Mr Wild; but, whether it was that nature and fortune had great designs for him to execute, and would not suffer his vast abilities to be lost and sunk in the arms of a wife, or whether neither nature nor fortune had any hand in the matter, is a point I will not determine. Certain it is that this match did not produce that serene state we have mentioned above, but resembled the most turbulent and ruffled, rather than the most calm sea.

I cannot here omit a conjecture, ingenious enough, of a friend of mine, who had a long intimacy in the Wild family. He hath often told me he fancied one reason of the dissatisfactions which afterwards fell out between Wild and his lady, arose from the number of gallants to whom she had, before marriage, granted favours; for, says he, and indeed very probable it is too, the lady might expect from her husband what she had before received from several, and, being angry not to find one man as good as ten, she had, from that indignation, taken those steps which we cannot perfectly justify.

From this person I received the following dialogue, which he assured me he had overheard and taken down verbatim. It passed on the day fortnight after they were married.

CHAPTER VIII

A dialogue matrimonial, which passed between Jonathan
Wild, Esq., and Lætitia his wife, on the morning of the day fortnight
on which his nuptials were celebrated; which
concluded more amicably than those debates generally do

Jonathan. My dear, I wish you would lie a little longer in bed
this morning.

Lætitia. Indeed I cannot; I am engaged to breakfast with Jack
Strongbow.

Jonathan. I don't know what Jack Strongbow doth so often at
my house. I assure you I am uneasy at it; for, though I have no
suspicion of your virtue, yet it may injure your reputation in the
opinion of my neighbours.

Lætitia. I don't trouble my head about my neighbours; and
they shall no more tell me what company I am to keep than my
husband shall.

Jonathan. A good wife would keep no company which made her
husband uneasy.

Lætitia. You might have found one of those good wives, sir, if
you had pleased; I had no objection to it.

Jonathan. I thought I had found one in you.

Lætitia. You did! I am very much obliged to you for thinking
me so poor-spirited a creature; but I hope to convince you to the
contrary. What, I suppose you took me for a raw senseless girl,
who knew nothing what other married women do!

Jonathan. No matter what I took you for; I have taken you for
better and worse.

Lætitia. And at your own desire too; for I am sure you never had
mine. I should not have broken my heart if Mr Wild had thought
proper to bestow himself on any other more happy woman. Ha,ha!

Jonathan. I hope, madam, you don't imagine that was not in my
power, or that I married you out of any kind of necessity.

Lætitia. O no, sir; I am convinced there are silly women
enough. And far be it from me to accuse you of any necessity for

a wife. I believe you could have been very well contented with the state of a bachelor; I have no reason to complain of your necessities; but that, you know, a woman cannot tell beforehand.

Jonathan. I can't guess what you would insinuate, for I believe no woman had ever less reason to complain of her husband's want of fondness.

Lætitia. Then some, I am certain, have great reason to complain of the price they give for them. But I know better things. *(These words were spoken with a very great air, and toss of the head.)*

Jonathan. Well, my sweeting, I will make it impossible for you to wish me more fond.

Lætitia. Pray, Mr Wild, none of this nauseous behaviour, nor those odious words. I wish you were fond! I assure you, I don't know what you would pretend to insinuate of me. I have no wishes which misbecome a virtuous woman. No, nor should not, if I had married for love. And especially now, when nobody, I am sure, can suspect me of any such thing.

Jonathan. If you did not marry for love why did you marry?

Lætitia. Because it was convenient, and my parents forced me.

Jonathan. I hope, madam, at least, you will not tell me to my face you have made your convenience of me.

Lætitia. I have made nothing of you; nor do I desire the honour of making anything of you.

Jonathan. Yes, you have made a husband of me.

Lætitia. No, you made yourself so; for I repeat once more it was not my desire, but your own.

Jonathan. You should think yourself obliged to me for that desire.

Lætitia. La, sir! you was not so singular in it. I was not in despair. I have had other offers, and better too.

Jonathan. I wish you had accepted them with all my heart.

Lætitia. I must tell you, Mr Wild, this is a very brutish manner in treating a woman to whom you have such obligations; but I know how to despise it, and to despise you too for shewing it me. Indeed, I am well enough paid for the foolish preference I gave to you. I flattered myself that I should at least have been used with good manners. I thought I had married a gentleman; but I find you every way contemptible and below my concern.

Jonathan. D—n you, madam, have I not the more reason to complain when you tell me you married for your convenience only?

Lætitia. Very fine truly. Is it behaviour worthy a man to swear at a woman? Yet why should I mention what comes from a wretch whom I despise?

Jonathan. Don't repeat that word so often. I despise you as heartily as you can me. And, to tell you a truth, I married you for my convenience likewise, to satisfy a passion which I have now satisfied, and you may be d—d for anything I care.

Lætitia. The world shall know how barbarously I am treated by such a villain.

Jonathan. I need take very little pains to acquaint the world what a b—ch you are, your actions will demonstrate it.

Lætitia. Monster! I would advise you not to depend too much on my sex, and provoke me too far; for I can do you a mischief, and will, if you dare use me so, you villain!

Jonathan. Begin whenever you please, madam; but assure yourself, the moment you lay aside the woman, I will treat you as such no longer; and if the first blow is yours, I promise you the last shall be mine.

Lætitia. Use me as you will; but d—n me if ever you shall use me as a woman again; for may I be cursed if ever I enter into your bed more.

Jonathan. May I be cursed if that abstinence be not the greatest obligation you can lay upon me; for I assure you faithfully your person was all I had ever any regard for; and that I now loathe and detest as much as ever I liked it.

Lætitia. It is impossible for two people to agree better; for I always detested your person; and as for any other regard, you must be convinced I never could have any for you.

Jonathan. Why, then, since we are come to a right understanding, as we are to live together, suppose we agreed, instead of quarrelling and abusing, to be civil to each other.

Lætitia. With all my heart.

Jonathan. Let us shake hands then, and henceforwards never live like man and wife; that is, never be loving nor ever quarrel.

Lætitia. Agreed. But pray, Mr Wild, why b—ch? Why did you suffer such a word to escape you?

Jonathan. It is not worth your remembrance.

Lætitia. You agree I shall converse with whomsoever I please?

Jonathan. Without control? And I have the same liberty?

Lætitia. When I interfere may every curse you can wish attend me!

Jonathan. Let us now take a farewell kiss, and may I be hanged if it is not the sweetest you ever gave me.

Lætitia. But why b—ch? Methinks I should be glad to know why b—ch?

At which words he sprang from the bed, d—ing her temper heartily. She returned it again with equal abuse, which was continued on both sides while he was dressing. However, they agreed to continue steadfast in this new resolution; and the joy arising on that occasion at length dismissed them pretty cheerfully from each other, though Lætitia could not help concluding with the words, 'Why b—ch?'

CHAPTER IX

Observations on the foregoing dialogue, together with a base design on our hero, which must be detested by every lover of GREATNESS

Thus did this dialogue (which, though we have termed it matrimonial, had indeed very little savour of the sweets of matrimony in it) produce at last a resolution more wise than strictly pious, and which, if they could have rigidly adhered to it, might have prevented some unpleasant moments as well to our hero as to his serene consort; but their hatred was so very great and unaccountable that they never could bear to see the least composure in one another's countenance without attempting to ruffle it. This set them on so many contrivances to plague and vex one another, that, as their proximity afforded them such frequent opportunities of executing their malicious purposes, they seldom passed one easy or quiet day together.

And this, reader, and no other, is the cause of those many inquietudes which thou must have observed to disturb the repose of some married couples who mistake implacable hatred for indifference; for why should Corvinus, who lives in a round of intrigue, and seldom doth, and never willingly would, dally with his wife, endeavour to prevent her from the satisfaction of an intrigue in her turn? Why doth Camilla refuse a more agreeable invitation abroad, only to expose her husband at his own table at home? In short, to mention no more instances, whence can all the quarrels, and jealousies, and jars proceed in people who have no love for each other, unless from that noble passion above mentioned, that desire, according to my Lady Betty Modish,[84] of *curing each other of a smile*.

We thought proper to give our reader a short taste of the domestic state of our hero, the rather to shew him that great men are subject to the same frailties and inconveniences in ordinary life with little men, and that heroes are really of the same species with other human creatures, notwithstanding all the pains they themselves or their flatterers take to assert the contrary; and that they differ chiefly in the immensity of their greatness, or, as the vulgar erroneously call it, villainy. Now, therefore, that we may not dwell too long on low scenes in a history of this sublime kind, we shall return to actions of a higher note and more suitable to our purpose.

When the boy Hymen had, with his lighted torch, driven the boy Cupid out of doors, that is to say, in common phrase, when the violence of Mr Wild's passion (or rather appetite) for the chaste Lætitia began to abate, he returned to visit his friend Heartfree, who was now in the liberties of the Fleet,[85] and had appeared to the commission of bankruptcy against him. Here he met with a more cold reception than he himself had apprehended. Heartfree had long entertained suspicions of Wild, but these suspicions had from time to time been confounded with circumstances, and principally smothered with that amazing confidence which was indeed the most striking virtue in our hero. Heartfree was unwilling to condemn his friend without certain evidence, and laid hold on every probable semblance to acquit him; but the proposal made at his last visit had so totally blackened his character in this poor man's opinion, that it entirely fixed the wavering scale, and he no longer doubted but that our hero was one of the greatest villains in the world.

Circumstances of great improbability often escape men who devour a story with greedy ears; the reader, therefore, cannot wonder that Heartfree, whose passions were so variously concerned, first for the fidelity, and secondly for the safety of his wife; and, lastly, who was so distracted with doubt concerning the conduct of his friend, should at this relation pass unobserved the incident of his being committed to the boat by the captain of the privateer, which he had at the time of his telling so lamely accounted for; but now, when Heartfree came to reflect on the whole, and with a high prepossession against Wild, the absurdity of this fact glared in his eyes and struck him in the most sensible manner. At length a thought of great horror suggested itself to his imagination, and this was, whether the whole was not a fiction, and Wild, who was, as he had learned from his own mouth, equal to any undertaking how black soever, had not spirited away, robbed, and murdered his wife.

Intolerable as this apprehension was, he not only turned it round and examined it carefully in his own mind, but acquainted young Friendly with it at their next interview. Friendly, who detested Wild (from that envy probably with which these GREAT CHARACTERS naturally inspire low fellows), encouraged these suspicions so much, that Heartfree resolved to attach our hero and carry him before a magistrate.

This resolution had been some time taken, and Friendly, with a warrant and a constable, had with the utmost diligence searched several days for our hero; but, whether it was that in compliance with modern custom he had retired to spend the honeymoon with his bride, the only moon indeed in which it is fashionable or customary for the married parties to have any correspondence with each other; or perhaps his habitation might for particular reasons be usually kept a secret, like those of some few great men whom unfortunately the law hath left out of that reasonable as well as honourable provision which it hath made for the security of the persons of other great men.

But Wild resolved to perform works of supererogation in the

way of honour, and, though, no hero is obliged to answer the challenge of my lord chief justice, or indeed of any other magistrate, but may with unblemished reputation slide away from it, yet such was the bravery, such the greatness, the magnanimity of Wild, that he appeared in person to it.

Indeed envy may say one thing, which may lessen the glory of this action, namely, that the said Mr Wild knew nothing of the said warrant or challenge; and as thou mayest be assured, reader, that the malicious fury will omit nothing which can anyways sully so great a character, so she hath endeavoured to account for this second visit of our hero to his friend Heartfree from a very different motive than that of asserting his own innocence.

CHAPTER X

Mr Wild with unprecedented generosity visits his friend
Heartfree, and the ungrateful reception he met with

It hath been said then that Mr Wild, not being able on the strictest examination to find in a certain spot of human nature called his own heart the least grain of that pitiful low quality called honesty, had resolved, perhaps a little too generally, that there was no such thing. He, therefore, imputed the resolution with which Mr Heartfree had so positively refused to concern himself in murder, either to a fear of bloodying his hands or the apprehension of a ghost, or lest he should make an additional example in that excellent book called *God's Revenge against Murder*;[86] and doubted not but he would (at least in his present necessity) agree without scruple to a simple robbery, especially where any considerable booty should be proposed, and the safety of the attack plausibly made appear; which if he could prevail on him to undertake, he would immediately afterwards get him impeached, convicted, and hanged. He no sooner, therefore, had discharged his duties to Hymen, and heard that Heartfree had procured himself the liberties of the Fleet, than he resolved to visit him, and to propose a robbery with all the allurements of profit, ease, and safety.

This proposal was no sooner made than it was answered by Heartfree in the following manner:

'I might have hoped the answer which I gave to your former advice would have prevented me from the danger of receiving a second affront of this kind. An affront I call it, and surely, if it be so to call a man a villain, it can be no less to shew him you suppose him one. Indeed, it may be wondered how any man can arrive at the boldness, I may say impudence, of first making such an overture to another; surely it is seldom done, unless to those who have previously betrayed some symptoms of their own baseness. If I have therefore shewn you any such, these insults are more pardonable; but I assure you, if such appear, they discharge all their malignance outwardly, and reflect not even a shadow within; for to me baseness seems inconsistent with this rule, OF DOING NO OTHER PERSON AN INJURY FROM ANY MOTIVE OR ON ANY CONSIDERATION WHATEVER. This, sir, is the rule by which I am determined to walk, nor can that man justify disbelieving me who will not own he walks not by it himself. But, whether it be allowed to me or no, or whether I feel the good effects of its being practised by others, I am resolved to maintain it; for surely no man can reap a benefit from my pursuing it equal to the comfort I myself enjoy: for what a ravishing thought, how replete with ecstasy, must the consideration be, that Almighty Goodness is by its own nature engaged to reward me! How indifferent must such a persuasion make a man to all the occurrences of this life! What trifles must he represent to himself both the enjoyments and the afflictions of this world! How easily must he acquiesce under missing the former, and how patiently will he submit to the latter, who is convinced that his failing of a transitory imperfect reward here is a most certain argument of his obtaining one permanent and complete hereafter! Dost thou think then, thou little, paltry, mean animal (with such language did he treat our truly great man), that I will forego such comfortable expectations for any pitiful reward which thou canst suggest or promise to me; for that sordid lucre for which all pains and labour are undertaken by the industrious, and all barbarities and iniquities committed by the vile; for a worthless acquisition, which such as thou art can possess, can give, or can take away?' The former part of this speech occasioned much yawning in our hero, but the latter roused his anger; and he was collecting his rage to answer, when Friendly and the constable, who had been summoned by Heartfree on Wild's first appearance, entered the room, and seized the great man just as his wrath was bursting from his lips.

The dialogue which now ensued is not worth relating: Wild was soon acquainted with the reason of this rough treatment, and presently conveyed before a magistrate.

Notwithstanding the doubts raised by Mr Wild's lawyer on his examination, he insisting that the proceeding was improper, for that a *writ de homine replegiando*[87] should issue, and on the return of that a *capias in withernam*,[88] the justice inclined to commitment, so that Wild was driven to other methods for his defence. He, therefore, acquainted the justice that there was a young man like-wise with him in the boat, and begged that he might be sent for, which request was accordingly granted, and the faithful Achates (Mr Fireblood) was soon produced to bear testimony for his friend, which he did with so much becoming zeal, and went through his examination with such coherence (though he was forced to collect his evidence from the hints given him by Wild in the presence of the justice and the accusers), that, as here was direct evidence against mere presumption, our hero was most honourably acquitted, and poor Heartfree was charged by the justice, the audience, and all others who afterwards heard the story, with the blackest ingratitude, in attempting to take away the life of a man to whom he had such eminent obligations.

Lest so vast an effort of friendship as this of Fireblood's should too violently surprise the reader in this degenerate age, it may be proper to inform him that, beside the ties of engagement in the same employ, another nearer and stronger alliance subsisted be-tween our hero and this youth, which latter was just departed from the arms of the lovely Lætitia when he received her hus-band's message; an instance which may also serve to justify those strict intercourses of love and acquaintance which so commonly subsist in modern history between the husband and gallant, dis-playing the vast force of friendship contracted by this more hon-ourable than legal alliance, which is thought to be at present one of the strongest bonds of amity between great men, and the most reputable as well as easy way to their favour.[89]

Four months had now passed since Heartfree's first confinement, and his affairs had begun to wear a more benign aspect; but they were a good deal injured by this attempt on Wild (so dangerous is any attack on a GREAT MAN), several of his neighbours, and particularly one or two of his own trade, industriously endeavouring, from their bitter animosity against such kind of iniquity, to spread and exaggerate his ingratitude as much as possible; not in the least scrupling, in the violent ardour of their indignation, to add some small circumstances of their own knowledge of the many obligations conferred on Heartfree by Wild. To all these scandals he quietly submitted, comforting himself in the consciousness of his own innocence, and confiding in time, the sure friend of justice, to acquit him.

CHAPTER XI

A scheme so deeply laid, that it shames all the politics of this our age; with digression and subdigression

Wild having now, to the hatred he bore Heartfree on account of those injuries he had done him, an additional spur from this injury received (for so it appeared to him, who, no more than the most ignorant, considered how truly he deserved it), applied his utmost industry to accomplish the ruin of one whose very name sounded odious in his ears; when luckily a scheme arose in his imagination which not only promised to effect it securely, but (which pleased him most) by means of the mischief he had already done him; and which would at once load him with the imputation of having committed what he himself had done to him, and would bring on him the severest punishment for a fact of which he was not only innocent, but had already so greatly suffered by. And this was no other than to charge him with having conveyed away his wife, with his most valuable effects, in order to defraud his creditors.

He no sooner started this thought than he immediately resolved on putting it in execution. What remained to consider was only the *quomodo*, and the person or tool to be employed; for the stage of the world differs from that in Drury Lane principally in this – that whereas, on the latter, the hero or chief figure is almost continually before your eyes, whilst the under-actors are not seen above once in an evening; now, on the former, the hero or great man is always behind the curtain, and seldom or never appears or doth anything in his own person. He doth indeed, in this GRAND DRAMA, rather perform the part of the prompter, and doth instruct the well-drest figures, who are strutting in public on the stage, what to say and do. To say the truth, a puppet-show will illustrate our meaning better, where it is the master of the show (the great man) who dances and moves everything, whether it be the King of Muscovy or whatever other potentate *alias* puppet which we behold on the stage; but he himself keeps wisely out of sight: for, should he once appear, the whole motion would be at an end. Not that any one is ignorant of his being there, or supposes that the puppets are not mere sticks of wood, and he himself the sole mover; but as this (though every one knows it) doth not appear visibly, i.e. to their eyes, no one is ashamed of consenting to be imposed upon; of helping on the drama, by calling the several sticks or puppets by the names which the master hath allotted to them, and by assigning to each the character which the great man is pleased they shall move in, or rather in which he himself is pleased to move them.

It would be to suppose thee, gentle reader, one of very little knowledge in this world, to imagine thou hast never seen some of these puppet-shows which are so frequently acted on the great stage; but though thou shouldst have resided all thy days in those remote parts of this island which great men seldom visit, yet, if thou hast any penetration, thou must have had some occasions to admire both the solemnity of countenance in the actor and the gravity in the spectator, while some of those farces are carried on which are acted almost daily in every village in the kingdom. He must have a very despicable opinion of mankind indeed who can conceive them to be imposed on as often as they appear to be so. The truth is, they are in the same situation with the readers of romances; who, though they know the whole to be one entire fiction, nevertheless agree to be deceived; and, as these find amusement, so do the others find ease and convenience in this concurrence. But, this being a subdigression, I return to my digression.

A GREAT MAN ought to do his business by others; to employ hands, as we have before said, to his purposes, and keep himself as much behind the curtain as possible; and though it must be acknowledged that two very great men, whose names will be both recorded in history, did in these latter times come forth themselves on the stage, and did hack and hew and lay each other most cruelly open to the diversion of the spectators, yet this must be mentioned rather as an example of avoidance than imitation, and is to be ascribed to the number of those instances which serve to evince the truth of these maxims: *Nemo mortalium omnibus horis sapit.*[90] *Ira furor brevis est*, etc.[91]

CHAPTER XII

New instances of Friendly's folly, etc.

To return to my history, which, having rested itself a little, is now ready to proceed on its journey: Fireblood was the person chosen by Wild for this service. He had, on a late occasion, experienced the talents of this youth for a good round perjury. He immediately, therefore, found him out, and proposed it to him; when, receiving his instant assent, they consulted together, and soon framed an evidence, which, being communicated to one of the most bitter and severe creditors of Heartfree, by him laid before a magistrate, and attested by the oath of Fireblood, the justice granted his warrant; and Heartfree was accordingly apprehended and brought before him.

When the officers came for this poor wretch they found him meanly diverting himself with his little children, the younger of whom sat on his knees, and the elder was playing at a little distance from him with Friendly. One of the officers, who was a very good sort of a man, but one very laudably severe in his office, after acquainting Heartfree with his errand, bade him come along and be d—d, and leave those little bastards, for so, he said, he supposed they were, for a legacy to the parish. Heartfree was much surprised at hearing there was a warrant for felony against him; but he shewed less concern than Friendly did in his countenance. The elder daughter, when she saw the officer lay hold on her father, immediately quitted her play, and, running to him and bursting into tears, cried out: 'You shall not hurt poor papa.' One of the other ruffians offered to take the little one rudely from his knees; but Heartfree started up, and, catching the fellow by the collar, dashed his head so violently against the wall, that, had he any brains, he might possibly have lost them by the blow.

The officer, like most of those heroic spirits who insult men in adversity, had some prudence mixt with his zeal for justice. Seeing, therefore, this rough treatment of his companion, he began to pursue more gentle methods, and very civilly desired Mr Heartfree to go with him, seeing he was an officer, and obliged to execute his warrant; that he was sorry for his misfortune, and hoped he would be acquitted. The other answered: 'He should patiently submit to the laws of his country, and would attend him whither he was ordered to conduct him'; then, taking leave of his children with a tender kiss, he recommended them to the care of Friendly, who promised to see them safe home, and then to attend him at the justice's, whose name and abode he had learned of the constable.

Friendly arrived at the magistrate's house just as that gentleman had signed the mittimus[92] against his friend; for the evidence of Fireblood was so clear and strong, and the justice was so incensed against Heartfree, and so convinced of his guilt, that he would hardly hear him speak in his own defence, which the reader perhaps, when he hears the evidence against him, will be less inclined to censure; for this witness deposed: 'That he had been, by Heartfree himself, employed to carry the orders of embezzling to Wild, in order to be delivered to his wife; that he had been afterwards present with Wild and her at the inn when they took coach for Harwich, where she shewed him the casket of jewels, and desired him to tell her husband that she had fully executed his command'; and this he swore to have been done after Heartfree had notice of the commission, and, in order to bring it within that time, Fireblood, as well as Wild, swore that Mrs Heartfree lay several days concealed at Wild's house before her departure for Holland.

When Friendly found the justice obdurate, and that all he could say had no effect, nor was it any way possible for Heartfree to escape being committed to Newgate, he resolved to accompany him thither; where, when they arrived, the turnkey would have confined Heartfree (he having no money) amongst the common felons; but Friendly would not permit it, and advanced every shilling he had in his pocket, to procure a room in the press-yard for his friend, which indeed, through the humanity of the keeper, he did at a cheap rate.

They spent that day together, and in the evening the prisoner dismissed his friend, desiring him, after many thanks for his fidelity, to be comforted on his account. 'I know not,' says he, 'how far the malice of my enemy may prevail; but whatever my sufferings are, I am convinced my innocence will somewhere be rewarded. If, therefore, any fatal accident should happen to me (for he who is in the hands of perjury may apprehend the worst), my dear Friendly, be a father to my poor children'; at which words the tears gushed from his eyes. The other begged him not to admit any such apprehensions, for that he would employ his utmost diligence in his service, and doubted not but to subvert any villainous design laid for his destruction, and to make his innocence appear to the world as white as it was in his own opinion.

We cannot help mentioning a circumstance here, though we doubt it will appear very unnatural and incredible to our reader; which is, that, notwithstanding the former character and behaviour of Heartfree, this story of his embezzling was so far from surprising his neighbours, that many of them declared they expected no better from him. Some were assured he could pay forty shillings in the pound if he would. Others had overheard hints formerly pass between him and Mrs Heartfree which had given them suspicions. And what is most astonishing of all is, that many of those who had before censured him for an extravagant, heedless fool, now no less confidently abused him for a cunning, tricking, avaricious knave.

CHAPTER XIII

Something concerning Fireblood which will surprise; and somewhat touching one of the Miss Snaps, which will greatly concern the reader

However, notwithstanding all these censures abroad, and in despite of all his misfortunes at home, Heartfree in Newgate enjoyed a quiet, undisturbed repose; while our hero, nobly disdaining rest, lay sleepless all night, partly from the apprehensions of Mrs Heartfree's return before he had executed his scheme, and partly from a suspicion lest Fireblood should betray him; of whose infidelity he had, nevertheless, no other cause to maintain any fear, but from his knowing him to be an accomplished rascal, as the vulgar term it, a complete GREAT MAN in our language. And indeed, to confess the truth, these doubts were not without some foundation; for the very same thought unluckily entered the head of that noble youth, who considered whether he might not possibly sell himself for some advantage to the other side, as he had yet no promise from Wild; but this was, by the sagacity of the latter, prevented in the morning with a profusion of promises, which shewed him to be of the most generous temper in the world, with which Fireblood was extremely well satisfied, and made use of so many protestations of his faithfulness that he convinced Wild of the justice of his suspicions.

At this time an accident happened, which, though it did not immediately affect our hero, we cannot avoid relating, as it occasioned great confusion in his family, as well as in the family of Snap. It is indeed a calamity highly to be lamented, when it stains untainted blood, and happens to an honourable house – an injury never to be repaired – a blot never to be wiped out – a sore never to be healed. To detain my reader no longer, Miss Theodosia Snap was now safely delivered of a male infant, the product of an amour which that beautiful (O that I could say virtuous!) creature had with the count.

Mr Wild and his lady were at breakfast when Mr Snap, with all the agonies of despair both in his voice and countenance, brought them this melancholy news. Our hero, who had (as we have said) wonderful good-nature when his greatness or interest was not concerned, instead of reviling his sister-in-law, asked with a smile: 'Who was the father?' But the chaste Lætitia, we repeat *the chaste*, for well did she now deserve that epithet, received it in another manner. She fell into the utmost fury at the relation, reviled her sister in the bitterest terms, and vowed she would never see nor speak to her more; then burst into tears and lamented over her father that such dishonour should ever happen to him and herself. At length she fell severely on her husband for the light treatment which he gave this fatal accident. She told him he was unworthy of the honour he enjoyed of marrying into a chaste family. That she looked on it as an affront to her virtue. That if he had married one of the naughty hussies of the town he could have behaved to her in no other manner. She concluded with desiring her father to make an example of the slut, and to turn her out of doors; for that she would not otherwise enter his house, being resolved never to set her foot within the same threshold with the trollop, whom she detested so much the more because (which was perhaps true) she was her own sister.

So violent, and indeed so outrageous, was this chaste lady's love of virtue, that she could not forgive a single slip (indeed the only one Theodosia had ever made) in her own sister, in a sister who loved her, and to whom she owed a thousand obligations.

Perhaps the severity of Mr Snap, who greatly felt the injury done to the honour of his family, would have relented, had not the parish-officers been extremely pressing on this occasion, and for want of security, conveyed the unhappy young lady to a place, the name of which, for the honour of the Snaps, to whom our hero was so nearly allied, we bury in eternal oblivion; where she suffered so much correction for her crime, that the good-natured reader of the male kind may be inclined to compassionate her, at least to imagine she was sufficiently punished for a fault which, with submission to the chaste Lætitia and all other strictly virtuous ladies, it should be either less criminal in a woman to commit, or more so in a man to solicit her to it.

But to return to our hero, who was a living and strong instance that human greatness and happiness are not always inseparable. He was under a continual alarm of frights, and fears, and jealousies. He thought every man he beheld wore a knife for his throat, and a pair of scissors for his purse. As for his own gang particularly, he was thoroughly convinced there was not a single man amongst them who would not, for the value of five shillings, bring him to the gallows. These apprehensions so constantly broke his rest, and kept him so assiduously on his guard to frustrate and circumvent any designs which might be formed against him, that his condition, to any other than the glorious eye of ambition, might seem rather deplorable than the object of envy or desire.

CHAPTER XIV

In which our hero makes a speech well worthy to be celebrated;
and the behaviour of one of the gang, perhaps more
unnatural than any other part of this history

There was in the gang a man named Blueskin, one of those merchants who trade in dead oxen, sheep, etc., in short, what the vulgar call a butcher. This gentleman had two qualities of a great man, viz. undaunted courage, and an absolute contempt of those ridiculous distinctions of *meum* and *tuum*, which would cause endless disputes did not the law happily decide them by converting both into *suum*. The common form of exchanging property by trade seemed to him too tedious; he, therefore, resolved to quit the mercantile profession, and, falling acquainted with some of Mr Wild's people, he provided himself with arms, and enlisted of the gang; in which he behaved for some time with great decency and order, and submitted to accept such share of the booty with the rest as our hero allotted him.

But this subserviency agreed ill with his temper; for we should have before remembered a third heroic quality, namely, ambition, which was no inconsiderable part of his composition. One day, therefore, having robbed a gentleman at Windsor of a gold watch, which, on its being advertised in the newspapers, with a considerable reward, was demanded of him by Wild, he peremptorily refused to deliver it.

'How, Mr Blueskin!' says Wild; 'you will not deliver the watch?' 'No, Mr Wild,' answered he; 'I have taken it, and will keep it; or, if I dispose of it, I will dispose of it myself, and keep the money for which I sell it.' 'Sure,' replied Wild, 'you have not the assurance to pretend you have any property or right in this watch?' 'I am certain,' returned Blueskin, 'whether I have any right in it or no, you can prove none.' 'I will undertake,' cries the other, 'to shew I have an absolute right to it, and that by the laws of our gang, of which I am providentially at the head.' 'I know not who put you at the head of it,' cries Blueskin; 'but those who did certainly did it for their own good, that you might conduct them the better in their robberies, inform them of the richest booties, prevent surprises, pack juries, bribe evidence, and so contribute to their benefit and safety; and not to convert all their labour and hazard to your own benefit and advantage.' 'You are greatly mistaken, sir,' answered Wild: 'you are talking of a legal society, where the chief magistrate is always chosen for the public good,[93] which, as we see in all the legal societies of the world, he constantly consults, daily contributing, by his superior skill, to their prosperity, and not sacrificing their good to his own wealth, or pleasure, or humour: but in an illegal society or gang, as this of ours, it is otherwise; for who would be at the head of a gang, unless for his own interest? And without a head, you know, you cannot subsist. Nothing but a head, and obedience to that head, can preserve a gang a moment from destruction. It is absolutely better for you to content yourselves with a moderate reward, and enjoy that in safety at the disposal of your chief, than to engross the whole with the hazard to which you will be liable without his protection. And surely there is none in the whole gang who hath less reason to complain than you; you have tasted of my favours; witness that piece of ribbon you wear in your hat, with which I dubbed you captain. Therefore pray, captain, deliver the watch.' 'D—n your cajoling,' says Blueskin: 'do you think I value myself on this bit of ribbon,[94] which I could have bought myself for sixpence, and have worn without your leave? Do you imagine I think myself a captain because you, whom I know not empowered to make one, call me so? The name of captain is but a shadow: the men and the salary are the substance; and I am not to be bubbled with a shadow. I will be called captain no longer, and he who flatters me by that name I shall think affronts me, and I will knock him down, I assure you.' 'Did ever man talk so unreasonably?' cries Wild. 'Are you not respected as a captain by the whole gang since my dubbing you so? But it is the shadow only, it seems; and you will knock a man down for affronting you who calls you captain! Might not a man as reasonably tell a minister of state: *Sir, you have given me the shadow only? The ribbon or the bauble that you gave me implies that I have either signalized myself, by some great action, for the benefit and glory of my country, or at least that I am descended from those who have done so. I know myself to be a scoundrel, and so have been those few ancestors I can remember, or have ever heard of. Therefore I am resolved to knock the first man down who calls me sir or right honourable.* But all great and wise men think themselves sufficiently repaid by what procures them honour and precedence in the gang, without enquiring into substance; nay, if a title or a feather be equal to this purpose, they are substance, and not mere shadows. But I have not time to argue with you at present, so give me the watch without any more deliberation.' 'I am no more a friend to deliberation than yourself,' answered Blueskin, 'and so I tell you, once for all, by G— I will never give you the watch, no, nor will I ever hereafter surrender any part of my booty. I won it, and I will wear it. Take your pistols yourself, and go out on the highway and don't lazily think to fatten yourself with the dangers and pains of other people.' At which words he departed in a fierce mood, and repaired to the tavern used by the gang, where he had appointed to meet some of his acquaintance, whom he informed of what had passed between him and Wild, and advised them all to follow his example; which they all readily agreed to, and Mr Wild's d—tion was the universal toast; in drinking bumpers to which they had finished a large bowl of punch, when a constable, with a numerous attendance, and Wild at their head, entered the room and seized on Blueskin, whom his companions, when they saw our hero, did not dare attempt to rescue. The watch was found upon him, which, together with

Wild's information, was more than sufficient to commit him to Newgate.

In the evening Wild and the rest of those who had been drinking with Blueskin met at the tavern, where nothing was to be seen but the profoundest submission to their leader. They vilified and abused Blueskin, as much as they had before abused our hero, and now repeated the same toast, only changing the name of Wild into that of Blueskin; all agreeing with Wild that the watch found in his pocket, and which must be a fatal evidence against him, was a just judgement on his disobedience and revolt.

Thus did this great man by a resolute and timely example (for he went directly to the justice when Blueskin left him) quell one of the most dangerous conspiracies which could possibly arise in a gang, and which, had it been permitted one day's growth, would inevitably have ended in his destruction; so much doth it behove all great men to be eternally on their guard, and expeditious in the execution of their purposes; while none but the weak and honest can indulge themselves in remissness or repose.

The Achates, Fireblood, had been present at both these meetings; but, though he had a little too hastily concurred in cursing his friend, and in vowing his perdition, yet now he saw all that scheme dissolved he returned to his integrity, of which he gave an incontestable proof, by informing Wild of the measures which had been concerted against him, in which he said he had pretended to acquiesce in order the better to betray them; but this, as he afterwards confessed on his deathbed at Tyburn, was only a copy of his countenance; for that he was, at that time, as sincere and hearty in his opposition to Wild as any of his companions.

Our hero received Fireblood's information with a very placid countenance. He said, as the gang had seen their errors, and repented, nothing was more noble than forgiveness. But, though he was pleased modestly to ascribe this to his lenity, it really arose from much more noble and political principles. He considered that it would be dangerous to attempt the punishment of so many; besides, he flattered himself that fear would keep them in order: and indeed Fireblood had told him nothing more than he knew before, viz. that they were all complete prigs, whom he was to govern by their fears, and in whom he was to place no more confidence than was necessary, and to watch them with the utmost caution and circumspection: for a rogue, he wisely said, like gunpowder, must be used with caution; since both are altogether as liable to blow up the party himself who uses them as to execute his mischievous purpose against some other person or animal.

We will now repair to Newgate, it being the place where most of the great men of this history are hastening as fast as possible; and, to confess the truth, it is a castle very far from being an improper or misbecoming habitation for any great man whatever. And as this scene will continue during the residue of our history, we shall open it with a new book, and shall therefore take this opportunity of closing our third.

BOOK IV

CHAPTER I

A sentiment of the ordinary's, worthy to be written in letters of gold; a very extraordinary instance of folly in Friendly, and a dreadful accident which befell our hero

Heartfree had not been long in Newgate before his frequent conversation with his children, and other instances of a good heart, which betrayed themselves in his actions and conversation, created an opinion in all about him that he was one of the silliest fellows in the universe. The ordinary himself, a very sagacious as well as very worthy person, declared that he was a cursed rogue, but no conjurer.

What indeed might induce the former, i.e. the roguish part of this opinion in the ordinary, was a wicked sentiment which Heartfree one day disclosed in conversation, and which we, who are truly orthodox, will not pretend to justify, *viz*. that he believed a sincere Turk would be saved.[95] To this the good man, with becoming zeal and indignation, answered, 'I know not what may become of a sincere Turk; but, if this be your persuasion, I pronounce it impossible you should be saved. No, sir; so far from a sincere Turk's being within the pale of salvation, neither will any sincere Presbyterian, Anabaptist, nor Quaker whatever, be saved.'

But neither did the one nor the other part of this character prevail on Friendly to abandon his old master. He spent his whole time with him, except only those hours when he was absent for his sake, in procuring evidence for him against his trial, which was now shortly to come on. Indeed this young man was the only comfort, besides a clear conscience and the hopes beyond the grave, which this poor wretch had; for the sight of his children was like one of those alluring pleasures which men in some diseases indulge themselves often fatally in, which at once flatter and heighten their malady.

Friendly being one day present while Heartfree was, with tears in his eyes, embracing his eldest daughter, and lamenting the hard fate to which he feared he should be obliged to leave her, spoke to him thus: 'I have long observed with admiration the magnanimity with which you go through your own misfortunes, and the steady countenance with which you look on death. I have observed that all your agonies arise from the thoughts of parting with your children, and of leaving them in a distressed condition; now, though I hope all your fears will prove ill grounded, yet, that I may relieve you as much as possible from them, be assured that, as nothing can give me more real misery than to observe so tender and loving a concern in a master, to whose goodness I owe so many obligations, and whom I so sincerely love, so nothing can afford me equal pleasure with my contributing to lessen or to remove it. Be convinced, therefore, if you can place any confidence in my promise, that I will employ my little fortune, which you know to be not entirely inconsiderable, in the support of this your little family. Should any misfortune, which I pray Heaven avert, happen to you before you have better provided for these little ones, I will be myself their father, nô shall either of them ever know distress if it be any way in my power to prevent it. Your younger daughter I will provide for, and as for my little prattler, your elder, as I never yet thought of any woman for a wife, I will receive her as such at your hands; nor will I ever relinquish her for another.' Heartfree flew to his friend, and embraced him with raptures of acknowledgement. He vowed to him that he had eased every anxious thought of his mind but one, and that he must carry with him out of the world. 'O Friendly!' cried he, 'it is my concern for that best of women, whom I hate myself for having ever censured in my opinion. O Friendly! thou didst know her goodness; yet, sure, her perfect character none but myself was ever acquainted with. She had every perfection, both of mind and body, which Heaven hath indulged to her whole sex, and possessed all in a higher excellence than nature ever indulged to another in any single virtue. Can I bear the loss of such a woman? Can I bear the apprehensions of what mischiefs that villain may have

done to her, of which death is perhaps the lightest?' Friendly
gently interrupted him as soon as he saw any opportunity, endeavouring to comfort him on this head likewise, by magnifying
every circumstance which could possibly afford any hopes of his
seeing her again.

By this kind of behaviour, in which the young man exemplified
so uncommon an height of friendship, he had soon obtained in the
castle the character of as odd and silly a fellow as his master.
Indeed they were both the byword, laughing-stock, and contempt
of the whole place.

The sessions now came on at the Old Bailey. The grand jury
at Hicks's Hall[96] had found the bill of indictment against Heartfree, and on the second day of the session he was brought to his
trial; where, notwithstanding the utmost efforts of Friendly and
of the honest old female servant, the circumstances of the fact
corroborating the evidence of Fireblood, as well as that of Wild,
who counterfeited the most artful reluctance at appearing against
his old friend Heartfree, the jury found the prisoner guilty.

Wild had now accomplished his scheme; for as to what remained, it was certainly unavoidable, seeing that Heartfree was
entirely void of interest with the great, and was besides convicted
on a statute the infringers of which could hope no pardon.

The catastrophe to which our hero had reduced this wretch was
so wonderful an effort of greatness, that it probably made Fortune
envious of her own darling; but whether it was from this envy,
or only from that known inconstancy and weakness so often and
judiciously remarked in that lady's temper, who frequently lifts
men to the summit of human greatness, only

ut lapsu graviore ruant;[97]

certain it is, she now began to meditate mischief against Wild,
who seems to have come to that period at which all heroes have
arrived, and which she was resolved they never should transcend.
In short, there seems to be a certain measure of mischief and
iniquity which every great man is to fill up, and then Fortune
looks on him of no more use than a silkworm whose bottom is
spun, and deserts him. Mr Blueskin was convicted the same day of
robbery, by our hero, an unkindness which, though he had drawn

on himself, and necessitated him to, he took greatly amiss: as Wild, therefore, was standing near him, with that disregard and indifference which great men are too carelessly inclined to have for those whom they have ruined, Blueskin, privily drawing a knife, thrust the same into the body of our hero with such violence, that all who saw it concluded he had done his business. And, indeed, had not Fortune, not so much out of love to our hero as from a fixed resolution to accomplish a certain purpose, of which we have formerly given a hint, carefully placed his guts out of the way, he must have fallen a sacrifice to the wrath of his enemy, which, as he afterwards said, he did not deserve; for, had he been contented to have robbed and only submitted to give him the booty, he might have still continued safe and unimpeached in the gang; but, so it was, that the knife, missing those noble parts (the noblest of many) the guts, perforated only the hollow of his belly, and caused no other harm than an immoderate effusion of blood, of which, though it at present weakened him, he soon after recovered.

This accident, however, was in the end attended with worse consequences: for, as very few people (those greatest of all men, absolute princes, excepted) attempt to cut the thread of human life, like the fatal sisters, merely out of wantonness and for their diversion, but rather by so doing propose to themselves the acquisition of some future good, or the avenging some past evil; and as the former of these motives did not appear probable, it put inquisitive persons on examining into the latter. Now, as the vast schemes of Wild, when they were discovered, however great in their nature, seemed to some persons, like the projects of most other such persons, rather to be calculated for the glory of the great man himself than to redound to the general good of society, designs began to be laid by several of those who thought it principally their duty to put a stop to the future progress of our hero; and a learned judge particularly, a great enemy to this kind of greatness, procured a clause in an Act of Parliament as a trap for Wild, which he soon after fell into.[98] By this law it was made capital in a prig to steal with the hands of other people. A law so plainly calculated for the destruction of all priggish greatness, that it was indeed impossible for our hero to avoid it.

CHAPTER II

A short hint concerning popular ingratitude. Mr Wild's arrival in the castle, with other occurrences to be found in no other history

If we had any leisure we would here digress a little on that ingratitude which so many writers have observed to spring up in the people in all free governments towards their great men; who, while they have been consulting the good of the public, by raising their own greatness, in which the whole body (as the kingdom of France thinks itself in the glory of their grand monarch) was so deeply concerned, have been sometimes sacrificed by those very people for whose glory the said great men were so industriously at work: and this from a foolish zeal for a certain ridiculous imaginary thing called liberty, to which great men are observed to have a great animosity.

This law had been promulgated a very little time when Mr Wild, having received from some dutiful members of the gang a valuable piece of goods, did, for a consideration somewhat short of its original price, re-convey it to the right owner; for which fact, being ungratefully informed against by the said owner, he was surprised in his own house, and, being overpowered by numbers, was hurried before a magistrate, and by him committed to that castle, which, suitable as it is to greatness, we do not choose to name too often in our history, and where many great men at this time happened to be assembled.

The governor, or, as the law more honourably calls him, keeper of this castle, was Mr Wild's old friend and acquaintance. This made the latter greatly satisfied with the place of his confinement, as he promised himself not only a kind reception and handsome accommodation there, but even to obtain his liberty from him if he thought it necessary to desire it: but, alas! he was deceived; his old friend knew him no longer, and refused to see him, and the lieutenant-governor insisted on as high garnish for fetters, and as exorbitant a price for lodging, as if he had had a fine gentleman in custody for murder, or any other genteel crime.

To confess a melancholy truth, it is a circumstance much to be lamented, that there is no absolute dependence on the friendship of great men; an observation which hath been frequently made by those who have lived in courts, or in Newgate, or in any other place set apart for the habitation of such persons.

The second day of his confinement he was greatly surprised at receiving a visit from his wife; and much more so, when, instead of a countenance ready to insult him, the only motive to which he could ascribe her presence, he saw the tears trickling down her lovely cheeks. He embraced her with the utmost marks of affection, and declared he could hardly regret his confinement, since it had produced such an instance of the happiness he enjoyed in her, whose fidelity to him on this occasion would, he believed, make him the envy of most husbands, even in Newgate. He then begged her to dry her eyes, and be comforted; for that matters might go better with him than she expected. 'No, no,' says she, 'I am certain you will be found guilty. *Death*. I knew what it would always come to. I told you it was impossible to carry on such a trade long; but you would not be advised, and now you see the consequence – now you repent when it is too late. All the comfort I shall have when you are *nubbed** is, that I gave you a good advice. If you had always gone out by yourself, as I would have had you, you might have robbed on to the end of the chapter; but you was wiser than all the world, or rather lazier, and see what your laziness is come to – to the *cheat*,† for thither you will go now, that's infallible. And a just judgement on you for following your headstrong will; I am the only person to be pitied; poor I, who shall be scandalized for your fault. *There goes she whose husband was hanged:* methinks I hear them crying so already.' At which words she burst into tears. He could not then forbear chiding her for this unnecessary concern on his account, and begged her not to trouble him any more. She answered with some spirit: 'On your account, and be d—d to you! No, if the old cull of a justice had not sent me hither, I believe it would have been long enough before I should have come hither to see after you; d—n me, I am com-

---

* The cant word for hanging.

† The gallows.

mitted for the *filing-lay*,* man, and we shall be both *nubbed* together. I' faith, my dear, it almost makes me amends for being *nubbed* myself, to have the pleasure of seeing thee *nubbed* too.' 'Indeed, my dear,' answered Wild, 'it is what I have long wished for thee; but I do not desire to bear thee company, and I have still hopes to have the pleasure of seeing you go without me; at least I will have the pleasure to be rid of you now.' And so saying, he seized her by the waist, and with strong arm flung her out of the room; but not before she had with her nails left a bloody memorial on his cheek: and thus this fond couple parted.

Wild had scarce recovered himself from the uneasiness into which this unwelcome visit, proceeding from the disagreeable fondness of his wife, had thrown him, than the faithful Achates appeared. The presence of this youth was indeed a cordial to his spirits. He received him with open arms, and expressed the utmost satisfaction in the fidelity of his friendship, which so far exceeded the fashion of the times, and said many things which we have forgot on the occasion; but we remember they all tended to the praise of Fireblood, whose modesty, at length, put a stop to the torrent of compliments, by asserting he had done no more than his duty, and that he should have detested himself could he have forsaken his friend in his adversity; and, after many protestations that he came the moment he heard of his misfortune, he asked him if he could be of any service. Wild answered, since he had so kindly proposed that question, he must say he should be obliged to him if he could lend him a few guineas; for that he was very *seedy*. Fireblood replied that he was greatly unhappy in not having it then in his power, adding many hearty oaths that he had not a farthing of money in his pocket, which was, indeed, strictly true; for he had only a bank-note, which he had that evening purloined from a gentleman in the playhouse passage. He then asked for his wife, to whom, to speak truly, the visit was intended, her confinement being the misfortune of which he had just heard; for, as for that of Mr Wild himself, he had known it from the first minute, without ever intending to trouble him with his company. Being informed, therefore, of the visit which

---

* Picking pockets.

had lately happened, he reproved Wild for his cruel treatment of that good creature; then taking as sudden a leave as he civilly could of the gentleman, he hastened to comfort his lady, who received him with great kindness.

CHAPTER III

Curious anecdotes relating to the history of Newgate

There resided in the castle at the same time with Mr Wild one Roger Johnson,[99] a very GREAT MAN, who had long been at the head of all the *prigs* in Newgate, and had raised contributions on them. He examined into the nature of their defence, procured and instructed their evidence, and made himself, at least in their opinion, so necessary to them, that the whole fate of Newgate seemed entirely to depend upon him.

Wild had not been long under confinement before he began to oppose this man. He represented him to the *prigs* as a fellow who, under the plausible pretence of assisting their causes, was in reality undermining THE LIBERTIES OF NEWGATE. He at first threw out certain sly hints and insinuations; but, having by degrees formed a party against Roger, he one day assembled them together, and spoke to them in the following florid manner:

'Friends and fellow-citizens, – The cause I am to mention to you this day is of such mighty importance, that when I consider my own small abilities, I tremble with an apprehension lest your safety may be rendered precarious by the weakness of him who hath undertaken to represent to you your danger. Gentlemen, the liberty of Newgate is at stake; your privileges have been long undermined, and are now openly violated by one man; by one who hath engrossed to himself the whole conduct of your trials, under colour of which he exacts what contributions on you he pleases; but are those sums appropriated to the uses for which they are raised? Your frequent convictions at the Old Bailey, those depredations of justice, must too sensibly and sorely demonstrate the contrary. What evidence doth he ever produce for the prisoner which the prisoner himself could not have provided, and often better instructed? How many noble youths have there been lost when a single *alibi* would have saved them! Should I be silent, nay, could your own injuries want a tongue to remonstrate, the very breath which by his neglect hath been stopped at the *cheat* would cry out loudly against him. Nor is the exorbitancy of his plunders visible only in the dreadful consequences it hath produced to the *prigs*, nor glares it only in the miseries brought on them: it blazes forth in the more desirable effects it hath wrought for himself, in the rich perquisites acquired by it: witness that silk nightgown, that robe of shame, which, to his eternal dishonour, he publicly wears; that gown which I will not scruple to call the winding-sheet of the liberties of Newgate. Is there a *prig* who hath the interest and honour of Newgate so little at heart that he can refrain from blushing when he beholds that trophy, purchased with the breath of so many *prigs*? Nor is this all. His waistcoat embroidered with silk, and his velvet cap, bought with the same price, are ensigns of the same disgrace. Some would think the rags which covered his nakedness when first he was committed hither well exchanged for these gaudy trappings; but in my eye no exchange can be profitable when dishonour is the condition. If, therefore, Newgate –' Here the only copy which we could procure of this speech breaks off abruptly; however, we can assure the reader, from very authentic information, that he concluded with advising the *prigs* to put their affairs into other hands. After which, one of his party, as had been before concerted, in a very long speech recommended him (Wild himself) to their choice.

Newgate was divided into parties on this occasion, the *prigs* on each side representing their chief or great man to be the only person by whom the affairs of Newgate could be managed with safety and advantage. The *prigs* had indeed very incompatible interests; for, whereas the supporters of Johnson, who was in possession of the plunder of Newgate, were admitted to some share under their leader, so the abettors of Wild had, on his promotion, the same views of dividing some part of the spoil among themselves. It is no wonder, therefore, they were both so warm on each side. What may seem more remarkable was, that the debtors, who were entirely unconcerned in the dispute, and who were the destined plunder of both parties, should interest themselves with the utmost violence, some on behalf of Wild, and others in favour of Johnson. So that all Newgate resounded with WILD *for ever*, JOHNSON *for ever*. And the poor debtors re-echoed *the liberties of Newgate*, which, in the cant language, signifies *plunder*, as loudly as the thieves themselves. In short, such quarrels and animosities happened between them, that they seemed rather the people of two countries long at war with each other than the inhabitants of the same castle.

Wild's party at length prevailed, and he succeeded to the place and power of Johnson, whom he presently stripped of all his finery; but, when it was proposed that he should sell it and divide the money for the good of the whole, he waived that motion, saying it was not yet time, that he should find a better opportunity, that the clothes wanted cleaning, with many other pretences, and within two days, to the surprise of many, he appeared in them himself; for which he vouchsafed no other apology than that they fitted him much better than they did Johnson, and that they became him in a much more elegant manner.

This behaviour of Wild greatly incensed the debtors, particularly those by whose means he had been promoted. They grumbled extremely, and vented great indignation against Wild; when one day a very grave man, and one of much authority among them, bespake them as follows:

'Nothing sure can be more justly ridiculous than the conduct of those who should lay the lamb in the wolf's way, and then should lament his being devoured. What a wolf is in a sheepfold, a great man is in society. Now, when one wolf is in possession of a sheepfold, how little would it avail the simple flock to expel him and place another in his stead! Of the same benefit to us is the overthrowing one *prig* in favour of another. And for what other advantage was your struggle? Did you not all know that Wild and his followers were *prigs*, as well as Johnson and his? What then could the contention be among such but that which you have now discovered it to have been? Perhaps some would say, Is it then our duty tamely to submit to the rapine of the *prig* who now plunders us for fear of an exchange? Surely no: but I answer; It is better to shake the plunder off than to exchange the plunderer. And by what means can we effect this but by a total change in our manners? Every *prig* is a slave. His own *priggish* desires, which enslave him, themselves betray him to the tyranny of others. To preserve, therefore, the liberty of Newgate is to change the manners of Newgate. Let us, therefore, who are confined here for debt only, separate ourselves entirely from the *prigs*; neither drink with them nor converse with them. Let us at the same time separate ourselves farther from *priggism* itself. Instead of being ready, on every opportunity, to pillage each other, let us be content with our honest share of the common bounty, and with the acquisition of our own industry. When we separate from the *prigs*, let us enter into a closer alliance with one another. Let us consider ourselves all as members of one community, to the public good of which we are to sacrifice our private views; not to give up the interest of the whole for every little pleasure or profit which shall accrue to ourselves. Liberty is consistent with no degree of honesty inferior to this, and the community where this abounds no *prig* will have the impudence or audaciousness to endeavour to enslave; or if he should, his own destruction would be the only consequence of his attempt. But while one man pursues his ambition, another his interest, another his safety; while one hath a roguery (a *priggism* they here call it) to commit, and another a roguery to defend; they must naturally fly to the favour and protection of those who have power to give them what they desire, and to defend them from what they fear; nay, in this view it becomes their interest to promote this power in their patrons. Now, gentlemen, when we are no longer *prigs*, we shall no longer have these fears or these desires. What remains, therefore, for us but to resolve bravely to lay aside our *priggism*, our roguery, in plainer words, and preserve our liberty, or to give up the latter in the preservation and preference of the former?'

This speech was received with much applause; however, Wild continued as before to levy contributions among the prisoners, to apply the garnish to his own use, and to strut openly in the ornaments which he had stripped from Johnson. To speak sincerely, there was more bravado than real use or advantage in these trappings. As for the nightgown, its outside indeed made a glittering tinsel appearance, but it kept him not warm, nor could the finery of it do him much honour, since every one knew it did not properly belong to him; as to the waistcoat, it fitted him very ill, being infinitely too big for him; and the cap was so heavy that it made his head ache. Thus these clothes, which perhaps (as they presented the idea of their misery more sensibly to the people's eyes) brought him more envy, hatred, and detraction, than all his deeper impositions and more real advantages, afforded very little use or honour to the wearer; nay, could scarce serve to amuse his own vanity when this was cool enough to reflect with the least seriousness. And, should I speak in the language of a man who estimated human happiness without regard to that greatness, which we have so laboriously endeavoured to paint in this history, it is probable he never took (i.e. robbed the prisoners of) a shilling, which he himself did not pay too dear for.

CHAPTER IV

The dead-warrant arrives for Heartfree; on which occasion
Wild betrays some human weakness

The dead-warrant, as it is called, now came down to Newgate for the execution of Heartfree among the rest of the prisoners. And here the reader must excuse us, who profess to draw natural, not perfect characters, and to record the truths of history, not the extravagances of romance, while we relate a weakness in Wild of which we are ourselves ashamed, and which we would willingly have concealed, could we have preserved at the same time that strict attachment to truth and impartiality, which we have professed in recording the annals of this great man. Know then, reader, that this dead-warrant did not affect Heartfree, who was to suffer a shameful death by it, with half the concern it gave Wild, who had been the occasion of it. He had been a little struck the day before on seeing the children carried away in tears from their father. This sight brought the remembrance of some slight injuries he had done the father to his mind, which he endeavoured as much as possible to obliterate; but, when one of the keepers

(I should say lieutenants of the castle) repeated Heartfree's name among those of the malefactors who were to suffer within a few days, the blood forsook his countenance, and in a cold still stream moved heavily to his heart, which had scarce strength enough left to return it through his veins. In short, his body so visibly demonstrated the pangs of his mind, that to escape observation he retired to his room, where he sullenly gave vent to such bitter agonies, that even the injured Heartfree, had not the apprehension of what his wife had suffered shut every avenue of compassion, would have pitied him.

When his mind was thoroughly fatigued, and worn out with the horrors which the approaching fate of the poor wretch, who lay under a sentence which he had iniquitously brought upon him, had suggested, sleep promised him relief; but this promise was, alas! delusive. This certain friend to the tired body is often the severest enemy to the oppressed mind. So at least it proved to Wild, adding visionary to real horrors, and tormenting his imagination with phantoms too dreadful to be described. At length, starting from these visions, he no sooner recovered his waking senses, than he cried out: 'I may yet prevent this catastrophe. It is not too late to discover the whole.' He then paused a moment; but greatness, instantly returning to his assistance, checked the base thought, as it first offered itself to his mind. He then reasoned thus coolly with himself: 'Shall I, like a child, or a woman, or one of those mean wretches whom I have always despised, be frightened by dreams and visionary phantoms to sully that honour which I have so difficultly acquired and so gloriously maintained? Shall I, to redeem the worthless life of this silly fellow, suffer my reputation to contract a stain which the blood of millions cannot wipe away? Was it only that the few, the simple part of mankind, should call me a rogue, perhaps I could submit; but to be for ever contemptible to the PRIGS, as a wretch who wanted spirit to execute my undertaking, can never be digested. What is the life of a single man? Have not whole armies and nations been sacrificed to the honour of ONE GREAT MAN? Nay, to omit that first class of greatness, the conquerors of mankind, how often have numbers fallen by a fictitious plot only to satisfy the spleen, or perhaps exercise the ingenuity, of a member of that second order of greatness the ministerial! What have I done then? Why, I have ruined a family, and brought an innocent man to the gallows. I ought rather to weep with Alexander that I have ruined no more, than to regret the little I have done.' He at length, therefore, bravely resolved to consign over Heartfree to his fate, though it cost him more struggling than may easily be believed, utterly to conquer his reluctance, and to banish away every degree of humanity from his mind, these little sparks of which composed one of those weaknesses which we lamented in the opening of our history.

But in vindication of our hero, we must beg leave to observe that Nature is seldom so kind as those writers who draw characters absolutely perfect. She seldom creates any man so completely great, or completely low, but that some sparks of humanity will glimmer in the former, and some sparks of what the vulgar call evil will dart forth in the latter: utterly to extinguish which will give some pain, and uneasiness to both; for I apprehend no mind was ever yet formed entirely free from blemish, unless peradventure that of a sanctified hypocrite, whose praises some well-fed flatterer hath gratefully thought proper to sing forth.

CHAPTER V

Containing various matters

The day was now come when poor Heartfree was to suffer an ignominious death. Friendly had in the strongest manner confirmed his assurance of fulfilling his promise of becoming a father to one of his children and a husband to the other. This gave him inexpressible comfort, and he had, the evening before, taken his last leave of the little wretches with a tenderness which drew a tear from one of the keepers, joined to a magnanimity which would have pleased a stoic. When he was informed that the coach which Friendly had provided for him was ready, and that the rest of the prisoners were gone, he embraced that faithful friend with great passion, and begged that he would leave him here; but the other desired leave to accompany him to his end, which at last he was forced to comply with. And now he was proceeding towards the coach when he found his difficulties were not yet over; for now a friend arrived of whom he was to take a harder and more tender leave than he had yet gone through. This friend, reader, was no other than Mrs Heartfree herself, who ran to him with a look all wild, staring, and frantic, and having reached his arms, fainted away in them without uttering a single syllable. Heartfree was, with great difficulty, able to preserve his own senses in such a surprise at such a season. And, indeed, our good-natured reader will be rather inclined to wish this miserable couple had, by dying in each other's arms, put a final period to their woes, than have survived to taste those bitter moments which were to be their portion, and which the unhappy wife, soon recovering from the short intermission of being, now began to suffer. When she became first mistress of her voice she burst forth into the following accents: 'O my husband! Is this the condition in which I find you after our cruel separation? Who hath done this? Cruel Heaven! What is the occasion? I know thou canst deserve no ill. Tell me, somebody who can speak, while I have my senses left to understand, what is the matter?' At which words several laughed, and one answered: 'The matter! Why no great matter. The gentleman is not the first, nor won't be the last: the worst of the matter is, that if we are to stay all the morning here I shall lose my dinner.' Heartfree, pausing a moment and recollecting himself, cried out: 'I will bear all with patience.' And then, addressing himself to the commanding officer, begged he might only have a few minutes by himself with his wife, whom he had not seen before since his misfortunes. The great man answered: 'He had compassion on him, and would do more than he could answer; but he supposed he was too much a gentleman not to know that something was due for such civility.' On this hint, Friendly, who was himself half dead, pulled five guineas out of his pocket, which the great man took, and said he would be so generous to give him ten minutes; on which one observed that many a gentleman had bought ten minutes with a woman dearer, and many other facetious remarks were made, unnecessary to be here related. Heartfree was now suffered to retire into a room with his wife, the commander informing him at his entrance that he must be expeditious, for that the rest of the good company would be at the tree before him, and he supposed he was a gentleman of too much breeding to make them wait.

This tender wretched couple were now retired for these few minutes, which the commander without carefully measured with his watch; and Heartfree was mustering all his resolution to part with what his soul so ardently doted on, and to conjure her to support his loss for the sake of her poor infants, and to comfort her with the promise of Friendly on their account; but all his design was frustrated. Mrs Heartfree could not support the shock, but again fainted away, and so entirely lost every symptom of life that Heartfree called vehemently for assistance. Friendly rushed first into the room, and was soon followed by many others, and, what was remarkable, one who had unmoved beheld the tender scene between these parting lovers was touched to the quick by the pale looks of the woman, and ran up and down for water, drops, etc., with the utmost hurry and confusion. The ten minutes were expired, which the commander now hinted; and seeing nothing offered for the renewal of the term (for indeed Friendly had unhappily emptied his pockets), he began to grow very importunate, and at last told Heartfree he should be ashamed not to act more like a man. Heartfree begged his pardon, and said he would make him wait no longer. Then, with the deepest sigh, cried: 'Oh, my angel!' and, embracing his wife with the utmost eagerness, kissed her pale lips with more fervency than ever bridegroom did the blushing cheeks of his bride. He then cried: 'The Almighty bless thee! and, if it be His pleasure, restore thee to life; if not, I beseech Him we may presently meet again in a better world than this.' He was breaking from her, when, perceiving her sense returning, he could not forbear renewing his embrace, and again pressing her lips, which now recovered life and warmth so fast that he begged one ten minutes more to tell her what her swooning had prevented her hearing. The worthy commander, being perhaps a little touched at this tender scene, took Friendly aside, and asked him what he would give if he would suffer his friend to remain half an hour? Friendly answered, anything; that he had no more money in his pocket, but he would certainly pay him that afternoon. 'Well, then, I'll be moderate,' said he; 'twenty guineas.' Friendly answered: 'It is a bargain.' The commander, having exacted a firm promise, cried: 'Then I don't care if they stay a whole hour together; for what signifies hiding good news? the gentleman is reprieved'; of which he had just before received notice in a whisper. It would be very impertinent to offer at a description of the joy this occasioned to the two friends, or to Mrs Heartfree, who was now again recovered. A surgeon, who was happily present, was employed to bleed them all. After which the commander, who had his promise of the money again confirmed to him, wished Heartfree joy, and, shaking him very friendly by the hands, cleared the room of all the company, and left the three friends together.

CHAPTER VI

In which the foregoing happy incident is accounted for

But here, though I am convinced my good-natured reader may almost want the surgeon's assistance also, and that there is no passage in this whole story which can afford him equal delight, yet, lest our reprieve should seem to resemble that in the *Beggar's Opera*,[100] I shall endeavour to shew him that this incident, which is indoubtedly true, is at least as natural as delightful; for we assure him we would rather have suffered half mankind to be hanged, than have saved one contrary to the strictest rules of writing and probability.

Be it known, then (a circumstance which I think highly credible), that the great Fireblood had been, a few days before, taken in the fact of a robbery, and carried before the same justice of peace who had, on his evidence, committed Heartfree to prison. This magistrate, who did indeed no small honour to the commission he bore, duly considered the weighty charge committed to him, by which he was entrusted with decisions affecting the lives, liberties, and properties of his countrymen. He, therefore, examined always with the utmost diligence and caution into every minute circumstance. And, as he had a good deal balanced, even when he committed Heartfree, on the excellent character given him by Friendly and the maid; and as he was much staggered on finding that, of the two persons on whose evidence alone Heart-free had been committed, and had since been convicted, one was in Newgate for a felony, and the other was now brought before him for a robbery, he thought proper to put the matter very home to Fireblood at this time. The young Achates was taken, as we have said, in the fact; so that denial he saw was in vain. He, therefore, honestly confessed what he knew must be proved; and desired, on the merit of the discoveries he made, to be admitted as an evidence against his accomplices. This afforded the happiest opportunity to the justice to satisfy his conscience in relation to Heartfree. He told Fireblood that, if he expected the favour he solicited, it must be on condition that he revealed the whole truth to him concerning the evidence which he had lately given against a bankrupt, and which some circumstances had induced a suspicion of; that he might depend on it the truth would be discovered by other means, and gave some oblique hints (a deceit entirely justifiable) that Wild himself had offered such a discovery. The very mention of Wild's name immediately alarmed Fireblood, who did not in the least doubt the readiness of that GREAT MAN to hang any of the gang when his own interest seemed to require it. He, therefore, hesitated not a moment; but, having obtained a promise from the justice that he should be accepted as an evidence, he discovered the whole falsehood, and declared that he had been seduced by Wild to depose as he had done.

The justice, having thus luckily and timely discovered this scene of villainy, *alias* greatness, lost not a moment in using his utmost endeavours to get the case of the unhappy convict represented to the sovereign, who immediately granted him that gracious reprieve which caused such happiness to the persons concerned; and which we hope we have now accounted for to the satisfaction of the reader.

The good magistrate, having obtained this reprieve for Heart-free, thought it incumbent on him to visit him in the prison, and to sound, if possible, the depth of this affair, that, if he should appear as innocent as he now began to conceive him, he might use all imaginable methods to obtain his pardon and enlargement.

The next day, therefore, after that when the miserable scene above described had passed, he went to Newgate, where he found those three persons, namely, Heartfree, his wife, and Friendly, sitting together. The justice informed the prisoner of the confession of Fireblood, with the steps which he had taken upon it. The reader will easily conceive the many outward thanks, as well as inward gratitude, which he received from all three; but those were of very little consequence to him compared with the secret satisfaction he felt in his mind from reflecting on the preservation of innocence, as he soon after very clearly perceived was the case.

When he entered the room Mrs Heartfree was speaking with some earnestness; as he perceived, therefore, he had interrupted her, he begged she would continue her discourse, which, if he prevented by his presence, he desired to depart; but Heartfree would not suffer it. He said she had been relating some adventures which perhaps might entertain him to hear, and which she the rather desired he would hear, as they might serve to illustrate the foundation on which this falsehood had been built, which had brought on her husband all his misfortunes.

The justice very gladly consented, and Mrs Heartfree, at her husband's desire, began the relation from the first renewal of Wild's acquaintance with him; but, though this recapitulation was necessary for the information of our good magistrate, as it would be useless, and perhaps tedious, to the reader, we shall only repeat that part of her story to which he is only a stranger, beginning with what happened to her after Wild had been turned adrift in the boat by the captain of the French privateer.

CHAPTER VII

Mrs Heartfree relates her adventures

Mrs Heartfree proceeded thus: 'The vengeance which the French captain exacted on that villain (our hero) persuaded me that I was fallen into the hands of a man of honour and justice; nor indeed was it possible for any person to be treated with more respect and civility than I now was; but if this could not mitigate my sorrows when I reflected on the condition in which I had been betrayed to leave all that was dear to me, much less could it produce such an effect when I discovered, as I soon did, that I owed it chiefly to a passion which threatened me with great uneasiness, as it quickly appeared to be very violent, and as I was absolutely in the power of the person who possessed it, or was rather possessed by it. I must, however, do him the justice to say my fears carried my suspicions farther than I afterwards found I had any reason to carry them: he did indeed very soon acquaint me with his passion, and used all those gentle methods which frequently succeed with our sex to prevail with me to gratify it; but never once threatened, nor had the least recourse to force. He did not even once insinuate to me that I was totally in his power, which I myself sufficiently saw, and whence I drew the most dreadful apprehensions, well knowing that, as there are some dispositions so brutal that cruelty adds a zest and savour to their pleasures, so there are others whose gentler inclinations are better gratified when they win us by softer methods to comply with their desires; yet that even these may be often compelled by an unruly passion to have recourse at last to the means of violence, when they despair of success from persuasion; but I was happily the captive of a better man. My conqueror was one of those over whom vice hath a limited jurisdiction; and, though he was too easily prevailed on to sin, he was proof against any temptation to villainy.

'We had been two days almost totally becalmed, when, a brisk gale rising as we were in sight of Dunkirk, we saw a vessel making full sail towards us. The captain of the privateer was so strong that he apprehended no danger but from a man-of-war, which the sailors discerned this not to be. He, therefore, struck his colours, and furled his sails as much as possible, in order to lie by and expect her, hoping she might be a prize.' (Here Heartfree smiling, his wife stopped and inquired the cause. He told her it was from her using the sea-terms so aptly: she laughed, and answered he would wonder less at this when he heard the long time she had been on board; and then proceeded.) 'This vessel now came alongside of us, and hailed us, having perceived that on which we were aboard to be of her own country; they begged us not to put into Dunkirk, but to accompany them in their pursuit of a large

English merchantman, whom we should easily overtake, and both together as easily conquer. Our captain immediately consented to this proposition, and ordered all his sail to be crowded. This was the most unwelcome news to me; however, he comforted me all he could by assuring me I had nothing to fear, that he would be so far from offering the least rudeness to me himself, that he would, at the hazard of his life, protect me from it. This assurance gave me all the consolation which my present circumstances and the dreadful apprehensions I had on your dear account would admit.' (At which words the tenderest glances passed on both sides between the husband and wife.)

'We sailed near twelve hours, when we came in sight of the ship we were in pursuit of, and which we should probably have soon come up with had not a very thick mist ravished her from our eyes. This mist continued several hours, and when it cleared up we discovered our companion at a great distance from us; but what gave us (I mean the captain and his crew) the greatest uneasiness was the sight of a very large ship within a mile of us, which presently saluted us with a gun, and now appeared to be a third-rate English man-of-war. Our captain declared the impossibility of either fighting or escaping, and accordingly struck without waiting for the broadside which was preparing for us, and which perhaps would have prevented me from the happiness I now enjoy.' This occasioned Heartfree to change colour; his wife therefore passed hastily to circumstances of a more smiling complexion.

'I greatly rejoiced at this event, as I thought it would not only restore me to the safe possession of my jewels, but to what I value beyond all the treasure in the universe. My expectation, however, of both these was somewhat crossed for the present: as to the former, I was told they should be carefully preserved; but that I must prove my right to them before I could expect their restoration, which, if I mistake not, the captain did not very eagerly desire I should be able to accomplish: and as to the latter, I was acquainted that I should be put on board the first ship which they met on her way to England, but that they were proceeding to the West Indies.

'I had not been long on board the man-of-war before I discovered just reason rather to lament than rejoice at the exchange of my captivity (for such I concluded my present situation to be). I had now another lover in the captain of this Englishman, and much rougher and less gallant than the Frenchman had been. He used me with scarce common civility, as indeed he shewed very little to any other person, treating his officers little better than a man of no great good-breeding would exert to his meanest servant, and that too on some very irritating provocation. As for me, he addressed me with the insolence of a bashaw to a Circassian slave; he talked to me with the loose licence in which the most profligate libertines converse with harlots, and which women abandoned only in a moderate degree detest and abhor. He often kissed me with very rude familiarity, and one day attempted further brutality; when a gentleman on board, and who was in my situation, that is, had been taken by a privateer and was retaken, rescued me from his hands, for which the captain confined him though he was not under his command, two days in irons: when he was released (for I was not suffered to visit him in his confinement) I went to him and thanked him with the utmost acknowledgement for what he had done and suffered on my account. The gentleman behaved to me in the handsomest manner on this occasion; told me he was ashamed of the high sense I seemed to entertain of so small an obligation, of an action to which his duty as a Christian and his honour as a man obliged him. From this time I lived in great familiarity with this man, whom I regarded as my protector, which he professed himself ready to be on all occasions, expressing the utmost abhorrence of the captain's brutality, especially that shewn towards me, and the tenderness of a parent for the preservation of my virtue, for which I was not myself more solicitous than he appeared. He was, indeed, the only man I had hitherto met since my unhappy departure who did not endeavour by all his looks, words, and actions, to assure me he had a liking to my unfortunate person; the rest seeming desirous of sacrificing the little beauty they complimented to their desires, without the least consideration of the ruin which I earnestly represented to them they were attempting to bring on me and my future repose.

'I now passed several days pretty free from the captain's molestation, till one fatal night.' Here, perceiving Heartfree grew pale, she comforted him by an assurance that Heaven had preserved her chastity, and again had restored her unsullied to his arms. She continued thus: 'Perhaps I give it a wrong epithet in the word fatal; but a wretched night I am sure I may call it, for no woman who came off victorious was, I believe, ever in greater danger. One night, I say, having drank his spirits high with punch, in company with the purser, who was the only man in the ship he admitted to his table, the captain sent for me into his cabin; whither, though unwilling, I was obliged to go. We were no sooner alone together than he seized me by the hand, and, after affronting my ears with discourse which I am unable to repeat, he swore a great oath that his passion was to be dallied with no longer; that I must not expect to treat him in the manner to which a set of blockhead land-men submitted. "None of your coquette airs, therefore, with me, madam," said he, "for I am resolved to have you this night. No struggling nor squalling, for both will be impertinent. The first man who offers to come in here, I will have his skin flea'd off at the gangway." He then attempted to pull me violently towards his bed. I threw myself on my knees, and with tears and entreaties besought his compassion; but this was, I found, to no purpose: I then had recourse to threats, and endeavoured to frighten him with the consequence; but neither had this, though it seemed to stagger him more than the other method, sufficient force to deliver me. At last a stratagem came into my head, of which my perceiving him reel gave me the first hint. I entreated a moment's reprieve only, when, collecting all the spirits I could muster, I put on a constrained air of gaiety, and told him, with an affected laugh, he was the roughest lover I had ever met with, and that I believed I was the first woman he had ever paid his addresses to. "Addresses," said he; "d—n your dresses! I want to undress you." I then begged him to let us drink some punch together; for that I loved a can as well as himself, and never would grant the favour to any man till I had drank a hearty glass with him. "Oh!" said he, "if that be all, you shall have punch enough to drown yourself in." At which words he rung the bell, and ordered in a gallon of that liquor. I was in the meantime obliged to suffer his nauseous kisses, and some rudenesses which I had great difficulty to restrain within moderate bounds. When the punch came in he took up the bowl and drank my health ostentatiously, in such a quantity that it considerably advanced my scheme. I followed him with bumpers as fast as possible, and was myself obliged to drink so much that at another time it would have staggered my own reason, but at present it did not affect me. At length, perceiving him very far gone, I watched an opportunity, and ran out of the cabin, resolving to seek protection of the sea if I could find no other; but Heaven was now graciously pleased to relieve me; for in his attempt to pursue me he reeled backwards, and, falling down the cabin stairs, he dislocated his shoulder and so bruised himself that I was not only preserved that night from any danger of my intended ravisher, but the accident threw him into a fever which endangered his life, and whether he ever recovered or no I am not certain; for during his delirious fits the eldest lieutenant commanded the ship. This was a virtuous and a brave fellow, who had been twenty-five years in that post without being able to obtain a ship, and had seen several boys, the bastards of noblemen, put over his head. One day while the ship remained under his command an English vessel bound to Cork passed by; myself and my friend, who had formerly lain two days in irons on my account, went on board this ship with the leave of the good lieutenant, who made us such presents as he was able of provisions, and, congratulating me on my delivery from a danger to which none of the ship's crew had been strangers, he kindly wished us both a safe journey.'

CHAPTER VIII

In which Mrs Heartfree continues the relation of her adventures

'The first evening after we were aboard this vessel, which was a brigantine, we being then at no very great distance from the Madeiras, the most violent storm arose from the north-west, in which we presently lost both our masts; and indeed death now presented itself as inevitable to us: I need not tell my Tommy what were then my thoughts. Our danger was so great that the captain of the ship, a professed atheist, betook himself to prayers, and the whole crew, abandoning themselves for lost, fell with the utmost eagerness to the emptying a cask of brandy, not one drop of which, they swore, should be polluted with salt water. I observed here my old friend displayed less courage than I expected from him. He seemed entirely swallowed up in despair. But Heaven be praised! we were all at last preserved. The storm, after above eleven hours' continuance, began to abate, and by degrees entirely ceased, but left us still rolling at the mercy of the waves, which carried us at their own pleasure to the south-east a vast number of leagues. Our crew were all dead drunk with the brandy which they had taken such care to preserve from the sea; but, indeed, had they been awake, their labour would have been of very little service, as we had lost all our rigging, our brigantine being reduced to a naked hulk only. In this condition we floated above thirty hours, till in the midst of a very dark night we spied a light, which seeming to approach us, grew so large that our sailors concluded it to be the lantern of a man-of-war; but when we were cheering ourselves with the hopes of our deliverance from this wretched situation, on a sudden, to our great concern, the light entirely disappeared, and left us in despair increased by the remembrance of those pleasing imaginations with which we had entertained our minds during its appearance. The rest of the night we passed in melancholy conjectures on the light which had deserted us, which the major part of the sailors concluded to be a meteor. In this distress we had one comfort, which was a plentiful store of provisions; this so supported the spirits of the sailors, that they declared had they but a sufficient quantity of brandy they cared not whether they saw land for a month to come; but indeed we were much nearer it than we imagined, as we perceived at break of day. One of the most knowing of the crew declared we were near the continent of Africa; but when we were within three leagues of it a second violent storm arose from the north, so that we again gave over all hopes of safety. This storm was not quite so outrageous as the former, but of much longer continuance, for it lasted near three days, and drove us an immense number of leagues to the south. We were within a league of the shore, expecting every moment our ship to be dashed in pieces, when the tempest ceased all on a sudden; but the waves still continued to roll like mountains, and before the sea recovered its calm motion, our ship was thrown so near the land, that the captain ordered out his boat, declaring he had scarce any hopes of saving her; and indeed we had not quitted her many minutes before we saw the justice of his apprehensions, for she struck against a rock and immediately sunk. The behaviour of the sailors on this occasion very much affected me; they beheld their ship perish with the tenderness of a lover or a parent; they spoke of her as the fondest husband would of his wife; and many of them, who seemed to have no tears in their composition, shed them plentifully at her sinking. The captain himself cried out: "Go thy way, charming Molly, the sea never devoured a lovelier morsel. If I have fifty vessels I shall never love another like thee. Poor slut! I shall remember thee to my dying day." Well, the boat now conveyed us all safe to shore, where we landed with very little difficulty. It was now about noon, and the rays of the sun, which descended almost perpendicular on our heads, were extremely hot and troublesome. However, we travelled through this extreme heat about five miles over a plain. This brought us to a vast wood, which extended itself as far as we could see, both to the right and left, and seemed to me to put an entire end to our progress. Here we decreed to rest and dine on the provision which we had brought from the ship, of which we had sufficient for very few meals; our boat being so overloaded with people that we had very little room for luggage of any kind. Our repast was salt pork broiled, which the keenness of hunger made so delicious to my companions that they fed very heartily upon it. As for myself, the fatigue of my body and the vexation of my mind had so thoroughly weakened me, that I was almost entirely deprived of appetite; and the utmost dexterity of the most accomplished French cook would have been ineffectual had he endeavoured to tempt me with delicacies. I thought myself very little a gainer by my late escape from the tempest, by which I seemed only to have exchanged the element in which I was presently to die. When our company had sufficiently, and indeed very plentifully feasted themselves, they resolved to enter the wood and endeavour to pass it, in expectation of finding some inhabitants, at least some provision. We proceeded therefore in the following order: one man in the front with a hatchet, to clear our way, and two others followed him with guns, to protect the rest from wild beasts; then walked the rest of our company, and last of all the captain himself, being armed likewise with a gun, to defend us from any attack behind – in the rear, I think you call it. And thus our whole company, being fourteen in number, travelled on till night overtook us, without seeing anything unless a few birds and some very insignificant animals. We rested all night under the covert of some trees, and indeed we very little wanted shelter at that season, the heat in the day being the only inclemency we had to combat with in this climate. I cannot help telling you my old friend lay still nearest me on the ground, and declared he would be my protector should any of the sailors offer rudeness; but I can acquit them of any such attempt; nor was I ever affronted by any one, more than with a coarse expression, proceeding rather from the roughness and ignorance of their education than from any abandoned principle, or want of humanity.

'We had now proceeded very little way on our next day's march when one of the sailors, having skipped nimbly up a hill, with the assistance of a speaking trumpet informed us that he saw a town a very little way off. This news so comforted me, and gave me such strength, as well as spirits, that, with the help of my old friend and another, who suffered me to lean on them, I, with much difficulty, attained the summit; but was so absolutely over-come in climbing it, that I had no longer sufficient strength to support my tottering limbs, and was obliged to lay myself again on the ground; nor could they prevail on me to undertake descending through a very thick wood into a plain, at the end of which indeed appeared some houses, or rather huts, but at a much greater distance than the sailor assured us; the little way, as he had called it, seeming to me full twenty miles, nor was it, I believe, much less.'

CHAPTER IX

Containing incidents very surprising[101]

'The captain declared he would, without delay, proceed to the town before him; in which resolution he was seconded by all the crew; but when I could not be persuaded, nor was I able to travel any farther before I had rested myself, my old friend protested he would not leave me, but would stay behind as my guard; and, when I had refreshed myself with a little repose, he would attend me to the town, which the captain promised he would not leave before he had seen us.

'They were no sooner departed than (having first thanked my protector for his care of me) I resigned myself to sleep, which immediately closed my eyelids, and would probably have detained me very long in his gentle dominions, had I not been awaked with a squeeze by the hand of my guard, which I at first thought intended to alarm me with danger of some wild beast; but I soon perceived it arose from a softer motive, and that a gentle swain was the only wild beast I had to apprehend. He began now to disclose his passion in the strongest manner imaginable, indeed with a warmth rather beyond that of both my former lovers, but as yet without any attempt of absolute force. On my side remonstrances were made in more bitter exclamations and revilings than I had used to any, that villain Wild excepted. I told him he was the basest and most treacherous wretch alive; that his having cloaked his iniquitous designs under the appearance of virtue and friendship added an ineffable degree of horror to them; that I detested him of all mankind the most, and could I be brought to yield to prostitution, he should be the last to enjoy the ruins of my honour. He suffered himself not to be provoked by this language, but only changed his manner of solicitation from flattery to bribery. He unripped the lining of his waistcoat, and pulled forth several jewels; these, he said, he had preserved from infinite danger to the happiest purpose, if I could be won by them. I rejected them often with the utmost indignation, till at last casting my eye, rather by accident than design, on a diamond necklace, a thought, like lightning, shot through my mind, and, in an instant, I remembered that this was the very necklace you had sold the cursed count, the cause of all our misfortunes. The confusion of ideas into which this surprise hurried me prevented my reflecting on the villain who then stood before me; but the first recollection presently told me it could be no other than the count himself, the wicked tool of Wild's barbarity. Good heavens! what was then my condition! how shall I describe the tumult of passions which then laboured in my breast? However, as I was happily unknown to him, the least suspicion on his side was altogether impossible. He imputed, therefore, the eagerness with which I gazed on the jewels to a very wrong cause, and endeavoured to put as much additional softness into his countenance as he was able. My fears were a little quieted, and I was resolved to be very liberal of promises, and hoped so thoroughly to persuade him of my venality that he might, without any doubt, be drawn in to wait the captain and crew's return, who would, I was very certain, not only preserve me from his violence, but secure the restoration of what you had been so cruelly robbed of. But, alas! I was mistaken.' Mrs Heartfree, again perceiving symptoms of the utmost disquietude in her husband's countenance, cried out, 'My dear, don't you apprehend any harm. – But, to deliver you as soon as possible from your anxiety – when he perceived I declined the warmth of his addresses he begged me to consider; he changed at once the tone of his features, and, in a very different voice from what he had hitherto affected, he swore I should not deceive him as I had the captain; that fortune had kindly thrown an opportunity in his way which he was resolved not foolishly to lose; and concluded with a violent oath that he was determined to enjoy me that moment, and therefore I knew the consequences of resistance. He then caught me in his arms, and began such rude attempts, that I screamed out with all the force I could, though I had so little hopes of being rescued, when there suddenly rushed forth from a thicket a creature which, at his first appearance, and in the hurry of spirits I then was, I did not take for a man; but, indeed, had he been the fiercest of wild beasts, I should have rejoiced at his devouring us both. I scarce perceived he had a musket in his hand before he struck my ravisher such a blow with it that he felled him at my feet. He then advanced with a gentle air towards me, and told me in French he was extremely glad he had been luckily present to my assistance. He was naked, except his middle and his feet, if I can call a body so which was covered with hair almost equal to any beast whatever. Indeed, his appearance was so horrid in my eyes, that the friendship he had shewn me, as well as his courteous behaviour, could not entirely remove the dread I had conceived from his figure. I believe he saw this very visibly; for he begged me not to be frightened, since, whatever accident had brought me thither, I should have reason to thank Heaven for meeting him, at whose hands I might assure myself of the utmost civility and protection. In the midst of all this consternation, I had spirits enough to take up the casket of jewels which the villain, in falling, had dropped out of his hands, and conveyed it into my pocket. My deliverer, telling me that I seemed extremely weak and faint, desired me to refresh myself at his little hut, which, he said, was hard by. If his demeanour had been less kind and obliging, my desperate situation must have lent me confidence; for sure the alternative could not be doubtful, whether I should rather trust this man, who, notwithstanding his savage outside, expressed so much devotion to serve me, which at least I was not certain of the falsehood of, or should abide with one whom I so perfectly well knew to be an accomplished villain. I, therefore, committed myself to his guidance, though with tears in my eyes, and begged him to have compassion on my innocence, which was absolutely in his power. He said, the treatment he had been witness of, which he supposed was from one who had broken his trust towards me, sufficiently justified my suspicion; but begged me to dry my eyes, and he would soon convince me that I was with a man of different sentiments. The kind accents which accompanied these words gave me some comfort, which was assisted by the repossession of our jewels by an accident so strongly savouring of the disposition of Providence in my favour.

'We left the villain weltering in his blood, though beginning to recover a little motion, and walked together to his hut, or rather cave, for it was underground, on the side of a hill; the situation was very pleasant, and from its mouth we overlooked a large plain and the town I had before seen. As soon as I entered it, he desired me to sit down on a bench of earth, which served him for chairs, and then laid before me some fruits, the wild product of that country, one or two of which had an excellent flavour. He likewise produced some baked flesh, a little resembling that of venison. He then brought forth a bottle of brandy, which he said had remained with him ever since his settling there, now above thirty years, during all which time he had never opened it, his only liquor being water; that he had reserved this bottle as a cordial in sickness; but, he thanked Heaven, he had never yet had occasion for it. He then acquainted me that he was a hermit, that he had been formerly cast away on that coast, with his wife, whom he dearly loved, but could not preserve from perishing; on which account he had resolved never to return to France, which was his native country, but to devote himself to prayer and a holy life, placing all his hopes in the blessed expectation of meeting that dear woman again in heaven, where, he was convinced, she was now a saint and an interceder for him. He said he had exchanged a watch with the king of that country, whom he described to be a very just and good man, for a gun, some powder, shot, and ball, with which he sometimes provided himself food, but more generally used it in defending himself against wild beasts; so that his diet was chiefly of the vegetable kind. He told me many more circumstances, which I may relate to you hereafter: but, to be as concise as possible at present, he at length greatly comforted me by promising to conduct me to a seaport, where I might have an opportunity to meet with some vessels trafficking for slaves; and whence I might once more commit myself to that element which, though I had already suffered so much on it, I must again trust to put me in possesssion of all I loved.

'The character he gave me of the inhabitants of the town we saw below us, and of their king, made me desirous of being conducted thither; especially as I very much wished to see the captain and sailors, who had behaved very kindly to me, and with whom, not-withstanding all the civil behaviour of the hermit, I was rather easier in my mind than alone with this single man; but he dis-suaded me greatly from attempting such a walk till I had recreated my spirits with rest, desiring me to repose myself on his couch or bank, saying that he himself would retire without the cave, where he would remain as my guard. I accepted this kind proposal, but it was long before I could procure any slumber; however, at length, weariness prevailed over my fears, and I enjoyed several hours' sleep. When I awaked I found my faithful sentinel on his post and ready at my summons. This behaviour infused some confidence into me, and I now repeated my request that he would go with me to the town below; but he answered, I would be better advised to take some repast before I undertook the journey, which I should find much longer than it appeared. I consented, and he set forth a greater variety of fruits than before, of which I ate very plentifully. My collation being ended, I renewed the mention of my walk, but he still persisted in dissuading me, telling me that I was not yet strong enough; that I could repose myself nowhere with greater safety than in his cave; and that, for his part, he could have no greater happiness than that of attending me, adding, with a sigh, it was a happiness he should envy any other more than all the gifts of fortune. You may imagine I began now to entertain suspicions; but he presently removed all doubt by throwing himself at my feet and expressing the warmest passion for me. I should have now sunk with despair had he not accompanied these professions with the most vehement protestations that he would never offer me any other force but that of entreaty, and that he would rather die the most cruel death by my coldness than gain the highest bliss by becoming the occasion of a tear of sorrow to these bright eyes, which he said were stars, under whose benign influence alone he could enjoy, or indeed suffer life.' She was repeating many more compliments he made her, when a horrid uproar, which alarmed the whole gate, put a stop to her narration at present. It is impossible for me to give the reader a better idea of the noise which now arose than by desiring him to imagine I had the hundred tongues the poet once wished for, and was vociferating from them all at once, by hollowing, scolding, crying, swearing, bellowing, and, in short, by every different articulation which is within the scope of the human organ.

CHAPTER X

A horrible uproar in the gate

But however great an idea the reader may hence conceive of this uproar, he will think the occasion more than adequate to it when he is informed that our hero (I blush to name it) had discovered an injury done to his honour, and that in the tenderest point. In a word, reader (for thou must know it, though it give thee the greatest horror imaginable), he had caught Fireblood in the arms of his lovely Lætitia.

As the generous bull, who, having iong depastured among a number of cows, and thence contracted an opinion that these cows are all his own property, if he beholds another bull bestride a cow within his walks, he roars aloud, and threatens instant vengeance with his horns, till the whole parish are alarmed with his bellowing; not with less noise nor less dreadful menaces did the fury of Wild burst forth and terrify the whole gate. Long time did rage render his voice inarticulate to the hearer; as when at a visiting day, fifteen or sixteen or perhaps twice as many females, of delicate but shrill pipes, ejaculate all at once on different subjects, all is sound only, the harmony entirely melodious indeed, but conveys no idea to our ears; but at length, when reason began to get the better of his passion, which latter, being deserted by his breath, began a little to retreat, the following accents leapt over the hedge of his teeth, or rather the ditch of his gums, whence those hedgestakes had long since by a batten been displaced in battle with an amazon of Drury.

* '... Man of honour! doth this become a friend? Could I have expected such a breach of all the laws of honour from thee, whom I had taught to walk in its paths? Hadst thou chosen any other way to injure my confidence I could have forgiven it; but this is a stab in the tenderest part, a wound never to be healed, an injury never to be repaired; for it is not only the loss of an agreeable

---

* The beginning of this speech is lost.

companion, of the affection of a wife dearer to my soul than life itself, it is not this loss alone I lament; this loss is accompanied with disgrace and with dishonour. The blood of the Wilds, which hath run with such uninterrupted purity through so many generations, this blood is fouled, is contaminated: hence flow my tears, hence arises my grief. This is the injury never to be redressed, nor ever to be with honour forgiven.' 'My — in a bandbox!'[102] answered Fireblood; 'here is a noise about your honour! If the mischief done to your blood be all you complain of, I am sure you complain of nothing; for my blood is as good as yours.' 'You have no conception,' replied Wild, 'of the tenderness of honour; you know not how nice and delicate it is in both sexes; so delicate that the least breath of air which rudely blows on it destroys it.' 'I will prove from your own words,' says Fireblood, 'I have not wronged your honour. Have you not often told me that the honour of a man consisted in receiving no affront from his own sex, and that of a woman in receiving no kindness from ours? Now sir, if I have given you no affront, how have I injured your honour?' 'But doth not everything,' cried Wild, 'of the wife belong to the husband? A married man, therefore, hath his wife's honour as well as his own, and by injuring hers you injure his. How cruelly you have hurt me in this tender part I need not repeat; the whole gate knows it, and the world shall. I will apply to Doctors' Commons[103] for my redress against her; I will shake off as much of my dishonour as I can by parting with her; and as for you, expect to hear of me in Westminster Hall; the modern method of repairing these breaches and of resenting this affront.' 'D—n your eyes!' cries Fireblood; 'I fear you not, nor do I believe a word you say.' 'Nay, if you affront me personally,' says Wild, 'another sort of resentment is prescribed.' At which word, advancing to Fireblood, he presented him with a box on the ear, which the youth immediately returned; and now our hero and his friend fell to boxing, though with some difficulty, both being encumbered with the chains which they wore between their legs: a few blows passed on both sides before the gentlemen who stood by stept in and parted the combatants; and now both parties having whispered each other, that, if they outlived the ensuing sessions and escaped the tree, one should give and the other should receive satisfaction in single combat, they separated and the gate soon recovered its former tranquillity.

Mrs Heartfree was then desired by the justice and her husband both, to conclude her story, which she did in the words of the next chapter.

CHAPTER XI

The conclusion of Mrs Heartfree's adventures

'If I mistake not, I was interrupted just as I was beginning to repeat some of the compliments made me by the hermit.' 'Just as you had finished them, I believe, madam,' said the justice. 'Very well, sir,' said she; 'I am sure I have no pleasure in the repetition. He concluded then with telling me, though I was in his eyes the most charming woman in the world, and might tempt a saint to abandon the ways of holiness, yet my beauty inspired him with a much tenderer affection towards me than to purchase any satisfaction of his own desires with my misery; if, therefore, I could be so cruel to him to reject his honest and sincere address, nor could submit to a solitary life with one who would endeavour by all possible means to make me happy, I had no force to dread; for that I was as much at my liberty as if I was in France, or England, or any other free country. I repulsed him with the same civility with which he advanced; and told him that, as he professed great regard to religion, I was convinced he would cease from all further solicitation when I informed him that, if I had no other objection, my own innocence would not admit of my hearing him on this subject, for that I was married. He started a little at that word, and was for some time silent; but, at length recovering himself, he began to urge the uncertainty of my husband's being alive, and the probability of the contrary. He then spoke of marriage as of a civil policy only, on which head he urged many arguments not worth repeating, and was growing so very eager and importunate that I know not whither his passion might have hurried him had not three of the sailors, well armed, appeared at that instant in sight of the cave. I no sooner saw them than, exulting with the utmost inward joy, I told him my companions were come for me, and that I must now take my leave of him; assuring him that I would always remember, with the most grateful acknowledgement, the favours I had received at his hands. He fetched a very heavy sigh, and, squeezing me tenderly by the hand, he saluted my lips with a little more eagerness than the European salutations admit of, and told me he should likewise remember my arrival at his cave to the last day of his life, adding, – O that he could there spend the whole in the company of one whose bright eyes had kindled – but I know you will think, sir, that we women love to repeat the compliments made us, I will therefore omit them. In a word, the sailors being now arrived, I quitted him with some compassion for the reluctance with which he parted from me, and went forward with my companions.

'We had proceeded but a very few paces before one of the sailors said to his comrades: "D—n me, Jack, who knows whether yon fellow hath not some good flip in his cave?" I innocently answered: "The poor wretch hath only one bottle of brandy." "Hath he so?" cries the sailor; " 'fore George, we will taste it"; and so saying they immediately returned back, and myself with them. We found the poor man prostrate on the ground, expressing all the symptoms of misery and lamentation. I told him in French (for the sailors could not speak that language) what they wanted. He pointed to the place where the bottle was deposited, saying they were welcome to that and whatever else he had, and adding he cared not if they took his life also. The sailors searched the whole cave, where finding nothing more which they deemed worth their taking, they walked off with the bottle, and, immediately emptying it without offering me a drop, they proceeded with me towards the town.

'In our way I observed one whisper another, while he kept his eye steadfastly fixed on me. This gave me some uneasiness; but the other answered: "No, d—n me, the captain will never forgive us: besides, we have enough of it among the black women, and, in my mind, one colour is as good as another." This was enough to give me violent apprehensions; but I heard no more of that kind till we came to the town, where, in about six hours, I arrived in safety.

'As soon as I came to the captain he enquired what was become of my friend, meaning the villainous count. When he was informed by me of what had happened, he wished me heartily joy of my delivery, and, expressing the utmost abhorrence of such baseness, swore if ever he met him he would cut his throat; but, indeed, we both concluded that he had died of the blow which the hermit had given him.

'I was now introduced to the chief magistrate of this country, who was desirous of seeing me. I will give you a short description of him. He was chosen (as is the custom there) for his superior bravery and wisdom. His power is entirely absolute during its continuance; but, on the first deviation from equity and justice, he is liable to be deposed and punished by the people, the elders of whom, once a year, assemble to examine into his conduct. Besides the danger which these examinations, which are very strict, expose him to, his office is of such care and trouble that nothing but that restless love of power so predominant in the mind of man could make it the object of desire, for he is indeed the only slave of all the natives of this country. He is obliged, in time of peace, to hear the complaint of every person in his dominions and to render him justice; for which purpose every one may demand an audience of him, unless during the hour which he is allowed for dinner, when he sits alone at the table, and is attended in the most public manner with more than European ceremony. This is done to create an awe and respect towards him in the eye of the vulgar; but lest it should elevate him too much in his own opinion, in order to his humiliation he receives every evening in private, from a kind of beadle, a gentle kick on his posteriors; besides which he wears a ring in his nose, somewhat resembling that we ring our pigs with, and a chain round his neck not unlike that worn by our aldermen; both which I suppose to be emblematical, but heard not the reasons of either assigned. There are many more particularities among these people which, when I have an opportunity, I may relate to you. The second day after my return from court one of his officers, whom they call SCHACH PIMPACH, waited upon me, and, by a French interpreter who lives here, informed me that the chief magistrate liked my person, and offered me an immense present if I would suffer him to enjoy it (this is, it seems, their common form of making love). I rejected the present, and never heard any further solicitations; for, as it is no shame for women here to consent at the first proposal, so they never receive a second.

'I had resided in this town a week when the captain informed me that a number of slaves, who had been taken captives in war, were to be guarded to the seaside, where they were to be sold to the merchants who traded in them to America; that if I would embrace this opportunity I might assure myself of finding a passage to America, and thence to England; acquainting me at the same time that he himself intended to go with them. I readily agreed to accompany him. The chief, being advertised of our designs, sent for us both to court, and, without mentioning a word of love to me, having presented me with a very rich jewel, of less value, he said, than my chastity, took a very civil leave, recommending me to the care of Heaven, and ordering us a large supply of provisions for our journey.

'We were provided with mules for ourselves and what we carried with us, and in nine days reached the seashore, where we found an English vessel ready to receive both us and the slaves. We went aboard it, and sailed the next day with a fair wind for New England, where I hoped to get an immediate passage to the Old: but Providence was kinder than my expectation; for the third day after we were at sea we met an English man-of-war homeward bound; the captain of it was a very good-natured man, and agreed to take me on board. I accordingly took my leave of my old friend, the master of the shipwrecked vessel, who went on to New England, whence he intended to pass to Jamaica, where his owners lived. I was now treated with great civility, had a little cabin assigned me, and dined every day at the captain's table, who was indeed a very gallant man, and, at first, made me a tender of his affections; but, when he found me resolutely bent to preserve myself pure and entire for the best of husbands, he grew cooler in his addresses, and soon behaved in a manner very pleasing to me, regarding my sex only so far as to pay me a deference, which is very agreeable to us all.

'To conclude my story; I met with no adventure in this passage at all worth relating, till my landing at Gravesend, whence the captain brought me in his own boat to the Tower. In a short hour after my arrival we had that meeting which, however dreadful at first, will, I now hope, by the good offices of the best of men, whom Heaven for ever bless, end in our perfect happiness, and be a strong instance of what I am persuaded is the surest truth, THAT PROVIDENCE WILL SOONER OR LATER PROCURE THE FELICITY OF THE VIRTUOUS AND INNOCENT.'

Mrs Heartfree thus ended her speech, having before delivered to her husband the jewels which the count had robbed him of, and that presented her by the African chief, which last was of immense value. The good magistrate was sensibly touched at her narrative, as well on the consideration of the sufferings she had herself undergone as for those of her husband, which he had himself been innocently the instrument of bringing upon him. That worthy man, however, much rejoiced in what he had already done for his preservation, and promised to labour with his utmost interest and industry to procure the absolute pardon, rather of his sentence than of his guilt, which he now plainly discovered was a barbarous and false imputation.

CHAPTER XII

The history returns to the contemplation of GREATNESS

But we have already, perhaps, detained our reader too long in this relation from the consideration of our hero, who daily gave the most exalted proofs of greatness in cajoling the *prigs*, and in exactions on the debtors; which latter now grew so great, i.e. corrupted in their morals, that they spoke with the utmost contempt of what the vulgar call honesty. The greatest character among them was that of a pickpocket, or, in truer language, a *file*; and the only censure was want of dexterity. As to virtue, goodness, and such like, they were the objects of mirth and derision, and all Newgate was a complete collection of *prigs*, every man behind desirous to pick his neighbour's pocket, and every one was as sensible that his neighbour was as ready to pick his: so that (which is almost incredible) as great roguery was daily committed within the walls of Newgate as without.

The glory resulting from these actions of Wild probably animated the envy of his enemies against him. The day of his trial now approached; for which, as Socrates did, he prepared himself; but not weakly and foolishly, like that philosopher, with patience and resignation, but with a good number of false witnesses. However, as success is not always proportioned to the wisdom of him who endeavours to attain it, so are we more sorry than ashamed to relate that our hero was, notwithstanding his utmost caution and prudence, convicted, and sentenced to a death which, when we consider not only the great men who have suffered it, but the much larger number of those whose highest honour it hath been to merit it, we cannot call otherwise than honourable. Indeed, those who have unluckily missed it seem all their days to have laboured in vain to attain an end which Fortune, for reasons only known to herself, hath thought proper to deny them. Without any further preface then, our hero was sentenced *to be hanged by the neck*: but, whatever was to be now his fate, he might console himself that he had perpetrated what

> *– Nec Judicis ira, nec ignis,*
> *Nec poterit ferrum, nec edax abolere vetustas.*[104]

For my own part, I confess, I look on this death of hanging to be as proper for a hero as any other; and I solemnly declare that had Alexander the Great been hanged it would not in the least have diminished my respect to his memory. Provided a hero in his life doth but execute a sufficient quantity of mischief; provided he be but well and heartily cursed by the widow, the orphan, the poor, and the oppressed (the sole rewards, as many authors have bitterly lamented both in prose and verse, of greatness, i.e. *prigism*), I think it avails little of what nature his death be, whether it be by the axe, the halter, or the sword. Such names will be always sure of living to posterity, and of enjoying that fame which they so gloriously and eagerly coveted; for, according to a GREAT dramatic poet:[105]

Fame

Not more survives from good than evil deeds.
Th' aspiring youth that fired th' Ephesian dome
Outlives in fame the pious fool who rais'd it.

Our hero now suspected that the malice of his enemies would overpower him. He, therefore, betook himself to that true support of greatness in affliction, a bottle; by means of which he was enabled to curse, and swear, and bully, and brave his fate. Other comfort indeed he had not much, for not a single friend ever came near him. His wife, whose trial was deferred to the next sessions, visited him but once, when she plagued, tormented, and upbraided him so cruelly, that he forbade the keeper ever to admit her again. The ordinary of Newgate had frequent conferences with him, and greatly would it embellish our history could we record all which that good man delivered on these occasions; but unhappily we could procure only the substance of a single conference, which was taken down in shorthand by one who overheard it. We shall transcribe it, therefore, exactly in the same form and words we received it; nor can we help regarding it as one of the most curious pieces which either ancient or modern history hath recorded.

CHAPTER XIII

A dialogue between the ordinary[106] *of Newgate and Mr Jonathan
Wild the Great; in which the subjects of death, immortality,
and other grave matters, are very learnedly handled by the former*

Ordinary. Good morrow to you, sir; I hope you rested well last night.

Jonathan. D—n'd ill, sir. I dreamt so confoundedly of hanging, that it disturbed my sleep.

Ordinary. Fie upon it! You should be more resigned. I wish you would make a little better use of those instructions which I have endeavoured to inculcate into you, and particularly last Sunday, and from these words: *Those who do evil shall go into everlasting fire, prepared for the devil and his angels.*[107] I undertook to shew you, first, what is meant by EVERLASTING FIRE; and, secondly, who were THE DEVIL AND HIS ANGELS. I then proceeded to draw some inferences from the whole*; in which I am mightily deceived if I did not convince you that you yourself was one of those ANGELS, and, consequently, must expect EVERLASTING FIRE to be your portion in the other world.

Jonathan. Faith, doctor, I remember very little of your inferences; for I fell asleep soon after your naming your text. But did you preach this doctrine then, or do you repeat it now in order to comfort me?

Ordinary. I do it in order to bring you to a true sense of your manifold sins, and, by that means, to induce you to repentance. Indeed, had I the eloquence of Cicero, or of Tully,[108] it would not be sufficient to describe the pains of hell or the joys of heaven. The utmost that we are taught is, *that ear hath not heard, nor can heart conceive*.[109] Who then would, for the pitiful consideration of the riches and pleasures of this world, forfeit such inestimable happiness! such joys! such pleasures! such delights? Or who would run the venture of such misery, which, but to think on, shocks the human understanding? Who, in his senses, then, would prefer the latter to the former?

Jonathan. Ay, who indeed? I assure you, doctor, I had much rather be happy than miserable. But† ·

·   ·   ·   ·

Ordinary. Nothing can be plainer. St ·   ·   ·

·   ·   ·   ·   ·

Jonathan. ·   ·   ·   ·   ·   ·   ·   If once convinced ·   ·   ·   ·   ·

·   no man ·   lives of ·   ·   ·

·   ·   ·   ·   ·   whereas sure the

clergy   ·   ·   opportunity   ·   ·   better

informed ·   ·   ·   ·   ·   all manner

of vice ·   ·

---

* He pronounced this word HULL, and perhaps would have spelt it so.

† This part was so blotted that it was illegible.

Ordinary. · · are · atheist. · · · deist · ari · ·
cinian · hanged · · burnt · · oiled · oasted. · · · dev ·
· his an · · · ell fire · · ternal da · · · tion.

Jonathan. You · · · to frighten me out of my wits. But the
good · · · is, I doubt not, more merciful than his wicked · ·
If I should believe all you say, I am sure I should die in inexpressible horror.

Ordinary. Despair is sinful. You should place your hopes in
repentance and grace; and though it is most true that you are in
danger of the judgement, yet there is still room for mercy; and no
man, unless excommunicated, is absolutely without hopes of a
reprieve.

Jonathan. I am not without hopes of a reprieve from the cheat
yet. I have pretty good interest; but if I cannot obtain it, you shall
not frighten me out of my courage. I will not die like a pimp.
D—n me, what is death? It is nothing but to be with Platos and
with Cæsars, as the poet says, and all the other great heroes of
antiquity. · · ·

Ordinary. Ay, all this is very true; but life is sweet for all that;
and I had rather live to eternity than go into the company of any
such heathens, who are, I doubt not, in hell with the devil and his
angels; and, as little as you seem to apprehend it, you may find
yourself there before you expect it. Where, then, will be your
tauntings and your vauntings, your boastings and your brag-
gings? You will then be ready to give more for a drop of water than
you ever gave for a bottle of wine.

Jonathan. Faith, doctor! well minded. What say you to a bottle
of wine?

Ordinary. I will drink no wine with an atheist. I should expect
the devil to make a third in such company, for, since he knows
you are his, he may be impatient to have his due.

Jonathan. It is your business to drink with the wicked, in order
to amend them.

Ordinary. I despair of it; and so I consign you over to the devil,
who is ready to receive you.

Jonathan. You are more unmerciful to me than the judge,
doctor. He recommended my soul to heaven; and it is your office
to shew me the way thither.

Ordinary. No: the gates are barred against all revilers of the clergy.

Jonathan. I revile only the wicked ones, if any such are, which cannot affect you, who, if men were preferred in the church by merit only, would have long since been a bishop. Indeed, it might raise any good man's indignation to observe one of your vast learning and abilities obliged to exert them in so low a sphere, when so many of your inferiors wallow in wealth and preferment.

Ordinary. Why, it must be confessed that there are bad men in all orders; but you should not censure too generally. I must own I might have expected higher promotion; but I have learnt patience and resignation; and I would advise you to the same temper of mind; which if you can attain, I know you will find mercy. Nay, I do now promise you you will. It is true you are a sinner; but your crimes are not of the blackest dye: you are no murderer, nor guilty of sacrilege. And, if you are guilty of theft, you make some atonement by suffering for it, which many others do not. Happy is it indeed for those few who are detected in their sins, and brought to exemplary punishment for them in this world. So far, therefore, from repining at your fate when you come to the tree, you should exult and rejoice in it; and, to say the truth, I question whether, to a wise man, the catastrophe of many of those who die by a halter is not more to be envied than pitied. Nothing is so sinful as sin, and murder is the greatest of all sins. It follows, that whoever commits murder is happy in suffering for it. If, therefore, a man who commits murder is so happy in dying for it, how much better must it be for you, who have committed a less crime!

Jonathan. All this is very true; but let us take a bottle of wine to cheer our spirits.

Ordinary. Why wine? Let me tell you, Mr Wild, there is nothing so deceitful as the spirits given us by wine. If you must drink, let us have a bowl of punch – a liquor I the rather prefer, as it is nowhere spoken against in Scripture, and as it is more wholesome for the gravel,[110] a distemper with which I am grievously afflicted.

Jonathan (*having called for a bowl*). I ask your pardon, doctor; I should have remembered that punch was your favourite liquor. I think you never taste wine while there is any punch remaining on the table?

Ordinary. I confess I look on punch to be the more eligible liquor, as well for the reasons I have before mentioned as likewise for one other cause, viz. it is the properest for a DRAUGHT. I own I took it a little unkind of you to mention wine, thinking you knew my palate.

Jonathan. You are in the right; and I will take a swinging cup to your being made a bishop.

Ordinary. And I will wish you a reprieve in as large a draught. Come, don't despair; it is yet time enough to think of dying; you have good friends, who very probably may prevail for you. I have known many a man reprieved who had less reason to expect it.

Jonathan. But if I should flatter myself with such hopes, and be deceived – what then would become of my soul?

Ordinary. Pugh! Never mind your soul – leave that to me; I will render a good account of it, I warrant you. I have a sermon in my pocket which may be of some use to you to hear. I do not value myself on the talent of preaching, since no man ought to value himself for any gift in this world. But perhaps there are not many such sermons. But to proceed, since we have nothing else to do till the punch comes. My text is the latter part of a verse only:

– To the Greeks FOOLISHNESS.[111]

The occasion of these words was principally that philosophy of the Greeks which at that time had overrun great part of the heathen world, had poisoned, and, as it were, puffed up their minds with pride, so that they disregarded all kinds of doctrine in comparison of their own; and, however safe and however sound the learning of others might be, yet, if it anywise contradicted their own laws, customs, and received opinions, *away with it – it is not for us*. It was to the Greeks FOOLISHNESS.

In the former part, therefore, of my discourse on these words, I shall principally confine myself to the laying open and demonstrating the great emptiness and vanity of this philosophy, with which these idle and absurd sophists were so proudly blown up and elevated.

And here I shall do two things: First, I shall expose the matter; and, secondly, the manner of this absurd philosophy.

And first, for the first of these, namely, the matter. Now here we may retort the unmannerly word which our adversaries have audaciously thrown in our faces; for what was all this mighty matter of philosophy, this heap of knowledge, which was to bring such large harvests of honour to those who sowed it, and so greatly and nobly to enrich the ground on which it fell; what was it but FOOLISHNESS? An inconsistent heap of nonsense, of absurdities and contradictions, bringing no ornament to the mind in its theory, nor exhibiting any usefulness to the body in its practice. What were all the sermons and the sayings, the fables and the morals of all these wise men, but, to use the word mentioned in my text once more, FOOLISHNESS? What was their great master Plato, or their other great light Aristotle? Both fools, mere quibblers and sophists, idly and vainly attached to certain ridiculous notions of their own, founded neither on truth nor on reason. Their whole works are a strange medley of the greatest falsehoods, scarce covered over with the colour of truth: their precepts are neither borrowed from nature nor guided by reason; mere fictions, serving only to evince the dreadful height of human pride; in one word, FOOLISHNESS. It may be perhaps expected of me that I should give some instances from their works to prove this charge; but, as to transcribe every passage to my purpose would be to transcribe their whole works, and as in such a plentiful crop it is difficult to choose; instead of trespassing on your patience, I shall conclude this first head with asserting what I have so fully proved, and what may indeed be inferred from the text, that the philosophy of the Greeks was FOOLISHNESS.

Proceed we now, in the second place to consider the manner in which this inane and simple doctrine was propagated. And here – But here the punch by entering waked Mr Wild, who was fast asleep, and put an end to the sermon; nor could we obtain any further account of the conversation which passed at this interview.

CHAPTER XIV

Wild proceeds to the highest consummation of human
GREATNESS

The day now drew nigh when our great man was to exemplify
the last and noblest act of greatness by which any hero can
signalize himself. This was the day of execution, or consummation, or apotheosis (for it is called by different names), which was
to give our hero an opportunity of facing death and damnation,
without any fear in his heart, or, at least, without betraying any
symptoms of it in his countenance. A completion of greatness
which is heartily to be wished to every great man; nothing being
more worthy of lamentation than when Fortune, like a lazy poet,
winds up her catastrophe awkwardly, and, bestowing too little
care on her fifth act, dismisses the hero with a sneaking and private
exit, who had in the former part of the drama performed such
notable exploits as must promise to every good judge among the
spectators a noble, public, and exalted end.

But she was resolved to commit no such error in this instance.
Our hero was too much and too deservedly her favourite to be
neglected by her in his last moments; accordingly all efforts for a
reprieve were vain, and the name of Wild stood at the head of
those who were ordered for execution.

From the time he gave over all hopes of life, his conduct was
truly great and admirable. Instead of shewing any marks of
dejection or contrition, he rather infused more confidence and
assurance into his looks. He spent most of his hours in drinking
with his friends and with the good man above commemorated. In
one of these compotations, being asked whether he was afraid to
die, he answered: 'D—n me, it is only a dance without music.'
Another time, when one expressed some sorrow for his misfortune, as he termed it, he said with great fierceness: 'A man can
die but once.' Again, when one of his intimate acquaintance
hinted his hopes, that he would die like a man, he cocked his hat
in defiance, and cried out greatly: 'Zounds! who's afraid?'

Happy would it have been for posterity, could we have retrieved any entire conversation which passed at this season, especially between our hero and his learned comforter; but we have searched many pasteboard records in vain.

On the eve of his apotheosis, Wild's lady desired to see him, to which he consented. This meeting was at first very tender on both sides; but it could not continue so, for unluckily, some hints of former miscarriages intervening, as particularly when she asked him how he could have used her so barbarously once as calling her b—, and whether such language became a man, much less a gentleman, Wild flew into a violent passion, and swore she was the vilest of b—s to upbraid him at such a season with an unguarded word spoke long ago. She replied, with many tears, she was well enough served for her folly in visiting such a brute; but she had one comfort, however, that it would be the last time he could ever treat her so; that indeed she had some obligation to him, for that his cruelty to her would reconcile her to the fate he was to-morrow to suffer; and, indeed, nothing but such brutality could have made the consideration of his shameful death (so this weak woman called hanging), which was now inevitable, to be borne even without madness. She then proceeded to a recapitulation of his faults in an exacter order, and with more perfect memory, than one would have imagined her capable of; and it is probable would have rehearsed a complete catalogue had not our hero's patience failed him, so that with the utmost fury and violence he caught her by the hair and kicked her, as heartily as his chains would suffer him, out of the room.

At length the morning came which Fortune at his birth had resolutely ordained for the consummation of our hero's GREAT-NESS: he had himself indeed modestly declined the public honours she intended him, and had taken a quantity of lauda-num,[112] in order to retire quietly off the stage; but we have already observed, in the course of our wonderful history, that to struggle against this lady's decrees is vain and impotent; and whether she hath determined you shall be hanged or be a prime minister, it is in either case lost labour to resist. Laudanum, therefore, being unable to stop the breath of our hero, which the fruit of hemp-seed, and not the spirit of poppy-seed, was to overcome, he was at the usual hour attended by the proper gentleman appointed for that purpose, and acquainted that the cart was ready. On this occasion he exerted that greatness of courage which hath been so much celebrated in other heroes; and, knowing it was impossible to resist, he gravely declared he would attend them. He then descended to that room where the fetters of great men are knocked off in a most solemn and ceremonious manner. Then shaking hands with his friends (to wit, those who were conducting him to the tree), and drinking their healths in a bumper of brandy, he ascended the cart, where he was no sooner seated than he received the acclamations of the multitude, who were highly ravished with his GREATNESS.

The cart now moved slowly on, being preceded by a troop of horse-guards bearing javelins in their hands, through streets lined with crowds all admiring the great behaviour of our hero, who rode on, sometimes sighing, sometimes swearing, sometimes singing or whistling, as his humour varied.

When he came to the tree of glory, he was welcomed with an universal shout of the people, who were there assembled in pro-digious numbers to behold a sight much more rare in populous cities than one would reasonably imagine it should be, viz. the proper catastrophe of a great man.

But though envy was, through fear, obliged to join the general voice in applause on this occasion, there were not wanting some who maligned this completion of glory, which was now about to be fulfilled to our hero, and endeavoured to prevent it by knock-ing him on the head as he stood under the tree, while the ordinary was performing his last office. They therefore began to batter the cart with stones, brickbats, dirt, and all manner of mis-chievous weapons, some of which, erroneously playing on the robes of the ecclesiastic, made him so expeditious in his repeti-tion, that with wonderful alacrity he had ended almost in an instant, and conveyed himself into a place of safety in a hackney-coach, where he waited the conclusion with a temper of mind described in these verses:

Suave mari magno, turbantibus æquora ventis,
E terra alterius magnum spectare laborem.[113]

We must not, however, omit one circumstance, as it serves to shew the most admirable conservation of character in our hero to his last moment, which was, that whilst the ordinary was busy in his ejaculations, Wild, in the midst of the shower of stones, etc., which played upon him, applied his hands to the parson's pocket, and emptied it of his bottle-screw, which he carried out of the world in his hand.

The ordinary being now descended from the cart, Wild had just opportunity to cast his eyes around the crowd, and to give them a hearty curse, when immediately the horses moved on, and with universal applause our hero swung out of this world.

Thus fell Jonathan Wild the GREAT, by a death as glorious as his life had been and which was so truly agreeable to it, that the latter must have been deplorably maimed and imperfect without the former: a death which hath been alone wanting to complete the characters of several ancient and modern heroes, whose histories would then have been read with much greater pleasure by the wisest in all ages. Indeed we could almost wish that whenever Fortune seems wantonly to deviate from her purpose, and leaves her work imperfect in this particular, the historian would indulge himself in the licence of poetry and romance, and even do a violence to truth, to oblige his reader with a page which must be the most delightful in all his history, and which could never fail of producing an instructive moral.

Narrow minds may possibly have some reason to be ashamed of going this way out of the world, if their consciences can fly in their faces and assure them they have not merited such an honour; but he must be a fool who is ashamed of being hanged, who is not weak enough to be ashamed of having deserved it.

CHAPTER XV

The character of our hero, and the conclusion of this history

We will now endeavour to draw the character of this great man; and, by bringing together those several features as it were of his mind which lie scattered up and down in this history, to present our readers with a perfect picture of greatness.

Jonathan Wild had every qualification necessary to form a great man. As his most powerful and predominant passion was ambition, so nature had, with consummate propriety, adapted all his faculties to the attaining those glorious ends to which this passion directed him. He was extremely ingenious in inventing designs, artful in contriving the means to accomplish his purposes, and resolute in executing them: for as the most exquisite cunning and most undaunted boldness qualified him for any undertaking, so was he not restrained by any of those weaknesses which disappoint the views of mean and vulgar souls, and which are comprehended in one general term of honesty, which is a corruption of HONOSTY,[114] a word derived from what the Greeks call an ass. He was entirely free from those low vices of modesty and good-nature, which, as he said, implied a total negation of human greatness, and were the only qualities which absolutely rendered a man incapable of making a considerable figure in the world. His lust was inferior only to his ambition; but, as for what simple people call love, he knew not what it was. His avarice was immense, but it was of the rapacious, not of the tenacious kind; his rapaciousness was indeed so violent, that nothing ever contented him but the whole; for, however considerable the share was which his coadjutors allowed him of a booty, he was restless in inventing means to make himself master of the smallest pittance reserved by them. He said laws were made for the use of *prigs* only, and to secure their property; they were never, therefore, more perverted than when their edge was turned against these; but that this generally happened through their want of sufficient dexterity. The character which he most valued himself upon, and which he principally honoured in others, was that of hypocrisy. His opinion was, that no one could carry *priggism* very far without it; for which reason, he said, there was little greatness to be expected in a man who acknowledged his vices, but always much to be hoped from him who professed great virtues: wherefore, though he would always shun the person whom he discovered guilty of a good action, yet he was never deterred by a good character, which was more commonly the effect of profession than of action: for which reason, he himself was always very liberal of honest professions, and had as much virtue and goodness in his mouth as a saint; never in the least scrupling to swear by his honour, even to those who knew him the best; nay, though he held good-nature and modesty in the highest contempt, he constantly practised the affectation of both, and recommended this to others, whose welfare, on his own account, he wished well to. He laid down several maxims as the certain methods of attaining greatness, to which, in his own pursuit of it, he constantly adhered. As:

1. Never to do more mischief to another than was necessary to the effecting his purpose; for that mischief was too precious a thing to be thrown away.
2. To know no distinction of men from affection; but to sacrifice all with equal readiness to his interest.
3. Never to communicate more of an affair than was necessary to the person who was to execute it.
4. Not to trust him who hath deceived you, nor who knows he hath been deceived by you.
5. To forgive no enemy; but to be cautious and often dilatory in revenge.
6. To shun povery and distress, and to ally himself as close as possible to power and riches.
7. To maintain a constant gravity in his countenance and behaviour, and to affect wisdom on all occasions.
8. To foment eternal jealousies in his gang, one of another.
9. Never to reward any one equal to his merit; but always to insinuate that the reward was above it.

10. That all men were knaves or fools, and much the greater number a composition of both.

11. That a good name, like money, must be parted with, or at least greatly risked, in order to bring the owner any advantage.

12. That virtues, like precious stones, were easily counterfeited; that the counterfeits in both cases adorned the wearer equally, and that very few had knowledge or discernment sufficient to distinguish the counterfeit jewel from the real.

13. That many men were undone by not going deep enough in roguery; as in gaming any man may be a loser who doth not play the whole game.

14. That men proclaim their own virtues, as shopkeepers expose their goods, in order to profit by them.

15. That the heart was the proper seat of hatred, and the countenance of affection and friendship.

He had many more of the same kind, all equally good with these, and which were after his decease found in his study, as the twelve excellent and celebrated rules[115] were in that of King Charles the First; for he never promulgated them in his lifetime, not having them constantly in his mouth, as some grave persons have the rules of virtue and morality, without paying the least regard to them in their actions: whereas our hero, by a constant and steady adherence to his rules in conforming everything he did to them, acquired at length a settled habit of walking by them, till at last he was in no danger of inadvertently going out of the way; and by these means he arrived at that degree of greatness, which few have equalled; none, we may say, have exceeded: for, though it must be allowed that there have been some few heroes, who have done greater mischiefs to mankind, such as those who have betrayed the liberty of their country to others, or have undermined and overpowered it themselves; or conquerors who have impoverished, pillaged, sacked, burnt, and destroyed the countries and cities of their fellow-creatures, from no other provocation than that of glory, i.e. as the tragic poet calls it,

a privilege to kill,
A strong temptation to do bravely ill;[116]

yet, if we consider it in the light wherein actions are placed
in this line:

Lætius est, quoties magno tibi constat honestum;[117]

when we see our hero, without the least assistance or pretence,
setting himself at the head of a gang, which he had not any
shadow of right to govern; if we view him maintaining absolute
power, and exercising tyranny over a lawless crew, contrary to all
law but that of his own will; if we consider him setting up an open
trade publicly, in defiance not only of the laws of his country but
of the common sense of his countrymen; if we see him first contriving the robbery of others, and again the defrauding the very
robbers of that booty, which they had ventured their necks to
acquire, and which without any hazard, they might have retained;
here sure he must appear admirable, and we may challenge not
only the truth of history, but almost the latitude of fiction, to
equal his glory.

Nor had he any of those flaws in his character which, though
they have been commended by weak writers, have (as I hinted in
the beginning of this history) by the judicious reader been censured and despised. Such was the clemency of Alexander and
Cæsar, which nature hath so grossly erred in giving them, as a
painter would who should dress a peasant in robes of state or give
the nose or any other feature of a Venus to a satyr. What had the
destroyers of mankind, that glorious pair, one of whom came into
the world to usurp the dominion and abolish the constitution of
his own country; the other to conquer, enslave, and rule over the
whole world, at least as much as was well known to him, and the
shortness of his life would give him leave to visit; what had, I say,
such as these to do with clemency? Who cannot see the absurdity
and contradiction of mixing such an ingredient with those noble
and great qualities I have before mentioned? Now, in Wild everything was truly great, almost without alloy, as his imperfections
(for surely some small ones he had) were only such as served to
denominate him a human creature, of which kind none ever
arrived at consummate excellence. But surely his whole behaviour

to his friend Heartfree is a convincing proof that the true iron or steel greatness of his heart was not debased by any softer metal. Indeed, while greatness consists in power, pride, insolence, and doing mischief to mankind – to speak out – while a great man and a great rogue are synonymous terms, so long shall Wild stand unrivalled on the pinnacle of GREATNESS. Nor must we omit here, as the finishing of his character, what indeed ought to be remembered on his tomb or his statue, the conformity above mentioned of his death to his life; and that Jonathan Wild the Great, after all his mighty exploits, was, what so few GREAT men can accomplish – hanged by the neck till he was dead.

Having thus brought our hero to his conclusion, it may be satisfactory to some readers (for many, I doubt not, carry their concern no farther than his fate) to know what became of Heartfree. We shall acquaint them, therefore, that his sufferings were now at an end; that the good magistrate easily prevailed for his pardon, nor was contented till he had made him all the reparation he could for his troubles, though the share he had in bringing these upon him was not only innocent but from its motive laudable. He procured the restoration of the jewels from the man-of-war at her return to England, and, above all, omitted no labour to restore Heartfree to his reputation, and to persuade his neighbours, acquaintance, and customers, of his innocence. When the commission of bankruptcy was satisfied, Heartfree had a considerable sum remaining; for the diamond presented to his wife was of prodigious value, and infinitely recompensed the loss of those jewels which Miss Straddle had disposed of. He now set up again in his trade: compassion for his unmerited misfortunes brought him many customers among those who had any regard to humanity; and he hath, by industry joined with parsimony, amassed a considerable fortune. His wife and he are now grown old in the purest love and friendship, but never had another child. Friendly married his elder daughter at the age of nineteen, and became his partner in trade. As to the younger, she never would listen to the addresses of any lover, not even of a young nobleman, who offered to take her with two thousand pounds, which her father would have willingly produced, and indeed did his utmost to persuade her to the match; but she refused absolutely, nor would give any other reason, when Heartfree pressed her, than that she had dedicated her days to his service, and was resolved no other duty should interfere with that which she owed the best of fathers, nor prevent her from being the nurse of his old age.

Thus Heartfree, his wife, his two daughters, his son-in-law, and his grandchildren, of which he hath several, live all together in one house; and that with such amity and affection towards each other, that they are in the neighbourhood called the family of love.

As to all the other persons mentioned in this history in the light of greatness, they had all the fate adapted to it, being every one hanged by the neck, save two, viz. Miss Theodosia Snap, who was transported to America, where she was pretty well married, reformed, and made a good wife; and the count, who recovered of the wound he had received from the hermit and made his escape into France where he committed a robbery, was taken, and broke on the wheel.

Indeed, whoever considers the common fate of great men must allow they well deserve and hardly earn that applause which is given them by the world; for, when we reflect on the labours and pains, the cares, disquietudes, and dangers which attend their road to greatness, we may say with the divine *that a man may go to heaven with half the pains which it costs him to purchase hell.* To say the truth, the world have this reason at least to honour such characters as that of Wild: that, while it is in the power of every man to be perfectly honest, not one in a thousand is capable of being a complete rogue; and few indeed there are who, if they were inspired with the vanity of imitating our hero, would not after much fruitless pains be obliged to own themselves inferior to MR JONATHAN WILD THE GREAT.

THE
TRUE AND GENUINE ACCOUNT
OF
THE LIFE AND ACTIONS
OF THE LATE

JONATHAN WILD

BY

DANIEL DEFOE

Not made up of fiction and fable,
but taken from his own mouth, and collected
from papers of his own writing.

LONDON
1725

THE PREFACE

The several absurd and ridiculous accounts which have been published, notwithstanding early and seasonable caution given, of the life and conduct of this famous, or if you please, infamous creature, JONATHAN WILD, make a short preface to this account absolutely necessary.

It is something strange, that a man's life should be made a kind of a romance before his face, and while he was upon the spot to contradict it; or, that the world should be so fond of a formal chimney-corner tale, that they had rather a story should be made merry than true. The author of this short but exact account of Mr Wild assures the world, that the greatest part of all that has hitherto appeared of this kind has been evidently invented and framed out of the heads of the scribbling authors, merely to get a penny, without regard to truth of fact, or even to probability, or without making any conscience of their imposing on the credulous world.

Nay, so little ground has there been for them, that except there was such a man as JONATHAN WILD, that he was born at Wolverhampton, lived in the Old Bailey, was called a thief-catcher, and was hanged at Tyburn, there is not one story printed of him that can be called truth, or that is not mingled up with so much falsehood and fable as to smother and drown that little truth which is at the bottom of it.

The following tract does not indeed make a jest of his story as they do, or present his history, which indeed is a tragedy of itself, in a style of mockery and ridicule, but in a method agreeable to the fact. They that had rather have a falsehood to laugh at, than a true account of things to inform them, had best buy the fiction, and leave the history to those who know how to distinguish good from evil.

INTRODUCTION

The undertaker of this work having easily foreseen that the story of this eminent criminal would be acceptable to the world, resolved sometime ago to publish it, but knowing at the same time it would be attempted over and over by our hackney Grub-street writers, upon the old pick-pocket principle of publishing anything to get a penny; they therefore took care not only to furnish themselves with authentic and full vouchers for the truth of what they have to say, but also to have the account of him be very particular, and such as may answer their title. Upon the assurance of their being thus provided, not only to give a true, but also a full and complete account of him, they took care to give the world an early and timely notice that such a work was preparing for the press, in order to prevent peoples being imposed upon. And to that purpose they advertised this work in several public prints, and they are satisfied that as on one hand, it has prepared the world to expect this account, so it will fully answer their expectation now it appears. They have not satisfied themselves in their enquiries, to take things upon the credit of common fame, which (generally speaking) is a common something; nor have they supplied by invention the particulars of what wanted such helps. The life of this unhappy wretch is too full of incidents, and that of an uncommon nature, to stand in need of any such helps; and we are so far from wanting matter to fill up this tract, and make the story out, that on the contrary, we are forced to abridge and contract some of the most considerable passages of his life, that we may bring it all into as narrow a compass as we can.

The life of Jonathan Wild is a perfectly new scene. As his conduct has been inimitable, so his employment has been singular to him, and is like to be so, for as it began, so it is like to die with him; no man among the most daring of the clan being, we believe, so hardy as to venture to take it up after him. Every step he took was criminal, and the very actions which he did with the greatest openness and an avowed professed allowance, merited the gallows even by the very letter. But pray note, when we say allowance, we mean his own allowance, for no other power or person could allow him in it. It is true, he had an inimitable boldness in his behaviour and by detecting some criminals, he assumed a kind of power to protect others, only the difference lay here, namely that he did the first publicly, and the last privately. So that in a word, he served the public in the first, and abused the public in the second, and was only deceived in this, that he thought his being useful in the first, would protect him in being criminal in the last. But here he was, we say, mistaken, and fell into a snare which all his pretended merit could not deliver him from.

Take him as a man, only he had a kind of brutal courage which fitted him to be an instrument in attacking some of the most desperate of the several gangs of rogues he had to do with. But as his courage also served to make him audacious in the other wicked things he undertook, he was rather bold than courageous, and might be called impudent, but we cannot say he was brave, as appeared in a more particular manner in his stupid and confused behaviour, during his lying in Newgate, and at his execution, of which in its place.

We have the advantage in this account to come at the particular of his story from unquestioned authority, for as he was sensible wrong accounts would be published of him, he was not backward to give materials from his own mouth which no body can contradict, and others fully conversant with him, having given the same stories or accounts of the same facts, we have the satisfaction to see them agree fully together, and thereby be assured of the truth of both. For in such cases there could be no combination to deceive us. Not that it is possible to obtain a full account of all the particular villainies of Jonathan Wild, during a series of sixteen years, in which he reigned in all wickedness with such success, as no age can produce the like. 'Tis enough if we give you a general view of his life, or a scheme of his practice, illustrated by examples; which examples likewise might be farther set forth by more examples and by stories full of an infinite variety, which if collected together, would make up a large volume in folio, and yet leave many of them unrelated.

It is true, as we shall take notice in its place, that the world does not charge Jonathan with being himself actually a highwayman or robber; or that when any of the gangs of prancers (as they are called in the Newgate cant) went out upon the grand design, he ever went with them, and we are assured he did not. He knew the trade too well to put his life into such a hazard. He knew how common a bite it was among such people to save their own lives at the expense of their companions. But he was too cunning for that. And he had likewise a so much better trade in hand, by which he was sure to make a prey both of the persons robbed, and of the rogues that robbed them, that he would have been worse than lunatic if he had been drawn in to be a party.

The part he acted in the fact for which he suffered was more than he ordinarily did, or that we ever find he ventured to do before. For here he was both thief and thief-catcher too, which he did not usually venture. But a secret infatuation was now upon him, and heaven who had determined his fate, no doubt left him to expose himself more in this one action, than he had done in many years before, and by this he fell. It is said that if this had not fixed him, there were other facts charged which would effectually have done; to that we shall say nothing, because those others have not been tried. 'Tis enough Jonathan died not in his own way of thief-catching, but by going out of his road and taking a share in the robbery as he did after in the reward. And here he was taken in his own snare, for the very thieves he employed, were the witnesses that hanged him. But we say no more of that, till we come to the story itself. We now proceed to the particular account of his life.

AN ACCOUNT OF THE LIFE
AND EMINENT ACTIONS, &C.

JONATHAN WILD, the wretched subject of this history, was born at Wolverhampton in Staffordshire; and to do justice to his original, his parents, though mean, had the repute of honest and industrious people, his father being a carpenter, and his mother sold herbs and fruit in the market of Wolverhampton. They had three sons and two daughters; the two daughters are yet living and married to honest tradesmen in Wolverhampton, one to a comb-maker, and the other a buckle-maker, and whose characters we do not hear are any way blemished. But the sons have all a different fame. The brothers, I say, were three in number, Jonathan, John and Andrew. John was a public officer in the town where they lived, being the crier of Wolverhampton. But stepping out of his employment in the time of the late Preston rebellion,[1] and making himself popular by heading and appearing among the rabble for pulling down the meeting-house at Wolverhampton; he was taken up for a rioter, brought to London, and put into custody of a messenger, where he continued sometime, till he was sent down again in custody to Stafford, to be tried at the assizes held there for the county. There he was convicted, and received sentence to be publicly whipped, and afterwards to lie in prison for a certain time, which sentence was accordingly executed. But the same John being afterwards at liberty, the time of his imprisonment being expired, died about four years ago, as did also his mother much about the same time, that is to say, within a month of one another.

The younger brother Andrew being by trade a Birmingham ware-man, or in particular a buckle-maker, left his own country and came up to London, what trade he has driven here we shall not meddle with, the man being yet alive. And as we are not writing his story, but that of his elder brother, so we are not willing to enter into anything that may be prejudicial to particular persons on any account whatever. 'Tis enough to say that we hear he is at this time a prisoner in the poultry-compter[2] for debt; so that it seems all the three brothers have had some acquaintance with the inside of a gaol, though on different accounts.

Jonathan as I have said, was the eldest brother, he was born about the year 1683, being at the time of his execution about two and forty years of age, of which something more than thirteen years has been spent in the most exquisite villainies, of which we shall give some account in this work. His education was suitable to his father's circumstances, being taught in the free school of Wolverhampton to read and write, and then his father put him apprentice to a Birmingham man, or as they call them there, a hardware man, and particularly a buckle-maker. Authors are not agreed in the name of his master, and as it is not material we also let it pass without any notice. Having served his time out, or as some say but part of it, he got into the service of one counsellor Daniel of Staffordshire, and came up with him to London as his servant; this was about the year 1704. But whether he did not please his master, or that he took ill courses so early we have not enquired; but that counsellor dismissing him, he went home again to Wolverhampton, and very honestly worked for some time at his trade. But his thoughts, as he said, being above his trade, though at that time he had had no taste of the life he afterwards led, yet he grew uneasie in the country, was sick of his work, and in short, after a few years came away to London to see if he could get into any business there. Here he found but little encouragement, and though he worked at his trade, yet what he could get at his day labour but ill served to maintain him, whose temper even then, was not much given to frugality. Which, with his being not inclined to sit very close to his work neither, made him run out pretty much, till at length it was his misfortune to be arrested for debt, and carried to Wood-street compter. Here he suffered great hardship, having no friends to help him out, or money to maintain him within, so that he was on the common-side, and fared as other people in those circumstances do fare, that is to say, very hard. However, after having lain a long time there, he at length having behaved himself well enough among the prisoners, got so much favour with the keepers, that he got the liberty of the gate, as they call it.

His business here was chiefly to attend in the night, in case any prisoners were brought in for disorders in the street; to wait upon them, and guard them with the officers to any justice of the peace, and so back again if they were committed. And in this he discharged himself to satisfaction, so that he was at length trusted to go on errands, and the like liberties to get a penny. Among the great variety of night-walking offenders which came into his custody, at length there comes in one Mary Milliner, who after having been carried before a justice, might be remanded to the compter for the present. But being a jade of some fame, she soon found her way out again, for we do not find she was reckoned to be a prisoner there at all. Whether it was that she was frequently brought in there in her night rambles, and might receive some favours from which on that occasion, it being much in his way to favour such as she was, he being as a kind of keeper set over them; or whether they contracted a friendship at first sight, or what other incident brought it about I know not. But Mr Wild not only became acquainted with her, but a more than common intimacy soon grew between them. Insomuch that she began to teach him a great many new, and to him unknown ways of getting money, and brought him into her own gang, whether of thieves or whores, or of both, is not much material.

By the advantage of this new correspondence Mr Wild soon cleared himself of his imprisonment, the debt for which he was thrust into the compter being but small. And though he had a wife at that time living at Wolverhampton, and had a son by her, which son is still living, as we shall hear presently; and though this new favourite he had pitched upon had also a husband then living, a waterman by his profession; yet they pretended to be married and lived together some time as man and wife, and this we are to call his second wife, for he had six of them in all. This Mrs Milliner as I am informed, is still living, so that Mr Wild has left several widows behind him at his exit, whether they go by his name or not, that he himself could not inform us.

During his intimacy with this Mrs Milliner, and by her means, he grew acquainted with some other of the wicked ways of living, which it seems she practised besides that of whoring. And first it seems she carried him out with her upon the TWANG.[3] This is one of the cant words for those who attend upon the night-walking ladies in their progress, and who keep at a distance, that if the lady they are employed by happens to fall into any broil, they may come in timely to her assistance, and making a noise and a quarrel, if possible fall afighting, and so give her an opportunity to walk off, which Jonathan often practised with good success. He improved his time during his acquaintance with this Mary Milliner to a very great degree, for she brought him acquainted with several gangs, or societies of the sharping and thieving world. In so much, that in a little time he knew all their several employments, and the several parts they acted, their haunts and their walks, how they performed, and how they managed their effects when they had met with success. And as he seemed to set up for a director to them, under the government of that dexterous lady his first instructor, so he found ways to make himself as useful to them, as if he had gone abroad with them, which however he always avoided. Nor, indeed, had he any occasion to run a hazard himself, he finding himself as much a gainer in the part he acted, as if he had shared in the adventure. So that, in a word he had the profit without the danger; and politically kept himself from the last, on pretence of his increasing the first, by his art in managing for them. Thus without being a thief or a receiver, he brought a gain to himself, and his business went on prosperously.

How he and his lady parted after this is a story which has nothing extraordinary in it. 'Tis enough to say that Jonathan became such a proficient in his business, that he stood no longer in need of her instructions. And as she had a trade of her own, which he began to be sick of assisting her in, they made no difficulty of separating, with as little ceremony as they came together. Though I do not find but that they kept a kind of remote correspondence after they were separated, as to cohabitation. And the other trade was carried on with mutual assistance, as well as to mutual advantage, for some time. And here it is very remarkable, that though during this intercourse of Mr Wild among these loose people (as above) many of them daily fell into the hand of justice, and some went off the stage, the high road, (as they call it) that is to say, by the gallows. Yet none of them had anything to say to Jonathan, or to his she friend, Mrs Milliner. But these always did their business so clean, with such subtlety, and so much to the advantage of the criminals, that it was of no use to them to charge him or her with anything.

In this dexterous way of managing, it came frequently in his way, where anything of value was stolen, to make it worth more money, both to himself and to the thief that had stolen it, by his private ways; which at the same time the criminal knew nothing of. The case was thus. It is not to be doubted that when a robbery was committed, the thieves sometimes run as much hazard in securing what they had got, as they did in the getting of it, and often times much more. Nay, they were very often discovered and detected in their attempts to turn what they had got into money, or to sell and dispose of it, when they had escaped the danger of the fact itself, and come off clean. There was a time indeed, when there were brokers and receivers whose business it was to take everything off of their hands as soon as they had gotten it; and a young shoplifter or housebreaker had no sooner got a booty, but he knew where to go and carry it in, as to a warehouse or repository; where he was sure to have money for it, and that something near the value of it too. And this was a great encouragement to the lightfingered gang. So that when it was a misfortune of a family or person to lose any goods, they were effectually lost, and seldom or never were they heard of any more. But there being an Act passed in the reign of the late King William making it felony to buy or receive any stolen goods, knowing them to be stolen; and one or two bold people having suffered on that very account, the receiving trade was spoiled all at once. And when the poor adventurer had, at the hazard of his neck, gotten any purchase, he must run all that hazard over again to turn it into money.

It is true, after some time, the temptation being strong and the profits great, there were persons frequently found again that did help the adventurers and took of their goods. But then the thief got so small a share, that the encouragement was very small; and had it continued so, the thieving trade might (for ought I know) have been in danger of being lost. For the receivers running so extreme a hazard, they got all the profit; and the poor lifter or housebreaker was glad to part with things of the greatest value for a trifle. But Jonathan and his director soon found out a way to encourage the trade again, and to make it worthwhile as they called it. And the first method was this: When a purchase was made, Jonathan enquired first where it was gotten, what house had been robbed, or who had lost the goods; and having learnt that, his next business was to have the goods deposited in proper places, always avoiding the receiving them himself, or bringing himself into any jeopardy as to the law. Then he found out proper instruments to employ to go to the persons who had been robbed, and tell them that if they could describe what they had lost, they believed they could help them to them again. For that there was a parcel of stolen goods stopped by an honest broker, to whom they were offered to be sold, and if their goods were among them they might have them again for a small matter of expense.

The people who had been robbed, it may be supposed, were always willing enough to hear of their goods again, and very thankful to the discoverer, and so readily gave an account of the things they had lost, with such proper descriptions of them as were needful. The next day they should be told there was such or such part of their goods stopped among other goods, which it was supposed were stolen from other people, and so upon assurance given on both sides to make no enquiry into the particular circumstances of stopping the goods, and a consideration to the person who went between, for helping the loser to his goods again, the things were restored, and the person received abundance of thanks and acknowledgements for their honesty and kindness. And this part always fell to Jonathan, or his mistress Milliner, or perhaps both, who always pretended they got nothing for their pains but the satisfaction of having helped the people to recover their own again, which was taken by a company of rogues; professing their sorrow that they had not had the good luck at the same time to detect the rogues that took them, and bring them to the punishment they deserved.

On the other hand, they acted as safe a part with the thief also, for rating and reproving the rogue for his villainy, they would pretend to bring them to an honest restoring the goods again, taking a reasonable consideration for their honesty, and so bring them to lodge them in such a place as should be directed. And sometimes, as I have been told, he has officiously caused the thief or thieves to be taken with the goods upon them, when he has not been able to bring them to comply, and so has made himself both thief and chapman, as the proverb says; getting a reward for the discovery, and bringing the poor wretch to the gallows too, and this only because he could not make his market of him to his mind. But I must be so just to Jonathan too, as to say he did not acknowledge this, so that this part was not had from his own mouth, yet perhaps it may not be the less true, nor do I think it would be very hard to prove the fact. As to the other part, he was never backward to own that it was his early practice, and boasted of it as doing a piece of service which none but himself could manage, and that he thereby assisted honest people in the recovery of their own. How far he acted honestly in the doing it, supposing he had no other hand in the robbery itself, I leave to the casuists to determine. No question, in their Newgate divinity, they might think it a mighty honest way of getting money, for as to the encouragement it was to the robbery itself, while the thief knew beforehand how to come off of the guilt and get money in his pocket, that they gave their thoughts no trouble about. This trade I found by his own discourse he carried on a great while, and had he gone no farther, I question whether it had been in any man's power to have hurt him to the last; nay, or that even the laws would have reached his life, notwithstanding the late act which seemed to be calculated on purpose to put a stop to his trade. But he knew no bounds to his gain, and therefore knew no restraint of laws, or at least considered of none, till he involved himself in a mass of crimes, out of which it was impossible he should recover. But to return to the first part of this unjust commerce, which, whatever gloss he might put upon it, was no other than an encouraging rogues to rob and plunder, and then demanding money for them to bring back what they had stolen, out of which he secured always a share for himself. This practice of giving people notice of their goods after they were robbed becoming pretty public, and especially several people recovering their lost goods upon the easy conditions of giving a gratuity to the discoverer, being known, it introduced another weak foolish practice as a consequence, namely that after this, when any person was robbed, they always published the particulars of their lost

goods, with the promise of a reward to those who should discover
them. It was reasonable indeed to suppose that this might occasion a discovery one way or the other, either by the thieves
betraying one another, or else by directing the buyers of goods,
who were honestly inclined, to stop such goods if they came to be
offered. And hence it was a usual practice in such advertisements
to add that if such goods were offered to be sold or pawned, they
were desired to stop both the goods and the persons and give
notice so and so, as directed. But this was every way an ineffectual
method, and indeed the latter part was particularly so, for indeed
it was neither more or less than giving a caution to the thief not
to venture to offer anything he had gotten to sale, for he should
be sure to be stopped as well as the goods. And indeed it was
strange that the people who published such advertisements
should not foresee the making such a publication would be an
effectual shutting the door against the discovery they designed it
for, and was therefore nothing but a throwing good money after
bad. On the other hand, neither was the advertising or publishing
their loss any real service, or of any use to the loser, for that the
only person who could assist in the recovery of the goods was
quite out of the question, having no need of the information, but
coming by his intelligence another way, *viz*. from the thief himself; and that if there had been no such information, I mean by
public print, he would as usual, have been sure to have sent an
account to the loser, and have come to a treaty with him another
way. For the thief giving an account to Mr Jonathan Wild where
the robbery was committed, and whose goods they were, the
cunning artist always made application to the loser first; and if it
was asked, how they come to know who the goods were taken
from? it was always answered, that it was merely providential.
Being, by mere accident at a tavern or at a friend's house in the
neighbourhood, they heard that such a gentleman had his house
broken open, and such and such goods stolen, and the like. This
was so plausible a story, and carried so much an appearance of
truth with it, that it left room for no enquiry. But on the other
hand, if the people to whom the discovery was made were too
inquisitive, the party sent presently seemed to take it ill, and
replied; 'Sir, I come to serve you. If you think to make any

discovery by me, of the thieves that robbed you, I must tell you that you are mistaken. I converse with no such cattle. I can give a very good account of myself to you, or anybody else. I only come to tell you that some goods being offered to sale by a suspected hand, the person to whom they were offered had the honesty to stop them, and the goodness to give you some notice of it, that you may see whether your goods are among them or not. If this is not enough to oblige you, I have done. If you have anything to say to me, or think to talk to me about the thief or thieves that robbed you, I have no more to say to you, but to let you know, my name is so and so; and I live in such a place. If you have anything to say to me, I am to be found, sir, at any time.' And thus they take their leave in a huff. And this never fails to bring the enquirer to a better temper; and either immediately, or soon after, to treat them with more civility. And indeed, the offer itself appears so good, and the appearance so above board, that not a magistrate or justice of the peace could find the least flaw in it. Only enquire where the goods are which are stopped, in which case a place and person is named, and goods produced when anyone is sent to view them. But then the party so cavilling at that offer is sure to find none of his own goods among them. And so being lost as it were in a wood, he is perfectly amused, and has not one word to say, for he neither sees his own goods, nor knows that the other goods are stolen, much less by who or from whom. And thus by his being too curious or rather impertinent, he loses his goods entirely, and has no second offer made him.

It must be confessed, Jonathan Wild played a sure game in all this; and therefore it is not to be wondered at that he went on for so many years without any disaster. Nay, he acquired a strange and, indeed, unusual reputation, for a mighty honest man; till his success hardened him to put on a face of public service in it, and for that purpose to profess an open and bare correspondence among the gang of thieves. By which his house became an office of intelligence for enquiries of that kind, as if all stolen goods had been deposited with him, in order to be restored. But even this good character of his, as it did not last long, so neither did it come all at once; and some tell us (how true it is, I will not affirm) that he was obliged to give up every now and then one or two of his clients to the gallows, to support his rising reputation. In which cases, he never failed to proclaim his own credit in bringing offenders to justice, and in delivering his country from such dangerous people. Some have gone so far as to tell us the very particulars which recommended any of the gangs to him for a sacrifice, and to divide them into classes: For example, (1) such as having committed the secret of a fact to him yet would not submit their purchase to his disposal. Or (2), would not accept reasonable terms of composition for restoring the goods: Or (3), used any threatening speeches against their comrades. These he would immediately cause to be apprehended, he knowing both their haunts, and where the goods were deposited; and in such cases, none so vigilant in the discovery, or so eager in apprehending the thief. And, generally speaking, he had his ways and means to bring in others of the gang to come in and confess, that they might impeach the person so intended to be given up to justice.

This, I say, some have affirmed was his practice, and assured me of the truth of it. And that in these cases, they add, that he managed with such dexterity that he always obtained public applause, as a mighty forward man to detect the villainies of those people, and bring offenders to justice. How many he murdered in that manner, (for as his end was only making a sacrifice to his own interest and fame, I can call it no other); I say, how many they were, I cannot learn. But if it has been a practice of so many years standing, and so frequent in that time, it cannot be doubted but the number has been very considerable. Nor does it a little contribute to the belief of the thing, that the fraternity of thieves in general were of late so exasperated against him; for though the method was in itself wicked in him, yet it certainly brought a great many criminals to just condemnation, who would otherwise have lived to do much more mischief than they did. And this occasioned him doubtless to push on with the more heat and fury against those who stood in his way, and where he could exert his power without fear of being touched himself, as particularly against the late J. Sheppard, Blueskin, and others, in the taking, re-taking, and prosecuting of whom, he was very officious. While at the same time, those audacious criminals exclaimed against him, as a man who had been the first great encourager of their villainies, or at least had been instrumental to draw them into the very practice itself. In revenge for which, the said Blue-skin bid fair for giving Jonathan his *quietus* in the very face of justice. But his fate was to die with more infamy than he would have gone off with, if he had been sent off at that time.

But to return to the history itself, whatever was at the bottom of his designs, 'tis evident he had two very clear pretences for what he did; and on these two pretences it was that he supported the credit of all his monstrous doings, and which indeed no man but himself could have shown his face in: 1. The Public Good, in taking and apprehending the most open and notorious criminals; and, 2. The procuring and restoring the goods again to the right owners, which had been stolen from them either by fraud or violence. It was allowed that neither of these could be done effectually as Jonathan did them, but by an avowed intimacy and acquaintance among the gangs and societies of thieves of every sort. And it was very hard to imagine that such an intimacy could be maintained without being really a party to their management, and without a criminal correspondence with them in the very facts. And Jonathan was often told so, as well by those who believed him really guilty of such a criminal correspondence, as those that did not. But be that as it will, Jonathan himself always denied it, and insisted not only on his innocence, but on his merit. And that as he was indeed acquainted with the wicked ways made use of by all the several classes of thieves, and by consequence with many of them personally, he only made use of that acquaintance to persuade and prevail upon them, when goods were offered for it, to restore the goods to the people who had lost them, placing himself so only in the middle, between the loser and the robber. As to capitulate for the latter, that if the goods were returned, the loser would keep promise, and give a reward without enquiry into the particulars, or persons, which would otherways put an end to all restorings or returnings of stolen goods for ever after. This part he insisted on as not only very honest, but very serviceable, always insisting that whatever he took on either side was no otherwise than as a solicitor takes his fee, on consideration from both parties for honestly putting an end to a lawsuit, and bringing the contending parties to a friendly accommodation. And had he gone no farther, I cannot say but he might be in the right. But he acted in a more difficult station, as placing himself in the middle, between the law and the offender, in a manner commuting the felony, and making a kind of composition where the fact was punishable; which punishment no man had power to anticipate, but the hand above, which had power also to remit the penalty; namely, the supreme magistrate.

It must be allowed to Jonathan's fame, that as he steered among rocks and dangerous shoals, so he was a bold pilot. He ventured in, and always got out in a manner equally surprising. No man ever did the like before him, and I dare say, no man will attempt to do the like after him. Two things indeed favoured him: (1) The willingness the government always shows to have criminals detected and brought to justice. And, (2) the willingness of the people who had been robbed, and lost things of considerable value to get their goods again.

1. The willingness of the government to bring rogues to their reward, as well to punish the persons, as to discourage the crime. All just governments discover a disposition to bring offenders to justice. And on this account they not only receive and accept of informations of the worst of crimes from the worst of criminals, and take knowledge of the offence from the offenders themselves, but encourage such criminals to come in and confess the offence, and discover their accomplices, promising as well pardon for the crimes as a reward for the discovery, even to those who are guilty. Now this willingness of the government to detect thieves seemed to be a kind of authority for Jonathan in his vigorous pursuit of those who he thought fit to have punished. Though 'tis true, it was no authority to him to draw poor fellows first into the crime, that he might afterwards obtain a reward from the government for detecting and apprehending them, and there indeed is the nice turn of Jonathan's case, and which indeed has turned him off of the stage at long run, as we shall see in its place.

He continued in the prosperous part of his business about ten year, without being so publicly taken notice of, or making himself so famous as he has been lately. And in this time it was not doubted but he got a large stock of money, as well as of credit; and had he contented himself with the same cautious wary way of acting, which his first instructor introduced him by, he might have grown rich, and been safe too. But as he was of a pushing, enterprising nature, he could content himself with nothing but everything he could get, nor could he act moderately in any part of his conduct. In this time of his prosperity he married a third wife, (his two former, *if they were wives*, being still living). Her name was Elizabeth Man, who, though she was a woman of the town was yet a very sensible and agreeable person; and her short history is this. He loved her above all the other women he had taken for wives, and lived publicly with her, which he did not with any of the rest. He had no children by her, but she was, as he himself confessed, a true penitent for all her former life, and made him an excellent wife. She expiated her former bad life by a formal full confession and penance, having on that occasion been persuaded to turn Roman Catholic, and having received absolution from her confessor, lived a very sober life for some years, after which she died and was buried at St Pancras in the Fields. And Jonathan retained such an impression of the sanctity and goodness of this wife, that he never forgot it as long as he lived; and ordered himself to be buried close to her when he died, which his friends took care to see performed, about two of the clock in the morning.

He had two wives, as they are called, besides this; and after her death, who I understand, he did not live with, or not long at a time, (*viz*):

Sarah Parrin, alias *Gregstone*, who I understand is yet living. *Judith Nun*, by whom he had a daughter who is now about ten years of age, and the mother also still living. Besides those five, he married his sixth and last wife about seven year ago, and with whom he lived to the time of his execution. Her maiden name was Mary Brown, but when he took her to wife, her name was Mary Dean, being the widow or relict of Skull Dean, a man of the trade who was executed for housebreaking, that is to say, for burglary, about the year 1716 or 1717. Some have taxed Jonathan with being instrumental to the execution of this Dean, her said first husband, that he might have the liberty to make court to his wife. But he denied it positively, and I see no reason for such a reproach. I shall not reflect on his memory without good evidence. The said Skull Dean, Mrs Wild's first husband, was a very dexterous fellow in his calling, and particularly expert in breaking into houses. After he was condemned, he got out of the prison on pretence of going to the necessary-house, and being gotten quite clear for a little while, he made his way as far as Giltspur street towards Smithfield. But being pursued by the keepers, and having his fetters on, he could not go long undiscovered, so they overtook him, and carried him back to prison.

This Mrs Dean is his present apparent relict, she has had the mortification to have had two husbands, and both hanged; and was so affected with the disaster of this last, that as Jonathan himself declared a few days before his execution, she had twice attempted to destroy herself, after she had the account of his receiving sentence of death. He had no children by this sixth venture. But we are assured, she has been an extraordinary wife to him on many accounts, and particularly in the way of his business, in which she could not be perfectly unacquainted, having had so extraordinary a husband before. Though we do not find that Jonathan himself wanted any assistance, being by this time perfect master of his trade. In the time of this wife, or on the marrying her, he removed from his former lodging, (a house in the little Old Bailey, where his said wife had lived before) and took a house in the Great Old Bailey, and there he lived to the last; and in no mean figure neither, for his wife made a very good appearance; and as to Jonathan, he carried on a very flourishing business, as the town well knows. He was now master of his trade. Poor and rich flocked to him. If anything was lost (whether by negligence in the owner, or vigilance and dexterity in the thief) away we went to Jonathan Wild. Nay, advertisements were published, directing the finder of almost everything to bring it to Jonathan Wild, who was eminently empowered to take it, and give the reward. How infatuate were the people of this nation all this while? Did they consider that at the very time they treated this person with such a confidence, as if he had been appointed to the trade, he had perhaps the very goods in his keeping, waiting the advertisement for the reward? And that, perhaps, they had been stolen with that very intention?

It was not a little difficult to give his eminence his true title. He was indeed called a thief-catcher, and on some extraordinary occasions he was so, as in the case of Sheppard, Blueskin and others. But this was no explanation of his business at all, for his profits came in another way, not in catching the thief, but more properly, in catching (that is, biting) the persons robbed. As for the thief, it was not his business to catch him, as long as he would be subjected to his rules; that is to say, as often as he had committed any robbery, to bring it to him to be restored to the owner. If the correspondence he kept was large, if the number of his instruments was very great, his dexterity in managing them was indeed wonderful. And how cleverly he kept himself out of the reach of the act for receiving stolen goods mentioned above, is hardly to be imagined; and yet we find he was never charged home till now, notwithstanding so many felons who he exasperated to the last degree, and made desperate by falling upon them to their destruction.

It is true, the young generation of thieves who as we may say, lived under him, were always kept low and poor, and could not subsist but by the bounty of their governor. And when they had a booty of any bulk or value, they knew not what to do with it, but to deposit it, and get some money for the present use, and then have a little more upon its being disposed the right way. For the managing this part he had his particular servants to take and receive, so that Jonathan received nothing, delivered nothing, nor could anything be fastened on him to his hurt, I mean for receiving stolen goods; and yet as things stood, almost all the stolen goods were brought to him, and put into his hands.

He openly kept his compting-house, or office, like a man of business, and had his books to enter everything in with the utmost exactness and regularity. When you first came to him to give him an account of anything lost, it was hinted to you that you must first deposit a crown; this was his retaining fee. Then you were asked some needful questions, that is to say needful not for his information, but for your amusement; as where you lived, where the goods were lost, whether out of your house, or out of your pocket, or whether on the highway, and the like. And your answers to them all were minuted down, as if in order to make a proper search and enquiry, whereas perhaps the very thing you came to enquire after was in the very room where you were, or not far off. After all this grimace was at an end, you were desired to call again, or send in a day or two, and then you should know whether he was able to do you any service or no, and so you were dismissed. At your second coming you had some encouragement given you, that you would be served, but perhaps the terms were a little raised upon you, and you were told the rogue that had it was impudent, that he insisted it was worth so much, and he could sell it when he would for double the money you offered; and that if you would not give him such a sum, he would not treat with you. 'However' says Jonathan, 'if I can but come to the speech of him, I'll make him be more reasonable.' The next time he tells you, that all he can bring the rogue to is that — guineas being paid to the porter who shall bring the goods, and a promise upon honour that nothing shall be said to him, but just take and give; the gold watch, or the snuff-box, or whatever it is, shall be brought to you by such a time exactly; and thus upon mutual assurances the bargain is made for restoring the goods. But then it remains to be asked what Mr Wild expects for his pains in managing this nice part, who answers with an air of greatness, he leaves it to you; that he gets nothing by what is to be given the porter, that he is satisfied in being able to serve gentlemen in such a manner, so that it is in your breast to do what you think is handsome by Mr Wild, who has taken a great deal of pain in it to do you a service.

It must be confessed that, in all this, if there was no more than is mentioned, such a part might be acted on all sides without any guilt fastened anywhere but on the thief. For example, a house is robbed, or a lady has lost her gold watch; Jonathan, by his intelligence among the gang finds out who has done it; that is to say he is told 'tis such a one, tis no matter how he hears it, he is not bound to the discovery upon a hear-say; nor is he obliged to prosecute a felony committed on he does not know who, by he knows not who, that's none of his business. However, having a kind of knowledge of the person, he sends to him to let him know that if he is his own friend, he will carry, that is, send the watch, or the cane, or the snuff-box, so and so to such a place; and that if he does so, and the porter receives ten guineas, or more or less, whatever it is that is offered, all will be well. If not he adds a threatening that he will be prosecuted with the utmost severity. Upon this the thief sends the goods, has the money, and never sees Jonathan nor any person else. What can Jonathan be charged with, in such an affair as this? I must confess I do not see it, no, nor if the thief sends him a present of four or five guineas out of the money, provided as he said it is without any conditions made beforehand, or being present at the time 'tis done. Nor, on the other hand, does the treating for delivering the goods as above, with a second or third person, give any room to fix any thing on Jonathan. So that, in short, he treats both with the thief and with the person robbed with the utmost safety and security. Indeed I do not see why he might not have carried on such a commerce as this with the greatest ease, I do not say honesty, in the world, if he had gone no farther. For he took none of your money for restoring your goods, neither did he restore you any goods; you gave him money indeed for his trouble in enquiring out the thief, and for urging his interest by awing or persuading to get your stolen goods sent you back, telling you what you must give to the porter that brings them, if you please, for he does not oblige you to give it.

But the danger lay on the other side of the question, namely, not being contented with what the person robbed gave upon the foot of a grateful acknowledgement for trouble, but impudently taking the goods of the thief, sending the porter himself, taking the money, and then capitulating with the thief for such a part of the reward; and then this thief coming in against him as a witness. This was the very case in the fact upon which Jonathan miscarried. So that, in a word, Jonathan's avarice hanged him. It is true, in the case he was tried for, it was apparent that he set the robbery, as they express it; that is, he directed the persons to the place, nay, went with them to show them the shop, described the woman and the business; and after all, received the goods, and gave them the money for returning them, reserving it in his own power to take what more he pleased for himself; and at last all this being testified by the thieves themselves.

It is not to be doubted but Jonathan, to carry on this commerce to such a height as he really had raised it, had a perfect understanding with all the professed thieves in the town; at least the young beginners, for these are a class generally more out of his power than others, and who are not so easily to be governed as the others are; and yet he finds ways to influence them too in the way of their practice. But the rest, I say, he had in his reach managed them as he thought fit; nay, he generally knew, or perhaps appointed them the quarter they should walk in; so that when ever any person came to enquire for his goods lost, he could make a tolerable guess at the thief by the quarter of the town you lived in, or where you were when you lost it.

I remember I had occasion, in a case of this kind, to wait upon Mr Jonathan with a crown in my hand as above, and having made a deposit, I was asked as above, where the thing was lost? At first he smiled, and turning to one, I suppose, of his instruments, 'Who can this be?' says he, 'Why, all our people are gone down to Sturbridge fair.'[4] The other answered, after some pause, 'I think I saw Lynx[5] in the street yesterday.' 'Did you?' says he. 'Then tis that dog, I warrant you. Well, sir,' says he, 'I believe we can find out your man; you shall know more of it if you let me see you again a Monday.' This was on the Friday. When the Monday came, truly I was told they could not see the young rogue, and they believed he was gone after the rest to the fair, it being about the beginning of September. After the fair I came again and again, but was put off from time to time, and could not at last be served in the case, it being only a silver-hilted sword, which the thief, it seems, had found means to turn into money, and then there was no coming at it; the time also having been lapsed by his honour having been gone to the fair.

Another person applying in another and more material affair was treated with respect by Mr Wild, and a pot of tea brought out in form; (*N.B.* the crown being first deposited as usual). The case related to a gold watch, with trinkets and some diamonds about either the watch, and the lady offered very considerably for the restoring it, as I remember, £30, but no advertisements had been published. Mr Wild, after the usual enquiries of when it was lost, and where; and being told it was at St Ann's church, Westminster, pauses a while, and calls up a servant and asks aloud, 'where was M—ll K——g[6] last Sunday?' 'About Westminster,' says the man, 'but the bi——h would not tell where.' 'Was she crank?'[7] says Mr Wild. 'I don't know,' says the fellow. However, turning to the lady, says he, 'Madam, I fancy I shall be able to serve you, and perhaps for less money than your ladyship speaks of. If it be M—ll K——g, that woman I have in my thoughts, as I believe 'tis, for she is a dexterous jade at the work, I'll have her safe before morning.' The lady, full of compassion returns, 'O sir! Don't take her up. I assure you I won't prosecute, I'll rather lose my watch than have any poor wretch hanged for it.' 'Why, madam,' says Mr Wild, 'We can't talk with her but by threatening. We must not make a bargain with her; that would be to compound a felony. If I can persuade her to come and bring your watch and ask your pardon, will that satisfy you?' 'Nay,' says the lady, 'I don't know whether that would be safe neither. If she will send it me, I had rather. And I'll forgive her, without asking pardon.' 'Well, madam, will you take it and give the porter that brings it 20 guineas, if you please, but not to oblige you to it.' 'Whatever you say, Mr Wild,' says the lady. 'Well madam,' says Mr Wild, 'if I may have the honour to see your ladyship again.'

Lady: Will it not do if I send anybody?

Wild: Why, truly, no madam: People that deal in these things do not care for witnesses.

Lady: Well, well, that's true. I'll come myself. What day would you have me come?

Wild: On Thursday, madam.

Lady: Well, Mr Wild, what must I do? What will satisfy you for your trouble?

Wild: It is time enough, madam, to speak of that when I am sure I can do you any service. These creatures are very loose, and I can't tell you how it may be.

Lady: Well, Mr Wild, I'll come furnished to pay my respects to you.

Wild: Madam, your most obedient servant.

(*Waits on her to her coach.*)

Accordingly, Thursday coming, the Lady appears. Mr Wild in his Callimancoe night-gown, (the same he was hanged in) receives her; and with a pleasant look tells her he is very glad to be able to say that he believes he shall serve her. That it was the same woman he suspected, and that the jade had already pawned the watch for some money, but that it was but a little, and he was glad she had.

Lady: Why, Mr Wild?

Wild: Because, madam, if she had kept it all this while, it would have been ten to one but she had broke something about it, or done it some mischief.

Lady: That's true, indeed. Pray, what has she pawned it for?

Wild: Not much, madam, she has got but seven guineas upon it yet.

Lady: Well, Mr Wild, what must be done?

Wild: Why, madam, if the people that have it, bring it safe and sound to your ladyship, will you give me your honour that you will ask no questions, or stop the person that comes with it?

Lady: I promise you, on my word, I will not.

Wild: The man that brings it may be a poor innocent fellow that knows nothing of it.

Lady: Well, well, he shall have no harm or interruption from me.

Wild: Then I believe your ladyship may hear something of it tonight.

Lady: And what must I give him?

Wild: I don't yet know, madam, but I'll bring them as low as I can. Not above 20 guineas, to be sure, madam.

Lady: That is very kind indeed. Well, Mr Wild, then I'll make it up to you. (*So the lady pulls out her purse in order to give him some money.*)

Wild: No, madam, not a farthing. Besides, you have not got your watch yet. Pray stay till you see whether the jade will perform; though I think, indeed, I am pretty sure of her.

Lady: Well, I'll take your word, Mr Wild.

(*Offers him money again.*)

Wild: By no means, madam. Let me see if I can serve you.

Lady: Well, Mr Wild, if it must be so, I must come again then.

Wild: It may be not. Will your ladyship be pleased to stay about half an hour?

Lady: Ay, with all my heart.

In about half an hour, Jonathan having been called hastily out, comes in again immediately. 'Madam,' says he, 'if your ladyship pleases to go into your coach, and drive gently up — street, perhaps a messenger may desire to speak with you as you go along.'

'Very well, Mr Wild, I understand you.'

Upon the lady's going along — street, a ticket-porter, with his hat in his hand, shows himself by the coach-side, and the lady taking the hint, stops her coach and lets down the glass, and speaking to the fellow, says, 'Would you speak with me, friend?'

The fellow says not a word, but delivers into her hand the watch with all the trinkets and diamonds perfectly safe; and when she had looked upon it a little, gives her a note, wherein was written nothing but thus in words at length,

Eighteen Guineas.

The lady immediately tells out the money to the porter, and he was going away. 'Hold, honest friend,' says the lady, 'there's somewhat for yourself,' and gives him half a guinea, and so dismissed him.

A day or two after she makes Mr Wild a visit, and presents him with 15 guineas more. But with great difficulty made him accept of it; telling her it was a great deal too much; that he would not take it by any means, but at last accepts it, with the ceremony of saying he would not take it on account of the watch, but for having been at some trouble in serving her ladyship, in which she was pleased to reward him much more than he deserved. When at the same time 'twas very likely (he) had part of the 18 guineas too from M—ll K——g, who he frighted out of the watch with threatening to have her put into Newgate for stealing of it.

This may serve for a sketch of *practice*, as I call it; and to let the world see in what manner this secret service was carried on; how the thieving trade was managed, how the people were gulled out of their money, and how a crew of hell-born rogues and whores, which is much the same, have been bred up to the trade by their grand patron and master of art, Jonathan Wild. It would be endless to give a particular of the many tricks and cheats of this kind that he has managed during a continued life of wickedness for about 16 years; among which it would be very instructing to give an account of the numbers of poor wretched creatures, like himself; who, he having first led them on in the road of crime for several years, as long as they would be subservient to him and put all their purchase into his hands, abandoned as soon as they offered to set up for themselves, and leaving them to the mercy of the government, made himself the instrument of their destruction and then pleaded the merit of it to the public. But these require a long history, rather than a pamphlet, and therefore I wholly omit them.

It is time now to enter into a particular account of the conclusion of this life of crime. It has been a kind of comedy, or a farce rather, all along, but it proved a tragedy at last. And Jonathan being brought to justice has summed up his account here in a most ignominious end, satisfied how in a manner not uncommon only, but such as history can not give one instance of the like, except lately, that of a murder at St Edmunds-Bury in Suffolk. The sum of the matter is this; Jonathan had long been so notorious, and his practice, though not within the compass of the law, was yet in its nature so criminal in itself, and above all, was so dangerous in its example, that the public began to be justly alarmed at it, and to consider of proper measures for putting a stop to it. [To] which purpose an Act of parliament, (the only remedy for growing evils of this kind) was passed the last session to make it felony, to take or receive any reward for the restoring of any stolen goods, knowing them to be stolen: The clause in the said Act is as follows.

'And whereas there are several persons who have secret acquaintance with felons, and who make it their business to help persons to their stolen goods, and by that means gain money from them, which is divided between them and the felons, whereby they greatly encourage such offenders: Be it enacted by the authority aforesaid, that wherever any person taketh money or reward, directly or indirectly, under pretence or upon account of helping any person or persons to any stolen goods or chattels, every such person so taking money or rewards as aforesaid, (unless such person do apprehend, or cause to be apprehended, such felon who stole the same, and cause such felon to be brought to his trial for the same, and give evidence against him) shall be guilty of felony, and suffer the pains and penalties of felony, according to the nature of the felony committed in stealing such goods and chattels, in the manner and with such circumstances as the same were stolen.'

This Act was so directly aimed at Jonathan's general practice that he could not be ignorant enough not to see it. But lest he should, a certain honourable person, too just to favour him, and yet too human not to warn him of his danger that he might avoid it, gave him notice that this very Act was made against his unlawful practice, and therefore in time warned him, in few but significant words, to take heed to himself and avoid the consequences by leaving off the trade of thief-catching, as it is unjustly called, that is of compounding for the return of stolen goods. But good advice to Jonathan Wild was like talking gospel to a kettledrum, bidding a dragoon not to plunder, or talking of compassion to a hussar. He that was hardened above the baseness of all cautionary fear scorned the advice, and went on in his wicked trade; not warily and wisely as he had formerly done, but in short, with more impudence and shameless boldness than ever. For as if he despised laws, and the governors, and the provoked justice of the nation, he now not only took rewards for returning goods stolen, but even directed the stealing of them, and making himself a party to the very robberies themselves, acted a part of the thief and the receiver also; and this in so many cases that we are told if the indictment had failed for which he was justly condemned, there were several others ready to have been brought on, and the witnesses ready to have been produced for proof of the facts. But one felony being fully proved was sufficient; and upon a full hearing he was convicted in so evident a manner that he really had nothing to say in his own behalf, not being able to deny the fact. His counsel would have pleaded that the offence was not within the late statute upon which he was indicted, but the court answered them fully, and overruled the plea; so that, being allowed to be within the statute, and the fact being fully proved by several witnesses, he received sentence of death the 15th of May last.

The circumstances of this fact seem to be so agreeable to the whole tenor of Jonathan's former practice, and so like other parts of his life, that we can not but observe the parallel, and conclude the particular accounts of other parts of his life to be true likewise. It has been said of him that if ever he was moved to promote any man, or to help any man to business, which he often pretended to do in compassion to their poverty, that still he did it always in his own way, that is to say, endeavoured to make thieves of them; to bring them to be hanged, to keep them from misery, and to make Newgate birds of them, to keep them out of the compters. This he practised principally upon young creatures and little destitute children, such as seemed to be left to wander about in want and beggary; and many a poor boy he has picked up in the street pretending charity and a willingness to do them good, which, when it has come to the issue, has been no more or less than to breed them up to thieving, and ripen them for the devil. But, which is still worse than all the rest, I have several stories by me at this time, which I have particular reasons to believe are true, of children thus strolling about the streets in misery and poverty, whom he has taken in on pretence of providing for them and employing them. And all has ended in this (*viz.*) making rogues of them. Horrid wickedness! His charity has been to breed them up to be thieves, and, still more horrid, several of these his own *foster children* he has himself caused afterwards to be apprehended and hanged for the very crimes which he first taught them how to commit.

I am not indeed to make a jest of these things. There is something shocking and dismal in the very relation, and therefore it is that this account of the life of Jonathan Wild, which in its nature is all a tragedy, is not related with an air of banter and ridicule as others are; 'tis hoped it will not be the less acceptable to men of sense. It is a solemn and terrible thing to look back on a life of such hardened, abominable practices; to see it carried on in defiance, either of God or Devil; and that with such success too, passing for so many years unpunished. And, though there are some things in the long series of his wicked life which may relish with the levity of a droll way of writing, yet to see a man turned into an incarnate devil, his life a scene of inimitable crimes, his very society a hell, and equally devouring both to soul and body; he that can read it without some horror must have very little of what we call Christianity about him. To see him take up an unthinking youth in the street, covered with dirt and rags, and willing on any terms to get out of his misery; to see this superlative wretch pretend charity to the child, and tell him he will provide for him, and thereby engage the lad to him, as to a gentleman that intends to do him good; and then, instead of providing for him, lead him by the hand to hell-gates, and after that, like a true devil, thrust him in! First to tempt, and then accuse, which is the very nature of the devil; first to make poor desolate vagabond boys, thieves, and then betray them to the gallows! Who can think of such a thing without just abhorrence; who can think it to be any less than the worst sort of murder. Such was the life, and such the practice of this wretched man, and in these very last scenes of his life, he grew so audacious, that it seemed as if he was really ripening up apace for his own destruction. It is said of him in the case of that hardened fellow Blueskin, that he should say Jonathan first made him a thief, and then abandoning him, left him to carry it on by himself; and it being necessary to his (Jonathan's) fame to have always some chase in his view, to build his own merit upon with the government, he kept a watch upon him, that he might at last bring him to the gallows, for which the said Blueskin was very near giving him a pass into another world by that desperate attempt to cut his throat in the face of a court of justice; which Jonathan, though surprised at then, has had leisure since to wish had been effectually done at that time, and said so publicly in the press-yard, two days before his trial.

But to come then to the particular fact for which he suffered, the story as it was related upon oath at his trial, and the several circumstances belonging to it stands thus.

Katherine Stetham deposed: That on the 22nd of January, between three and four in the afternoon, a man and woman came into her shop under pretence of buying some lace. They were – said she – so very difficult, that I had none below that would please them; and so, leaving my daughter in the shop, I stepped upstairs and brought down another box. We could not agree about the price, and so they went away together; and in about half an hour after I missed a tin box of lace that I valued at £50. The same night, and the next, I went to Jonathan Wild's house; but not meeting with him, I advertised the lace that I had lost, with a reward of 15 guineas and no questions asked. But hearing nothing of it, I went to Jonathan's house again, and then met with him. He desired me to give a description of the persons that I suspected, which I did as near as I could; and then he told me that he'd make enquiry, and bade me call again in two or three days. I did so, and then he said that he had heard something of my lace, and expected to know more of the matter in a little time. I came to him again on that day that he was apprehended, (I think 'twas the 15th of February). I told him that though I had advertised but 15 guineas reward, yet I'd give 20 or 25 rather than not have my goods. 'Don't be in such a hurry' says he, 'I don't know but I may help you to it for less; and if I can, I will. The persons that have it are gone out of town. I shall set them to quarrelling about it, and then I shall get it the cheaper.' On the 10th of March he sent me word, that if I would come to him in Newgate, and bring 10 guineas in my pocket, he could help me to the lace. I went. He desired me to call a porter, but I not knowing where to find one, he sent a person who brought one that appeared to be a ticket-porter. The prisoner gave me a letter which he said was sent him as a direction where to go for the lace. But I could not read, and so I delivered it to the porter. Then he desired me to give the porter the 10 guineas, or else, (he said) the persons that had the lace would not deliver it. I gave the porter the money; he went away, and in a little time returned, and brought me a box that was sealed up, but not the same that was lost. I opened it, and found all my lace but one piece.

'Now, Mr Wild,' (says I) 'What must you have for your trouble?' 'Not a farthing,' (says he) 'not a farthing for me. I don't do these things for worldly interest, but only for the good of poor people that have met with misfortunes. As for the piece of lace that is missing, I hope to get it for you ere be long; and I don't know but that I may help you not only to your money again, but to the thief too; and if I can, much good may't do you. And as you're a good woman and a widow, and a christian, I desire nothing of you but your prayers, and for them I shall be thankful. I have a great many enemies, and God knows what may be the consequence of this imprisonment.'

This is a black story indeed, and it was very remarkable, that the fact was really committed, that is to say, the felony was contracted, or that part which the late Act in particular reached (*viz.*) the delivering the goods, and taking the money for discovering them; all this part was acted I say after his being committed to Newgate.

It was likewise very remarkable that there was another case much of the same nature which lay ready to have been brought to a hearing if this had not intervened, namely, of a pocket-book stolen from Mr Tidman, a corn-chandler in Giltspur street, near Newgate, in which was a bank bill for £116 in which the witnesses were two persons who had pleaded to their pardons. We come now to his behaviour after this condemnation, and at the place of execution; at which last place he indeed scarce said a word to God or man, being either dozed with the liquid laudanum which he had taken, or demented and confused by the horror of what was before him, and the reflection of what was within him. Nor even before he took the dose of laudanum was he in any suitable manner sensible of his condition, or concerned about it, very little sign appeared of his having the least hope concerning his future state. But as he lived hardened, he seemed to die stupid. He declined coming to the chapel, either to the sermon or prayers, pleading his lameness by the gout, but chiefly the crowds and disorders of the people discomposing or disordering him. In the condemned hold, or place where malefactors are kept after their sentence, they had prayers as usual; and he seemed to join with them in a kind of form, but little or nothing of the penitence of a criminal, in view of death, appeared upon him. His principal enquiries seemed to be about what kind of state was to be expected after death, and how the invisible world was to be described; but nothing of the most certain judgement which is there to be expected, righteous and terrible, according to the deeds done in the body, or of a saviour to whom to have recourse, as the slayer in the old law had to the city of refuge, to save him from the avenger of blood. As his time shortened he seemed more and more confused, and then began to entertain discourses of the lawfulness of dismissing ourselves out of the present misery, after the example of the ancient Romans, which, as he said, was then esteemed as an act of bravery and gallantry, and recorded to their honour.

This kind of discourse was indeed sufficient to have caused the keepers to have had an eye to him, so as to prevent any violence he might offer to himself, and they did watch him as narrowly as they could. However, he so far deceived them, as that the day before his execution he found means to have a small bottle with the liquid laudanum conveyed to him unseen, of which he took so large a quantity, that it was soon perceived by the change it made upon him, for he was so drowsy that he could not hold up his head, or keep open his eyes, at the time of reading the prayers. Upon this two of his fellow prisoners endeavoured to rouse him (not suspecting that he had taken enough to hurt him) and taking him by the hands, they persuaded him to stand up, and walk a little about the room, which he could not do without help because of his gout. This walking, though it did a little waken him, had several other operations at the same time. For first it changed his countenance, turning it to be exceeding pale, then it put him into a violent sweat, which made them apprehend he would faint, upon which they offered to give him something to keep up his spirits, but he refused it, telling them he was very sick; soon after which he vomited very violently, and this in all probability prolonged his life for the execution, For by their stirring him, and making him vomit, he brought up the greatest part of the laudanum which he had taken, before it had been long enough in his stomach to mix with the animal spirits or blood, which if it had done but one hour more, he would certainly have taken his last sleep in the prison. But nature, having thus discharged itself of the load, he revived again, and though still dozed and insensible of what he said or did, yet he was able to walk about, speak, and act sufficiently for the part that remained to him, namely, for the last scene of his life at the gallows.

Accordingly on Monday the 24th of May, he was conveyed in a cart to Tyburn, and though it was apparent he was still under the operation of the laudanum, and that which was left in his stomach had so far seized upon his spirits as to make him almost stupid, yet it began to go off, and nature getting the mastery of it, he began to be more sensible of what he was going about; but the scene was then short, and he had little to do but to stand up in the cart, and, the needful apparatus being made, be turned off with the rest, which was done about 3 a-clock in the afternoon. The rudeness of the mob to him, both at his first going into the cart, and all the way from thence to the place of execution, is not to be expressed, and shows how notorious his life had been, and what impression his known villainies had made on the minds of the people. For, contrary to the general behaviour of the street in such cases, instead of compassionate expressions, and a general cast of pity, which ordinarily sits on the countenances of the people, when they see the miserable objects of justice go to their execution; here was nothing to be heard but cursings and execrations. Abhorring the crimes and the very name of the man, throwing stones and dirt at him all the way, and even at the place of execution; the other malefactors being all ready to be turned off, but the hangman giving him leave to take his own time, and he continuing setting down in the cart, the mob impatient, and fearing a reprieve, though they had no occasion for it, called furiously upon the hangman to dispatch him, and at last threatened to tear him to pieces, if he did not tie him up immediately.

In short there was a kind of an universal rage against him, which nothing but his death could satisfy, or put an end to, and if a reprieve had come, it would have, twas thought, been difficult for the officers to have brought him back again without his receiving some mischief, if not his death's wound from the rabble. So detestable had he made himself by his notorious crimes, and to such a height were his wicked practices come.

Thus ended the tragedy, and thus was a life of horrid and inimitable wickedness finished at the gallows, the very same place where, according to some, above 120 miserable creatures had been hanged whose blood in great measure may be said to lie at his door, either in their being first brought into the thieving trade, or led on in it by his encouragement and assistance; and many of them at last betrayed and brought to justice by his means, upon which worst sort of murder he valued himself, and would have had it passed for merit, even with the government itself.

FINIS

APPENDIX

The Lives and Deaths of Jonathan Wild

On the day before his trial, 14 May 1725, Wild played his trump card. He circulated a printed list of the names of sixty-four men and one woman who had been 'discovered, apprehended and convicted' by him, and subsequently hanged at Tyburn. He also added the names of a further nine persons caught by him and transported. The plan misfired. Rather than convincing the court of his public service as a thief-catcher, it convinced his accusers of his callous inhumanity. These were the names:

For Highway Robbery

Humphrey Angier
James Butler
Henry Checkley
William Colthurst
Darville, *alias* Chapman
William Duese
Timothy Dun
John Dykes
John Easton
Mathew Flood
Footman *alias* Goodman
Butler Fox
John Herrington
John Holmar
Joseph Hutton
Edward Joice
John Levee

James Lincoln
Richard Oakey
Thomas Piggot
Jeremiah Rann
James Reading
James Shaw, *alias* Smith *alias* Thompson
Thomas Sinnament
Thomas Smith
Edward Spencer
John Thomas
Thomas Thurland
William White
John Wigley
Robert Wilkinson
William William
James Wilson

For House Breaking

John Allen
Joseph 'Blueskin' Blake

Henry Browne
John Chance

Samuel Davis
Thomas Draper
Thomas Eades
Robert Evans
John Fairbone
John Harris
James Harvey
William Hoskins
John Latherington

John Parrot
Arnold Powell
William Rigglesdon
Jack Sheppard
Elizabeth Shirley
Samuel West
John Wheeler
Thomas Wynne

For Returning from Transportation

William Bond
James Filewood
Robert Godfrey, *alias* Perkins
Martin Grey
Old Harry, *alias* Williams

Charles Hinchman
William Holaday
John Meffe
Samuel Whittle
Henry Woodford

Transported, after having returned from Transportation

Edward Catornes
James Dalton
John Jones
Mary King
John Hall

John Mason
William Smith
Thomas Stanton
Sarah Wells

The extent of the public fascination with Wild's exploits can be demonstrated in part by this list of works devoted mainly or exclusively to his life and actions, which were published in the three months from April to July 1725.

1. *British Journal*, 27 February to 27 March. Four articles by *Philanthropos* (Bernard de Mandeville) later expanded into a pamphlet, *An Inquiry into the Cause of the frequent Executions at Tyburn* (April 1725).

2. *An Authentic Narrative of the Parentage, Birth, Education and Practices of Jonathan Wild, Citizen and Thief Taker of London.* Sold by A. Moor (April 1725).

3. *An Authentic Narrative of the Life & Actions of Jonathan Wild* etc.

4. *An Authentic History of the Parentage etc. of the Famous Jonathan Wild* etc. 'Printed from the London Copy at Stamford.' Text same as 3.

5. *The Ordinary of Newgate's Accounts of the Behaviour of the Printers* etc. Probably a pirate reprint of the Ordinary's authentic account in *The Political State of Great Britain*, vol. 29, pp. 507–10.

6. *The Funeral Procession of Jonathan Wild*. A satirical print (May 1725).

7. *Jonathan Wild's Complaint or England's Ingratitude*. A Dublin reprint of the poem on 6.

8. *Jonathan Wild's Last Farewell to the World*. A ballad.

9. *The Whole Proceedings of the Trials of Jonathan Wild* etc. (15 May 1725). A highly misleading title.

10. *The Thief-Taker Taken*. A broadsheet of engravings advertised in the *Daily Journal*, 20 May 1725.

11. *The Life of Jonathan Wild, from his Birth to his Death* by 'H. D. Clerk to Justice R—' (29 May and 6 July 1725).

12. *The Life and Glorious Actions of the Most Heroic and Magnanimous Jonathan Wilde, Generalissimo of the Prig-Forces in Great Britain and Ireland*. Sold by H. Whitbridge. Advertised in the *Daily Post*, 31 May 1725. Obviously an influence on Fielding's version.

13. *The Life of Jonathan Wilde* etc. Sold by W. Dicey of Northampton. Almost identical to 11.

14. *The Life & Actions of Jonathan Wilde* (Gloucester, May or June 1725).

15. *The True and Genuine Account of the Life and Actions of the*

Late Jonathan Wild ... Defoe's version. Printed and sold by John Applebee (8, 10 and 12 June 1725).

16. *Life of Jonathan Wild* by *Chronicon Newquissimus.*

17. *Weighley alias Wild, a Poem etc.* by N. P. (July 1725).

NOTES

In preparing the notes for this edition I gratefully acknowledge a general indebtedness to the erudition of Douglas Brooks, in his notes to the Everyman edition (1973), and of Gerald Howson in *Thief-Taker General* (Hutchinson, 1970). I am also indebted to Professor H. K. Miller of Princeton University for supplying the reference for Note 116.

NOTES: JONATHAN WILD

1. (p. 39) *Plutarch, Nepos, Suetonius*: Plutarch (*c.* AD 46–after 119), author of the *Parallel Lives*; Cornelius Nepos (*c.* 99–31 BC), author of *De Viris Illustribus* (*Concerning Famous Men*); Suetonius (born AD 69), author of *The Twelve Caesars*.

2. (p. 39) *Aristides ... Brutus ... Lysander ... Nero*: Aristides is cited by Plato in the *Gorgias* as a rare example of a virtuous politician. Marcus Junius Brutus was another type of virtue. Fielding names him alongside Socrates as an example of 'the great and good' in the Preface to the *Miscellanies*, vol. i (1743). Lysander, the Spartan commander, and Nero the Roman emperor are examples of the opposite qualities of vanity and brutality.

3. (p. 40) *the histories of Alexander and Cæsar*: See especially Plutarch's parallel lives of the two men. Fielding had also compared the two men in his *Essay on Nothing*: 'What did *Alexander, Cæsar*, and all the rest of that heroic Band, who have plundered, and massacred so many Millions, obtain by all their Care, Labour, Pain, Fatigue and Danger? – ...*Nothing*.' (*Miscellanies*, vol. i, ed. H. K. Miller, Oxford University Press, 1972, p. 188.)

4. (p. 41) *The Great*: The phrase is an allusion to Walpole, generally referred to as 'the great man' during his period as Prime Minister, 1721–42. Fielding often plays with and comments upon the phrase in his writings, see for example his poem 'Of True Greatness' (*Miscellanies*, vol. i, ed. Miller, pp. 19 ff.). In his 'Modern Glossary', in the *Covent Garden Journal* for 14 January 1752, Fielding defines 'Great' thus: 'Applied to a thing, signifies bigness; when to a man, often littleness, or meanness.'

5. (p. 42) *Prince Prettyman*: This character in Buckingham's burlesque comedy *The Rehearsal* (1672) has a rather confused parentage being thought 'sometimes a fisher's son, sometimes a prince'. His plight parodies that of Leonidas in Dryden's *Marriage à la Mode* (1672). *The Rehearsal* served as a model for many of Fielding's own early comedies.

6. (p. 42) *Nemet eour Saxes ... take out their purses*: Fielding's Anglo-Saxon, as revealed in this pun, is really surprisingly good. To be strictly correct, 'take out your swords' should be '*nimad eower seax*', and 'take out their purses/bags' '*nimad hira saccas*'.

7. (p. 43) *Snap*: The term is explained by Eric Partridge in *A Dictionary of Slang and Unconventional English* (Routledge & Kegan Paul, 1937; 5th edition, 1961) as 'a thief claiming a share in booty'.

8. (p. 44) *went ... abroad to one of our American colonies*: Was transported. See Note 33 below.

9. (p. 44) *Westminster Hall*: The chief English law court.

10. (p. 44) *oranges*: Sexual favours, in the tradition of Nell Gwyn. In *Shamela* Parson Oliver writes that 'her mother sold oranges in the play-house'.

11. (p. 44) *Hockley-in-the-Hole*: A bear-garden and arena just to the north-west of Clerkenwell Green. In addition to bull and bear-baiting, it was a favourite venue for cock-fights, dog-fights and prize-fights. Not surprisingly, it was notorious for drunkenness and brawling.

12. (p. 44) *Venienti occurrite morbo*: Persius, *Satires*, III, 64: '... go out and meet the approaching disease'.

13. (p. 44) *Astyages ... Asia*: Herodotus, I, 108; *Hecuba ... flames*: Cicero, *De Divinatione*, I, 21.

14. (p. 45) *Priapus*: The god of fertility, whose cult had spread from the East to Greece and Rome. Said to be the son of Aphrodite and Dionysus, he was represented as a grotesque figure with an erect phallus. Statues of Priapus often graced the doorways or gardens of great houses. Mrs Wild's mispronunciation seems intended to hint at a bawdy pun, 'pri-a-pus' or 'prick-a-puss', 'pussy' being a cant term for the vagina. Mr Wild might have heard of Mercury either as the planetary god of thieves or as the usual treatment for syphilis.

15. (p. 45) *house of an orbicular or round form*: Roundhouses, or night-prisons, were among the several public and private gaols in London. Defoe estimated that there were more houses of confinement in London than in any other city in Europe, 'perhaps as many as in all the capital cities of Europe put together'. He listed the following public prisons (not counting private mad-houses, or 'tolerated prisons'):

The Tower	King's Bench
Newgate	The Fleet
Ludgate	Bridewell
Marshalsea	The Dutchy
The Gatehouse	St Katherine's
Two Counters in the City	Bale-Dock
One Counter in the Borough	Little-Ease
St Martin's le Grand	New Prison
The Clink	New Bridewell
Whitechapel	Tottil-Fields Bridewell
Finsbury	

Five night prisons, called roundhouses, &c.

(Daniel Defoe, *A Tour through the Whole Island of Great Britain*, ed. Pat Rogers, Penguin, 1971, p. 321)

16. (p. 45) *Titus Oates*: Titus Oates (1649–1705) was the central figure in the 'Popish Plot' scare of 1679. Together with Israel Tonge,

Oates made a lengthy deposition in September 1678 to Sir Edmund Berry Godfrey, J.P., describing in detail an alleged Jesuit plot to murder Charles II and re-establish Roman Catholicism in England. These fabricated allegations received apparent corroboration when Godfrey was found murdered the following month. During the ensuing panic, Oates gained considerable wealth and reputation from his further denunciations of prominent Catholics. In 1684 he was tried and imprisoned for perjury; in 1685 James II had him flogged from Aldgate to Newgate, and then from Newgate to Tyburn. He gained some partial rehabilitation after the Glorious Revolution of 1688, and went on issuing dark hints of Jacobite plots for the rest of his life.

17. (p. 46) *Gradus ad Parnassum*: A collection of Latin synonyms, epithets, quotations, etc.

18. (p. 47) *eleventh Iliad ... a sum of money*: *Iliad*, XI, 143–5. In Pope's translation:

> These on the mountains once Achilles found
> And captive led, with pliant osiers bound;
> Then to their sire for ample sums restored.

19. (p. 47) *Nestor ... Eleans*: The plunder of the Eleans is described in the *Iliad*, XI, 816–901.

20. (p. 47) *Cacus ... a better way*: *Aeneid*, VIII, 223–5.

21. (p. 47) *the late King of Sweden*: Charles XII of Sweden, whose life of continual warfare and conquest concluded in defeat and poverty, was a familiar object lesson in the futility of earthly ambitions. Voltaire's biography of Charles, which was popular in England, accused him of the error of extremism – of exaggerating his many virtues until they became vices. 'His life', Voltaire concluded, 'may be a lesson to kings, and teach them that a peaceful and happy government is more to be desired than so much glory.' Johnson agreed, choosing Charles XII as one of his examples in *The Vanity of Human Wishes*.

> He left a name at which the world grew pale,
> To point a moral, or adorn a tale.

Swift was an admirer of the Swedish monarch, having once, he claimed, 'intended to have begged my bread at his court'. Instead he dedicated his *Abstract of the History of England* to Charles.

22. (p. 47) *Spanish Rogue ... Cheats of Scapin ... favourite play*: Mateo Aleman's picaresque *Guzman de Alfarache* had first been translated into English in 1622, and then again in the early eighteenth century under the title *The Spanish Rogue, Or, The Life of Guzman de Alfarache*. There was also an undistinguished verse comedy by Duffett entitled *The Spanish Rogue*, produced at Lincoln's Inn Fields in 1673. *The Cheats of Scapin* is Otway's English version of

Molière's *Les Fourberies de Scapin*, written in 1676. The central
character, a quick-witted, rascally servant with a flair for outrageous
lies, would naturally have appealed to Wild.

23. (p. 48) *Mr Snap*: Snap may be modelled in part on Charles Hitchen,
Under City Marshal from 1712. Positions such as Hitchen's were
clearly understood to be offices of profit. He paid £700 for his post
in January, but quickly recouped that amount in fees, gratuities and
'garnish' exacted from prisoners. Prison inmates were required to
pay for their accommodation, and cells were available to suit a range
of pockets. A cell in the most prestigious part of Newgate, the Press
Yard, from which the fortunate prisoner might actually catch a brief
glimpse of sunshine for a short time in the afternoon, would cost a
deposit of £500, with a rent, including fixtures and fittings, of 22
shillings a week. This made Press Yard the most expensive address
in London – suitable only for great men. 'Garnish' or gratuities paid
to turnkeys, keeper or marshal might easily double these charges.
Hitchen was soon able to boast of a network of some 2,000 thieves
in London who brought their stolen goods to him to dispose of, and
he also ran a protection racket for taverns, gin-shops and brothels.
These underworld activities brought him to the notice of the Court
of Aldermen, who temporarily suspended him from duty. At about
the same time Wild became Hitchen's deputy or partner. In 1714
the two men quarrelled, and thereafter they ran rival criminal organ-
izations.

24. (p. 49) *whisk and swabbers*: Variations on whist. 'Swabbers' is a
highest hand of ace of hearts, knave of clubs, and the ace and deuce
of trumps.

25. (p. 49) *play the whole game*: Cant term for cheating.

26. (p. 51) *I had rather stand ... in Paradise*: Wild here, and on the following page, echoes the sentiments of Milton's Satan (*Paradise Lost*,
I, 263):

> Better to reign in Hell, than serve in Heav'n.

27. (p. 52) *Tower Hill ... Tyburn*: Tyburn, now Marble Arch, was the
place of execution for common criminals. The scaffold consisted of
three posts, ten or twelve feet high, held apart by three connecting
cross-bars at the top, and was known as the 'nubbing-cheat,' the
'cramping-cheat' or simply the 'cheat'. The regular progress of condemned prisoners westwards through London from Newgate to
Tyburn was a frequent and popular spectacle. Crowds gathered to
cheer and jeer. Lamplighters offered vantage-points on top of their
ladders for a better view of the executions; 'dying speeches' were
hawked about for sale, even as the noose tightened. The whole brutal
carnival was sometimes rounded off by an undignified struggle
between the dead man's relatives and the hired thugs of the Surgeons'
College for possession of the body. (See Peter Linebaugh, 'The

Tyburn Riot against the Surgeons', in Douglas Hay *et al.*, *Albion's Fatal Tree*, Allen Lane, 1975; Penguin, 1977.) Tower Hill was the place of execution for state prisoners, usually of higher social status, who were beheaded, not hanged.

28. (p. 53) *cog a die*: Cant term for cheating at dice.

29. (p. 53) *the Cant Dictionary*: Most of the chroniclers of criminal lives liked to indulge in the colourful thieves' argot of the period. *The New Canting Dictionary*, a comprehensive glossary of the terms used by 'all the clans of cheats and villains', which appeared in 1725 at the height of Wild-mania, is a fascinating guide through the undergrowth of slang. It takes us, for example, from 'Adam Tilers' (lookouts) to 'zanies' (mountebanks or jesters); or from 'autem-mort' (a married woman – 'autem' is a church) to 'wapping' (one of the many cant terms for sexual intercourse). Fielding is not entirely accurate in his use of the terms here. A 'buttock-and-file' is not a shoplifter, but, as the name suggests, a whore who also picks her clients' pockets. This is the only time that Fielding makes such a deliberate display of these cant terms. Unlike Defoe, or the author of *The Life and Glorious Adventures of the most heroic and magnanimous Jonathan Wilde* (1725), Fielding is less interested in the local colour and authentic atmosphere that such terms confer than in their euphemistic similarity with other forms of jargon that bleed language of its moral content.

30. (p. 55) *night-cellar*: 'A cellar serving as a tavern or place of resort during the night for persons of the lowest class' (OED).

31. (p. 56) *plain Spanish*: Ready money. (See Eric Partridge, *A Dictionary of Slang and Unconventional English*.)

32. (p. 57) *sneaking-budge*: Once again, *The New Canting Dictionary* (1725) gives a rather fuller definition: 'one that robs alone, and deals chiefly in petty larcenies.'

33. (p. 58) *His Majesty's plantations in America*: Seven years was the minimum period of transportation for those who could claim 'benefit of clergy' in their defence. Otherwise the minimum sentence was fourteen years. 'Benefit of clergy', once a privilege of those in Holy Orders, was now extended to all who could read. If found guilty, a prisoner would 'seek the bible'. He would then be required to read out verse 1 of Psalm 51, known accordingly as the 'neck-verse'. As it was always the same verse, a number of illiterate felons took the trouble to learn it by heart. Having 'proved' literacy a prisoner might be whipped, branded and transported, but was spared hanging. The branding was to ensure that his claim could only be made once. It was officially abandoned as a plea in 1705, but continued in use for some years thereafter.

34. (p. 59) *hazard-table*: Hazard was 'a game at dice in which the chances are complicated by a number of arbitrary rules' (OED).

35. (p. 59) *Bob Bagshot*: Fielding recalls a character from Gay's *Beggar's*

Opera, 'Robin of Bagshot, alias Gorgon, alias Bluff Bob, alias Car-
buncle, alias Bob Booty'. The aliases refer to nicknames of Walpole,
hence Fielding's interest.

36. (p. 60) *the labourer worthy of his hire*: Luke x, 7.

37. (p. 61) *Aristotle ... cattle*: A rather forceful interpretation of
Aristotle's division of society into labourers and intellectuals in *The
Politics* Bk I, ch. 2.

38. (p. 62) *hanger*: 'A kind of short sword, originally hung from the belt'
(OED).

39. (p. 63) *Qui color ... albo*: Ovid *Metamorphoses,* II, 541: 'which once
was white, but is now the opposite of white'.

40. (p. 65) *pinchbeck plate*: Pinchbeck is an alloy of copper and zinc used
to resemble gold in cheap jewellery, clocks, etc. Named after its inventor, Christopher Pinchbeck.

41. (p. 65) *dimity*: 'A stout cotton fabric woven with raised stripes or
fancy figures' (OED).

42. (p. 66) *nothing, not even a louse, is made in vain*: A tongue-in-cheek
restatement of the theory of universal plenitude that finds its most
notable expression in Pope's *Essay on Man* (I, 245–6 and 267–8):

> From Nature's chain whatever links you strike,
> Tenth or ten thousandth, breaks the chain alike ...
> All are but parts of one stupendous whole,
> Whose body Nature is, and God the soul.

43. (p. 69) *speaking with him*: *Speaking with* is italicized to remind us that
this is a cant term for stealing. However, the appropriateness of the
double meaning here is not entirely clear.

44. (p. 71) *blown up*: betrayed, informed upon (OED).

45. (p. 73) *Conv—n*: The Convocations of Canterbury and York, the
representative assemblies of the Church of England, had been pro-
rogued by the ministry in 1717, and again in 1741.

46. (p. 73) *some other such persons*: The reference is to Colley Cibber
(1671–1757), perennial butt of Fielding's satire. Cibber was the
colourful actor-manager of Drury Lane Theatre who was appointed
Poet Laureate in 1730, much to the rage and astonishment of Pope,
Swift, Fielding and their Tory friends. In 1740 Cibber published a
rambling, conversational autobiography entitled *Apology for the Life
of Mr Colley Cibber, Comedian*, a work which Fielding parodied re-
peatedly both for its style and its content.

47. (p. 74) This debate on the nature of honour owes as much to Locke
as it does to Falstaff. In his *Essay Concerning Human Understanding*
Locke devoted considerable thought to the problems of abstract
moral vocabulary: 'When we speak of *justice* or *gratitude*, we frame
to ourselves no imagination of anything existing which we would
conceive, but our thoughts terminate in the abstract *idea* of those
virtues ...' (III, v). Fielding was preoccupied with the dangers of the

euphemistic misuse of such terms as 'honour' and 'virtue' throughout his career. His 'Modern Glossary' in the *Covent Garden Journal* (14 January 1752) is a kind of cant dictionary for fashionable society. In it he defines *honour* simply as 'duelling', a *patriot* as 'a candidate for a place at court', and *politics* as 'the art of getting such a place'. Mrs Honour in *Tom Jones* is a typically ironic personification of this ambiguous quality. (See G. W. Hatfield, *Henry Fielding and the Language of Irony*, University of Chicago Press, Chicago, 1968.)

48. (p. 74) *it is not in the lie's going from us*: One is reminded of the advice which that devious secret service agent Daniel Defoe offered his master, Robert Harley: 'A lie does not consist in the indirect position of words, but in the design by false speaking, to deceive and injure my neighbour' (*Letters of Defoe*, ed. G. H. Healey, Oxford University Press, 1955, p. 42).

49. (p. 77) *the hills near Bath*: Fielding was often a guest at Prior Park, near Bath, the home of the wealthy and benevolent entrepreneur Ralph Allen, and may well have spent some time there while composing *Jonathan Wild* in 1741–2. Allen has often been mentioned as the model for Allworthy in *Tom Jones*. Pope was another of his literary friends who spent time at Prior Park.

50. (p. 78) *Sic, sic juvat*: '*Sic, sic iuvat ire sub umbras*' ('Thus, thus it is pleasing to pass beneath the shades'). The words of the dying Dido (*Aeneid*, IV, 660).

51. (p. 78) *whole nations ... GREAT MAN*: Alexander wept because he had not conquered one of the infinite number of worlds. (See Plutarch, 'On Tranquillity of Mind', 466, D–E.)

52. (p. 84) *Mr Thomas Heartfree*: Unworldly as he seems, Heartfree may be at least partly modelled on Fielding's friend and fellow-dramatist, George Lillo. As well as pioneering the form of domestic tragedy in *The London Merchant* (1731), Lillo was a jeweller by trade. Fielding's admiration is obvious in this obituary panegyric: 'He had the spirit of an old Roman, joined to the innocence of a primitive Christian; he was content with his little state of life, in which his excellent temper of mind gave him a happiness beyond the power of riches' (*The Champion*, 26 February 1739/40).

53. (p. 91) *Miss Molly Straddle*: This may glance at Walpole's relationship with his mistress Molly Skerret.

54. (p. 92) *Rummer and Horseshoe*: 'Rummer' is a large drinking-glass; 'horseshoe' is a cant term for the vagina.

55. (p. 92) *red clocks*: The reference is to Penelope in the *Odyssey*, XIX. 'Clocks' are ornamental patterns embroidered in silk on the sides of stockings.

56. (p. 94) *the fair of Bartholomew*: This fair continued from the Middle Ages through to the nineteenth century. It was held in Smithfield on St Bartholomew's day, 24 August.

57. (p. 94) *Derdæus Magnus*: William Deard (d. 1761), a well-known

jeweller and toy-maker. He is referred to in *Joseph Andrews*, III, vi, and the *Covent Garden Journal* of 4 January 1752.

58. (p. 96) *sneaker*: A small bowl (of punch) (OED).

59. (p. 102) *Mr Ketch*: The hangman, after Jack Ketch, public hangman from 1663 to 1686.

60. (p. 102) *politics*: Cf. Fielding's *An Essay on the Knowledge of the Characters of Men*: '... as it is impossible that any man endowed with rational faculties, and being in a state of freedom, should willingly agree, without some motive of love or friendship, absolutely to sacrifice his own interest to that of another; it becomes necessary to impose upon him, to persuade him, that his own good is designed, and that he will be a gainer by coming into those schemes, which are, in reality, calculated for his destruction. And this, if I mistake not, is the very essence of that excellent art, called *The Art of Politics*' (*Miscellanies*, vol. i, ed. Miller, p. 155).

61. (p. 102) *nab or trencher hat*: A 'nab' is a broad-brimmed hat; a 'trencher' is a flat-topped hat, of the academic type.

62. (p. 103) *shakebags, oldnolls*: 'Shakebag' is 'a rogue or scoundrel' (OED); 'oldnoll' derives from a nickname for Oliver Cromwell.

63. (p. 103) *Sophocles ... no very honourable sense*: 'Sophocles ... cheating in hats': *Ajax*, 1285 ff., on the casting of lots; 'Achilles ... dog's eyes': *Iliad*, I, 159; 'old hat': yet another cant term for the vagina.

64. (p. 107) *Peter Pounce*: A character in *Joseph Andrews*, modelled on the wealthy miser Peter Walter (1664?–1746) of Stalbridge Park, Dorset.

65. (p. 109) *Drawcansir-like*: Drawcansir was a character in Buckingham's *The Rehearsal*, given to such outbursts as the following (IV, i):

> I drink, I huff, I strut, look big and stare;
> And all this I can do, because I dare.

Fielding adopted the pseudonym of Sir Alexander Drawcansir – a combination of two fearless elements – when he began the *Covent Garden Journal* in 1752.

66. (p. 114) *struck*: To strike one's colours signifies surrendering at sea.

67. (p. 117) At this point in the 1743 *Miscellanies* edition of *Jonathan Wild* there is a digressionary chapter, 'Of PROVERBS. A chapter full of very cunning and curious learning'. It is a facetious exercise in the Scriblerian vein of ridicule of false learning, and is only very loosely linked with the concerns of *Jonathan Wild*. Two examples of the proverbs, with their accompanying commentaries, will give an indication of the lameness of the wit.

PROVERB VII: The sensible man and the silent woman are the best conversation.
Here is noted that a woman talks best who says nothing.

PROVERB IX: A young fellow who falls in love with a whore may be said to fall asleep in a hog-sty.

NOTES

Here is observed the likeness or resemblance between a whore and a hog-sty.

68. (p. 117) *Nec Deus ... nodus*: Horace, *Ars Poetica*, 191: 'Let not a god intervene unless the difficulty be worthy of his assistance.' Also cited in *Tom Jones*, VIII, i, and IX, v.

69 (p. 118) *Naturam expellas ... recurret*: Horace, *Epistles*, I, x, 24: 'You may drive Nature out with a pitchfork, but she will always return.'

70. (p. 118) NATURALS: Idiots, simpletons.

71. (p. 119) *ab effectu*: From the performance.

72. (p. 124) *Cræsus ... stupid and motionless*: Herodotus, *The Histories*, III, xiv.

73. (p. 127) *as the excellent poet says*: The quotation is from Edward Young, *The Complaint, or Night Thoughts on Life, Death and Immortality* (1742–5), 'Night', I, 376–8. Fielding appears to quote from memory; the correct reading is:

> Where is tomorrow? In another world.
> For numbers this is certain; the reverse
> Is sure to none.

74. (p. 129) *Socrates ... death*: See the opening of Plato's *Crito*.

75. (p. 130) *God's revenge against murder*: See Note 86 below.

76. (p. 132) *Achates ... Alexander*: Achates, usually styled 'fidus', was Aeneas' armour-bearer and loyal friend. Hephaestion was a close friend of Alexander and one of his generals.

77. (p. 134) *what was said ... labour*: 'Labor omnia vincit' (Virgil, *Georgics*, I, 145).

78. (p. 137) *should be first approved and licensed by the said great men*: The Licensing Act was rushed through Parliament in June 1737 as Walpole's reaction to Fielding's satiric attacks upon his administration in such plays as *Pasquin* and *The Historical Register for the Year 1736*. Its requirement that the Lord Chamberlain should read and either approve or censor all plays before they were performed put an effective end to Fielding's career as a dramatist. The Act remained in force until 1968.

79. (p. 137) *Socrates ... open*: See Plato's *Crito, passim*.

80. (p. 138) *marriage ... at Smithfield*: a 'Smithfield match' is a marriage for money, so called after the cattle market. See *Joseph Andrews*, II, vi.

81. (p. 139) *the great Bubble-boy*: A 'bubble' is a trifle, or a cant term for a fool, gull or victim. However, the reference here is probably to the South Sea Bubble of 1720, when stocks in the South Sea Company rose from £150 to £1,000 in a matter of months, only to crash, even more rapidly, down to £300. It was Walpole's dexterity in clearing up the mess of this débâcle that laid the basis for his long years in power. It would therefore be unfair to apply this term to him, as if he had presided over the Bubble. Yet I suspect that that is exactly

what Fielding intends, relying on the gap of more than twenty years to have clouded people's memories of Walpole's exact role in the affair.

82. (p. 139) *academy of compliments*: *The Academy of Complements: or, a New Way of Wooing* appeared in 1685 and was reprinted in the mid eighteenth century.

83. (p. 141) HURGOS: 'Hurgo' was the Lilliputian term for a great lord. The *Gentleman's Magazine*, under the resourceful proprietorship of Edward Cave, had hit on an ingenious way to circumvent the resolution of the House of Commons of 13 April 1738 that it was 'a notorious breach of the privilege of this house' for debates to be reported and published. The *Gentleman's Magazine* instead published reports on the 'Debates in the Senate of Lilliput', with accounts of proceedings both in the House of *Hurgos* (Lords) and in the House of *Clinabs* (Commons). What Fielding says here about the lack of authenticity of the reported speeches is largely correct, for by far the majority of the speeches in the 'Debates in the Senate of Lilliput' were written by Samuel Johnson, who was then on the magazine's staff. He did not attend the galleries of parliament himself, but got reporters to bring him careful notes of the speeches made. 'The whole was afterwards communicated to me, and I composed the speeches in the form which they now have in the Parliamentary debates' (quoted in Murphy, *Life and Genius of Samuel Johnson*, 1792). It's hardly surprising that the Hurgos seem more eloquent in Johnson's prose than they were in real life. But at least Fielding did not object to the political bias in the reports, for, as Johnson admitted, 'I took care that the Whig dogs should not have the best of it' (quoted in Murphy, op. cit.).

84. (p. 148) *Corvinus ... Camilla ... Lady Betty Modish*: Stock characters, whose personalities are revealed in their names. More specifically, Corvino (the raven) is a character in Jonson's *Volpone*; Camilla was a Volscian princess who aided Turnus against Aeneas (*Aeneid*, vii, 808 *et seq.*); *Lady Betty Modish* is the coquette in Colley Cibber's play *The Careless Husband* (1704).

85. (p. 148) *liberties of the Fleet*: The Fleet was a debtors' prison; the 'liberties' were areas immediately outside the city walls which enjoyed certain exemptions and privileges because they had once been the sites of monasteries, and which consequently became 'bastard sanctuaries' inhabited by debtors, refugees, and criminals of all sorts. By 1712 only one 'liberty', that of the 'Mint' in Southwark, remained. Nevertheless the sites of the liberties of the Fleet, Whitefriars, etc., remained criminal areas.

86. (p. 150) *God's Revenge against Murder*: Fielding possessed a copy of the 1635 edition of *The Triumphes of God's Revenge against the crying and execrable Sinne of Murther* by John Reynolds (1622).

87. (p. 152) *writ de homine replegiando*: The same as a 'writ of replevin',

where replevin is 'the restoration to, or recovery by, a person of goods or chattels distrained or taken from him, upon his giving security to have the matter tried in a court of justice and to return the goods if the case is decided against him' (OED).

88. (p. 152) *capias in withernam*: 'In an action of replevin, the reprisal of other goods in lieu of those taken by a first distress and eloigned; also, the writ (called *capias in withernam*) commanding the sheriff to take the reprisal' (OED).

89. (p. 153) *at present one of the strongest bonds ... favour*: Fielding may well be making a sniping reference to Walpole's close connection with Queen Caroline. It was common practice for the Queen and Walpole to agree policies which she would subsequently discuss with King George, leading him to believe they had been his own ideas. This firm alliance made Walpole's position almost impregnable until the Queen's death in 1737.

90. (p. 155) *Nemo ... sapit*: Pliny, *Natural History*, VII, xl, 131: 'no mortal is wise all the time'. A favourite tag, also found in *Joseph Andrews*, III, v, and *Tom Jones*, XII, xiii.

91. (p. 155) *Ira furor brevis est*: Horace, Epistles, I, ii, 62: 'anger is brief madness'.

92. (p. 156) *mittimus*: 'a warrant by which a justice commits an offender to prison' (Johnson's *Dictionary*).

93. (p. 161) *chief magistrate is always chosen for the public good*: An enduring concern of Fielding's, who became a magistrate himself in 1748. His half-brother John Fielding, who succeeded to the magistracy at Bow Street, was one of the most influential magistrates of the century, helping to build up an effective and legal detective force and paying an unusual attention to the causes of crime. In the *Covent Garden Journal* (7 January 1752) Fielding (Henry) quoted Plato's *Republic* to the effect that 'a true Magistrate is not so constituted that he may consult his own good, but that he may provide for the good of the subject'.

94. (p. 161) *this bit of ribbon*: Compare Swift's satire on the system of political honours in Lilliput: 'Whoever performs his part with most agility, and holds out the longest in leaping and creeping, is rewarded with the blue-coloured silk; the red is given to the next, and the green to the third ...' (*Gulliver's Travels*, I, iii).

95. (p. 165) *a sincere Turk would be saved*: Parson Adams's similar belief in *Joseph Andrews* (I, xvii) provokes much the same reaction. Fielding is echoing the remark in Bishop Hoadley's sermon 'The Good Samaritan' that 'an honest Heathen is much more acceptable to [God] than a dishonest and deceitful Christian'.

96. (p. 167) *Hicks's Hall*: Situated in St John's Street, this was the Shire House for the Middlesex Sessions. Named after Sir Baptist Hicks, who gave the money for its erection.

97. (p. 167) *ut lapsu graviore ruant*: Claudian, *In Rufinum*, I, xxiii: 'that they might tumble down with a more severe fall'.

98. (p. 168) *a clause in an Act ... soon after fell into*: Sections 5 and 6 of the Transportation Act 1718 (4 George I c. 2) aimed at stopping all traffic in stolen goods, even through agents such as Wild, who claimed never to have such goods in their possession. The text of the relevant sections is given in Defoe's *True and Genuine Account*.

99. (p. 172) *Roger Johnson*: The historical Roger Johnson was born in 1695. He lived for some while with Mother Jolly, the proprietress of the King's Arms tavern and brothel in Drury Lane. He also gained money by posing as a clergyman. In 1718 he escaped hanging by impeaching his own mother. In November 1720 he was again arrested for 'the kidlay', a kind of confidence trick. Again he escaped hanging, and soon afterwards he became the captain of Wild's newly acquired ship, used for smuggling. It was Wild's ill-advised raid to release Johnson from custody in February 1725 that led to his imprisonment in Newgate and eventual execution. (See Gerald Howson, *Thief-Taker General*, Hutchinson, 1970.)

100. (p. 181) *Beggar's Opera*: In the last scene of *The Beggar's Opera* Macheath is reprieved, on the player's plea that the work must 'comply with the taste of the town'. The beggar agrees, adding this comment which Fielding obviously recalled when writing *Jonathan Wild*: 'Through the whole piece you may observe such a similitude of manners in high and low life, that it is difficult to determine whether (in the fashionable vices) the fine gentlemen imitate the gentlemen of the road, or the gentlemen of the road the fine gentlemen. Had the play remained as I first intended, it would have carried a most excellent moral. 'Twould have shown that the lower sort of people have their vices in a degree as well as the rich: And that they are punished for them.' That was what it *would* have shown. What it does show is something far closer in ironic spirit to Fielding's message in *Jonathan Wild* about the wilful self-deception of the people.

101. (p. 192) At this point in the 1743 edition, Fielding indulges a vein of whimsical satire at the expense of the fantastic exaggeration of many travellers' tales in the Sir John de Mandeville tradition. Mrs Heartfree and her sailor companions encounter an elephantine monster which she describes as 'not unlike Windsor Castle' in size and shape. Having slain this creature, the whole company march through its body, with the exception of Mrs Heartfree, who declines on the grounds of delicacy, 'the monster being of the male kind'. Although an entertaining episode, Fielding was right to cut these paragraphs from the 1754 edition of the work. The tone is quite different from the rest of the novel, and the jokes at Mrs Heartfree's delicacy rather undercut her pose of resilient chastity. It is an isolated episode of a free-wheeling wit that recalls the burlesque comedies of the 1730s.

102. (p. 198) *My — in a bandbox*: 'My arse in a bandbox', meaning 'that won't do'. (See Eric Partridge, *A Dictionary of Slang and Unconventional English*.)

103. (p. 198) *Doctors' Commons*: The courts to the south of St Paul's Cathedral that housed the registries of the Archbishop of Canterbury and the Bishop of London. The Faculty Court of Doctors' Commons could grant permission for speedy marriages, without banns having been called in church for three successive weeks.

104. (p. 204) *Nec Judicis ...vetustas*: Ovid, *Metamorphoses*, XV, 871–2: 'Neither Jove's wrath, nor fire, nor sword, nor devouring old age could destroy.'

105. (p. 204) *a* GREAT *dramatic poet*: None other than Colley Cibber. The words quoted are Gloucester's at the end of Cibber's 'improved' version of *Richard III* (III, i).

106. (p. 205) *the ordinary*: The Ordinary, or chaplain-in-ordinary, to Newgate prison was at this time the Rev. Thomas Purney. Like several of his predecessors, Purney profited from the notoriety of his parishioners by publishing his official versions of their last days, dying speeches, etc. (See *The Ordinary of Newgate's Accounts of the Behaviour of the Prisoners etc.*, May 1725.)

107. (p. 206) *Those who do evil ... angels*: Matthew xxv, 41.

108. (p. 206) *Cicero, or of Tully*: Both the same man, of course.

109. (p. 206) *ear hath not heard, nor can heart conceive*: Paraphrasing 1 Corinthians II, 9.

110. (p. 208) *the gravel*: 'A term applied to aggregation of urinary crystals' (OED).

111. (p. 209) *To the Greeks* FOOLISHNESS: 1 Corinthians I, 23.

112. (p. 212) *laudanum*: A tincture of opium in alcohol. Wild was an inexperienced drug-taker who took far too large a dose and vomited it up again.

113. (p. 213) *Suave mari magno ... laborem*: Lucretius, *De Rerum Natura*, II, i–ii: 'It is pleasant, when there are stormy waters, to gaze from the land on another's struggles.'

114. (p. 215) HONOSTY: In *The Vernoniad* (1741) Fielding refers to Walpole as 'a certain Magician called (Osonos) or (Usonos), or, according to the *Laconians* (Usonor), in Latin *Hishonour* – this Magician is said to have invented a certain *Aurum potabile*, by which he could turn men into Swine or Asses, whence some think he had his Name; (Us) signifying a Swine, and (Onos), Laconicè (Onor) an Ass'. (See M. C. Battestin, 'Pope's *Magus* in Fielding's *Vernoniad*: The Satire of Walpole', *Philological Quarterly*, xlvi, 1967, p. 139.)

115. (p. 217) *twelve excellent and celebrated rules*: These rules, supposed to have been found in Charles I's study after his death, were well known throughout the eighteenth century from their appearance on a woodcut of the execution. Versions could be found in cottages and taverns (cf. Goldsmith's *Deserted Village*, I, 232).

116. (p. 218) ... *a privilege to kill,/A strong temptation to do bravely ill*:
This appears to be a conflation, typical enough of Fielding's quo-
tations from memory, of two passages from plays. One is from
Boyle's *Mustapha* (Act I):

> *Haly*: ... I can less doubt the Justice of your will,
> Than that you here have privilege to kill.

The other is from Nathaniel Lee's *Sophonisba* (I, i):

> *King Massinissa*: ... The lust of power
> Like glory, boy, it licenses to kill;
> A strong temptation to do bravely ill ...

117. (p. 218) *Lætius est ... honestum*: Lucan, *The Civil War*, IX, 404:
'virtue is pleased to be preserved at a high price'. Ironically, the
sentiments are those of Cato, patriotically encouraging his troops to
cross the African desert.

THE TRUE AND GENUINE ACCOUNT
OF THE LIFE AND ACTIONS
OF THE LATE JONATHAN WILD

1. (p. 229) *the late Preston rebellion*: A force of some 5,000 Jacobites was defeated at Preston on 13 November 1715. This defeat meant the effective end of the Old Pretender's hopes of unsettling the Hanoverian succession.

2. (p. 229) *poultry-compter*: The two compters or 'counters' of Poultry and Wood Street were the ancient debtors' prisons of the city of London. They were divided into 'sides' or 'wards' according to the costs for accommodation: 'Master's-side', 'Knight's-side', 'two-penny-ward' and 'common-ward'.

3. (p. 231) *the* TWANG: Captain Smith describes, in *The Memoirs of the Life and Times of the famous Jonathan Wild, together with the History and Lives of Modern Rogues*, (1726), how Moll Raby and her husband Humphrey Jackson went out on the *'Buttock and Twang'*: 'So whilst the decoy'd fool is groping her with his breeches down, she picks his fob, or pocket, of his watch or money. And giving a sort of *Hem!* as a signal she has succeeded in her design, then the fellow with whom she keeps company, blundering up in the dark, he knocks down the gallent [*sic*] and carries off the prize.'

4. (p. 246) *Sturbridge fair*: This fair took place annually in September on the Chesterton side of Cambridge. It was, according to Defoe, 'not only the greatest [fair] in the whole nation, but in the world'. He went on: As for the people in the fair, they all universally eat, drink, and sleep in their booths, and tents; and the said booths are so intermingled with taverns, coffee-houses, drinking-houses, eating-houses, cooks-shops, &c, and all intents too; that there's no want of any provisions of any kind, either dressed or undressed. In a word, the fair is like a well fortified city, and there is the least disorder and confusion (I believe) that can be seen any where, with so great a concourse of people' (*A Tour through the Whole Island of Great Britain*, 1724–6).

5. (p. 246) *Lynx*: Alias Samuel Linn; he belonged to Obadiah Lemon's gang. He was hanged on Friday 13 February 1719, having almost certainly been betrayed by Wild. It was also the date of Wild's fifth wedding.

6. (p. 246) *M–ll K––g*: Moll King was almost certainly a main source for Defoe's *Moll Flanders*. (See Gerald Howson's discussion of the point in *Thief-Taker General*, Hutchinson, 1970.)

279

7. (p. 248) *crank*: Various meanings as a cant term. Usually a confidence trick or a disguise of some sort. 'Confek crank' was a term for someone feigning madness or epilepsy.

Discover more about our forthcoming books through Penguin's FREE newspaper...

READ MORE IN PENGUIN

In every corner of the world, on every subject under the sun, Penguin represents quality and variety – the very best in publishing today.

For complete information about books available from Penguin – including Puffins, Penguin Classics and Arkana – and how to order them, write to us at the appropriate address below. Please note that for copyright reasons the selection of books varies from country to country.

In the United Kingdom: Please write to *Dept. JC, Penguin Books Ltd, FREEPOST, West Drayton, Middlesex UB7 0BR.*

If you have any difficulty in obtaining a title, please send your order with the correct money, plus ten per cent for postage and packaging, to *PO Box No. 11, West Drayton, Middlesex UB7 0BR*

In the United States: Please write to *Consumer Sales, Penguin USA, P.O. Box 999, Dept. 17109, Bergenfield, New Jersey 07621-0120.* VISA and MasterCard holders call 1-800-253-6476 to order all Penguin titles

In Canada: Please write to *Penguin Books Canada Ltd, 10 Alcorn Avenue, Suite 300, Toronto, Ontario M4V 3B2*

In Australia: Please write to *Penguin Books Australia Ltd, P.O. Box 257, Ringwood, Victoria 3134*

In New Zealand: Please write to *Penguin Books (NZ) Ltd, Private Bag 102902, North Shore Mail Centre, Auckland 10*

In India: Please write to *Penguin Books India Pvt Ltd, 706 Eros Apartments, 56 Nehru Place, New Delhi 110 019*

In the Netherlands: Please write to *Penguin Books Netherlands bv, Postbus 3507, NL-1001 AH Amsterdam*

In Germany: Please write to *Penguin Books Deutschland GmbH, Metzlerstrasse 26, 60594 Frankfurt am Main*

In Spain: Please write to *Penguin Books S. A., Bravo Murillo 19, 1° B, 28015 Madrid*

In Italy: Please write to *Penguin Italia s.r.l., Via Felice Casati 20, I–20124 Milano*

In France: Please write to *Penguin France S. A., 17 rue Lejeune, F–31000 Toulouse*

In Japan: Please write to *Penguin Books Japan, Ishikiribashi Building, 2–5–4, Suido, Bunkyo-ku, Tokyo 112*

In Greece: Please write to *Penguin Hellas Ltd, Dimocritou 3, GR–106 71 Athens*

In South Africa: Please write to *Longman Penguin Southern Africa (Pty) Ltd, Private Bag X08, Bertsham 2013*

READ MORE IN PENGUIN

A CHOICE OF CLASSICS

Matthew Arnold	**Selected Prose**
Jane Austen	**Emma**
	Lady Susan/The Watsons/Sanditon
	Mansfield Park
	Northanger Abbey
	Persuasion
	Pride and Prejudice
	Sense and Sensibility
William Barnes	**Selected Poems**
Anne Brontë	**Agnes Grey**
	The Tenant of Wildfell Hall
Charlotte Brontë	**Jane Eyre**
	Shirley
	Villette
Emily Brontë	**Wuthering Heights**
Samuel Butler	**Erewhon**
	The Way of All Flesh
Thomas Carlyle	**Selected Writings**
Arthur Hugh Clough	**Selected Poems**
Wilkie Collins	**The Moonstone**
	The Woman in White
Charles Darwin	**The Origin of Species**
	The Voyage of the *Beagle*
Benjamin Disraeli	**Sybil**
George Eliot	**Adam Bede**
	Daniel Deronda
	Felix Holt
	Middlemarch
	The Mill on the Floss
	Romola
	Scenes of Clerical Life
	Silas Marner
Elizabeth Gaskell	**Cranford/Cousin Phillis**
	The Life of Charlotte Brontë
	Mary Barton
	North and South
	Wives and Daughters

READ MORE IN PENGUIN

A CHOICE OF CLASSICS

Charles Dickens	**American Notes for General Circulation**
	Barnaby Rudge
	Bleak House
	The Christmas Books (in two volumes)
	David Copperfield
	Dombey and Son
	Great Expectations
	Hard Times
	Little Dorrit
	Martin Chuzzlewit
	The Mystery of Edwin Drood
	Nicholas Nickleby
	The Old Curiosity Shop
	Oliver Twist
	Our Mutual Friend
	The Pickwick Papers
	Selected Short Fiction
	A Tale of Two Cities
Edward Gibbon	**The Decline and Fall of the Roman Empire**
George Gissing	**New Grub Street**
	The Odd Women
William Godwin	**Caleb Williams**
Thomas Hardy	**The Distracted Preacher and Other Tales**
	Far from the Madding Crowd
	Jude the Obscure
	The Mayor of Casterbridge
	A Pair of Blue Eyes
	The Return of the Native
	Tess of the d'Urbervilles
	The Trumpet-Major
	Under the Greenwood Tree
	The Woodlanders

READ MORE IN PENGUIN

A CHOICE OF CLASSICS

READ MORE IN PENGUIN

A CHOICE OF CLASSICS

William Hazlitt	**Selected Writings**
George Herbert	**The Complete English Poems**
Thomas Hobbes	**Leviathan**

Samuel Johnson/
  James Boswell
	**A Journey to the Western Islands of
	  Scotland and The Journal of a Tour of
	  the Hebrides**

Charles Lamb	**Selected Prose**
George Meredith	**The Egoist**
Thomas Middleton	**Five Plays**
John Milton	**Paradise Lost**
Samuel Richardson	**Clarissa**
	Pamela
Earl of Rochester	**Complete Works**
Richard Brinsley Sheridan	**The School for Scandal and Other Plays**
Sir Philip Sidney	**Selected Poems**
Christopher Smart	**Selected Poems**
Adam Smith	**The Wealth of Nations**
Tobias Smollett	**The Adventures of Ferdinand Count Fathom**
	Humphrey Clinker
Laurence Sterne	**The Life and Opinions of Tristram Shandy**
	A Sentimental Journey Through France and Italy
Jonathan Swift	**Gulliver's Travels**
	Selected Poems
Thomas Traherne	**Selected Poems and Prose**
Sir John Vanbrugh	**Four Comedies**

READ MORE IN PENGUIN

A CHOICE OF CLASSICS